ENIGMA
of the
Second Coming

A novel by

Stan I.S. Law

INHOUSEPRESS, MONTREAL, CANADA

2nd Edition
Published in Canada in 2014 by
INHOUSEPRESS
http://www.inhousepress.ca

Design and layout
Bozena Happach

2nd Edition
ISBN-13: 978-0-981301594

This book is a work of fiction.
Names, characters, titles, places and incidents are either the products of the
author's imagination or are used fictitiously.

Printed and bound in the USA

For my wife
Bozena
In gratitude

[na imieninki]

ZERO MINUS 30

ZERO MINUS 20

ZERO MINUS 10

NOW

EPILOGUE

ZERO MINUS 30

1

A Near Miss

It didn't really start with the Enigma. The errant asteroid came before it. There were also those sporadic meteor showers that started a minor panic at the Moon Base that our friends from NASA had been attempting to build – but that came even later. There were also those earthquakes that didn't quake, inundations that submerged some lands only to expose others, and a number of other events that didn't make much sense. Scientific sense, that is. They were things that defied logic. That belonged in Hollywood tabloids.

Then came the viral diseases – more like plagues really. It was as though Nature had taken over and decided to run things her own way, relegating man to the role of a dumbfounded spectator, powerless and basically unprepared. But what really upset John Hydon was that I, his own little Hey, wasn't disturbed by any of this. Ever. Or so it seemed to him. Even JJ found his own escape from the mounting dilemmas. Only John Hydon, Ph.D., the man others referred to as The Brain, seemed progressively more lost with each day.

"Even now I just don't understand it," my father muttered to himself. I remember: he was looking out through the triangular latticework of aluminium tubes that kept us alive. The view was breathtaking. But all that came later. Many years later.

That's as close as I remember it from my dreams. The rest is conjecture. Mostly derived from talking to about two thousand people. Sometimes I can't be sure. Lately I seem to be losing the distinction between what is real and what isn't. Did it all really happen? I strongly suspect that all things are real. All events, all feelings, ideas... Whatever we perceive as such. Even dreams. Isn't the Universe infinite? Maybe there's no limit to the versions of reality.

Occasionally, my perception of reality takes off on a tangent. I don't seem to have too much control over it. Never did. You'll just have to bear with me.

And by the way. If you were expecting a fast-paced sci-fi story, you would better think again. This is the story of my life. It really happened. And if some parts sound as if they were figments of my imagination, then let me tell you: they may have taken place just in my mind, but to me they are as real as the hand in front of my face. Trust me.

But now we really are well ahead of the story. We would better take a deep, a really deep, breath and start at the beginning. Some thirty years ago. About the time I was born.

For three days, the atmosphere in the lab had been electrifying. In spite of numerous red-rimmed eyes, stifled yawns and innumerable cups of black coffee, all fourteen scientists had remained glued to their computer screens, tracking the motion of an object that measured the length of two football fields, and with the mass of the Empire State Building. That's minute by cosmological standards. Simultaneously, the laser printouts hummed with an ever-growing flood of data. In days to come, tens of thousands of numerical data would be dissected with surgical precision. In astronomy, not to mention in astrophysics, the smallest items often open the gates of the unknown. And out there, there was the infinite field of the unknown still waiting to be discovered. A truly infinite field. A field of dreams.

Now and then John Hydon looked up from his desk, gave terse instructions to one of his assistants and then froze, again, in rapt attention. Apart from those brief moments, his eyes did not waver from the computer screen. Now and then his fingers would stab the keyboard, staccato, like a fragment of a brief *rondo cappricioso*, automatically, then revert to their previous rigid immobility on the desk. His face remained a mask of concentration. His hazel eyes that turned brown in the dimmed light of the Observatory shone unblinking, narrowing behind the outsized spectacles, determined to catch information before it was even recorded by the electronic memory. Billions of megabytes a minute. He seemed lost in his private world of astrophysics. Astro-speculation, he called it in his lighter moments. But this wasn't one of them. For Dr. Hydon this was work, glorious, absorbing work. No one knows how a genius mind works. There were those who thought that John Hydon could think faster than a computer. Than a whole army of them. He had a reputation of using machines only for confirmation of what he'd already decided. Or suspected. He'd proven this capacity in the past. His assistants imagined that, right then, he might be attempting to predict the orbit and ultimate destiny of the tiny satellite.

It was already the third day.

The Monster Eye, as the staff affectionately called the largest optical telescope in the world, moved with the precision of an atomic clock, following the course of the chunk of rock, metal and ice as it glided silently from beyond the asteroid belt, past us and on to nowhere. At least to nowhere until the computers calculated its precise mass and exact velocity as expressed by its angular motion. They also had to allow for the Earth's gravitational pull, the motion of the Earth itself, and half a dozen other factors that influenced this chunk of rock. For three days Dr. Hydon, his dedicated assistants, and the array of computers linked into a single giant electronic brain worked to answer as least some of these question. Finally the contours of the object lost their definition and, moments later, melted into the darkness of the great beyond. For now, their work was done.

"You may go now," Dr. Hydon muttered stretching his back. "Get some sleep."

With that Dr. John Hydon rose to his feet and left the observatory. The computers would continue to churn out detailed calculations of the data they'd gathered over the last three days. They needed neither sleep nor food. Just power. Men needed rest. They'd earned it.

As Dr. Hydon left the dome the diffused lights came on. They signified that no more observations would be carried out that night. As he entered the lush garden, his face assumed its usual mask of studied indifference. He had worn it now for almost three years. Since his wife, my mother, had died. A mask that hid both, that which was and that which wasn't there. In those days I found it hard to think of him as my father. It hurt too much. Not that I did much thinking at that age. But I did feel. Mostly loneliness. And absence.

The next day, things got back to normal.

There was no surprise when the asteroid missed the earth by a mere 300,000 kilometres. Whatever gods designed and maintained the orbits of the thousands, possibly millions, of chunks of matter populating our solar system must have done a good job. Again. It was the third time in as many years, that minor, irregularly shaped interplanetary nuggets of matter had been observed by the scientific community. The first two had not even been reported. They'd missed us by too wide a margin. By astronomical standards 300,000 kilometres was a mere hair's breadth, a light-second, a distance travelled by light in a single second. A light-hour would represent about one billion kilometres. Yet in terms of safety of life on earth it was as though it had never happened. There was absolutely no danger to anyone, even to the array of satellites suspended in their gyrations around our mother planet.

Following the press release by the Canadian National Observatory, the dailies carried a note on the third page, and that only because it was a *Canadian* astronomer who had provided the data. Not one of our money-stacked cousins south of the 50th parallel had even spotted the event. No doubt the Hollywood dream spinners would have been inspired to put out another series of disaster films. I can just see the placards: "The Last Days on Earth", "The Human Dinosaur", or "The Asteroid!!!", yes, with three exclamation marks, or something equally as ridiculous. Lots of explosions, lots of electronic noise and flashing lights. The juvenile delinquents liked this sort of thing. By the time Mozart was five, he'd composed a symphony. It would be ludicrous to compare his genius to ordinary mortals. Not because the human genius had died with Amadeus, but because by the time the youth of today reached this age, they were already half-deaf. Over-amplified hullabaloo was the essence of their concept of having fun. Noise and flashing lights. For the immature mind, this appears to serve as some sort of escape. From what, no one knows.

I shouldn't really talk like that. Makes me sound old. I suspect, in my own way, I'd soon begin indulging in my own escapes. I can picture Dad's, the famous Dr. Hydon's, brilliant if tired mind straying to his children.

"They really are my children," he must have sighed. "I sired them. Will I ever start acting like their father?"

His forehead bruised into tiny vertical chasms as the silent question found its way to his frontal lobe. "Will I ever do them justice?"

And a voice deeper than conscious awareness shrugged with studied indifference. "Not yet," it seemed to say. "I need time. More time!"

Even though I was only a new born at the time, I can still see his pain...

I can see him shaking his head. "Excuses!" he muttered under his nose. He hated himself in such moments. Deep down, he knew what he had to do. Deep down things were simpler. But in the light of day, they were different. Usually people see ghosts at night. John spent his nights in the Observatory. Ghosts surrounded him in the daylight. Especially in the early morning, when the stars began to recede into the advancing grayness, but before the dawn gave reality to the here-and-now. There, in the Monster Eye, the stars were never here and now. The light he studied had been born when the universe was young. Even when our own little home was young. Billions of years before the dinosaurs ruled the Earth. The stars belonged to the way back when. They bore witness to a past so distant as to be hardly imaginable. In some ways, he worked in the realm of the dead. Of the long gone and forgotten.

The same ghosts visited him towards the end of the day. When light was waning. When he could no longer distinguish the sharp, hard contours around him, yet before his beloved stars claimed his undivided attention. At those times his children, their faces innocent, seemingly so very indifferent, sauntered across his vision. He would rather work day and night, provide for them, pay for their every need, pay for the best nanny he could find. He would do anything rather then face either one of them. As a father.

"Not yet," his lips formed the silent words. "Please, Heidi, not yet..."

How do I know all this? After all, at the time, I'd only just been born. At the very beginning. But I know. I know and I feel. As though it were yesterday. As though I'd witnessed it all first hand.

Even as I sit here, my fingers poised lightly over the keyboard of my computer, my eyes drift up, towards the sunset, where the gossamer cobwebs of scattered clouds hang suspended, effortlessly, over the blue and the green. How beautiful she is. Was?

Used to be?

Am I imagining this as I had so many things over the last thirty years? Isn't reality that which we perceive as real? Is not the wondrous globe suspended in an ocean of sparkling black velvet – the Earth, my home?

Is not this beauty, beyond all that is beautiful, not drifting away from me? Slowly, almost imperceptibly?

Within the Enigma there is no time. Things, events, even ideas are all jumbled up. So is space. There is no sequential order of any kind. There are no terms of reference until events are arranged chronologically. It is a little like life flashing before your eyes at the moment of death – all events are there, stored in the Enigma, waiting to be recognized. Organized. We experience it as the process of becoming. And it takes time.

Well, time, it seems, I've got in abundance. Perhaps forever. Isn't this what immortality is all about? Anyway, even then, in the fullness of time, the events only make relative sense when placed in the context of transformation. Even our senses or feelings are only relative. Like a point of view. One can only see one side of things – at a time.

But I am ahead of myself again.

Enough said that since, at the time, I'd hardly been born, I did not recognize my father as an individual towards whom I felt any affinity. When recalling those days, I prefer to refer to him in the third person singular. I can hardly refer to him as Dad before he'd become one. Can I?

For Dr. Hydon neither of the Hollywood made-for-TV-movies, which appeared within two months of the asteroid event, was very likely to happen at all. The world was not about to be torn apart by a shower of meteorites, nor would life be destroyed by the resulting climatic changes. Space was both empty and full of junk. Events with any dire consequences were expected to occur once in every 100,000 years at most. Global disasters, meteoric cataclysms, remained the domain of the earlier universe or of the doomsday thrill seekers. Or as David had said, of the special effects department.

There had been some celestial 'accidents', like those that left their imprints in Barringer, Arizona, a crater of 1200 meters in diameter, or almost as large an indentation in Lona, India. Or even the 850-meter Wolf Creek Crater, in West Australia. There were another half-dozen authenticated impact craters scattered around the globe, ranging in diameter from 90 to 250 meters, but those hardly threatened the survival of humanity. We had no idea, of course, how many had splashed into our extensive oceans, but that was another matter. For now, we had nothing to worry about.

If there had been any danger to anyone or anything, it was to the slightly inflated ego of Dr. John Hydon Ph.D., who detected the presence of the inoffensive object hurtling through space in our "immediate" vicinity only *after* it had missed us, and was already receding into outer space. His only consolation was that no one, not even one other astronomer had detected its passing presence at all. Not until he had announced his data. Then his colleagues hastily confirmed the sighting, but with conflicting data. They had to say something if they were to qualify for the movie screenplays. Dr. Hydon did not suffer from such ambitions. Astronomy was his life. Years had passed since he'd wasted any of his time on the dream spinner's offerings. He had dreams of his own. Aplenty.

What might have happened had the rock come much closer to our atmosphere remained a moot question. Dr. Hydon dealt in hard-nosed reality, not in idle speculation. Work for him served as an escape from wandering thoughts. Most who knew him better, guessed as much. He never talked about it. Only those closest to him knew that behind the mask of studied indifference there beat the heart of a poet, a philosopher, perhaps even of an incontrovertible dreamer.

This is awkward.

I think I shall refer to John Hydon as father, or Dad. After all, what is time? Since it is a matter of record that, in the fullness of it, he did become my father. Outside the constraints we choose to impose on time by our need for a sequential order, he is my father *in esse* as well as *in futuro*, so to speak. It is a question of 'I am', versus 'I was' or 'I shall be'. Did I not chose him, as well as my mother, to be the instruments through which I would experience, once more, my mode of becoming? They were my parents even before time began. Or to put it differently, in the 'now' they *are* my parents. There is an infinite number of possible futures for each one of us. But all those futures are no more than projections of the eternal now. This is the true meaning of immortality. And in this particular version of my becoming, they will always be my parents.

A week later, Dad got excited again.

This time he was sure that he'd spotted a celestial body just outside the orbit of Pluto. He and his staff had been directing the brand-new, the most sensitive optical telescope in the world, at the segment of space just outside Pluto's orbit. Perhaps it was the location of the Observatory that gave it an edge over other sky-gazers. The climate in the Yukon Territory generally, let alone atop Ogilvy Mountain, offered a purity of air quite remarkable by modern standards. Not only did the cool temperature assure very low moisture, but there was minimal pollution of any kind, and certainly no city lights to interfere with the star light. Except for the Hubble, the National Observatory had an edge, an advantage, other astronomers could only dream of.

Three times already father had photographed a wispy shape that corresponded to a sphere, perhaps a large comet or a small planetoid, travelling in, what appeared to be a regular orbit, just outside our solar system. The reason the suspected celestial body remained invisible, at least most of the time he reasoned, was that its course seemed synchronized with that of Pluto. It was as though it was using Pluto to shield itself from human eyes. Only planetoids don't do that. Unless, of course, it was trapped by Pluto's gravitational pull which would have to have been greater than scientists had heretofore imagined. What father feared was that his discovery might simply be a reflection of Pluto in some transient cloud of space dust or of interstellar gas that had drifted towards our solar system and became trapped by the gravitational pull of our sun.

Whatever the cause, the Observatory was the only place where Dad got excited. The rest of his life seemed of little or no consequence. It did not matter. Outside his lab, father moved like an automaton, a polite if aloof robot, asking for nothing, giving nothing in return. He did his duty. He didn't really care if anyone approved his behaviour or not. He was a good scientist – he knew that. Everyone knew that. If his personal life was in shambles, it was none of anyone's business.

Not for a long while. Not for three years. Three years of abject emptiness.

When my father examined the computer printouts the next morning, his excitement grew to unprecedented heights. Astronomers live for discoveries. They spend innumerable hours peering at photographs, superimposing them one over the other to detect any changes in pattern, compute endless data – columns upon columns of numbers – all in the hope of spotting something, some unaccounted for movement, a change, a variable, that no one had spotted before. Luckily for Dad, the overwhelming majority of the peering, superimposition and computation were done by the latest generation of dedicated computers. A new comet, an undiscovered galaxy heretofore hidden by interstellar dark matter – its light diluted by thousands of light-years, or any anomaly in the established order of things were enough to make any astronomer's day. Or father's day, for that matter.

After the initial excitement, his mind under control, father gave instructions to his staff to study the photographs and reverted to his private dream world. That's right. In those years, more than ever father had needed an escape. Astronomical discoveries were few and far between. What he liked to do, especially at night when only a skeleton staff remained, was to scan the sky looking for ghosts. Not with the Monster Eye, of course. The main telescope's time was too precious. It worked full time. There was a long waiting list for its unique services. There were scientists galore waiting in line for the privilege of taking a peek at their favourite segment of space.

No. Father ventured into space on his own very private wings.

What Dad used was one of the three sixty-centimetre optic telescopes, one of which he'd founded himself. There was seldom a waiting list for the smaller spyglasses. Like the ancient Greeks, Dad searched for constellations. He had, of course, an enormous advantage over the early Greeks. He could puncture holes in the sky much deeper than the Greeks had ever imagined possible. Even, Nicolaus Copernicus and Galileo Galilei would have given their right arms for the toys Dad had to play with. Not even counting the Monster Eye. He would set his lenses to record only stars at specific distances from Earth. At least they alone would remain in focus while others receded into oblivion. He was looking for something that would bring back an image, a shadow, a fragment of a memory he'd lost. An image of his wife. Sometimes, when his soul cried out the loudest, he was sure he'd found a vague contour, a silhouette, an ephemeral shadow of my mother Heidi's face, or the curve of her neck, or a contour of her presence adorning the speckled darkness. A vague, ethereal contour, yet so very real to him, a lingering memory, a dream....

Yet even then, when he'd found something, the pain would not recede.

The pain was a mixture of love and hatred, a feeling that, in its irrepressible dichotomy, tore him apart. The pain, the cause of his pain, was his daughter. Me. The tiny copy of his late wife. The mother I'd never met. The constant reminder of her absence. I can't say that at the time I was really aware of any of this. But babies can sense things. Or emotions. Believe me.

The first time round, my father had married late. He was already forty years old. He had been appointed to lead a team of scientists at the brand new CNO. The Canadian National Observatory. That's what they called it then. Later it became known as the Canadian Science Centre. The CSC. At that time it consisted of seven geodesic domes, with virtually unlimited expansion possibilities in the future. The architectural and engineering design was breaking new ground in every way imaginable. Experimental in location, in scope, in the nature of construction, in every way anyone could think of. If it hadn't been for that day's technology, it couldn't have worked. Communication is imperative to successful operations of any scientific endeavour. No experimental work can function without it. Internet, global viphone link, instant exchange of ideas are what makes Science work. And the Centre was the very state of the art. One could still smell fresh paint. Those were the early days. One could call them the beginning. Yet for father, in so many ways, they were also the end. The end of a time in his life that he wanted to, but couldn't, leave behind. Not till much, much later. Poor Dad.

All this was some thirty years ago.

The first three years were the last during which I and JJ remained neutral. Later... later, so much happened. Beyond my wildest imagination. Beyond what anyone could possibly have imagined. Later, all three of us, Dad, JJ and myself, took off on our own particular tangents. Like comets that hold disdain for regular orbital order. But, as you'll see, the universe, even space itself, curves upon itself. No matter where you go, you end up close to where you started. Only your perception of the place will have changed. In some ways, you would never have moved. It was the world that had spun on its intricate orbit.

Those first three years were also the last years during which neither JJ nor myself managed to influence the ramblings of father's vacillating mind. At least, not in the scientific sense. In father's psyche, those three years marked the end of an era.

The end of the beginning.

**

2

Hey

They had chosen my name not in honour of my mother, but my great-great grandmother. Since the early nineteenth century, all the first daughters in my mother's family had been named Heidi. It had become a cherished tradition. Since then, whenever any Heidi, worldwide, had been accorded any achievement, Heidi's family took it as personal honour. This too became a tradition. My mother's family had more celebrations than any family my father had ever come across. They were a happy lot.

Until little Heidi arrived. That's me.

In my particular case, the family tradition was practically all for nothing. A few weeks after I'd uttered the first, proverbial Dada, all too natural in the absence of a mother, I've been told that I began referring to myself as Hey. Hey wants this, Hey wants that. Or else... Hey whaaaaa...

My grandmother had been an operatic soprano. In spite of the tiny capacity of my lungs, I had inherited a powerful resonance. So much so that Dad put a spare bedroom between himself and his little daughter's room. Father usually slept during the day. He needed all the rest he could get after a long night of stargazing.

Little Hey wasn't Dad's only child, but she was the only child my parents had together. When I was born, John Junior, JJ, was already three years old. He was the product of father's previous

marriage, still in England. Soon after JJ was born Dad's first marriage ended in divorce. He felt that not just Margaret, his first wife,
had died, but all things associated with her had died also. (In fact,
to the best of my knowledge, Margaret has remained in robust
health.) Nevertheless, in spite of JJ, father was hard put to recall
any memories he missed. There was no animosity. Just a lingering
sense of indifference.

My parents immigrated to Canada. When little Hey arrived,
things changed. For everyone. At forty-three, Dad became a widower twice over.

Other than that, there was virtually no feeling at all.

JJ likewise felt doubly abandoned. Like his father, he blamed
his sister, me, for his second mom's sudden departure. He'd only
just learned to trust Heidi like a real mom. More so. As for little
Hey, from the moment she'd begun crawling along the floor of her
playroom she must have felt even more forsaken. At least I imagine
that's what I must have felt. On some level of perception that only
the smallest children can feel, she must have sensed an inherent
resentment, or perhaps a repressed hostility, or even a sense of
blame directed at herself. Not understanding what it all meant she
began, nevertheless, even during those first years, or months, to
start building for herself a sanctuary where no one could hurt her.
She was forced to crawl into a tiny world, to conjure imagery, a
reality that was kinder and warmer. She soon learned that, whatever is earthly, associated with other people, whatever is made up
of anything tangible that she could see or touch with her senses, is
likely to be transient, ephemeral, not deserving of her attention.
She felt that the world she had been brought into was cold and unforgiving. Even before her father's nightly escapes, she'd set out
on the long journey into the realm of her private dreams.

By the time Hey was three, she seemed secure in her own
realm. Or nearly so.

For my father, the second tragedy, second death as he thought of
it, so soon after the previous dissolution, was infinitely more painful than the loss of his first wife. Margaret – never Marge or Mag-

gie, always Margaret – a girl from good Stafford stock, had been punctilious, very proper, and always supportive of her husband's aspirations. Having been raised by nannies and private teachers herself, she'd never experienced real family life. She had no worldly knowledge to contribute. Not knowledge based on personal experience. Other than what she'd acquired at an expensive Finishing School in Switzerland. While Margaret was invariably 'very correct' in public, when they were on their own, particularly during the first few months, she was a veritable hellcat; in the nicest way possible, of course.

Another thing that the Finishing School had accomplished was to get rid of the last remnants of any sexual hang-ups. Margaret, on their very first weekend together, which was only two days after they'd met, took the concept of freedom of action between two consenting adults to a new level. Both, up and down. The whole gamut. Margaret had shown him what adult movies were made of and perhaps given new meaning to the word 'adult'. Father, who'd been no angel during his time at Cambridge, had felt strangely inadequate, timid, reserved, even shy. To do her justice, she'd performed all the contortions in the best possible taste, with the exception, perhaps, of insisting on all the lights being turned on. She was not after romance. She was after sating her cravings, after releasing her pent up, repressed desires that were held in check during her usual and abnormally repressed, proper, punctilious, cold behaviour. We all pay for our repression. Margaret found a number of innovative methods to extract payment from father as well.

After she had given my father a son, as a good wife should, she believed that, at least for now, her marital obligations had been fully discharged. The fire of the first few weeks was displaced by apathy, even distaste toward any sexual activity. With her, it was an all-or-nothing proposition. For the rest of their marriage, father settled for virtually nothing. A state of limbo. In spite of all this, Dad thought he loved her until, supposedly on the rebound after the divorce, he'd met my mother.

Only six months after he'd regained his bachelor status, John Hydon came across Heidi, to be honest, quite by accident. Literally. He'd fished her out of the lake, like a mysterious and beauti-

ful mermaid, and instantly fell in love. Or at least as fast as he'd
managed to clear his eyes from all the splashing and from the water
dripping from his still abundant hair. He cleared his vision, he saw,
he conquered. Actually, he had been conquered. Veni, vidi, Heidi
vincit. He'd fallen proverbially head-over-heels, which, appropriately, was the way he'd met her. Wet head over wet heels.

For Dad, his second marriage, was like the Second Coming. It
gave him a new lease on life. It made him alive again. It shook
him out of an emotional stupor. It opened a new colourful world.
A world both vibrant and filled with love, with caring, with step-
ping outside himself. It was a world where time was of little consequence. Life flowed with a renewed current, fed by springs that
seemed eternal. Father felt as though he'd been born again, to a
new wondrous life of serenity and happiness.

Until that fateful time, Dad had never realized what true love
could be like. Heidi, my mother, not only filled a gaping hole in
his life, but she filled an emptiness he hadn't known existed. In
finding Heidi, Dad had found himself. Not surprisingly, his new
wife became a loving mother to JJ, a woman Dad could count on,
consult on his day-to-day problems, rest in her presence. In her
arms. Her arms seemed in constant demand. She asked for little
yet was an inexhaustible source of giving. She made Dad feel like
an enchanting lover, a dutiful husband, an excellent provider, a
good father. She was full of laughter, a ray of sunshine on an overcast day, particularly because on such days, or nights rather, he
couldn't get on with his astronomic observations, but was forced to
catch up on paperwork that the computers churned out with unparalleled regularity.

My mother was the very antithesis of the cool, perfectly controlled, always correct Margaret. In no time at all, all memory of
Dad's first wife receded into the hazy, uneventful, unemotional
past. As with outer space, it got cooler as it receded from the sun.
Heidi was his sun. His blinding nova. My mother had been too
good to last...

At the time, father could hardly cope with his emotions. Usually men fall in love with such abandon before they turn twenty,
twenty-five at most. Dad had been almost forty, at the time. But
his heart beat with the euphoria of an adolescent.

I find it vaguely amusing how distant memories saunter into my mind, in bits and pieces, little unordered snippets, like disjointed strips of lace, woven loosely into the fabric of my life.

There was a time, albeit a very short period, when I was no more than six or seven, that my father managed to inspire the same awe in my heart when observing the Milky Way as he'd held when in his early twenties. Dad regarded the expanse of some fifty billion visible stars held together in a vise of still inexplicable attraction at the centre of our galaxy as his personal backyard, his home within the home of the entire Universe. To John, to Dr. Hydon, not just planets but even individual stars were as atoms of his own body – expedient, necessary, holding a beauty in their own right, but virtually insignificant constituents of his whole, physical self. Nearby, for the most part, all else was puny. Nearby, for Dad included our Solar System, up to and including Pluto, though the outer planet, which some years ago some eggheads attempted to relegate to the status of a planetoid, travelled an orbit that averaged almost six million kilometres from the sun.   He would spend hours, each night when the conditions permitted, staring at 'The Galaxy, that Milky Way... Powdered with Stars,' as Milton referred to it in Paradise Lost. Only Dad's paradise was still there, awaiting him, drawing him into its cold, fiery embrace, night after night, month after month....

Every night that weather permitted.

Later, at least for a time, his interest shifted to astrophysical theories. Not really at the expense of his prime passion, but to broaden his field. He rationalized that he did so to establish himself among his peers. At that time, he succumbed to what was fashionable, to what enabled him to publish more papers in the scientific Journals. But only for a while. A few years. When his original passion returned, it did so with renewed force. After sauntering through the whole of the visible universe, he returned to Via Lactis. To the River of billions of silvery fish. He dove into its currents, studied its depth and breadth, he swam deep in its waters. The Milky Way was the path he revisited to recapture his lost happiness.

It seems to have worked.

Since then, his personal antagonism towards me waned and then all but disappeared. But it took a miracle to consolidate his new state of mind. It was during such serene nights that he'd first won, and then lost his daughter's heart.

But, yet again, we are running ahead of ourselves. All this came later. It seems like ages into the distant future.

Little Hey never met her mother. The complications began during the sixth month of pregnancy. They exacerbated considerably as mother neared my delivery. Dad wanted his wife to abort the child. That's right, to abort me. Men do not feel the same nearness to the unborn child as women do. How could they? All that mattered to father was his wife. She was his life, his inspiration, his *raison d'être*. There was nothing he wouldn't have done for her. As cruel as it may sound, it included losing a daughter. An almost daughter. My mother refused.

"If we are to be her parents, nothing will stop us. If not...?" She left the question hanging.

Father knew his wife well enough to finish the sentence for her. "...we can waste energy fighting a losing battle, but nothing will change whatever is written in the stars for us." That was the romantic postulate my mother had lived by. Father had disagreed. He thought Shakespeare was right when he said that it is not in our stars but in ourselves that we are underlings. Mother did not oppose this sentiment. She only thought that we should have the equanimity to accept our destiny with grace. That we should never despair, nor oppose the inevitable, but know that all is for the best.

"Well, it wasn't. Nor for me," Dad must have thought, his jaws set sternly. "Nor for me, my love." I can picture my father's face set in repressed anger. I've seen it as such since. Remember, at the time I hadn't been born yet.

But no one had listened to Dad. Neither my mother nor the doctors. "There is a chance," they said.

Apparently there is always a chance. But for mother there wasn't. No one had listened to father any more. He must have felt

incredibly alone. Deserted. JJ was much too young, and Mary,
well, Mary had her job to do.

Father didn't really have any friends. With the exception of
the Mendels. Perhaps because it was too soon after arrival in
Canada. Relatively speaking, Dad was still a newcomer. Perhaps
he suffered from the proverbial English reserve; perhaps he really
was shy. Then. In addition he was also a little too senior, too well
positioned, professionally – riding herd just a little too high over
his staff. It's hard to make friends when you're the boss. Whatever his faults, Dad was popular enough. He was invited to all the
usual drinks after work, although, often enough, he finished working in the early hours of the morning. Not many people invite you
for a drink at sunrise. Such limitations notwithstanding, father had
no one he could really call close. Not a man, nor woman, he could
call a friend. A real friend. As much as he liked David and Miriam
Mendel – they had been so very kind – he was hardly disposed to
opening his heart to them. Perhaps he didn't know how. Perhaps
I've inherited this seeming inability from my father. It could be
that Dad had never shared his inner desires with anyone. Not before he'd met Heidi and not since she died. And during those brief
moments they shared together, much less than a year, they hardly
noticed the world around them. At least, this was true of John Hydon. Of my father. I know. I've seen him in those days. In my
own way. In the Enigma. When my mother died, Dad had still
been in the process of discovering his wife.

It had been mother, already carrying his child, who wanted
them to emigrate. It was still before any trouble had started. Before the complications.

"Here, darling," she'd said, "you'll wait for decades before Dr.
Penderton retires." She was referring to the snail's pace of advancement in England. "By then you'll have lost your passion for
the stars. You will be too set in your ways to branch out on your
own." Dr. Penderton, Dad's immediate superior in Cambridge Institute, was only fifty years old. It would have been a long wait.

Mother had been talking about Dad's ambition to make his
mark on the Astronomical Establishment. He thought he could
prove that, at the centre of our galaxy, there is a Black Hole. There

have been some loose theories to that effect, but none backed up by
hard scientific data. He thought that, given a free hand, he could do
it. But it would take years of observations. He would have to direct his own team. Men he could trust not to steal his results. She
had been right, of course. Heidi, my mother, was always right.
Especially in matters that concerned father's welfare.

She gazed at him like a teenager on her first date. They'd
been married for just over three months. And mother was little
more than a teenager. I've spent timeless hours staring at them in
that moment. Up there. In my dreams.

It was true that Heidi had been a country girl. Dad had met
her in the Midlands, in the Lake District, on a sailing holiday.
She'd fallen overboard and he pulled her out.

"I owe you my life!" she'd exclaimed. She would have been
more convincing if her eyes hadn't shone with unabashed pleasure
as he put his arm around her to pull her into his Flying Dutchman.
Only later father had learned that she was an excellent swimmer.
She wouldn't have drowned if she'd gone overboard in the middle
of the Pacific Ocean.

Well, if reasonably close to the ship.

A rare smile widened Dad's mouth as he recalled those precious moments. That was what he'd lived on, those first few years.
On memories. They'd sustained him. They allowed him to do his
work like an efficient automaton, a robot that managed to switch
off its emotional circuits. But he couldn't face his own daughter.
He couldn't face me.

Mary was not a professional nurse but she did her best. After
the nine months of security that only a mother's womb can provide,
Heidi, little Hey, had emerged into the world, and weaned herself,
by force, into the reality she'd neither wanted nor asked for. My
father, whose renewed attraction to the stars to escape the reality of
his wife's death, continued to keep his distance. Dad was too crestfallen, too numb, to be able to transfer his love from Heidi to little
Hey. From Heidi to Heidi – even the names sounded offensive to
him. On some level of his shattered psyche he held his daughter
responsible for his wife's death. Not consciously, of course. Yet

even his eyes, which were used to staring at the icy starlight, would not soften when he looked at his baby – its arms raised as though saying, pick me up, Daddy. Please, pick me up.

I'm glad I don't really remember that. Not really. Just....

Heidi wasn't a she. To him, it was a baby. She was an 'it'.

Father couldn't pick her up. As beautiful as she was, as tiny and innocent, his heart was so filled with pain that he would walk away, quickly, without looking back. After he'd leave his daughter's presence, he would walk directly to his laboratory, day or night, regardless of the weather. There was always plenty to do. Plenty to occupy his mind. That was what he needed most. Less than a kilometre up the hill, he'd walk through the carefully laid out gardens he barely noticed, and then immerse himself in the avalanche of data, which the computers had been churning out in a constant, impassive, unemotional way. This indifference, this clarity, was what he craved. To overcome his sorrow he sought to eradicate his capacity to feel. Such were the first three years of his daughter's life. My first three years. Three years to the day. The pain may have lifted gradually. His reticence to forgive his daughter took longer.

As for little Hey, there were advantages to her assumed stance – to the protective shell I'd erected for myself. I was the very inverse of that with which my father had to deal on a daily basis. He had lost so much. I was unaware of ever having lost anything. I had nothing to lose. My tiny, private universe obeyed its own private laws. I had never experience any other reality. Love, in the maternal sense, was unknown to me. For that matter I was a stranger to any form of love. My heart was untouched, unblemished, emotionally virginal.

Later, things changed, of course. All things change. Lately more so than ever. But my first real memories actually start on or about my third birthday.

On my third birthday, a miracle happened.

No. No angels swooned from the sky, no heavenly choirs influenced Dad's state of mind. On her third birthday, Hey fell from
the balcony. It was only from the second floor and she fell on top
of the thick branches of a juniper bush. Its mature, tightly inter-
woven twigs broke her fall. Other than a few tiny scratches, she
was safe and sound. Yet even that near escape wasn't the miracle.
It, the wonder of wonders, took place in her father's heart. He realized, suddenly, that if it hadn't been for sheer luck, he would have
lost the only person he held dear in the whole world. There was JJ,
of course, and in his own way, Dad loved his son also. But there
were other skeletons in the cupboard of his tormented soul. And
anyway, it was not the same type of love – towards a boy. Dad's
heart had been starving for the only link to his only real love. To
my mother. I had my mother's eyes. Her mouth. Even her hair.

"How come I've never noticed this before?" I could feel his
heart speaking.

He kept looking at me as though seeing me for the very first
time. In a way it was. And it was also my first conscious memory.
Upon seeing me, my father's eyes filled with wonder.

Heidi was Heidi. She was her mother's image. It had taken
three years, but in that perilous moment of her fall from that balcony – in that single instant – little Heidi, the tiny Hey, had become
his daughter. No longer a culprit who was even partially responsible for her mother's death, but the only cherished link to her
mother, to his wife, to the memory of her still anchored in the emptiness of his heart.

Many years passed before I met my mother. Many long
years. But Dad had been right. She and I did look alike. Still do.

For the very first time, John Hydon picked up his daughter and
held her in his arms. He wanted this magical moment to last forever. Finally, after some long minutes, Mary suggested that he
might put me down. For a while he appeared not to hear her. Only
when the starched and proper nanny put her hands around little Hey
and placed her on the floor, had Dad returned to reality.

"Begging you pardon, Sir, but the little sweetheart couldn't
breathe very easily. With you holding her so tight and all..." Mary
admonished sternly.

She would never admit it, but she would protect her charge with her life, even against father's inexperience. The nurse, nanny, was a precious import from the Old Country where she was born, where she had lived, and if it hadn't been for my mother, where she would have died. Mary had lived near Sheffield.

If fact, she was born in Spinkhill, a forgotten village in whose borough father had gone to school, at the Mount St. Stanislaus Kostka's College. A Jesuit institution. Prison, he called it then. And for years after. But that was almost three decades ago; it had been even longer since he'd immigrated to Canada and married Heidi. His wife had given her life to present him with this wondrous angel. A gift he'd rejected, for three full years, out of hand.

Until she fell. Until she'd fallen from the balcony. A few inches to the left, and she would not have survived. He was sure of that. As sure as he was that he held her in his arms. For the very first time.

Dad had been wrong. I had been meant to live on. I know that now.

It was from that fateful birthday that Dad's attitude toward his daughter changed diametrically. It was as though he needed to catch up on the lost years. He not only spent every free moment with her, in her playroom, or in their tiny garden, but took her to his office where he'd arranged a playpen for her. Not a rectangular cage to constrain her movement, but he'd rearranged his office in such a way that I could romp free everywhere, yet keep my busy fingers from innumerable electrical connections, and, almost as importantly, from the computer keys. Dad and I, Hey as he called me, became as inseparable as is possible for a little girl and the Director of the Observatory, an Astronomer of some repute, a man conducting constant research with the newest, the best and the most expensive telescope in the history of Canadian science.

In no time at all members of his staff were finding excuses to knock on his door. They had no business with Dr. Hydon; they all wanted to steal a glance at Hey, who willingly showed off 'her' office to all-comers.

"And this is co-puter with keeeys," I vaguely recall explaining gravely. "And here are the movies," as I pointed to the screen. "You can see stars in there, did you know that?"

Most of them did, but every single visitor had been enchanted. I say that with all modesty. In no time at all Heidi had stolen a lot more than just her father's heart. She was becoming the sweetheart of the Observatory. A mascot.

During all this time, Dad and JJ had grown further and further apart. Often enough, JJ had been present when Dad played with his sister. Sometimes, when she was asleep, Dad would even throw the ball with him. Or they would go for a walk together. But... the estrangement that Hey must have felt, subconsciously, during her first three years, now began to drive JJ away also. First, my dear brother had lost his mother. Then, his second mother. And now Dad was showering attention on his sister. He felt like a child adopted by a man who loved both his children but only one was of his true blood.

JJ had been only six years old when the change occurred on my third birthday. Before that fateful day, he'd taken his father's coolness as a natural form of behaviour. The English Nanny, Mary, would cuddle him up in bed, dress him and feed him, cater to his every need. Except to the needs of his heart. He had little idea of what he was missing, other than his mother, until he saw the change in Dad towards Hey. Then suspicions that he was an odd cog in the family wheel grew in him. Again, it was only a feeling, an undefined suspicion, but he'd begun to erect a protective barrier between himself and his father. In order not to miss paternal love, he had to learn not to need it.

In time he succeeded.

***

3

JJ

Amazing though it may have seemed at the time, JJ took the loss of his first, natural mother in his stride. At the time of his parents' divorce, he was almost three years old. Even then he was being treated by his mother, as well as by the rest her family, as an adult. A little adult. As the only male descendant to the Stafford dynasty to-date, he was afforded all the benefits that Margaret's breeding and heritage could provide. He was raised by the best professional staff, all fully accredited by the best British Institutions. They treated him with all the due respect. His slightest whim was taken care of. But in all this abundance there was little room for love. Unfortunately for JJ, and for all other boys in his circumstances, love was not for sale. No matter how affluent your parents. No matter how much love mama and papa deposited into their bank accounts.

Of course, JJ was not JJ in those days. Not even John Junior. He was John Percival Sebastian Hydon. John after his father, Percival after his grandfather, and Sebastian after the forefather who had first been named the Earl of Stafford by King George IV, way back in the 1820's. Lord Percival had not earned his title like some common money-maker. He had inherited his breeding. He was the

Earl of Stafford, as his forefathers before him. If just eleven members in line to the succession of the Staffords' earldom met with a
sudden death, JJ would inherit the title. Lord JJ, he could become.
But only under certain, rather special, circumstances. Unfortunately or not, only William Shakespeare knew how to get rid of
eleven inconvenient members of one's family with impunity.
Shakespeare and, perhaps, Agatha Christie.

No matter. JJ was happy just being JJ.

By the time his father remarried, little John Percival Sebastian,
aka JJ, had already learned to be reasonably self-sufficient. Emotionally, that is. After all, at the time, he was only three years old.
JJ's father (my own *in futuro*), for his part, was as inexperienced in
the mysteries of parenthood as any man whose total energies had
been poured into self-betterment. Presumably, if subconsciously, to
close the colour gap between his blood and his wife's. But the
Staffords were not after his blood, only after it's colour. They bled
blue. An assistant professorship at the University of Cambridge
Institute of Astronomy did little to raise his social status. He
worked for a living – which was bad enough. That he was a member of the working class was inexcusable. One can work for a living providing one doesn't actually need to or in fact do anything.
A sort of Sino-British version of *wu-wei*. Literal meaning of the
Taoist expression is 'without action.' The British version would be
'the gentleman's way', meaning maximum effect with minimum
effort – although serious scholars would doubtless hang me on the
nearest branch for such an over-simplification. Nevertheless, the
Staffords held, some professions might be acceptable. Like a
Prime Minister, or a politician, or any member of the House of
Lords. But teaching?

"Too much like work, old chap. Must get you a better position. Perhaps a deanship, or something of that nature, what?"
There was always a perfunctory question mark on the end of a sentence as though no one was listening anyway.

They all cared about John, the father of John Percival Sebastian. The eleventh down-the-line heir. You could never tell.... Yet
even then JJ's father often wondered if he had been appointed to
his position at Cambridge only after some confidential intervention
by his father-in-law, Lord Percival, who while denying any such

action on his part, did so with a pronounced wink. The old *wu-wei?*

"Don't shortchange yourself, my boy," the moustachioed magnate would say, his mouth contorted in a vaguely cantankerous cross between a grin and an almost permanent sneer. "You will go, ah... a long way, what?" his Lordship would add, the index finger of his left hand brushing both sides of his thin lips as if to underscore the feeble growth over the upper part of his aristocratic mouth. And then he would wave his hand dismissing the matter, or perhaps John himself, from his illustrious presence.

Somehow whenever Lord P offered assurance regarding his future, father had expected him to add: "I'll see to that, old boy, what?" It had been obvious even if unsaid. The son-in-law of Lord P was destined to go a long way. At least I thought that was what father would have detected in his tone. I have to make up some of these things to make them real. Well, sort of.

Eventually John Hydon did go a long way. To Canada. Without Lord P's assistance, though ostensibly with a sigh of blue-blooded relief.

Of course, none of this had anything to do with little JJ, other than the proud genes that he'd inherited from his patrician mother.

To my future father it came as a pleasant surprise that, after the divorce, neither Margaret, nor any other member of her family, laid any claim to JJ. He was treated as *corpus delicti* of their daughter's misdemeanour, an unfortunate product of misalliance at best. If John wanted to emigrate and take JJ with him, it was fine with them. In fact, the sooner the better. They all felt that Margaret had made a grave mistake in marrying John Hydon, a junior astronomer no one had ever heard of.

"Nice enough fellow, you know," they all said of John, for the want of something better to say. But just not quite a chip off the old block, so to speak.

The real but less known reason for the wedding bells – even among the cognoscenti – was that Margaret had been in her second month with John's child. A little misadventure after a little too much Champagne at Ascot. Lord P's 'Ladybird', a magnificent

filly bred in Lord P's stables, had won. And one simply had to
drink Champagne at Ascot. And after such a victory? Well, really!
Don't you know, darling?

For some years after the divorce, Dad wondered why Margaret
had agreed to marry him at all. To this day this question remained
unanswered. It never crossed his mind that John Hydon, in his late
thirties, struck a superb figure of a man. A man as handsome as he
was tall and athletic. At least in appearance. In fact, he alone in
the house of Lord P displayed an easy, effortless aristocratic bearing. His posture, his chiselled features, slightly hawked nose and
high forehead crowned with abundant dark hair just a little too
long, were all more suited to Stratford on Avon, or the Old Vic,
than to astronomy. His charisma flowed from the total lack of
awareness of his obvious attributes, obvious to any and every woman, while raising pangs of jealousy among most men he met. If
anything, it had been Lady P's side of the family who shared some
of John's physical traits.

Whatever Margaret may or may not have been, she and John
cut a splendid couple. Actually, I've never seen them together.
Remember that all this took place before I was born. I felt no com-
pulsion to search that far back in my dreams. I did in the Enigma,
but that came later. For his part, John had been taken by Margaret's refinement, by the subtle filigree of *society*, which could not
really be penetrated and which, until he'd met Margaret, had kept
him at bay. To be blunt, for society, John looked good in tails – for
Margaret, in his swimming trunks.

It couldn't have lasted. Perhaps on the French Riviera? In
England, the climate was too cold. Still is. Cold and wet.

Had Margaret suffered through the divorce? John doubted it.
In hindsight, he thought Margaret should be accorded a measure of
pity, compassion if need be. Not for having suffered a loss, though.
More like for inconvenience. She was no more capable of feeling
deep pain than the deadwood that had been seasoned for generations in her family's cupboards. That which enables one to suffer
also empowers one to love. Pain is the penalty for loving too well.
Love is the reward in itself. Margaret could experience neither of
these extremes. She was a creature of her kind. Still, poor Margaret.

After an initial period of adjustment, JJ grew immensely attached to his father's new wife, Heidi. His new mother adored him. She was everything Margaret hadn't been. Perhaps she loved JJ because he was John's son. Perhaps because he'd lost his 'real' mother, who seemed neither to think nor care about him. But most of all Heidi loved JJ because he needed love. What boy doesn't?

JJ's world, heretofore drab, colourless, devoid of the kaleidoscope of emotions of a real family, suddenly became rich and enchanting. He blossomed from a shy, reserved child to a boy full of self-assurance, confident of his place in their little tight-knit family. Even John had learned that his son was not a little man, but a child in need of care and attention. He'd learned that a father's job was not just to provide for his son's physical needs, but to acquaint him with the male version of love. As necessary, yet surely, so different from that of a woman's. Not that he would ever try to compete with Heidi. She was as much a mother as a companion, a friend, a nurse if need be, and most of all a guardian angel to JJ. And then it stopped. Suddenly.

JJ felt cheated.

He felt that he must have done something wrong to deserve such a fate. In this he differed little from his father. Dad, having been brought up by the Jesuits in his college days, did not quite manage to eradicate the dogmas instilled in his psyche. In moments of weakness, John was sure that he'd lost Heidi as punishment for having divorced Margaret. Despite the fact that it had been Margaret who, at the instigation of her family, had initiated the proceedings for separation, John felt that he had to bear part of the blame. He'd merely suggested that a divorce seemed a more equitable solution. He'd felt like adding, "After all, we do have nothing in common." But he'd kept quiet. He didn't want to use the word 'common'.

"It takes two to tango," he thought bitterly, looking at JJ. "Your mother and I both carry a share of the blame. I took your mother away from you and then your guardian angel as well. Now

we are alone, you and I. And Heidi..." he added to himself, trying
hard to hide his distaste. This was before the balcony incident.

God, I felt that disdain! It was like a dark cloud that allowed
no light to enter.

John's mind refused to formulate the words 'the culprit', 'the
cause of it all', but, at the time, his heart still burned with anger.
Mostly at himself. Yet it was a sensation of constant, nagging guilt
that drove him away from his own son. With me, his daughter, his
emotions bordered on some sort of inordinate if subliminal hatred.
With JJ it was a sense of unrequited guilt. In the single moment of
mother's death he'd lost not two, but three people. His wife and
both of his children.

I am referring to Dad as John because it seems more impersonal that way. Easier for me to talk of his limitations.

This all took place before my third birthday. Before the miracle that restored me in Dad's heart. And therefore, all of the above
is just hearsay. I wasn't around, at the time. My personal countdown could be defined as minus three years. Perhaps, three-and-a-
half. After all, some of this happened even before JJ was born.
What I am telling you here I learned mostly from Mary, a little
from JJ, and later, much later from Dad. And, of course, from my
visits to the Enigma. In time father learned to trust me. To accept
me.

JJ had to wait longer for his turn. It took father a lot longer.
Guilt has a longer shelf-life than hatred. Some years later, after
father had buried his feelings of guilt towards JJ, my brother asked
me if I had ever hated my father. I was stunned. "Hating Dad for
having loved mother too much?" I recall asking. "I am too busy
rejoicing in having found him. It is as though he'd been dead and
was alive again."

I think JJ understood me.

Then, some months after that fateful birthday, help came to JJ
from unforeseen quarters. It was little Heidi, that's me, who drew
JJ to her newly effervescent heart. It must have been a purely in-
stinctive reaction, but Hey apparently had decided that now that she

was happy, she'd make JJ happy too. She must have inherited this trait from her mother. Like mother like daughter. Just a bundle of love.

I vaguely remember those days. Just vaguely.

I've since visited that part of my past many times to make sure I did my job. I remember the shadows that still engulfed those early years. Slowly the light has penetrated the intricate mists. I'm glad I was part of that dawning.

For a while, I recall, I couldn't break through little John Jr.'s ramparts. He'd erected them, day by day, over the years, so as to protect himself from yet another loss. There was only so much a boy could take. But I'd persisted. Finally after almost a year, JJ would talk to me as though we were friends. I thought I'd been very clever about it. Whenever my father invited me to go anywhere, to do anything, I persistently asked if JJ would be coming also. If he couldn't, other than because of schooling, I would also decline. In time it grew on JJ that I preferred his company to that of my father. It hadn't been necessarily true, but JJ's needs had been greater than mine. There developed a certain covert conspiracy of shared emotions between us. I loved my father as much as ever, but not at the expense of JJ. He, in turn, knew he could trust me. Years later, when JJ grew to lead a dedicated group of people, I suspect I remained the only one with whom he would speak freely. With childlike trust. Though, even then, he was anything but a child. He was a little adult.

I also benefited from this new friendship. Already during those early days, nights really, I'd been experiencing strange, irrepressible dreams. Always mysterious, sometimes repetitive. While JJ was in no position to explain or interpret them for me, he was at least a willing ear. Even though he hardly listened, I shamelessly unloaded my mysterious visions on my brother. I had to. Whenever we suffer a nightmare, most of us feel compelled to share it with someone. The same is true of a vivid, persistent dream. I've had many of those. Not nightmares, but my dreams often seemed more vivid than my waken reality. I was much too young to understand them, often even unable to put them into words. But speaking about them took the edge off the emotions, which they stirred, in my young heart. JJ became my bouncing board. My release of pent up feelings.

It was all quite innocent, of course.

I suppose a trained psychologist would enumerate a number of explanations for my childish imagination turning inwards. Not the least of them would have been total absence of other children to play with. Other than JJ, of course, and there was precious little of that. When you're an adult, a difference of three years is negligible. When you are three or four, it is a chasm one simply cannot bridge. Emotionally, or in any other way.

In spite of this, I never thought of myself as victimized or short-changed for never having participated in a sleepover, a pyjama party, or any number of pastimes which, I learned later, girls hold so dear. At the time, I was neither a girl nor a boy. I was what my father had initially thought of me – an 'it'. He referred to me as she, but didn't treat me as such. For the first three years, I had been an irreconcilable appendage to the family. A come-along. But I repeat, I never felt short-changed. At my conscious level I was not aware that it could be any other way. That I was treated in a way in which a normal family would frown upon. If it hadn't been for Mary, I would probably have ended up in an asylum specializing in children starved of affection. My mother knew exactly what she was doing when she'd imported Mary from the Old Country. My mother must have been quite a woman.

On the other hand, I feel certain that it was only thanks to my emotionally starved childhood that my world of dreams has unfolded so richly before me. Or rather, within me. It was through the ecstasy of grief that the walls of my sensual universe crumbled – the walls that held me in my self-imposed prison limited to my five senses. What I discovered, and continue to discover, cannot be experienced until one frees oneself from the fetters of expectations, desires and demands, and particularly of confining traditions. I have learned that infinity begins where limitations cease.

In hindsight, I would never have agreed to substitute my infancy or adolescence for what is usually regarded as 'normal' childhood. I believe that one always gets what one pays for. Judging by the rewards, I must have paid my dues in full.

As for my girlishness, my one sin, or tacit claim to incipient femininity, was to spend hours in front of a mirror, in my bedroom, arranging my hair up or down, or pleating my abundant tresses into intricate forms and cascading shapes. Some girls like dolls, prams and suchlike. I liked my hair. Frankly, I still do.

JJ learned another escape. He told me, that as early as he could remember, he'd developed an interest in electronics. Computers, to be precise. Our father's hardware was constantly being updated and Dad needed little persuasion to let JJ have some of the old models that had been replaced by the latest technology. By the time JJ was nine, he could reprogram his three computers with his eyes closed. By the time he was twelve, he could take almost any computer apart, put it together again, and make it better in the process. While other boys played computer games, he would spend hours tinkering with both hardware and software, until he'd removed all mystery from his electronic toys.

There was another reason for this predilection of his. He found a strange affinity with the orderly fashion in which electronic impulses yield predictable results. Maybe he wanted something that resembled a human brain, yet which was devoid of all feelings. Without any emotions. With no emotions at all.

In the meantime, life at the Science Centre went on.

Before the year was out, men on Dad's staff had recorded two more near misses. The rocks seemed to fly straight at our mother Earth. Then, at the last moment, within less than seven astronomical units, a little over one million kilometres, the errant chunks of matter seemed nudged by some invisible force and missed us by a good three to four hundred thousand kilometres. There were theories of solar winds, of variable magnetic radiation, of an imperceptible wobble in the earth's axis of rotation. Many theories. Each was vaguely plausible. None had been proven.

The errant rocks kept coming, and kept missing us. Perhaps it had been always so, for generations, only scientists hadn't paid any attention. After all, a rock whizzing by at tens of thousands of kilometres per hour, some half a million kilometres from our orbit is not easy to spot. Now, father had the biggest Eye on Earth. The Monster Eye. And, many had suggested, an awful lot of luck.

Father had other suspicions. But he regarded them as too absurd to make public. For now. As for little *moi*, I felt inexorably drawn into the intricacies of astronomical hypotheses. Not in any scientific way, of course – I was too young at the time – but in my own special way. I'd close my eyes and see the rocks as they sailed the outer reaches of the Earth, waiting to be nudged, prodded this way and that. Just for fun.

***

4

Via Lactis

Our galaxy is a very complex organism. A full on view of our
home galaxy would look like a double spiral wrapping itself around
a spherical halo that spans some twenty thousand light-years
across. We, the earthlings, abide behind two of those spiral arms
which, together with part of the Great Rift spanning from Sagitta-
rius to Cassiopeia, make the central halo both invisible to the naked
eye and even inaccessible to our instruments.

Even to the Monster Eye.

To put it yet another way, our home star, our life giving sun,
with its attendant array of planets, hovers between the second and
the outer spiral arm, some 30,000 light-years from the mysterious
core. Seen from the side, we would see the spiral arms winding
their way around each other, like two serpents caught in the grip of
a cyclone, drawn towards the central hub, where the monstrous vi-
pers continue to swallow each other. Each arm consists of millions
upon millions of stars, nebulae, gas and dust, all spinning, all in
constant, seemingly perpetual motion. This is what we would see
if we could only step out into space and admire our home from
afar.

Our galaxy is definitely a very complex organism.

By the time Hey was eight, she'd demanded that her father treat her like an adult. I say Hey and not I, because placing demands on anyone is now categorically against my nature. Anyway, I'd asked Dad to do so at least in his area of expertise. He could no longer fool me with some old wives' tale about the Green Man on the Moon, even less so with little lights which are switched on in the sky at night. By this time, Hey had had five years of experience in the field of astronomy. I still think of her as some other girl, close to me, yet not quite my own self. So much has happened since....

"I am eight years old, Daddy," she assures him, as if that alone qualifies her to be told the truth. "EIGHT," she spells out staccato in her still childish voice.

"Then you don't want to hear about how the ancients saw our galaxy?"

"You can tell me, providing it's *really* serious," she acquiesces.

So he told her, as best he could. From memory. I remember those stories, those legends and myths to this day. I can close my eyes and see little Hey sitting on a low stool; her eyes fixed on Dad's face, spellbound. I can also hear Dad's voice....

"From ancient times men raised their heads towards the Milky Way – to stare and wonder. The Anglo-Saxons of yore worshipped it as the *Waetlinga Straet*, the Street of the Giant of Waetla. It was also known to the Vikings as the Path of Odin, who was their god of gods. They called it the *Wuotanes Weg*. The Midland Dutch saw in the starry marvel the *Vronelden Straet*, the Women's Path, which seemingly lead those chosen maidens to the divine altar, with their long, snowy veils of intricate starry lacework streaming behind them. The Finns, on the other hand, saw a flock of birds migrating towards a single luminescent nest. They called it the *Linnunrata*."

Hey's eyes remain riveted on her father's face. She seems transported to a different reality, perhaps to that of the ancients of our race. "Go on, Daddy," she urges when her father stops for a sip of water. He too looks enchanted, only in his case it is I who apparently am the spell-caster.

"There have been many names for our home of homes. Some persist to this day."

He opens a large book with illustrations of the Milky Way.

"The Chinese saw in our galaxy a river teeming with silvery fish running away from the threatening hook of the crescent Moon. They called it *Tien Ho*, the Celestial River. The Hindus thought of it as the Bed of Ganges, the most holy of rivers. Lord Shiva directed the tempestuous currents of Ganges to flow through his hair and thus feed the streams of Earth. To the ancient Arabs it was *Al Nahr*, while the Hebrews thought of it as the River of Light, the *N,her di Nur*. Is that enough?" he asks quietly.

Hey gives him a dirty look. "I'll tell you when it's enough," she assures him nodding fiercely.

Father must have shrugged. It seems that, at the time, I had exactly the same insatiable attitude towards the stars as he had when about my age. I could tell that he was becoming very proud of his daughter. And then I see his face again. He smiles, kisses my hair, and continues. By now I've moved from the stool to his knee. Yes... I can see it even now....

"The ancient Polynesians scattered across the islands of the South Pacific saw in the sky a great shark consuming the clouds floating over the endless ocean. The Canadian Indians from the environs of Ottawa saw a celestial turtle roiling the muddy currents of the very same Celestial River. We took our name from the Romans. *Via Lactis* or *Via Lactea* means the Milky Way, or the Road of Milk. Possibly the North Frieslanders also reached out to Rome for their inspiration; their name of *Melkpath* speaks for itself."

"But why milky, Daddy?" I must have been insatiable even in those days.

"Well, the Greeks had many gods and goddesses. One day, Hera decided to adopt and nurse Hercules, a very, very strong mortal. In fact Hercules was so strong, that he hurt Hera's nipple, and she was forced to pull him away. Inadvertently, she spilled some of her divine breast milk. And there you have it. From these droplets arose the Milky Way. After all, Hercules was Hera's son, and

Hera was the consort of Zeus, the god of gods in the Greek
heaven."

"I like this story," I said. I still do.

"And so the Greeks called our galaxy the *Galaxias Kuklos*,
meaning the Milky Band. The Romans always liked to borrow
ideas from the Greeks, so they changed the name a little, to *Via
Lactea*, or the Road of Milk. And that's all there is to it."

Dad's private lecture went on well into the night. Finally, he
picked me up and carried me to bed. I struggled, weakly, for him
to continue. But by the time he laid me down, I must have been
fast asleep. I checked on that later. It's strange how every single
incident in my life lives on in the realm where neither space nor
time can displace it. It has its being suspended in nowhere, in the
never. In the unchangeable eternity of the ubiquitous now.

If Alice had walked on a road paved with golden bricks,
shouldn't the path of gods be strewn with myriads of diamonds,
leading the way back to paradise? A street sparkling with the light
of two hundred billion suns....

It was only when little Hey stepped into his laboratory that
Dad allowed his mind to stray from the path of science and in-
dulged in such rare thoughts such romantic illusions, joining our
forefathers in their holy quest for the lofty reaches of gods. For
years now he had taught his long lost daughter the wonders of the
ancients, still hiding a million mysteries in their floating veils. I
still recall how enchanted I was by my first glimpse of the starlight
enhanced by the magical lenses of Dad's telescopes. Even when
still less than four years of age, my questions taxed my father's scientific mind to the limit. Not that he lacked the answers, but how
does one tell a child that the miraculous universe really and truly
exists in all its glory? That what even the largest telescope in the
world is capable of showing is but an infinitesimal fragment of the
glory of... God?

"Daddy, why are the stars shining?"

"Are they cold, Daddy? As ice-cold as the freezing rain?"

"Daddy, why can't I touch them?"

"Is Mommy up there, among them? Is she, Daddy? Is she?"

Dad felt sure that Mommy was indeed amongst them. Among the stars. He'd told me as much. Where else could she be? Don't angels roam the celestial realm? Isn't the *Vronelden Straet* hers to explore? Even if only gods were allowed to tread the path strewn with billions of diamonds, was she so inferior to them? She had been a true goddess on earth. Could she be any less in heaven?

"Yes, darling," he said drawing me closer to his heart. "She is right there, waiting for us. You may be sure...."

And from that moment on, Dad and I shared this secret knowledge. Just he and I. We never wavered from our firm belief: mother was there – waiting for us. Among the stars. Forever.

But *Via Lactis* still hid more secrets than she divulged.

Twelve billion years ago a giant, protogalactic sphere, perhaps a million light-years across, spun about its centre. It was made up of energy held in a vice of angular momentum. Slowly, after eons of time, the sphere began to condense into clouds of gas and rarefied dust. None of the heavier elements necessary for life were present. Just hydrogen and helium. As density increased, billions of furnaces flared under the increased pressure. The sphere began to collapse into a disc of rotating matter, some hundred thousand light-years across. Yet, even to this day, over a hundred and twenty-five globular clusters of stars, each home to a million suns, linger behind, defining the shape of the original protogalactic sphere. These globular clusters, nebulae and dust clouds, still remain bound to the enigmatic halo at the centre of our galaxy. In such a realm as this the first stars were born.

"What are the stars made of, Daddy?"

John Hydon smiled at his daughter. He recalled his own first visit to the observatory in Suffolk. He hadn't been much older than Heidi. Yet there and then he'd known that stars would enter and define his life. Now, his own daughter was in great danger of contracting the same incurable affliction. The stars, galaxies, nebulae, clouds of yet unstructured matter, made up the realm he lived in. Perhaps not yet bodily, but his heart and mind dwelled there for many hours daily. And now Heidi....

He felt like answering: 'of sugar and spice and everything that's nice.' But it wouldn't be true. There was nothing sweet or nice about the heat and pressure even at the surface of our own sun. And there were many suns, many times bigger and hotter than ours.

"It's not so much a question of what the stars are made of, Hey," even his own voice was dreamy. "It is more a question of what we are made of, sweetheart."

Normally, when father was at work in the observatory, he acted like a hard-nosed scientist. But whenever I came, whenever I was present, his voice would become introspective, his heart would get all mixed up with his mind. He would become everything he hadn't been for the first three years of my life. A loving, concerned, single-minded father. It wasn't just that his mind was centred on my presence. It seems that he saw the whole world, literally, through my eyes. It certainly felt like it. I had become his Muse. His Urania, often his Erato. His inspiration.

"What are we made of, Daddy?"

"Star stuff. We're made up of star-stuff, darling," he said, pronouncing the two as one word. And having said it, he wondered at his own answer.

In all essence he was right. The early stars in our galaxy had been made up of three-quarter parts of hydrogen and one quarter helium. Their life span had often been less than a million years. They had been unimaginably huge giants, which had soon collapsed under their own gravitational force. As their internal pressures increased their temperatures climbed. Gradually the gasses condensed into heavier elements. As the giants collapsed still further under the unimaginable pressures of their own weight, those early inhabitants of our galaxy exploded with a fury that seeded the heavier elements – carbon for our bodies, iron for our blood, and many other constituents indispensable for our survival – throughout the early galaxy. In time those new wandering clouds of star-stuff, of intergalactic dust, condensed again, forming the second generation of stars, later adorned with planets, like vassals gracing a royal court. That prehistoric period marked the birth of our own star. Some four-and-a-half to five billion years ago. Twelve billion since the protogalaxy began its long evolution.

Tempus fugit. But what is time in terms of eternity?

Father had tried, as best he could, to explain to a four-year-old that if it hadn't been for the stars, we would not have been born. That the inseparable bond of evolution inexorably links the stars and us. Linked by the very elements that had once emerged from the same source. From the first generation of stars – now long extinct. Yet to this day new stars are being born in the midst of gigantic dust-clouds. Stars that one day could provide building blocks for yet new life, new intelligence, which would appreciate the wonder of becoming. Indeed, if it hadn't been for the stars, we would have remained ghosts, discarnate spirits, angels, entities suspended in the eternal stasis, in the interminable void. Perhaps we would have been formed of sugar and spice, only without any sugar and surely, without any spice....

I never grew tired of listening to my father.

Unlike other girls my age I felt no need for dolls. I liked to play, well enough, but I liked to play with other people. Or even talk, or just listen. I tried hard to engage JJ in some childish games, but he was too old for me. I didn't run fast enough, couldn't climb even the lowest branches of the apple tree, didn't throw the ball far enough. Three years is a life span at that age. JJ remained alone, as did I. Except when father took me to the lab. The one concession I'd made for toys were little figurines of animals. I had a vast collection. It had started with teddy bears, stuffed pandas, then I progressed to other wild and domestic creatures. I talked to them as though the toys were real, and more so, as though they were people. Particularly when I talked to figurines of monkeys and apes, and of those, the chimpanzees had been by far my favourites.

Mary, the English Nanny, as we called her, was helpful enough; carried out her duties to the letter, but... well, Mary was an old maid. She wasn't old, as yet, but she was an unfulfilled maid in the making. She'd never developed any maternal instincts. And now, rather than taking the opportunity to get closer to both children, she shirked away from more intimate contact, fearing that one day she might be dismissed and forced to leave part of herself behind. Poor nanny. She seemed more alone than anyone of us. For three years we formed a highly dysfunctional family with a dysfunctional nanny providing the feminine element. Those had been hard years. Yet, for the children, this early period was the most formative of all. Father tried to use the information on child-raising he'd gathered when Margaret had been pregnant with JJ, but emotions took over. Or the lack of them. A void. As deep and as cold as Outer Space. In a way, he'd experienced both. The inner and the outer void. Those first three years affected me in many peculiar ways. And for JJ, those years were even longer. Perhaps it was meant to be.

"Are there just stars out there, Daddy? Just many, many stars? Everywhere?"

Father had no idea what had precipitated such questions. "What else could there be, darling?" Was she thinking of monsters or angels, he'd probably wondered? But he would have been wrong on both counts. While he was busy, I stole a glimpse of some discarded photographs, lying on the floor. In them I saw strange shapes of convoluting clouds of dust and gas, of bright nebulae and dark ghostly outlines that obliterated the view of what lay beyond. Later father confessed to me that he'd been amazed at the way children notice things adults often ignore.

"Our galaxy is a home for many..." his voice wavered as though unsure of himself, "...for many beings."

I knew he'd wanted to say 'things' but that wouldn't have been right either. The nebulae, the clouds, the dust filled with star-stuff, had their being in the galactic environs. Who was he to say that they were not possessed of intelligence we knew nothing about? How can we, who are aware of the universe for a few puny years, define the nature of giants who stare at us through aeons upon aeons? Even if one lived to be a hundred, the giants count their lives in billions of years. The funny thing was that until I had asked the question, Dad had never given such problems any thought. Such posers didn't influence his work. Had no bearing on it. And now? Now, belatedly, he had become a father. He had questions to answer.

"What is it that you want to know, Heidi?" He may have thought that he'd misunderstood me.

"If we are made up of star-dust, then are there other star-dust people living among the stars?"

I really remember that question. I also remember that Dad had smiled at the eternal quandary.

"Very likely, darling," he'd answered gravely. He couldn't help nodding his head. "I really believe that it's very likely."

In spite of his scientific training, or perhaps because of it, Dad really did believe that out there, beyond the reach of his telescope, there were other beings wondering, even as he was, about others like themselves. In some ways, the galaxy was a lonely place.

John Hydon wished Heidi had asked him something for which he had a ready answer. Something requiring statistical knowledge. Like the number of stars in the galaxy, their size, their life span, their movement.... There was much knowledge man had already accumulated. And even some of the big questions of the day were easy to explain to a four-year-old. His colleagues speculated on the size of that original protogalaxy from which the galaxy appeared as a disc of some 100,000 light-years across. They all agreed that originally the protogalaxy must have been many times larger. The astrophysicists said that the universe was expanding, but in John's experience it was mostly shrinking. Shrinking into a hard, physical reality. That's how he thought of the Milky Way. And, after all, there were trillions of other galaxies, millions of light-years away. All shrinking, condensing, maybe even being swallowed, whole, by the mysterious beings dwelling in their centres.

Dwelling within the Black Holes.

Our early home had shone with the brightness of a trillion suns. Yes. One thousand billion suns. Now, we are in awe of the luminescence of a mere two hundred billion. A mere two hundred billion suns such as ours. It still seemed like an unimaginable number. Yet viewed from a distance of a few galactic diameters, some three or four hundred thousand light-years, we would appear no more than a faint brightening in the midnight sky. John could never grasp the significance of this scale. That is why, early in his career, he'd decided to concentrate his research on optical telescopes. While limited in their range, at least what he saw was real. Real to him. Real some millions of years ago. When the light had first left its source. He felt that what he could see with his eyes, he could touch with his other senses. Even if only in his imagination.

Two hundred billion stars whirling, near-endlessly, around the invisible, obscure, unknown hidden core. There lay the true mystery. What held this abundance of stars together? What stopped the centrifugal force from slinging them all out into the endless darkness? Some of his colleagues insisted that what held them together must be a giant Black Hole. A monster of unimaginable mass. But black holes were no more than euphemisms for the unknown. In essence they were meaningless. Defining a black hole was like trying to define God. Spinosa refused to do so, lest he negated the very essence of the Divine. And John had long given up any attempts to define those realms of infinite darkness. But not their existence. And he never lost his fascination for them. For the greatest unknown.

"Let the theoretical astrophysicists speculate on their nature," he thought.

He meant of both God and the black holes. Both were as enigmatic. Both beyond the known laws of physics. If there were black holes at the centre of each galaxy, and the theorists speculated there were some trillions of them – were there as many gods? And when one galaxy cannibalized another, what happened to the gods? Or their black holes? Did it really matter?

He prayed that I, Heidi, would not ask him such questions. Ever.

I didn't.

Somehow, even then, though a child, I could sense his dilemma. I can sense it again now, as I sit here recording those early days. I raise my arms to reach out and hold onto the fluffy wisps of cotton hovering over the home of my youth, as it continues to spin on its axis, day after day, season after season, year after year....

This enchanted sphere doesn't need us on its journey, on its endless gyrations. Neither do we, the individualized fragments of Omnipresent Consciousness endowed with rudimentary self-awareness, continue in our own rotations, in our own cyclic journey of eternal becoming. The eternal Wheel of Awagawan.

Yet even now, I love my Earth.

I love this verdant haven, suspended so effortlessly in the incomprehensible vastness of infinite space, on the outer fringes of an insignificant galaxy. It was there that I learned to dream, to wonder. To reach out by reaching within. It was there that I took my first tentative steps towards the ephemeral reality of the Enigma.

***

5

Home within a Home

I'm sure Dad sometimes thought that life was unfair. While he
and his men dedicated their lives to peering into the distant Universe, there was only an infinitesimal chance that anyone, anyone
at all, was taking even a cursory glance at us. More's the pity, he
thought, although he had to admit that this idea of the lack of reci-
procity, as so many ideas of late, had been planted in his head by
his own daughter. By me.

As I've already mentioned, the images from my early childhood are not really memories. I recount them when they come to
me as flashes, as visual as they are audible, snippets taken from
someone else's life. Those flashes are of what must have been,
rather than what has been. And thus, it is not really I that appear in
those evocative visions. It is a little girl who, in due time, became
'I'; became the sum total of what I am today. These images belong
to a girl called Hey, a little girl about whom I am learning even as
you are.

"Does he wave hello to you, Daddy?" Hey asked her father
one day.

*For a moment he seemed lost. He'd just directed his Monster
Eye to follow the course of Pluto, and record any deviations in the
established orbit. The computer would keep up with our distant
planet for as long as the planet remained visible. Before the*

earth's spin augmented by Pluto's orbit placed it below the hori-
zon. Then the telescope would automatically sound an alarm.
"Who darling?"
"The man you are looking at," and she giggled as if to add
"silly, who else?"
"I don't think he can see me," he said with mock sadness.
"He can see you if you can see him," she affirmed.

It couldn't have been easy to have me for a daughter. I'm sure some said I was the proverbial pain in the back side. But by then, Dad just loved me too much. Can one have too much love?

It must have been after that conversation that Dad had decided that whenever he left the operational seat at the gyro setters, and I was around, he would wave to the 'man' on the other side of the telescope. I am sure that Hey liked that. It must also have been on that occasion that Dad had decided that maybe I was right. Why shouldn't some advanced race zero in on his lens and see him struggling to see them?

Father laughed. He realized that I was beginning to get under his skin. I don't think he really believed anyone could be that ad-vanced. Ever. But he had to admit that my questions were at least refreshing.

"What do we look like to him, father?"

Poor Dad. What could he have told me?

From a fair distance, through an optical devise as advanced from the Monster Eye as the latter was from Galileo's primitive telescope, who knows what they, the alien intelligences, would see.

"On a very clear night..." he began, "on a very, very clear night they might compare our Observatory to a distant galaxy seen edge on." His voice was dreamy, tentative, his brow furrowed in concentration.

Father punched a few buttons and an image appeared on one of his monitors.

"NGC 891," he said. "The galaxy we can actually see edge-on," he added unnecessarily. From the age of eight I could recognize all the better known galaxies. I was my father's daughter.

The NGC 891 was a big, a gargantuan ball of cotton, a sphe-roid brightness squashed at its poles into a shimmering puff of cream. Cutting it in half was a line of darkness, of mystery, which

extended light-years on either side. This was the Great Rift, such
as our galaxy has, consisting of gas and dust.

"We would look something like this," Dad added again.

*"That's real pretty, Daddy," Hey approved nodding her head.
She'd seen the image many times before.*

From afar, even on some photos produced by the USA spy
satellites, the crystal domes, when illuminated from within, appeared as pearly clusters of feeble stars, of a magnitude of say +15.
They resembled a string of Red Dwarfs, but no less so than galaxies some four to five thousand light-years away.

Cutting through the Science Centre, along its long axis, was an
equally dark line, a Tiny Rift, which served as the communication
corridor, linking all the various Departments. Its solid roof, a rain-
water collector, allowed no light to escape, hence its darkness from
outside.

The reason the complex looked so much like the objects of father's study, a galaxy edge-on, had been arrived at by necessity. A
bright spheroid centre, lesser domes along its long axis, cut by a
line of relative darkness. Due to the climatic conditions of the
Yukon, all buildings were enclosed in giant geodesic domes, originally conceived by R. Buckminster Fuller. Already in the early
sixties of the last century, the Gentle Giant, as Fuller had been
known to his admirers, proposed geodesic domes as a solution for
overcoming the constraints of extreme climates. Now, a near half-
century later, with the genius long departed to the big-dome-in-the-
sky, the Canadian engineers had decided that the time for his idea
had come. Ten years after its construction, the inhabitants of the
Canadian Science Centre were able to stroll through verdant gardens, gently rolling landscapes and scattered waterfalls – in the
middle of a harsh Canadian winter. The 'jungle', as JJ once called
it, was further enhanced by the many balconies protruding from
individual cottage-condos which were literally overflowing with
greenery in full bloom, creepy and climbing lianas, and perennials
which never ceased to flower.

The Hanging Gardens of Babylon came to mind.

The sun poured its energies through the triangular and hexag-
onal panels of glass and plastic, letting the light in, while prevent-
ing the heat from escaping. Over the years new domes had been

added, as the Centre continued to spread along its long axis for almost eleven kilometres. The many individual domes, the largest approaching a kilometre in diameter, some overlapping, others some distance apart, were linked and served by a conveyor belt, like a moving sidewalk, which was also powered by solar energy. It wove its way through those year-round gardens, so necessary to keep up the morale of the scientists and the ancillary staff. No one thought of going south for winter vacations. Three oversized swimming pools, designed to look like natural lakes, had been carefully integrated along the central axis, rivalling the best that the hotels down south had to offer.

People, who had originally been drawn to the vast outdoors, who had thought that in such relatively confined surroundings they would suffer from acute claustrophobia had, in no time at all, become acclimated to the ravishing indoors. Not I. At least, not at first. Until I'd learned to go where no one had gone before, I stole lonely walks outside under the starry sky, or sneaked out just to feel the rain touch my face. But that too passed. The indoors was just too entrancing.

This cluster of geodesic domes was, and remains, the home of the many that work there. For my father, home was much, much further away. It was also much greater in size and aspiration.

It was about that time, I must have been about seven, that the line between hard reality and the world of my imagination lost its traditional sharpness. The events, as I recall them, retained their sharpness, but the chronological sequence to which they were anchored seems to have lost its prerogatives. *What* happened became more important than *when*. Time was loosing its rigidity. It was becoming more flexible, more elastic – stretching both ways – forward and into the past. It didn't make much sense to me, at the time. There! There goes that *time* thing again. It didn't make much sense. Period.

While father's heart remained mesmerized by the Milky Way, he was not immune to the activities of his more immediate environs. No, not the Ogilvy Mountain Science Centre and its 'hanging gardens', nor even Canada or the Planet Earth. Dad held a warm spot in his heart for the Solar System. He called it his little nook in the Milky Way. His private backyard. His home within a home. Like a den within a house.

If one were to arrange Dad's interests in order of priorities, his family life would come a distant last. Even though of late he'd become acutely aware of his shortcomings as a father, those concerns were hardly what stirred his blood, or roiled his mental juices. While enjoying the rebirth of our emotional union to the full, he still felt free to let his mind revert to its previous ruminations. After all, he was the youngest director of the largest optical observatory in the world. *Noblesse oblige*. While the Hubble Space Telescope, launched to probe the depths of time and space, could be compared to a dessert, his Mount Ogilvy Monster Eye was the bread and butter, often the main course of astronomical research.

In recent years, NASA and its European and Asian counterparts had been deeply preoccupied with Mars. There was an array of rockets directed at our second nearest neighbour, in a concentrated effort to find out if it had ever supported life. At least, that was the official reason. Father knew, from his personal contacts, that there was another underlying cause motivating many scientists engaged in the pursuit of Mars' mysteries.

"If Mars held life, at any time in the past, then what caused its disappearance?"

It was I, once again, who'd asked this probing question. Unwittingly, I'd put my finger on the scientists' prime motivation. I'd put my thumb in the pie. My question had been phrased differently, of course. I couldn't have been more than eight, at the time. What I actually said was: "Can the man on Mars see us?" And when Dad replied that there were no men on Mars, I followed up with another very reasonable question: "What happened to him Daddy?"

And that was it. Their true motivation.

What cataclysms must have occurred to rid Mars of its water, and thus atmosphere, which in turn converted the planet, seemingly well positioned in relation to its sun, into the arid wasteland we could see? After all, they reasoned, if it happened to Mars, and few doubted that it had, it could happen to Earth. Had it been sudden? Cataclysmic? Internal? Caused by external influences? Had the process been gradual, over millions of years, rather than a sudden event?

"We don't know yet, Hey," father admitted contritely.   "We just don't know yet, Pet."

In the Northern Hemisphere, the inherent regularity of terrain as examined by an army of automated probes, which crawled over Mars's surface, seemed to indicate a uniform and, in astronomical terms, speedy termination of whatever had been there before. Like some kind of enormous flattening explosion. Or the Northern Hemisphere could well have had ranges of mountains which, after millions and millions of years had eroded, gradually brought down to their present flatness.

Examining the Southern half, geophysicists argued just the opposite. In the South, there were mountains that reached higher than any other in the Solar system. If there had been an explosion then it had flattened only one hemisphere. And if erosion had been responsible for the apparent flatness of the Northern part, then it was a kind of erosion that only existed on one half of the planet. Not a very likely hypothesis.

Few astronomers or planetary geologists doubted that the topographical demise had been fairly sudden. Much less than a billion years. Perhaps as little as a million or two. But before the planet cooled – had there been earthquakes? Had there been unprecedented inundations by the still abundant oceans? Had Mars been subjected to an overwhelming bombardment of asteroids or other space debris? After all, Mars is much closer to the asteroid belt than Earth is, and thus had much greater exposure to errant rocks being captured by its gravitational field.

There were many questions.

Within a year or two I could have told them how to find out. But would anyone have listened? A little girl with no formal training in astronomy? And I would never have been able to tell them the source of my knowledge. Not then.

The topography of Inner Planets was not my father's principal field of interest, but he kept abreast of the latest data from the many interplanetary robots, which sent back a continuous stream of information for the scientists to examine. Frankly, they all confirmed a similar conclusion. Yes, Mars was suitable for life. All it needed was a little water. A little evaporation to reconstitute a heavier atmosphere. Later, a few seeds of flora to generate more oxygen and, in no time at all, you would be able to buy a lot at your favourite resort on the shores of the 'Red Sea' on the Red Planet – as far away from the Sinai Peninsula as anyone could wish. 'No time at all' in cosmological terms, of course. Say a couple of thousand years. Or maybe sooner if more ice were to be found under Mars' surface.

"Daddy, when can we go to Mars?" Hey wanted to know.

I was nine then and Dad couldn't distract me with a few facile explanations. For some time now father felt embarrassed when he couldn't answer his daughter's direct questions. Not that there hadn't been an answer, but there were just too many variables.

"We could go tomorrow if our spaceship was big enough, darling."

It wasn't really a lie. For over fifty years they'd been experimenting with the renewable, closed environment inside geodesic domes. A sort of total recycling. A closed ecosystem. I don't mean at Mount Ogilvy but in Arizona, down south. A similar complex but designed for environmental testing. Should we choose to construct such a sphere in space, and attach to it some solar sails, perhaps collect enough solar energy to steer our ship and supply it with energy, we could go tomorrow.

Dad always thought in cosmological terms. After all, wasn't Earth just such a ship? Travelling through space, fed by energy collected from the sun, which it managed to store below the dome of its atmosphere. We could have emulated such a system with relatively little imagination. The technology was already there. Given time. And money. And time. Yes, mostly time...

"Will you go with them?"

"Where darling?"

"Will you go with them to Mars?"

Hey tried hard to ask the question in a carefree tone, but a single glance at her face would have revealed grave concern. Evidently father had understood instantly.

"No, darling. Daddy will stay with you right here on Earth."

For as long as you want, he'd nearly added. This is only partially a conjecture. In fact, I remember the moment quite well. At the time father had been acutely aware that the next parting of ways would not be precipitated by his own immature idiosyncrasies but by my inevitable growing up. She'll go her way, and I shall stay behind, he thought. A moment later he realized that he also missed JJ. He had missed his chance to grow closer to him. Why have I been so stupid, he asked himself?

"Who is stupid, Daddy?"

The last thought had escaped his lips in a murmur. There was nothing wrong with Hey's hearing. There was nothing wrong with Heidi at all. Perhaps a little precocious or maybe even just a shade eccentric. But, who isn't? I mean really?

The next day was Sunday, which did not stop father from working. Dr. David Mendel visited him in his office.

"You should come and see my fish," he said without any preamble.

I was playing behind the desk. I liked Dr. Mendel. Soon he became Uncle David. He was nice. But not as nice as Aunt Miriam.

Dr. Mendel was in charge of seismographic research. His department of Geology and Tectonics was located in the third dome east of the Observatory. The Monster Eye was, appropriately I thought, in the centre. Dave Mendel was the nearest father had come to a friend, particularly since Mom died. When mother had been pregnant with me, Uncle David had invited my parents to dinner. Since then, it became a ritual. Once a month at the Hydons, on alternate fortnights at the Mendels. During one of the early dinners, Dad told Uncle Dave about Margaret and the unpleasant circumstances of divorce.

"I bet," David said with forced enthusiasm. "I would much rather be a widower."

They all laughed though Aunt Miriam, Dr. Mendel's wife, pulled on her left ear with her right hand. Just in case. Unfortunately Miriam's superstitious ministrations didn't work.

Within four months of that dinner my mother died and my father became a widower. Dad had long forgotten the ill-timed joke,
while David seemed to stoop under its weight. Though he'd never
mentioned it, he felt a lingering sense of guilt. He was one of the
few people, outside of Dad's own department, who attended
mother's funeral. Father appreciated the gesture. David and his
wife stood apart, dressed in severe black, serious to the point of
despair. It was Dad who approached them.

"We are so sorry, John," was all he could mutter. "We're so
very, very sorry..." and both David and Miriam shed real tears
while each embraced Dad with both arms. I told you they were
nice, didn't I? Dad related that story to me some years later, while
we sat under the weeping willow by the pond.

Over the next eight years the dinners at the Mendels continued
on every first Sunday of the month. After mother died, father
hardly knew how to reciprocate. He took with him the best wine he
could find. He brought Miriam flowers. He brought presents for
their two children. Their two boys were much older than JJ or I.
The Mendels had married early.

Now and then father invited the Mendels to the best restaurant
in 'town', just outside the science complex. It was little better than
a greasy spoon joint. It was also the best he could do. He couldn't
force himself to invite them to the vastly superior restaurant inside
the Centre. Somehow it would have been too much like work. Too
many spying eyes. No privacy at all.

David and Miriam contrived to make each of the Sunday dinners into a special occasion. The food was excellent, the wine first
class, the conversation stimulating. Of course JJ and I didn't drink
wine. Not then. In fact, usually, we stayed home. Mary would
cook us a dinner – just for the three of us.

At the Mendels the table was invariably adorned with two
large silver candelabras supporting five long, tapering candles each.
It gave the dining room an agreeable glow of family warmth.

"Back home, in Europe," David told Dad on one early occasion, "we couldn't always afford electricity. Here," he waved his
hands in a broad arc, "people often cannot afford candles."

Dr. Mendel came from central Europe though he, like Dad, had completed his studies in England. Father wasn't quite sure if David was from Poland or the now defunct Czechoslovakia, or even Ukraine. He'd moved around. His Jewish ancestors may have sojourned in all of these countries. Dad could never remember because really he just didn't care where Dr. Mendel was from. He was the best tectonics expert in Canada. And there was quite a choice since the Canadian graduate scientists no longer had to flee to the USA for lack of jobs. Not since the Yukon Science Centre had opened its doors.

When David asked father to come and see his fish, Dad was sure that there would be a special treat that night. He'd already tasted an array of fish at the Mendel's table. Lake trout, Pacific and Atlantic salmon – cooked, fried, baked or smoked. For special occasions Miriam prepared the traditional *gefüllter fisch*, which David pronounced with a thick German accent. Dad had learned later that David was most at home in Yiddish, in preference to Hebrew – that's when he wasn't speaking slightly accented English. Accented with a mixture of British and mid-European accents. It was a cocktail not unpleasant to the ear. At any rate, the gefilte fish was a mixture of pike and carp, or some other sweet water offering, finely chopped with onion and other seasoning, and then carefully returned into the original skin before boiling. It was neither Dad's nor my favourite, but it was a dish requiring the most work. We both appreciated the effort. It always looked impressive. It was a fish one didn't just come to eat, but to see.

"Were the fish biting this morning?" father asked with a wink.

"You'll come and see?"

"The usual time?"

"Come earlier. I want to talk."

They met at six. David served Dad his usual summer quaff – a pint of imported ale – and sank down into his armchair. He looked worried. That was of relatively little consequence because David often looked worried. In fact, most of the time. Father suspected this might have something to do with his Semitic background. Jews worry. Often. Almost on principle. "Why do I worry?" Dave looked surprised when Dad commented on his

frown. "Why not?" he replied. And then seeing that Dad hadn't
accepted that as a sufficient reason, he'd added, "Just in case."

After some general small-talk, David directed the discussion
to the subject that prayed on his mind. It lay in the area of his expertise. He asked father if he knew anything about the traditional
Japanese methods for predicting earthquakes. Dad confessed his
ignorance.

"You should, my friend," David assured him. His forehead
was furrowed with concentration or apprehension. Dad could no
longer tell the expressions apart. Had I been there, I would have
seen Uncle Dave's face, slightly distorted, through the glass of the
aquarium. "Their methods save them many lives," David added
seeing that Dad didn't take up the challenge. John waited for
David to continue.

"I don't have any catfish," David muttered inconsequentially.

"I am sorry to hear that..." Dad raised an eyebrow.

"What?" Dr. Mendel looked a little nonplussed. "Ah, yes. I
don't have any catfish," he repeated, "but I do have a very nice
aquarium with goldfish. As you know."

Dad knew. The large glass tank was his friend's pride and
glory and my favourite hiding place. I'd spent hours staring at the
rich underwater world uncle Dave had created for his silent pets.
That day I'd stayed home with JJ watching our favourite program
on TV. But later, much later, Dad told me all about that particular
visit. Word for word. I may have embroidered some of it a little to
make it more interesting, but just a little. The essential facts are
accurate.

"I'm sorry," David started again. "I'm a bit absentminded
lately. It's those damn fish."

Father waited for more. David cleared his throat and started
again. "There are about a hundred members of the Japanese
Namezyu No Kai or the Catfish Club, who spend a lot of time
watching their tanks. They've chosen catfish, because these particular fish are said to create tremors below the earth when angry.
So says their legend. Whatever you may think of their methods,
the Japanese have a lot more earthquakes than we do. Over the
years, they've noticed that the fish actually pickup the minute

changes in the earth's electrical, or possibly magnetic field, which precede an earthquake."

Dr. Mendel stopped to see Dad's reaction. There was none coming though Dad lost the slight smirk which had played about his lips at the beginning of David's *exposé*. It was evident that Dr. Mendel, an expert in tectonics, was deadly serious. Only father still had no idea why.

"Come!" David rose and led the way to the room adjacent to the dining room where he kept his aquarium. "Usually," he said after Dad stared at the tank for a little while from a respectable distance, "when you tap the tank, the fish come towards your fingers, in expectation of feeding. Now watch."

David waited for Dad to come closer and peer into the greenish water. He then gently tapped the glass with his fingernail. The fish began darting about, in a near frenzy, as though chased by some unknown predator. Eventually they calmed down and settled into their usual lackadaisical mode of existence. Father was duly impressed.

"What exactly happened here?" he asked noncommittally.

"According to them," Dave said pointing to the fish while he glanced at his wristwatch "we are about to experience an earthquake within two to three hours. They began this strange behaviour about an hour after the noon feeding. I was finishing my lunch when I tapped the tanks... as a sort of 'so-long'. I was on my way back to the office, when the little rascals gave me their command performance."

"And you say that the Japanese have positive, confirmed results of the correlation..."

"There is no doubt. This afternoon I called my friend who is watching her cockroaches. Same results. The tiny monsters have been exhibiting strange behaviour since two this afternoon. Finally, about three, it's already night there, I called my Japanese colleague, who in turn telephoned someone at the Namezyu No Kai club. He called me back at four. The catfish are in a frenzy."

"Isn't it rather far for the electrical or magnetic variations to reach them from a single epicentre?"

"It is much too far. If it is a single epicentre," David said. "In fact, it is absolutely impossible..."

"Coincidence?"

"You don't really believe that, do you?"

Father didn't. In the field of science, coincidences are few and
far between. Nature much prefers the cause and effect modus op-
erandi. "No, my friend. I don't."

Finally Miriam called them to the dinner table, interrupting the
dragging silence. She brought a ray of sunshine to the pensive atmosphere.

"You are not bothering John with your golden toys, are you
my husband?"

The rest of the dinner was uneventful. Two hours later father
and Dr. Mendel left together for David's office. There was a good
chance that the seismographs would indicate some agitation. Assuming that the period of the fish and cockroach commotion pre-
ceded the actual tremor by a maximum of eight hours, the seismographs should have begun to register it by now.

They had – although the needles were moving in a strange
wavy pattern, growing and subsiding like the swell of an ocean.
There were no sudden variations in the graph usually associated
with a major earthquake. No sharp peaks and dips. After a good
half-hour, David was beginning to suspect that something was
wrong with his instruments. Earthquakes don't last that long. And
certainly not with such controlled and regular intensity.

The printouts were different from anything Dr. Mendel, or father for that matter, had ever seen. While the epicentre must have
been far away, the duration of the quake went way beyond any acceptable scale. The deep tremor lasted, continuously, for two
hours, seventeen minutes and eleven seconds. By far the longest
earthquake on record. It seemed that some mighty gods had been
making major adjustments in the earth's crust. At the same time
the vibrations had been so small, that only the most delicate seismographs registered anything at all.

On his way home, Dad remained as pensive as David had been
when they'd met earlier that evening. He had no idea what to make
of the events. The tremor was truly extraordinary. And then, for
no reason at all, his mind switched to the increased incidence of
asteroids diligently missing the Earth's orbit, and, equally for no

reason, to the strange reading he was getting from behind the orbit of Pluto.

Halfway home he shook his head and chuckled to himself. Surely, there couldn't possibly be any connection. The events were worlds apart. Literally.

Then he slowed down and wondered, "why am I thinking about it at all?"

That last was probably my fault, again. I had been telling Dad about the Enigma.

***

6

Dreaming the Dream

I told Dad about it in bits and snippets. I remembered it all, but I
didn't want to share it all at once. Dad told me that a lot of what I
had to say sounded as strange as what my mother had told him,
when she and Dad were alone.

"Funny that," he said, "your mother described an almost identical vision; to her it was so very real."

"You and Uncle Dave," I said somewhat miffed, "you both
always separate the tangible from the intangible. Science from po-
etry. The visible from the invisible. There is no such separation in
the Enigma. Reality is one. Perception of reality is limitless."

Of course, I did not say all that in as many words. I must have
been about nine or ten at the time. But evidently I managed to
make an impression on Dad in some other way. Years later, he
said that the substance of what I'd said was the same. It must have
been my schooling; the primary school at the Centre was outstanding. When the time came, I was to attend the high school in
Whitehorse, some hundred and fifty kilometres down the Mayo
Road.

When I told father about my dream, Dad and I were sitting
alone, he nursing a stein of lager, quietly thinking about the old
days. His old days. For me, all the days were still young.

I was telling Dad about the Enigma, the 'whatever it was that
was hiding behind Pluto'. I couldn't have been making much

sense. "Just how did it all start?" he wondered aloud. "Some sort of reflection of what shouldn't be there, and the next thing you're making up all these stories."

I'd first mentioned the Enigma thing some four years earlier. At the time he ignored me. I hadn't shared my dreams with him since. I decided to try again and keep trying. I needed to share my inner life with someone. I was older, I thought, he might take me more seriously. Neither then nor on this occasion, did we call it the Enigma. That came much later. At least we had started taking to each other. One on one. Dad had opened up a great deal over these last few years. And just when I thought that I finally had his undivided attention, his mind shifted to JJ.

"He too has a mind of his own," he mused taking another sip.

JJ, now almost thirteen, had been stashed safely away in a boarding school, in Brompton. Though father wouldn't admit it to anyone, it came as a shock to him that his one and only son wanted to attend a Catholic College. JJ had read up on the Internet all about Canadian schools that offered residences to their students. Almost from the start he'd become dead set on attending one. He'd actually written to a number of headmasters, or directors, as some preferred to be called, to find out if they would have him. He'd used every Ph.D. researcher he'd met at the Centre as his reference. He'd signed the letters with his father's name, using the official Observatory URL. To be sure, JJ and Dad share their initials. JJ merely omitted to add Jr. after his signature. E-mail lends itself to such tiny peccadilloes. To be honest, JJ's tactics had hurt no one, other than precipitating slight twinges in, or to, his father's ego. On the plus side, he'd saved Dad a lot of time. Other than discussing the matter with David, just once, Dad had done nothing to find a school suitable for his firstborn. Yet the very idea of going to a Jesuit College 'of one's free will' was enough for father to seriously consider taking his son to see a child psychiatrist.

After JJ's repeated pleas, father succumbed to his son's choice. Under protest. Practically in near, if quiet, desperation. After his own experiences in England, and all things considered, John Hydon refused to impose his will over that of his son. That would have been, in his mind, a greater harm.

"Somehow we always place greater value on our child's life, than on his mind and soul," he told David the Sunday after JJ's departure. "It must be our scientific training," he concluded.

David nodded, having no idea what his friend was talking about.

Two weeks later, Dad was still mulling over his son's adamant choice of schooling. Father had rebelled against the Jesuits' methods that seemed closer to a boot camp than to an institution of learning. He couldn't reconcile himself to the idea of having his son grow up to be a well-trained chimpanzee. Although, from what he'd heard, JJ could do a lot worse. According to one of his close acquaintances at the Centre, there were some very smart chimpanzees.

Father did not count his own sojourn with the Jesuits, at Mount St. Stanislaus Kostka's, among his favourite experiences. As Dad recalled, when faced with JJ's choice of schooling, the British, or at least the Jesuits in Great Britain, had the habit of training their charges, in preference of offering them an education. They seemed unable to distinguish between the two. John despised everything that was compulsory. As a boy, he'd once spent a whole summer training to extend the time he could spend under water holding his breath, just so that he wouldn't be forced to breathe like other boys. To free himself from being a sheep. An obedient sheep.

He survived his attempt at self-liberation, though he'd failed to incite his masters to respect his preference for being taught, not trained. To be inspired, not impelled. To be noticed as an individual, not an obedient member of a flock. He'd given up, early on, in his attempts to explain to the masters at Mount St. Stanislaus Kostka Einstein's thesis that in order to be an immaculate member of a flock of sheep, one must, above all, be a sheep oneself.

Baaaa... baa...

He'd spent his early years, the years preceding his matriculation as they called it then, being sequestered behind stone walls which in no way differed from his idea of a prison. The daily Mass, the biweekly Vespers, and particularly the compulsory sports, including boxing, rugby and cricket, did little to enhance his stay there. No one, not a single master or father, as the illustrious

members of the Society of Jesus insisted on being addressed, believed that in spite of his robust physique he did not like sports.
Any sports.

"It's just not British," he'd overheard one master crying on his
parents' shoulders. "It's just not British, you know."

Rugger, as they'd referred to rugby in his day, and boxing
were good for building a boy's character, they'd said. Boys had to
partake in it, and that was that. But cricket...? Cricket was quite
another story. The British boys had to *like* cricket. Liking cricket
was what being British was all about. No matter how boring, ardu-
ous and singularly unimaginative the game was. It was probably
even worse than baseball, which Dad rated only one step above
induced nausea. He would rather watch an overcast night sky for a
chance of a momentary clearing, than being compelled to look at a
bunch of indolent millionaires in tight pyjamas spitting all around,
running in circles, and occasionally striking a ball with a primitive
weapon.

"What an absurd way to spend one's free time," he'd commented to me at the time. His opinion hasn't changed to this day.

This singular aversion to the asinine game of cricket, as well
as for the inherent need of the British to compel their offspring to
watch, or partake in, anything against his or her will remained with
him for years to come. Yet this method underscored the British
concept of discipline.

"This is precisely, my boy, how we built the Empire!" his father-in-law had once assured him. "Don't you know?"

John Hydon was lucky. He didn't know.

Not surprisingly, when Dad's second wife, my mother, had
suggested that they emigrate to Canada, the idea came to him as a
long awaited relief. Somewhere at the back of his mind a silent
thought rejoiced: *no more cricket.* Of course, he hadn't heard of
baseball then.

Years after his final exams liberated him from the fetters of
the Jesuits, Margaret's family had been, he found to his horror,
very punctilious about watching cricket matches on Sunday afternoons. For hours. Long cigars, smelly pipes, and abundant Scotch,
all but destroyed by the injection of bubbly soda, helped, nevertheless, to alleviate the tedium to some degree.

At least he'd been spared the ignominy of making a spectacle of himself on the Village Green. That would have killed him. "Bad knee", he'd said over his shoulder. "A bad knee... Really, old boy. Had it for years, you know..." and all that sort of nonsense. A convenient injury, probably originating in one of a thousand wars the British fought while building the Empire. Although, the Empire was long gone, the convenient 'injuries' remained.

Sometimes father got mixed up and limped on the wrong leg. No one seemed to notice.

The school in Brompton, or the Brompton School, as really it was a village that grew around the boarding school, was one of only three educational institutions JJ could have chosen in the adjoining Provinces of British Columbia or Alberta. Once JJ expressed his desire to attend one of them, his choice seemed to have resolved a lot of problems. While I still liked to visit father's observatory at least twice a week, father, even as Professor Doctor John Hydon, Ph.D., the Director, could hardly have a bunch of kids running around his office. The electronics were delicate and expensive to say the least. And, contrary to his Dad's youthful predispositions, JJ just loved to swing a bat. It seems to have given him a sense of power. Maybe he imagined people he didn't like on the receiving end. But since JJ had been given a bat for his tenth birthday, he seldom walked around without it.

To do JJ justice, other than Brompton being on a hill, a mount if you will, there was no other similarity between his father's old College in Spinkhill, England, and JJ's choice of school. To start with, the buildings at JJ's school were modern, bright, and located in unique surroundings. The rolling countryside, for the most part richly covered with Douglas fir, hemlock and cedars, was situated at the foot of the Rocky Mountains. Originally a trading post, the Jesuits converted it (including the resident Indians) and expanded the settlement into one of the top residential schools in the country. The fact that it was located miles from anywhere gave the parents a sense of security. The boys, stimulated by their effervescent hormones, would be unlikely to stray into dens of iniquity, so prevalent in most major cities. The curriculum offered and encouraged guided hikes through the secluded nature trails, most of them quite inaccessible to road traffic. If you liked Mother Nature, there was little not to like about Brompton.

On the other hand, a mere six-hour drive along the Alaska Highway would get father to the JJ dorm.

The first time father arrived at Brompton to deposit his son into the Jesuits' care, he was pleasantly surprised. He noticed the absence of mustiness he associated with his own Jesuit College. He'd half expected to inhale a combination of dampness and old age, intermingled with infrequently washed socks he remembered only too well from his own schooldays. Not to criticize the past, but in Dad's youth running hot water was a luxury, especially in old English buildings. Even though, in his day, washing was resolutely encouraged, in fact strictly enforced, hot water had been, on most days, conspicuous by its absence.

In addition, the Brompton Jesuits allowed lay teachers in a number of subjects, giving the school a less monastic atmosphere. While attending the religious services was warmly encouraged, the school was, to a degree at least, non-denominational, in the sense that one did not have to be a Christian, let alone a Catholic, to attend. Needless to say, the vast majority of pupils were Christians, but in this day and age, parents grounded their children more on the articles of faith than the articles of religion. In father's day, few would admit that there was a difference.

In the months preceding father's driving JJ to Brompton, he and JJ had begun to grow closer. It had begun one afternoon when Dad, flipping channels, had been about to express his disdain for the baseball on TV. He caught himself just in time when he saw a strange glint in JJ's eyes. Mary also noticed the look.

"You might take the young master onto the village green," she advised father, using the old English terminology. Maybe Mary was worried about the amount of cleaning she would have if JJ swung his bat indoors.

Dad, on the other hand, cringed at the very idea of any sort of playing field. Of course, there was no such thing as a village green in Canada, let alone at the CSC. Not to his knowledge. But he remembered David telling him about his son practising on a baseball field; a diamond, just outside the Chemistry Pavilion. With guilt still lingering at the periphery of his consciousness, father shrugged as he turned to JJ.

"I can show you where it is, Dad?" It was as much a question, as a plea, as a statement. JJ's eyes were shining.

"You've been there before?"

JJ was on his feet, the bat poised to deliver a mighty whack.

"What now?" Father sounded crestfallen, but no one seemed to hear the agony in his voice.

JJ was on his way to the door.

For the next two months, father threw the ball, while JJ did his damnedest to smash it with all his might. Towards the end of the two months, JJ had connected with some mighty good swings. To father's utter amazement, it turned out that he, himself, had a pretty good throwing arm. He was even more amazed, that he actually enjoyed playing with his son. Perhaps there was a difference between playing and watching the game. Maybe the British were on to something after all.

As it sometimes happens, this new concord between father and son evolved from most unexpected and certainly undefined quarters. It arose from father's need to make up to his son for his paternal shortcomings, and the son's love of hitting things. Perhaps the frequent explosive contacts between the ash wood and the hard ball diffused the anger and loneliness which had been simmering subliminally in JJ for a number of years. Baseball seemed to release both these emotions. So much so that the parting at Brompton – meant to be JJ's final escape – turned out to be another loss in JJ's life.

John Junior, JJ, had inherited his father's looks and his mother's disposition. He inherited the high forehead from both his parents, and the patrician posture from his mother. Quite unwittingly, he gave an impression of looking down at his peers, including those taller than himself. His piercing hazel eyes formed a barrier hard to cross even for some people he knew well. He also inherited his mother's aloofness without much of his father's charm.

Respected, if not all that liked. Was it the half-blue blood that was showing?

"He might yet grow up to be a good leader," father said after one of JJ's visits. "Or he might have been better off had we stayed in England."

There was a tinge of sadness in Dad's voice.

But after the very first term at Brompton, JJ returned to Ogilvy Mountain with a firm resolve to go back to school as soon as he could. Never having any sustained friendships at home, there, at the Jesuits, he'd quickly learned to manipulate boys so as to surround himself with a cadre who were ready to follow him. JJ had found his milieu. He needed a strict organization in which he could flourish.

The priests thought him an example of what a well-behaved boy should be. They soon began calling him *Arbiter Exemplarum*, which had something to do with good behaviour. No one, neither master nor pupil, seemed able to see through the mask that JJ had developed in just three months. It stuck to him as naturally as a dog collar stuck to the black-cassocked priests. They seemed two of a kind. Or perhaps, he'd just belonged to them, or would have, if they hadn't attempted to impose their will on him. In that respect JJ had followed in his father's footsteps. But unlike his father he refused to suffer because of it. He would cheat, lie if need be, to get his own way.

Oh, yes. He'd also inherited his father's exceptional intelligence. On the other hand, he did like baseball. Father always thought the two were self-exclusive.

For now, JJ's problems remained under control. Father was amazed how confident his son looked. On that first trip back after the first term, they strolled the Observatory gardens like adults, discussing this and that, never touching the subject of baseball. Next term, to celebrate JJ's thirteen's birthday, Dad took me to visit JJ at Brompton. The deputy Headmaster had given Dad permission to take JJ out for the day, just to give him a break in the routine. JJ had given the impression of being pleased, but little enthusiasm registered on his face. Some time later he confessed that he'd been afraid other boys might accuse him of favouritism

from the headmaster. That wouldn't sit well in his scheme of
things. He wanted all the advantages on his side.

I recall father asking JJ if he was reading anything interesting
in school. JJ hesitated, and shook his head. Just school stuff, he
implied. He then looked away. But John Hydon was beginning to
learn, even if belatedly, the body-language of his children. He
nudged gently.

"Well, Dad, there is one book I found.... But you wouldn't
like it," JJ confessed.

"Try me?" Dad looked genuinely interested. Not so much
about the book, but for JJ's hedging.

"The Prince," JJ said at last.

The only 'Prince' father had ever heard of was *The* Prince by
Niccolo Machiavelli. John had read the book but only when he
was in his early thirties. He decided to let it drop. He wasn't at all
sure that thirteen year-olds should read books like that but...

For the birthday outing father took us to a forested area with a
glade where the children could play, swim in a feral pond and raise
Cain to their hearts' content. Once outside the school walls, JJ
immediately shed his rigid, distinctly formal behaviour. It was as
though he'd stopped acting and reverted to being himself. He
finally started behaving like a boy on his day off from school.
Boisterous. Carefree.

I must admit that in those days, I looked up to my brother as
though beholding an idol. There must have been open admiration
in my eyes. Dad, on the other hand, seemed preoccupied with trying to figure out which was the real JJ. The perfectly balanced,
poised, unemotional young man, mature beyond his years, he'd
seen this morning, or the lad turning somersaults into the pond over
his screaming sister's head – a mere hour later. Or maybe a mix of
both. For an instant, Margaret's face hovered in his memory. The
next moment he dismissed the idea. Whatever JJ was, he would
grow up to be his own man. Neither his genes nor his paternal
hopes would have great influence on the outcome.

And then Dad's face clouded over. "I hope it's not just wish-
ful thinking," he muttered to himself. "Now, why would such a
thought cross my mind," he mused out loud.

But the cloud wouldn't go away. He was still new to the parenting game. He didn't find it easy, and he had started very late in life.

It was there, after a sumptuous picnic, that I told them both about my latest dream. Or at lest, how it had started. Dad and JJ were lying down, resting on their elbows absently chewing on the last of the chicken wings. My mouth still full of chicken, I looked into the sky and pointed almost straight up, slightly east of the sun. "It was right there," I said. "Behind Pluto."

JJ continued munching while Dad caught his breath. He was aware that I knew very well where Pluto was. When its orbit brought it to the northern celestial hemisphere, that is. At night. I couldn't possibly have known in the middle of the day where Pluto would be at this particular moment. He had to give it some considerable thought, in order to place the position of the distant planet during daylight. After all, it would remain quite invisible not only for the rest of the day, but this night also. Its orbit would take it to the other side of Earth. But now – he glanced at his watch – it would be exactly where I'd pointed. In broad daylight.

"What was up there?" Dad asked noncommittally.

"The other planet. The silver ball, Daddy."

Pluto had not been in the northern sky during the night for two weeks. What I had seen, he thought, could only have been in a dream.

"Were you dreaming, darling?"

"Of course, Daddy. I was dreaming the dream."

"And just when have you been dreaming, darling?"

"I took a nap after lunch, Daddy. Like you often do."

That was quite true. As father usually worked most of the night, his sleeping schedule had been scattered throughout the day. He often took five or six hours in early morning, and then made up for the missing hours with a nap after lunch. On occasion, I, who at the time followed his every move, joined him. It was quite true that at about one p.m. Pluto's orbit would place the planet directly overhead.

JJ finished his last chicken wing and ran off after a bird which was making a racket in a bush overhanging the water. The next moment he was soaking wet. No matter. The bird was gone. The moment JJ climbed ashore, the thrush, probably a bluebird, sat down again and continued its lilt. JJ gave it a long look and came back. He was definitely not pleased with the recalcitrant singer, but he refused to get involved in battles he couldn't win. Father looked fascinated by his son's behaviour. He'd never really observed him before.

As I continued with my story, JJ began paying attention. Without interrupting. A rare occasion indeed.

"It was very dark, Daddy."

"Your eyes were closed?" Dad offered.

"Yes, Daddy. But when I opened them it was even darker. It was nothing."

"What was nothing?"

"It. There. Where I was nothing."

"You were in nothing?"

"No, Daddy. Where I was it was nothing, and I was nothing. Everything was nothing."

I can hardly blame my father for not knowing how to formulate the next question. Frankly, he still couldn't decide if I was recounting a dream or making up the story as I went. He decided to wait and see. What he found strange was that JJ didn't scramble for attention. It looked as if he was waiting for me to continue. Dad had no idea that I had already shared a number of my dreams with my brother.

"And then I stopped being afraid. I... I... didn't keep, I didn't hold on..."

"You let go? Stopped holding on to being afraid?"

"Yes! And then I was light. Just a little light. Like a firefly. I was flying in the dark. In nothing."

"That's a lovely story, Hey..." father started but I ignored him.

"And then there was a big light. And the big light broke up into little lights. Not little like me, but into smaller lights. Then there was ten.. no, ele... And then there were twelve lights." I know I must have sounded as if I was still counting them.

When I remained silent for a while, father prompted me gently. "And then...?"

"And then I woke up, Daddy. It was already two-thirty. We always get up at two-thirty, you know that?"

"Of course," he nodded, none the wiser.

He knew what time we usually got up. What he didn't know at all was what to make of my dream. In a way, the way I'd told it, it sounded as though I was still dreaming the dream.

So there.

Now you see what problems I've faced in trying to convey to my father my early experiences with the Enigma. It is not easy to describe 'Nothing'. I put together this story, from Dad's, JJ's and my own memories. It is pretty accurate. I didn't want to tell it from only my point of view, or it might have been slanted. As for JJ, he really was an incredible boy. He was just thirteen, so I must have been almost ten. I thought JJ was like a prince. A prince from some fables Mary had read to me.

Dad was nice too. Dad was getting nicer every day. But as far as the Enigma was concerned, he had no idea what I was talking about.

Nor would he have for a long time.

I should mention one other thing. From the time I turned twelve, I'd spent a great deal of my time in Dad's office. I also followed him whenever and wherever I could. By then, I could already recite all the main characteristics of our planetary system. I was also attending Uncle Dave's Sunday dinners, although I never took part in any of the discussions. I spent most of my time at the fish tank. My golden friends held my eyes, but my ears were always attuned to the dining room. When I wasn't around, they spoke more freely. That way I learned things I would never have heard otherwise.

Wasn't I a smart girl?

***

ZERO MINUS 20

7

A Real and Present Danger

Father knew how to handle problems connected with his work. Not just concerning his beloved Via Lactis, but other events much closer to home. He, for the most part, understood them to be events that needed analysis and mental dissection. In due time, the process of synthesis, consisting of integration of the new data, resulted in the gradual dissolution of mysteries. And there were mysteries galore. Not of any profound order of magnitude. Not discoveries of new galaxies, globular clusters, or heretofore unseen patches of dark matter. Not even the discovery of uncharted stars or planets, or even comets, but rather an array of minor events, vaguely annoying, in as much as their occurrence disturbed the smooth, day-to-day operation of the Observatory.

The chunks of matter, presumed asteroids, which continued to miss Earth, in increasing numbers, were just some of such disturbances. Their increased number was not the problem in itself. Since the Canadian Science Centre boasted the largest optical telescope in the world, new and heretofore unseen objects were expected to become visible. After all, the Monster Eye was not only the largest, the most advanced, the most electronically equipped telescope the human race had ever possessed, but it was also fully automated. When properly set, it scanned the night sky by itself, latching onto any movement in the deeps, up to 2.5 million kilometres away, and then followed the object logging any changes of direction, velocity

or variations in observable size. That was how the first near miss
had been discovered and how the growing number of near colli-
sions came to be noticed and recorded.

There were so many of them that competing astronomers had
grown quite *blasé* about father's reports. Dad didn't like that at all.

There was another item that caught our attention after a detailed spectroscopic examination. We presumed these chunks to be
of dirt and ice originating in the Asteroid Belt, but they turned out
to be lumps of matter rich in rare minerals, some of which had abstruse military applications. Our friends down south, especially
those hiding behind the ramparts in the star shaped dungeon known
as the Pentagon, began wondering. They started to suspect that the
variations in the trajectory of those clumps of matter weren't
caused by some underground source in China, or North Korea, or
some other place that President Twigg's predecessor had referred
to as the Axis of Evil. Neither Twigg, nor his successor, realized
that no one on Earth would possess the technology to shift these
asteroids even a fraction of what we had observed for at least another hundred years.

"I think they are all paranoid, down south," Dad concluded.

David Mendel, who participated in the spectroscopic examin-
ations, had been listening to father's explanations with a whimsical
expression.

"Alas," he said at length, "paranoia is not a malady with which
one should beat around the bush. Or, ah, Twigg, for that matter."

Father didn't laugh. He was just a little annoyed. Not at
David, nor even at the Pentagon, but at his scientific fraternity. He
hated being ignored.

"Another of your pebbles, John? Well, thanks for letting us
know..." Dad mimicked the voice of the head of NASA. "That's
all they said."

There followed a moment of silence. Profound, pensive silence replete with strained connotations. Three published papers
and a number of lectures, and all he got was 'thanks for letting us
know'. No one seemed impressed with the interplanetary missiles
which continued to change direction in mid-flight. As Dad turned
his attention to the Monster Eye, the telephone rang again. Once
more, it was the Pentagon.

"You are not making this information public, Dr. Hydon, are you?" It was the Two-Star General who'd spoken to father before. He sounded much more formal.

"What information?" Dad's mind was already drifting to some other part of our galaxy.

"Good man! Never mind. Just keep it to yourself." This last, Dad said later, sounded like an order.

"Of course!" father replied, still having no idea what the pompous *generalissimo* had been talking about. It was probably too secret to be divulged.

Usually, the change in trajectory was a mere .0002 to .0003, or two to three millionth of a meter. A tiny fraction, to be sure, but, in Dad's judgement, a significant amount. When you allow that the change of direction occurred at say, a 1.5 to 2 million kilometres from Earth, and after working into the equation Earth's orbital movement and her gravitational attraction, the deviation of say .0003 of a meter could result in about a 300,000 kilometre miss. Father also found it significant that the near misses were all too regular. The near misses stayed in the range of 280,000 to 300,000 kilometres. Why not 500,000 or 150,000 kilometres? Too good to be true, or to be a coincidence.

With such a margin of safety, no one deemed it necessary to pay too much attention to father's reports, even if the errant missiles were all well inside the moon's orbit around the earth. Much too close for comfort by any standards. One could but hope that the moon's gravitational pull was too week to draw the wandering asteroids towards its surface. At any rate, at the time, American activities on the Moon were not as yet making the headlines.

As for Dad's colleagues, all respectable and established astronomers, well... they just seemed glad that the extraterrestrial chunks were missing us. That, they said, was the most significant thing of all.

"This sort of thing must have been happening for millions of years, John. Only we didn't have the benefit of your Monster Eye, ha, ha..."

As for the sudden changes in trajectory, they blamed that on the instrumentation. After all, there was no other logical explanation.

Father suspected that their lackadaisical reaction had something to do with professional jealously. He stopped calling them. He didn't mind being ridiculed, but what he was looking for was a scientific opinion, not jocularity. What he really hated even more was that he was at a loss as to how to provide a reasonable explanation for his observations. Had he discovered a new law of nature? Did something happen to make large objects repel smaller ones? This was even more absurd than the comments offered by his colleagues.

I could have told him, there and then, that his answers lay in the Enigma. That Enigma would explain all this. But I had neither the words nor the experience to do so. I was still just a ten-year-old. And frankly, there were no appropriate scientific terms. Science was simply not yet sufficiently advanced enough. I wonder if it ever will be.

Poor Dad.

Thanks to his friend David Mendel, father's expertise in the field of tectonics was growing day by day. Not that there were any more of the *legato sustinuto* earthquakes, stretching for two hours at a time. Just the opposite. After the initial unexplainable lengthy tremor, which was recorded the world over, no one claimed to have discovered its epicentre. It was as though there had been a global adjustment of the tectonic plates. Of the whole crust.

"It's ridiculous, my friend," David claimed with considerable exasperation. "The crust just doesn't behave like that. It prefers a nudge here, a tuck there. Tectonics work more like a plastic surgeon. After all, we are dealing with the Earth's skin. With external cosmetics."

"Which reach quite deep under the epidermis?" John suggested.

"Yes, but skin, is skin, is skin. Or if you prefer, a crust is a crust. You do not remove or disturb the whole skin to make minor adjustments. And you don't operate on the whole body at once. I'm telling you, if it hadn't been for the countless instruments reporting the same occurrences, I wouldn't have believed my own seismographs. Never!"

Poor David had been completely crestfallen.

"You have your plastic surgery, I have my deviations..." father mused aloud.

"What's that?"

"I said we both need medical help! You – a plastic surgeon... never mind." He shrugged. He might well end up on the psychiatrist's coach, but not without a fight.

Father told David about his frustrations with other astronomers who trivialized his findings. While David had full support for the inexplicable readings from an army of geologists, Dad stood alone. Sometimes he wondered if he was born to be alone. What with Margaret, then Heidi, then us, his children... although the latter he'd regained. To some degree. Though for quite different reasons, both JJ and I remained, in some ways, strangers to him. We all seemed to live in worlds of our own making. JJ with his Machiavellian ideas, I with my Enigma, my dreams, my ideas about my mother.... It was all getting to be too much. There was a hazy distinction between the reality most people lived in and my own inimitable Universe. They were both, the same and they weren't. Father had hoped I would snap out of it. Out of my perception of reality. Soon. But even then, no one could hand back the years he'd lost with JJ and me.

"Is this my punishment?" he wondered. I heard him say that. The Catholic concept of guilt dies a slow death.

"How come you've never told me about your problems with NASA and the others, John? Isn't that what friends are for?"

There was chagrin in David's tone. He sounded really hurt. And then he remembered just how private a person John had always been. In the beginning, it had taken two years before John had even alluded to the problems he'd been having with his children. At that time Dad had really needed to unburden himself. He knew he'd been a lousy father and he needed advice. Now it was different. This was his area of expertise. It was his riddle to solve. Yet John had waited almost ten years since the first sighting before sharing his frustrations with David.

"Listen to me, John," David put his hand on Dad's shoulder. "I am not trying to solve your problems for you. I am only offering a friendly ear. Sometimes it helps to talk things out. Even if you do all the talking."

"Thanks, Dave."

From that time on the Sunday dinners had advanced to a new level. Every fortnight they met, early, and spent the first hour or so just bellyaching, as Dad called it, at the stupid crust, the stupid errant asteroids, the stupid fish in the tank, the stupid love JJ developed for baseball, and the stupid world in general. After the second Scotch, which during the winter months replaced beer, they both felt much better and ready to face any adversity. Miriam would look at them through an open door and shake her head, concern showing on her motherly features.

"Boys!" she said more than once looking up at the ceiling in mock desperation. She would then close the door with an exaggerated shrug.

And then there was the problem of the elusive shadow behind Pluto. It was Dad who started referring to it as the 'Enigma' because the shadow was playing an enigmatic 'now you see me, now you don't' game with Dad's cameras. It didn't make any sense. Like the wandering asteroids. Like our friends down south.

Was the world going crazy?

Father had occasion to contact some of his professional friends in New Mexico. The scientists there scanned the sky for distant elliptical galaxies and proved of little help. The NASA people looked more promising. Their Infrared Astronomy Satellite with its 57-centimetre infrared telescope could reach where Dad had little access. Infrared wavelengths are near impossible to observe from Earth, as our atmosphere filters most of them out.

Father asked his counterpart at NASA to direct their telescope at Pluto and report any deviations. He'd waited two months to hear that, after repeated scans of Pluto and it's immediate vicinity, they had nothing to report. No new, additional, or unexplained radiation in the infrared range. Nothing new at all.

So that was that.

Father felt understandably rejected by his colleagues. No one would confirm his elusive sightings behind Pluto. Whether the elusive globe was just a reflection or had other substance was of no consequence. No one knew anything about its existence. He'd all but decided to give up his histrionics, or what others regarded as such, and return to his original love. To Via Lactis. There was only one problem left. Little Hey. *Moi.*

As a reasonably proud scientific mind, Dad didn't like puzzles. Actually he loved them, but only in so far as they were solvable. When logic, mathematics and all the scientific paraphernalia at his disposal failed, he didn't like puzzles at all. And I had, with a single dream created the Enigma, or at least an enigma, which seemed beyond his capacity to resolve. Not my dream, nor my visions of nothing or nothingness, nor even of my expanding circle of lights. What troubled my father more was my apparent ability to point my finger at the 'precise' location of Pluto, in broad daylight. Repeatedly. Once could have been luck. But I'd done it four times. I seemed to have Pluto's orbit ingrained in my brain. Dad had questioned me about it a number of times. I managed to shed little light. I remember the first time he questioned me.

"Just how did you know where the planet Pluto was on that day in Brompton?" he asked me, his tone sounding hopeful.

"It was there, Daddy," I replied.

"Yes, sweet, but how did you know that?" He encouraged me as gently as he could.

"You know it's there, Daddy. So why shouldn't I?" Apparently that wasn't very helpful at all. He face grew stern.

At this, he told me later, my mouth had turned into a pout and my eyes began getting misty. He had to drop the subject. He wondered it there was any other way to get at the truth. Finally, he had to give up.

About two years later, I came to his rescue myself.

"Look, Daddy, look!" I was sitting up on my bed, my eyes wide in sheer wonderment. It was Saturday and Dad and I had been taking our afternoon nap.

"What is it, dear?" He was still groggy.

By then I realized that I'd been asleep. I rubbed my eyes, looked up at the ceiling and lay back. Then I rubbed my eyes again. For some strange reason, Dad was sure that I'd had another of my, for the want of a better word, experiences with Pluto.

"What happened?" he persisted.

"I was looking for Mommy," I explained.

At this father sat up. I was eleven then and we hadn't talked about my mother for some time. Probably, not for at least a year. Rather than pushing me, Dad waited for me to continue. I appreciated that. I needed to find the right words.

"She's everywhere," I said finally.

"Care to explain?"

"She is nowhere," I said, apparently quite unaware of having contradicted myself.

Father vaguely remembered my terminology from the time I'd related my previous dreams. I'd spoken of great darkness and something about it being nothing, and she, my mother, being nothing also. I'd said, then, that everything was nothing. And now here it was again. "She is nowhere," I'd said. But also that she was everywhere. Dad had no idea how to ask a question that would shed any light on my quandary. Yet to me, it had all been very real.

"Do you miss Mommy?"

"Not now, Daddy. Not anymore," I recall assuring him.

"How come?"

"Well, Daddy, now I know she's everywhere."

"And nowhere?" he'd asked looking into my eyes.

"Well, yes. Everywhere is nowhere."

That was not the way my father thought the conversation should evolve. I was older then, but, in his opinion, I still didn't make any sense. So few things made sense these days.

"Care to explain?" he tried again.

"When you are no-thing, you are everywhere," I offered.

"When you are nothing..."

"No Daddy. When you are *no* thing. When you are *not anything*, then you are everywhere. When you are nothing. Not a thing. Nothing, not anything at all." Dad was not getting any closer.

I was getting exasperated.

"You will see, Daddy," I assured him. "You will see."

And that was all that father managed to get out of me on that occasion.

That was my first real contact with the alternative reality. I mean real in the sense that I could recall every detail, every minute fragment of that dream. At the time I saw it, became part of it, I had no idea that it might have been an illusion. I began to doubt myself. I didn't know, then, that men and women, and apparently little girls, create realities all the time. All realities are real in their particular context. What I also didn't know was that each present shapes its own future. That I had to be careful. I recall reading somewhere: "Be careful what you wish for – it just might come true." But that was years later.

At that particular moment I began to doubt the reality of my whole life. Was father really a famous astronomer? Perhaps he'd just imagined the Enigma? Did aunt Miriam really bake those marvellous cakes? Had my mother really died when I was born? Or had I seen her smile, heard her voice, touched her hand, her face, just a few minutes ago?

The week after JJ came home for Thanksgiving. It wasn't a normal holiday, but some years ago the Jesuits decided to allow the boys to spend the festive day with their parents. It was probably a concession for the boys from the USA, who regarded Thanksgiving as a feast on par with Xmas and Easter. The Jesuits' attempt at public relations misfired when they realized that Canadians and Americans observed Thanksgiving on different dates. Nevertheless, the tradition remained.

JJ took the train to Whitehorse and from there a bus, along highway 2, which brought him to Ogilvy Mountain. Since the CSC was now well established, access to the Centre improved dramatically. JJ insisted on coming to see us on his own.

"I'm old enough, Dad. I can find my own way," he'd assured both of us.

Indeed, JJ was fourteen now and he did find his way without any trouble. The trouble came later. A real and present danger.

The Jesuits, in their effort to make the school accessible to youth from as far and wide as possible, took a very ecumenical attitude towards their pupils. This, of course, substantially broadened their recruiting base. They had almost doubled their enrolment. After all, all church organizations needed money. The governments had been cutting the free ride, which all the religions had enjoyed, from time immemorial. The definition of a non-profit organization had been considerably refined. If they made no profit, they had to open their books and prove it. If they didn't, the auditors did it for them. The free religious lunch, which lasted for hundreds, or was it thousands of years, was over.

The consequences of this new policy were staggering. Not only did the various churches stop fighting each other, but there developed a new air of cooperation. You scratch my back and I'll scratch yours became the official ecumenical policy. It all sounded quite reasonable. Almost Christian.

But there was a snag.

The more traditional orthodox sects had absolutely no experience in cooperation. Their policy had always held that 'we' were right and 'they' , whoever 'they' were, were invariably wrong. When the need for cooperation brought them closer to the mainstream, they lacked the know-how to protect their own, and be more generous to others.

On this premise of mutual cooperation preachers from various sects had been given (almost) equal time on the Brompton podium. Not in the church as such, but in the amphitheatre which was often attended by boys in preference to the Catholic rites. The priests seldom took time to explain the 'mysteries' of their own services and ceremonies, let alone to demystify them. Heretofore, boys attended them out of obligation, not out of interest. When the preachers of various Protestant denominations took the dais, boys flocked to the amphitheatre as though to a school play. They heard stories of wonders, and miracles, and hair-raising prophecies about the end of the world. Like inventive, if on occasion grotesque,

Hollywood sagas. Some Baptists, Jehovah Witnesses, and Seventh-Day Adventists were particularly good at scaring the wits out of the impressionable young minds.

When the Jesuits caught on to the surreptitious fundamentalist propaganda, it was already a little too late.

While the Catholics relied mostly on the stick, the new generation of preachers preferred the carrot. To hell with hell, let's live well and go to heaven. Stick with us and you won't need a stick, and will be saved to boot. You want that in writing? I'll send you a certificate with a number of quotations certifying the authenticity of our offer. Join now and save on fees. Etc., etc., etc..

It was all above board, clean, hands on the table.

It sounded pretty convincing. A number of boys were already hooked and JJ, the little JJ who only three years ago wouldn't go near a church unless compelled or bribed, now began to give a portion of his time to the professional proselytizers. And professional they were. JJ, without telling the preachers anything, took it upon himself to organize his own branch of the Adventist movement.

What this idea really gave JJ was a sense of belonging. He didn't really acknowledge it but his emptiness, his lack of affiliation to any group was the big black hole in his personal life. The Adventists, keen to recruit new members, welcomed JJ with open arms.

"You want to organize? Why, this is exactly what we expect from young lads like you! To participate! To get involved!"

Their eyes shone with the fervour of having saved yet another soul from a fate worse than... they didn't say exactly from what. But they did welcome JJ with open arms.

JJ had been given a number of small gifts, the title of an acolyte, a membership card and instructions on how to spread the word. Within a single school term JJ had become the official spokesman. He became a prophet for the Second Coming of Christ. He felt there was a future in the movement. Within a mere two months he gathered a dozen followers, boys who also wanted to be singled out, who found Mass and Vespers rather boring. They still attended the Jesuit services, but their own organization grew exponentially. It was all reminiscent of a secret club, of an underground army, where they and only they knew things.

JJ was expanding his fledgling organization with precision and determination. He would have made Niccolo proud.

Father heard about his son's activities from the deputy Headmaster at Brompton. JJ never suspected that his ambitions were known to anyone but his own inner circle, but the Jesuits weren't born yesterday. They made it very clear to Dr. Hydon that, unless JJ discontinued his underground activities, he, Dr. John Hydon, would be asked to remove John Hydon Junior from the school. The matter was not negotiable.

"I am sorry, Sir," Father Martin had said, his voice taking on a suitably sorrowful inclination. "But we must recognize the difference between ecumenism and an underground network directed against the Holy Church."

"Ah, surely, the boys should be encouraged..." father tried to intervene. Suddenly, Dad felt like an altar boy at Mount St. Stanislaus Kostka's College trained not to ask questions but to obey.

"We try to be as tolerant as we can, Dr. Hydon, really, but without endangering the souls of boys in our charge." The deputy Headmaster continued as though Dad hadn't spoken. "I am sure you understand. Please feel free to call us whenever you feel that we can be of any assistance."

Assuring himself that no assistance would be called for, Father Martin promptly hung up the receiver. During this conversation I had been hiding in my favourite place, behind the bookshelf. I saw father's facial expression change. I don't think he was angry with the priest for ignoring his attempt to speak on behalf of his son. He was angry, very angry, at himself, for allowing the callous Jesuit to browbeat him into silence. "It's the last time," he hissed under his breath. "The last time I allow them to put me down," he promised himself. Dad felt more rebellious than he'd ever felt since his school days. At least I think he must have. He looked deadly pale. I'd never seen Dad's face turn such colour.

There had been a number of things father wanted to tell the priest. He was going to suggest that if they wanted to inspire the boys to 'stay within the faith', then they might try treating them like young men, students if need be, but never like recruits at the lowest level of conscription. He also wanted to tell the garrulous Jesuit that the Christian way is supposed to be the way of love and compassion, not of the carrot and the stick. Heidi, my mother, had told him that, when they were first married. There was a great deal more he could have told Father Martin – but didn't. He'd become a docile boy, a malleable bit of clay in the priest's hands. Once again.

"No more," he swore to himself. "Never, never again!"

The last three words Dad said out loud. The rest I've made up. Mostly. But I'm sure I'm right. Really.

JJ arrived at Ogilvy Mountain full of beans. Energy radiated from him like a halo around a full Moon on a misty night. Father would have preferred to refer to his son as a minor Nova, but he thought that would have been a little presumptuous. Enough said that the rather withdrawn, almost shy boy had blossomed into a lad brimming with confidence. JJ had no idea that anyone had telephoned his father about his activities at Brompton. Unless it might have been about his achievements in sports. He'd collected more kudos, more praise from the masters than practically any other boy. He'd been appointed the arbiter in boys' disputes; he was fostered as the paradigm of scholastic behaviour (though at first, JJ had no idea what the word meant).

But all of that was just a game. Frankly, sports was the only thing of which he felt really proud. Sports were his passion. Sports and leadership, which, at this stage of his development, coincided. He was the youngest captain ever of the school's baseball team, with the highest number of home runs in school history. He had nothing to worry about.

Nothing at all.

Then father spoke to him. Dad was very down to earth. He told JJ how to conduct himself behind enemy lines. He told him how to avoid detection. He told him that if he got caught, again, he would be on his own. He was quite tough on his son.

JJ felt convinced that he'd found a powerful ally.

***

8

The Game

During the following two years, JJ reread Machiavelli's The Prince. He didn't make notes. He'd decided not to leave any evidence of his more abstruse or perhaps eccentric tastes. On one of his visits to Mount Ogilvy, he'd also gotten hold of a copy of Marx's Manifesto and had spent hours in the library scanning through the English version of *Das Capital* which Engels had helped put together. He was a fast learner.

JJ had absolutely no interest in communism. What he was after was the frame of mind of people who wanted to impose their will on others by the use of surreptitious if not underhanded means. He learned a lot. He tried to follow in Engels' footsteps and apply the method developed by Hegel which Engels, together with Marx, applied to their Dialectical Materialism. His own version was more akin to Dialectical Adventism, he thought, smiling at his practically oxymoronic play on words. To apply extremes of materialism to sell the idea of the Second Coming was JJ's idea of a joke. Particularly when done under the noses of the recognized Guardians of Orthodoxy at Brompton.

Only this time, he would not get caught.

He never spoke of his ideas. He was conspicuously present at any and every religious service or ceremony the Jesuits dreamed up. He served as an altar boy at the Holy Mass with the same overt dedication he displayed when swinging a baseball bat. He excelled at school in Religion, with particular interest in Apologetics. He could prove the Jesuits right even when they doubted their own probity. He did his utmost to live up to the expectations; he became every mother's dream: a straight shooting, honest, upright, direct and punctilious student. After that single call from Father Martin, JJ had changed his ways. It was obvious. Self-evident. A blind man could see it. Or a blind priest. Like Father Martin, S.J., the Deputy Headmaster.

JJ had indeed changed. Substantially. Only it wasn't in the way his masters had anticipated.

He was determined that, one way or another, he would get even with the Jesuits. "JJ screws SJ." He liked the sound of it.

Divide and conquer is an old adage.

JJ's opposition remained conveniently united. What he did divide were his own followers. First, he told them all that he no longer espoused the Adventists' creed. Then, he decided not to do anything on his own. To prove his honesty, he no longer accepted any titles, gifts, positions of authority, or other perks from the group with whom he'd started. There was great disappointment in the ranks that he'd left. There was great regret.

JJ decided that if he were to succeed in his game, he had to become and remain the Power behind the Throne. Under an assumed name he appointed three lieutenants, making sure that each one would spy on the other two and report to him personally. By e-mail. It was all so delightfully hush-hush that the boys fell for it like a bunch of chimps on bananas. Within a week following Father Martin's phone-call to his father, JJ had withdrawn into the dark panelling adorning the Headmaster's private office. The Principal's principle lair, the Jesuits' Holy of Holies. A place where angels feared to tread. (JJ amused himself making up alternate names for his quarry).

It was all rather simple.

For a time, JJ's quiet passion for computers had lain dormant. There had been no reason to explore his abilities further. The school had provided so many new and exciting interests that he'd felt no need to escape into his world of emotional sterility.

Then an opportunity presented itself.

He learned that no one ever looks at a uniformed man's face. He managed to get a suit of overalls from a cleaning-cupboard, including a cap that covered half his face. Then, pretending to be a regular cleaner, he installed two tiny listening devices in the Headmaster's wood panelling. The devices broadcast on an elusive band directly to a tiny receiver inserted into JJ's ear. The bug had been his own adaptation of a miniaturized two-way system. The idea was that knowing in advance the Headmaster's needs, he could, quite innocently, present himself to offer help, thus ingratiating himself to the Principal Father. Or Father Principal officially known as Father Sylvester O'Neil, S.J., Ph.D. etc., etc., the Big Kahuna himself. By the same token he could find ways of dodging any activities which Father Martin might dream up.

It was all very cloak and dagger, and JJ loved every minute of it. After all, it was not as if he was planning a robbery, a major desecration, or murder. It was all good, clean fun. It did require him to work twice as hard at his studies, but, having examined his life carefully, he realized what an enormous number of hours people wasted during the day. He watched the other boys. They took too long to get out of bed, to wash, to dress, to eat breakfast, to go to classes, to find their allotted desk and so on until going to bed.

Like his father, JJ was a Titan for work.

By the time he'd turned fifteen, he was the best-organized lad on the campus. He had time for everything – including his underground activities, which were conducted exclusively by his three lieutenants through the Internet. He devised a system of communication wherein the e-mail message, once opened, had a screen time of eleven seconds. Once read, it erased itself with an eerie efficiency but not till the message had been passed on to all the addresses saved in the computer. A sort of exponential bug. Even ludicrous warnings like "The End is at Hand" carries extra weight, when the words on the screen fade and disappear, as though by magic. Basically, JJ was a very successful but inconspicuous nerd,

in direct contrast to his outer persona. His cover was to be as un-
nerdy as could be. And he was.

Finally, his machinations bore fruit. He had a chance to ingra-
tiate himself to Father O'Neil's secretary by removing a bug from
her computer. Needless to say, it had been JJ who'd sent her the
bug initially. It all happened quite suddenly. To Father Martin's
anguish, Father O'Neil had recently been appointed as the new
Principal of Brompton. The secretary kept her job. The Pope has
male secretaries and nuns, working as maids. The Jesuits preferred
not to demean men by relegating them to women's tasks. Anyway,
'everyone knows that women are better at typing', he heard one of
them assure another. Or it may have had something to do with
ecumenism or equal rights. JJ didn't really care.

They should know. They were pretty bad typists.

JJ had learned about the eventual discovery of the computer
bug thanks to his tiny listening device. The rest was easy. In Father O'Neil's absence, he found a way to worm his way into the
Principle's room, by delivering a fictitious, untraceable message to
the secretary. Having sent it himself, JJ knew, of course, that the
bug was already in the computer memory, but he had to wait for it
to be discovered.

According to Fr. O'Neil's secretary, JJ's services had been
nothing short of miraculous. He'd removed all traces of the bug,
rebooted the computer and left without a word.

"Modesty is my second nature," he muttered on his way out
from the Holy of Holies with an ill-concealed grin on his otherwise
studiously bland face.

Soon, the word about JJ's electronic dexterity spread until he
was in danger of loosing his anonymity. As luck would have it, Fr.
Martin's computer developed a similar, not to say.... identical
problem. It didn't take long before JJ was called to appear before
the Deputy Director.

"I hear you're very good at this sort of thing," Father Martin
smiled, his thin lips in grave danger of cracking.

JJ's nemesis was probably calculating how much money he
would save by not calling in a professional 'de-bugger'. JJ remained silent. He stood at near-attention, close to the door, his

head slightly bowed. He preferred this stance in case the good father would notice a sardonic smile fighting to part his lips.

"Yes, Father. I mean, no Father. I don't really know much
about those things at all," he managed to lie glibly.

"No need for false modesty, my boy. Come. See what's
wrong with this infernal machine."

Like most people – cassocked or otherwise – Father Martin
thought a computer a work of the devil. It works well enough
when it wants to, but if it doesn't...?

"Really Father, I have no formal training. I was lucky that
once..."

"Then come and be lucky twice."

The smile on Father Martin face looked positively painful. In
the old days Fr. Martin would have been among those who meted
out long and painful corporal punishment. "I hate it, but someone
has to do it," he would have said, adding a few extra whacks for
good measure.

"Yes, sir. Father," JJ succumbed to the commanding voice.

For the next three hours JJ made a complete examination of
the Deputy Director's computer. He planted two new bugs, and
performed a very crafty manoeuvre whereby should anyone take
the trouble to search, he or she would trace the Adventist's ponderous, End-of-the-World messages to Fr. Martin's computer, as
the original source. And he reset the calendar just to confuse the
issue. The 'source' would now have begun before JJ first arrived at
the school. It would stand to reason, that he, JJ, must be innocent
of any subterfuge. All this time while JJ amused himself, Father
Martin was busy with his paperwork. When JJ was satisfied with
his gallant venture, he threw his hands up in desperation.

"I just can't do it, Father. I'm sorry."

Father Martin got up and approached the computer.

"Show me," he commanded, a little grit added to the ice in his
voice.

JJ restarted the computer. It worked perfectly. Like new.

"I thought you couldn't do it, lad?" There was just a suggestion of suspicion in his tone.

"I guess I was lucky again, Father," JJ replied humbly.

"I guess you were," Father Martin confirmed. "You may go now."

"Thank you, Father."

JJ bowed and disappeared down the corridor. He turned two corners before he dared to release the laughter constricting his stomach. When he finally let go, the convulsions shook his whole body. Tears streamed from his eyes. He hadn't had so much fun since he first stood before Father Martin that time after his father was called.

"I had words with your father, John. I'm sure you and I shall find a better understanding. From now on."

The smile on Father Martin's face had been positively unnerving. JJ also remembered the ice-cold stare that seemed devoid of any human compassion. It was really then that he'd decided to play the game to the fullest. That day marked the creation of the First World Electronic Church of the Adventist. The FWECA. It had no Elder, no Pope, no Lord Bishop in charge. It was guided by the Unholy Spirit of Tomfoolery. Electronic Spirit. For now, it had the beginnings of the world-wide crusade to scare the wits out of gullible people.

All in good fun, of course. Really!

The last time he'd visited us at CSC, he had described to me some of the antics he'd gotten up to in school. He'd also told me that he was waiting to get even with the offensive master.

"You shouldn't JJ," I'd told him. He was treating the whole affair as a joke.

"And just why not?"

"Your prey is too easy. You can do better."

But, as I recall, I couldn't elaborate. Frankly, I was twelve at the time, and I hardly knew why I wanted him to stop. I just felt it was the right thing to do, and I had to say so. More and more often I found myself acting on impulse. Perhaps it was intuition. So many things were happening in my life that I didn't understand. Not till many years later.

As for JJ, he did understand my viewpoint, though not until a few weeks later. It took a few months before JJ felt a rare, unaccustomed, and brief feeling of compassion. He realized he could win with such a one as Father Martin with his hands tied behind his back. At the time, I hadn't known about Father Martin's call to my father. I wished he'd explained his game to me. I could hardly ask him though, could I?

JJ never admitted to anyone, including himself, that he missed me, his little sister, more than anybody or anything in his young life. I'd dreamt about it. Oh, yes. I dreamed about JJ quite often. He felt he shared something intangible with me that no one else could possibly understand. He realized, belatedly, that no matter how successful he would be with his undercover stratagems, they would never be nearly as much fun if he had no one to share them with. And by the same token, he had, or would have had no one with whom to share his moments of glory. Except for his sister. And I didn't approve.

And now, he wasn't even sure if I would appreciate the significance of the 'game'.

In the middle of the next term, he visited Mount Ogilvy again. He wanted to bounce some of his Machiavellian ideas off his father. JJ was still convinced that he was amusing himself with a perfectly innocent game. Even if, in his mind, he spelled the word Game with a capital G. After all, who could possibly take warnings of an impending end of the world seriously? Surely, no one with an ounce of grey matter between his or her ears. Yes. It was definitely a game. He wondered where it would take him.

When the opportunity presented itself, JJ gave Dad an outline of his Internet ruse. He found father's reaction staggering. Instead of sharing in the fun, Dad started hedging, skirting the issue, and trying to create nonexistent problems. He sounded most discouraging, and this after JJ had been sure that Dad was his silent ally.

It was only some time later that the truth began to dawn on JJ. He reached his conclusions after a lot of soul searching. JJ had been brought up virtually without any religious conditioning. Dad had nothing against any particular religion, not in so many words, though he didn't see, in any of them any intrinsic value. He accepted that the possessor of strong faith might enjoy psychological advantages, that a 'good' confession might release some pent up sense of guilt. But these were practical matters, not necessary for men who found satisfaction in their work.

Now, for the first time JJ looked at what he was doing, and not just to Father Martin. Surely, the countless recipients of his Adventist Internet messages were fair play. Yet for a brief moment he felt sorry for the thousands of deadbeats who may well find some sort of sick satisfaction in the idea of bringing Earth to an untimely demise. No doubt they believed that they alone would be spared. Fr. Martin was quite another story, he felt. After all, it had been he who'd started it. At the same time, JJ felt that he shared, if just peripherally, in his father's apparent sense of guilt. He knew that his father had been brought up a Catholic. Only John Hydon Sr. was no longer a 'real' Catholic. Not in the sense the Jesuits were Catholic. His father had no desire to control anyone. Nor to command them. Nor to tell them what to do and what not to do. His father was truly 'catholic', the kind that did not exist any more.

According to Webster, the word catholic meant universal, general, from splitting the Greek word *katholikos* into *kata* meaning down, and *holos* whole. The Concise Oxford Dictionary defined the word as: universal, *of interest or use to all men; all-embracing, of wide sympathies, broadminded, tolerant.*

Tolerant!

The Jesuits did not meet any of these requirements and, supposedly, they were more Catholic than the Pope. JJ's father, Dad, had long freed himself from any such oxymorons as 'Catholic Church'. If the word catholic espoused universal, all-embracing, broadminded and tolerant values, then, the two words seemed, to JJ, to be self-exclusive. Yet, the Church, had produced 'real' saints. Perhaps, he wondered, we can only elevate our soul in the most adverse environment. If so, then the Church surely provided such. With vengeance!

Nevertheless, his father had been brought up a Catholic. Of the old variety. Catholics, like their Jewish predecessors, thrive on a sense of guilt. JJ refused to share this sentiment.

I referred to Dad as *his* father, because *my* Dad is a completely different entity. I sometimes wonder if we not only create realities but also populate them with people we wish to have around.

There is one other thing worth mentioning that happened about that time. It was another of my strange dreams. Or perhaps visions, as it happened in broad daylight. I felt myself suspended in the air, seemingly in the middle of nowhere, when a dark cloud appeared on the horizon. It approached me at great speed. I was frightened. Just then JJ put his arms around me, as though to protect me.

The cloud was so near now that I could distinguish individual clumps of something, little irregular chunks of dirt, hurtling towards us. I blinked my eyes and the clumps of dirt sprang wings, and changed direction to avoid us. By the time they'd passed us, they looked like a large group of ducks retreating before an approaching winter. I'd seen such ducks once, some years ago. But this was the wrong time for the ducks to fly south. It was only May. When I last saw them, they shrunk to the size of bees, later gnats, until they dissolved into the clear dark sky.

I wondered why the sky was so dark.

Something was wrong. Or perhaps no longer so.

I didn't find out what it was for another fifteen years.

At least I think I found out. Fifteen years from then I was no longer sure of anything. It was all clear and it wasn't. Does this make any sense?

Later I wondered if what I'd seen or imagined had something to do with my future. Can a future exist without the present? It didn't seem so. Each present can develop into infinite versions of futures. In this sense, nothing tangible could ever be taken as real. When I look ahead, I don't see a future; I see a possible future. One of many. Each minute change today must, surely, result in a diametrically different future. Rather like fractal equations with their endless arabesques, or like that butterfly which can flap its wings over the Amazon jungle and, in the fullness of time, be the cause of a hurricane that batters our Atlantic coast.

Yes. I feel only the present is real. And even then I have my doubts.

***

9

Pure Science

Since last year, the monthly feasts had grown to include five more
heads of other departments. In addition to David's own Department of Geology, which included Tectonics and, more interest-
ingly, a fairly new branch of Planetary Geology, there was now in
attendance the fulcrum of the Science Centre. Departments of Astronomy, Physics, Molecular Chemistry and Theoretical Mathematics comprised the original nucleus. Physics, of course, included
Theoretical Physics, which was inexorably tied to Astronomy,
while Molecular Chemistry could hardly be distinguished from Nu-
clear Physics. The Department of Mathematics dealt with such
subjects as the Theory of Numbers, Fractals and Abstract Patterns.
So while officially only five men attended, depending on the subject that tickled David's fancy for the particular evening discussion,
the guests could grow in number to at least nine. For some reason,
at that time, there were no women at the departmental head level,
although they adorned the Humanities in vast numbers. Regrettably, the arts only complemented the CSC later.

Miriam, with only one girl to assist her, took these fluctuations
of guests in her stride though she would be the first to admit that

David was as handy with a ladle as he was with his seismographs. This girl, to whom David referred to jovially as the handmaiden, was what is commonly referred to as a 'looker'. All the scientific eggheads turned their balding pates to stare whenever she crossed the dining room. She was probably the single most compelling reason why the later departments of Arts & Applied Sciences had been introduced. These included Archeology, Palaeontology, as well as Linguistics, Philosophy, History and such like. With the influx of Humanities, women came into their own and joined Miriam gracing the dinner table. Men no longer dared to crane their necks at the voluptuous charms of the single, later two sweet things, serving the illustrious congregation.

In those days, I continued to do my best to remain reasonably invisible. I would eat with Uncle Mendel's sons, when they were home from school, or be mesmerized by the deep-sea activities of the voluminous fish tank.

I'd usually overhear enough of the discussion at the dinner table to tell my story.

Dad returned from Ottawa on Tuesday, where he'd attended a number of conferences. He'd also added weight to Mr. Fairview's presentation of the next budget. Mr. Fairview MBA, the Chief Administrator, more correctly known as the Director of the Canadian Science Centre, leaned heavily on my father with regards to many of the principal administrative decisions of the Centre. Father was rapidly becoming the most experienced resident scientist. David Mendel had been waiting anxiously for Dad's return, insisting that father atone for his absence at dinner the previous Sunday, and visit his home for a make up supper the very next day. When Dr. Mendel got excited about anything, he could be quite persuasive. He was. He added weight to his request in person, walking briskly into Dad's office.

"Must report to you on the gathering I had last Sunday. I'll expect you at six."

His tone sounded like a senior addressing his assistant. He stressed the word *must* so firmly as to preclude any further discussion. He did this sort of thing often. Miriam tried hard to assuage her husband's ardour, but often failed.

"Yes, Sir!" Father saluted clicking his heels, but uncle Dave had already left.

I remember that moment because I giggled.

There is another reason why this particular period left an indelible mark on my psyche. Around that time I'd been studying a flamboyant nebula on my own computer. It was from that time on that I'd been invited to visit Dad's office more often, although no longer to play. I'd been drawn to the stars with the same dedication as a young lad named John Hydon, back home in England, just after he'd successfully defended his doctoral thesis.

Dr. Mendel's professional motivation behind this particular dinner with Dad, with me at his coattails, did not stop Miriam. The table set for just the four of us was ready and waiting. The Sterling silver glistened even before the candles in candelabras gave it an additional noble glow. Kissing Miriam's cheek at the door, Dad smiled his appreciation. I was no longer picked up off the floor and hugged by my adoptive aunt and uncle. I solemnly shook hands with both of them and ran to the fish tank. Apparently Miriam wanted to join the men for aperitifs.

"I missed too much of Dave's Sunday discussion," she confessed, in the way of an excuse. Not that she needed one. If she missed some discussion it must have been due to her self-assumed duties of a perfect hostess.

For some reason, father had always given an impression that he felt very much at home at the Mendel's. I knew that he liked our own condo well enough, but it served as little more than a resting place where he could hide from the exigencies of his work. At the Mendel's he felt more like being at home. A real home. Like his own house had felt way back when mother was alive. I hadn't witnessed those days, of course, but there was no doubt about it. It took a woman's touch to convert a house into a home. God knows Mary had tried hard enough. To this day there were the fresh flowers, which "Madam had liked so much." The place was kept spotless. The refrigerator was always well stocked. There was nothing for which Dad could possibly criticize Mary. And yet?

A home is not a home when its heart is missing.

I was still too young to introduce that elusive feminine element into the, even more elusive, equation of a true family hearth. It wasn't anything one could buy or rent. It was the influence, the presence of a woman, wherein she, by her intrinsic individuality and magic contrived to convert an impersonal space into a nest exuding warmth. Dad only vaguely remembered how it had once been. Yet now, at the Mendel's, he evidently found that very air. It was as intangible as it was palpable. Quite different from the one he'd remembered, but still unmistakable. It was undeniably Miriam's spiritual imprint.

As usual on arrival, father looked around, scanning the apartment for any changes. Perhaps a new picture, a new photograph of the boys, or just to reclaim his own space in the room. He found all as it should be. He always did. That was what made it a home for him. Finally at ease, he sat down. I helped myself to an orange juice and wandered off to the fish tank.

"The usual?"

I could both see and hear them from my hiding place behind the tank. Uncle David held up a glass of Scotch. His own was already half-full at the sideboard. Aunt Miriam was awaiting her cocktail on the settee. Dad took note that David had already started. Rarely if ever did he drink alcohol on his own. Something must be making his friend nervous.

Dad nodded. The last Scotch he'd had was right here, over two weeks ago. Now, as then, he was sitting in 'his' chair, a small stool thrust under his feet. Also as usual, he was being pampered. Should he attempt to get up to help with anything, his friend would unceremoniously push him right back into the armchair's soft embrace.

The bureaucratic red-tape of Ottawa seemed a million miles away. It almost was. Father felt contented. For once, he felt he'd earned the right to relax. After nearly a week in the Capital City, endlessly waiting at the doors of minor mandarins, some dull-faced bureaucrats filled with self-importance, he'd been on the brink of desperation. When he'd finally met with the Minister of Finance, it felt like an anticlimax. They settled the budget within ten minutes.

The Rt. Hon. Brian McDuff had promised to get it through the House by next week.

"Leave it to me, my friend," Brian said with a reassuring smile. "You know you can trust me."

Father knew he could. McDuff had pushed like a medieval ramrod for his previous requests for funds. Few people, and that included all the honourable members of the Opposition, dared oppose him. Not because McDuff was so powerful, but because his caustic humour could ruin a man's reputation for months to come. McDuff was a master of the forgotten art of elocution.

As for Dad, he liked to either work or to rest. What he really hated was waiting. The nature of his work demanded patience to the limits of his fortitude. He'd been forced to do too much waiting, too often, because of the fickle temperament of the Canadian climate. Even if Mt. Ogilvy had been chosen specifically for its micro-climatic conditions that were deemed favourable for astronomical research. For Dad any waste was bad waste. And waste of time was by far the worst.

"You missed an interesting dinner, my friend," David started after he resumed his seat and allowed a respectful moment for a sip of the golden nectar. "There were six of us, and some interesting questions arose, even in your absence."

Father remained silent enjoying his Scotch. He knew David well enough to know that he would get to the point in his own good time. It was obvious that his friend was gathering his thoughts to be as concise as possible.

"I think we are in trouble," was Dr. Mendel's next declaration. "Probably, big trouble."

"Perhaps John would prefer to eat first?" Miriam's concern for Dad's welfare was always disarming. "You shouldn't worry him like that on an empty stomach."

Dad smiled his thanks. "I believe, Miriam, that my stomach is quite safe in your hands, so to speak." Then he turned to David, "Let's have it, Dave."

"We had an extra guest last Sunday, from the Ministry of Agriculture. He'll be presenting his case to you and Fairview tomorrow."

Father looked up. He hadn't been told. The memo must be still lying on his desk. There was too much in his IN basket lately. It interfered with his work. Real work.

David continued. "He came to inquire if we would consider adding a department representing his interests. After he pleaded his case, I was inclined to back him up."

"Out with it, Dave," Dad encouraged.

For some reason Uncle David was beating about the bush. And he would not be rushed. He got up, paced up and down the sitting room and finally looked father directly in the eye.

"You know me, John. I am not one for doomsday scenarios. I've always been pragmatic. Had to be. It's my work." He then lowered his voice to a conspiratorial level. "According to him, to Adam Brown, a vast percentage of the population of Earth will be starving by the beginning of the next decade."

"In four years?"

I watched and listened from my vantage point by the aquarium. My father raised an eyebrow. He'd heard pessimistic prognoses before.

"Or sooner."

"I presume this Brown fellow substantiated his thesis?"

David burst into a short, high-pitched peal of laughter. He sounded more nervous than amused. "He gave us reasons enough to take him seriously."

"I presume you'll share some of them with me?"

"We are quite isolated here, at the Centre," he ignored Dad's remark. "Do you remember the mad cow problems we had some years ago, first in England, then in Canada, finally in the USA and Brazil?"

Dad nodded. "Vaguely," he conceded. At the Centre's restaurant they seldom served meat.

"Well, there is evidence that the gene carrying the disease is more wide-spread than our biologists had suspected. According to AB, the Brown fellow, the gene is carrying a dormant strain. There is evidence that within the next year or two it will erupt all over the world."

"A pandemic spread? So we shall stop eating cows. Can we still drink their milk?"

"This is not a laughing matter, John. Wait till you hear the rest."

"Not till after dinner, my good husband," Aunt Miriam declared. She had given her girl the evening off and decided that the roast beef was ready. I hurried over to help her. As Miriam placed the platter on the table, David remarked with a crooked smile, "Enjoy it John, it may be your last."

Over dinner they talked about father's trip. Later, Uncle Dave briefed Dad on the remainder of the troubling scenario. The more he talked the less amusing it sounded. Apparently there was a connection between big herds, such as held and administered by mega-farms, and the spread of the pernicious gene. This not only applied to large herds of cows but to all livestock, which had been mass-produced to fill the insatiable stomachs of North Americans and their European cousins. There was also evidence that some strains of the virus were making inroads into the human immune system. Especially to those who liked to eat a lot more than they should. Some sort of cumulative effect. Although there is absolutely no connection between mad cow disease and overeating, the degree of obesity had increased during the last ten years to pandemic proportions. Diabetes and other attendant diseases had already run wild. Particularly in North America and Europe, but other countries were not far behind.

"Perhaps Mother Nature is fighting back?" father offered.

"Perhaps. But if she's doing so, then her department of communications must be functioning in overdrive. In addition to the renewed strain of the Mad Cow virus, a similar, though not the same bug has been discovered in sheep, chicken, ducks, geese, and, as I already mentioned, all livestock which has been extensively mass produced."

"Mass produced?"

"There seems to be a connection."

They lapsed into silence. Aunt Miriam looked worried, and I excused myself to return to the tank. The fish fascinated me. They didn't talk, of course, but I sensed a distinct mode of communication between them at a level just below my own awareness. I was determined to get a deeper grasp of it. It was like music that expressed a great deal without words. Only, this was not so emotional.

Behind me the silence stretched longer. Uncle Dave offered Dad some cognac. He refused. Dad always refused alcohol when he was trying to think. And he'd already enjoyed an excellent Pomard with the roast beef.

"What of the small farmers?"

"So far, so good. But this could be misleading. They can't afford the tests the mega-farmers are obliged by law to carry out. Random testing has been the governments' policy since the second outbreak of the virus."

"Looks like we shall revert to being vegetarians?" For the first time Miriam joined in the discussion. "Pauling would have liked that."

"Pauling?"

"Linus Pauling. The only man ever to have won two individual Nobel Prizes, peace and chemistry. He claimed that the human race developed on a vegetable diet. In evolutionary terms, we became omnivores only recently."

Neither of the men laughed. They both remained pensive. After a good minute Dad looked up from his shimmering wineglass. "Perhaps we were always meant to evolve as vegetarians," he murmured.

That sounded strange to me. Dad was anything but a superstitious man, and this sounded on the borderline.

The worrying news was at odds with the warm atmosphere and the relaxed dinner. I moved from behind the tank and stood in the doorway. Dad continued to study the glittering reflection in his wineglass, back-lit by the flickering candlelight. He was a little too tired to be at his best. His neurons needed a rest.

"Anything else?" he asked at length.

"Actually, yes."

Miriam got up to clear the table. Dad immediately jumped to his feet in order to help her but she pushed him back into his chair. She let me give her a hand.

"This is just between us, John. I heard about this on Sunday."

"So there really is more?"

The men went back to the sitting room and sank into their respective armchairs.

"I have given it to you all at once... but...."

"Get on with it, Dave."

"I got an e-mail from NASA that the last of the robots we put on Mars have stopped sending messages. The base on the Moon has been hit, twice, by sizable meteors. That's after not a single hit has ever been recorded in seventy-four years. That in itself is amazing. That nothing has hit its surface even without an atmosphere to protect it. And now two hits. On a different tack, your own man told me that the probe they sent out to study the outer limits of the solar system four years ago reported no significant or unusual sightings in the vicinity of Pluto, but did suggest some fluctuations in Pluto's orbit. There are...."

"And all this in the four days I've been away?!"

"There is more. My colleague from Planetary Geology said that there is unprecedented activity in the outer atmosphere of outer planets. Saturn and Jupiter seem angry about something or other. They've noted extraordinary planetary storms. The Red Spot has doubled in size. They haven't figured out, as yet, what the devil's going on."

"Didn't my men have anything to add?"

"You usually represent your men. You weren't here. I only met George once." Dr. George Moore was father's right-hand man.

Miriam brought in a tray with coffee and Dad's favourite Belgian chocolates. Dad got up to thank her. Thank heaven for Miriam, he must have thought. "What no meat? Let them eat chocolate," he muttered under his breath. Marie Antoinette would have liked that. Finally, after the second mouth-watering cube, he relaxed once more.

"Looks like I have some work to do."

For a while they sipped coffee from the dainty, antique demitasses. Father inquired about their two sons at the university, Miriam about JJ. But the atmosphere was not conducive to small talk. When father rose to go, David took him to the door, and then evidently changed his mind. For a moment I had a distinct impression that they'd both forgotten about me.

"I need some air," he said, "I'll walk you home."

We were about half way to our condo when David stopped. He pointed to the shimmering dome above them. "It's a beautiful world we inhabit," he said. "We really should take better care of it, don't you think?"

Father nodded. "You're thinking of pollution?"

"Pollution, pandemics, the anarchists attempting to spread terror..." David said quietly.

"We no longer need any terrorists. With a little effort, we are all quite capable of destroying our planet on our own."

Uncle Dave nodded. "We treat the terrorists the way our doctors treat our diseases. We try to remove the symptoms without taking care of the disease. The disease that drives men and women to sacrifice their lives to accomplish their aims remains," he said, his tone barely above a whisper.

Father noticed something very sad about his friend. It was as though David blamed himself for the state of the world. It wasn't fair.

Uncle Dave continued looking up at the shimmering dome. "It seems so magnificently serene... I wonder why my fish are so agitated. They have such a beautiful tank... don't you agree?" He turned to me. I nodded. Then he looked over his shoulder. "I'll let you be, John. You had enough surprises for one day. Good night!"

They shook hands. I got on tiptoe and gave Uncle Dave a kiss on his bearded cheek. I always thought he looked like Father Christmas. A beautiful beard but somewhat less of a paunch. Lately, poor uncle was looking quite slim.

Dad's eyes followed his friend as he strolled back towards his own home. Something had changed in Dave, over these last few months. And then I had it. Uncle David had begun to stoop. He was growing old. Too quickly. Too soon.

Dad said that just before he left for Ottawa, he'd read about inordinate inundations in the Far East. Vast areas of Bangladesh and southern India were underwater. The Himalayas have been melting at an alarming rate, ocean levels were rising. "What next," he wondered aloud. "What's next, Pet?" he asked me in an undertone.

His mouth was smiling but his eyes looked very serious.

"It's at moments like this that I wish I'd taken up literature, or history or music." Dad sounded as though he was talking to himself. "There is less joy in pure science. And it's no longer so pure, either," he added as we continued home. At the door he said he was going to take another stroll. "I want to think a little, Hey. Give me an hour."

I knew the symptoms. Dad was getting depressed. He had to do something. Anything. Walking helped.

An hour later his world changed diametrically. I ran out to meet him. I fell into his arms like a hurricane in search of an eye. He suddenly remembered that he was still the only one to whom I could run to find solace or peace in my young life. He was my haven in an ocean of discord and fragmentation, in the ferment that seemed to be engulfing our beautiful planet.

"Love you Daddy," I purred, my arms around his neck.

"Love you too, Pet," he returned.

And suddenly the world didn't seem so bad after all. Maybe I am wrong, he thought. Maybe this is what it's all about. Just living. Doing one's best. Maybe it's about love, and compassion, and lending a helping hand to one's fellowman. And finding beauty everywhere. At the end of the telescope. Or in the eyes of my daughter.

At least I think that was what he thought.

That night I dreamt I was in an incredibly beautiful world, replete with magnificent trees, overflowing with flowers, with the sun smiling between soft, cotton-ball clouds drifting along the serene sky. Just before I woke up, I wondered why there wasn't a single man, woman or child, or even a single animal with whom I could share all this beauty. In the midst of all this Paradise, I was all alone.

How sad, I thought. How very sad. So much beauty and no one to share it with.

***

10

Memories

Mary, the English Nanny, planned it all on her own. She'd invited three of my closest friends from school, two girls from the Conservatory of Music (yes, we now had one), Dr. and Mrs. David Mendel and two of father's youngest trainees from the Observatory. All in honour of my 15th birthday. I've been told that I looked seventeen, and both of my father's assistants from the Observatory begged my dear ol' nanny to be invited.

Mary, after being assured that I would never leave her sight, acquiesced.

Years had passed since the 'English Nanny' performed any duties remotely related to a nanny – English or otherwise. She had emancipated herself well beyond her station. She'd also matured in most unexpected ways. Her long hair was now pinned up into a severe knot. Her flowery dresses had given way to more sedate patterns. She was only a little over forty, but in Spinkhill, women over forty were expected to behave as was becoming their stage of life. It was customary to assume a degree of demeanour, of quiet authority, befitting one who, by Mary's age, under normal circumstances, would have been a mother of at least six little Heidis and/or JJs.

But our Mary had never married. First, there had been no one she'd really wanted. Her home village consisted of no more than six or seven hundred people, knit tightly into an introverted society, a ghetto where everyone knew each other. She'd wanted more. When, sixteen years ago, my father gave her the opportunity to go to Canada, Mary had taken it as a sign from heaven. As I've already mentioned, over the years, she had changed beyond recognition, and not just physically. She'd metamorphosed, apparently quite painlessly, from a country girl for whom being a nanny for Madam's children was a meteoric rise in social status, into a proficient housekeeper, then into an indispensable member of our little family; it was only Dr. Hydon, myself, and occasional visits from JJ, who by now had reached the ripe old age of eighteen and was in his last year at Brompton. JJ was completing the High School and preparing for University in Calgary.

When father's second wife, my mother, had died, Mary had inherited two children to look after. Father had been invariably busy with his work, and Mary had raised the two of us practically on her own. For many years she would not risk developing an emotional attachment to us lest it be cut off by father's will, by a dismissal from service. After all, by the time I was 15, neither JJ nor I had really needed a nanny for a number of years. Yet neither alternative ever happened. At first she'd succeeded in remaining aloof from any emotional attachments, and later father wouldn't dream of parting with her. Strange though it may seem, she remained one of all too few links father needed to his own past. I think all people who emigrated from their own country have such a need. Especially if they emigrated when already adults.

Later, Mary could have left of her own will. Over the years, she'd saved enough money. As the Director of the Observatory, Dr. Hydon, Dad, had been more than generous in this regard. She could have bought a little shop, or started a kindergarten of her own. But by then, however, it was already too late. Completely against her will, she'd grown attached not only to JJ and me, but also to Dr. Hydon himself. Not in any sexual or even sensual way. Although she was a good many years younger than Dad, the feelings she'd developed towards him, her employer, were maternal. The attachment she wouldn't allow herself to give to JJ and me, she bestowed on Dad. No one lost by this turn of events. Father had gained a caring housekeeper, JJ and I, a devoted grandmother.

Miss Heidi, my mother, and Mary had met in Spinkhill, their village near St.Stanislaus College. They'd practically grown up together. Mother's parents owned the local farm, an estate really, a fairly large tract of land by English standards. Mary's parents looked after the stables and equipment: cars, tractors and such like. On Sunday afternoons, all children of the people employed on the estate were invited to the mansion for scones and cakes or whatever sweets were available. They played games, swapped stories, became personal friends. My mother and Mary had grown to know and like each other. When mother needed help with JJ, she'd immediately thought of Mary. Mary, as we already know, had relatively little to lose. Whereas she could go back home, to England, anytime, she wisely chose to benefit from a visit to a foreign country and get paid for it besides. She'd come at once.

Within less than a year of her coming to Canada, my mother had died. Mary never lost the feeling that her Madam had had suspicions regarding her approaching demise. She remembered the day when Mrs. Hydon had called her to her side.

"You must promise me, Mary, that you will not leave my children for as long as they need you."

At the time, Mary had had no idea what Madam was talking about. She'd agreed instantly. Mrs. Hydon, as well as her parents, had always been really nice to her. Really nice to all the village children. In fact, they'd helped with her schooling. Mary could read and write better than any of her brothers. And she certainly read more books than all of them put together.

Three times Mary had visited her parents in Spinkhill. The last time it had been to attend her father's funeral. Three times she'd flown with expectations of.... she knew not what. They, her family, never appeared to have missed her. Not that much. She'd suspected that having eight children might have had something to do with it. And now with her father dead... She'd loved him most of all.

"Ah, there you are, Mary," her mother had said at her first visit. "We missed you girl. Didn't we, lads?"

Her mother had repeated almost the same words on each succeeding occasion. "Ah, there you are, Mary..." There she was;
there indeed, but not for long.

The three lads, now men, her brothers, standing against the
wall of their family cottage agreed punctiliously. The three looked
like carbon copies of each other. Her other brothers and sisters had
left home long ago. Two of the men went to live in Sheffield, one
got a job in the north of London and two of the sisters followed
their husbands to Australia. There was no work in Spinkhill.

But there was no conviction in her brothers' greeting. It was
friendly enough, but they did not bear witness to the old adage that
absence makes the heart grow fonder. It makes the heart forget.
That's all. Just forget. Also, the room she'd shared with her sister
looked so much smaller than it used to. And the water in the tap
wasn't as hot, and the w.c. didn't flush properly, and the windows
were single-glazed and there was no air-conditioning and...

Yes, and the ceilings had definitely been too low.

Mary had outgrown her old abode. She'd also outgrown her
family. When the two weeks were over and she climbed aboard the
Air Canada 747, she told herself with a sigh of relief: "I'm going
home." When she looked through the tiny oblong window, one last
time, she remembered that it had rained nine of the thirteen days
she'd been in Spinkhill. "Yes," she repeated to herself with growing conviction, "I am going home." She smiled even though she
felt sad.

And now Mary Bodkins was the unofficial grandmother, the
well established, liked-by-all, even admired for her efficiency, female major-domo. She knew her place – yet her place was anywhere she chose it to be. She wasn't told what to do, she frequently told others how to behave. Often she remonstrated the
children, occasionally even Dr. Hydon. Like that time she'd told
him that it was time to visit JJ at Brompton. Or to take me camp-
ing, or renew his invitation for me to visit his office. Or to invite
the Mendels to his house, for a change, not just to that awful cafe.

But even then, she was so much more than that. Since Madam
died, Mary had become the only stable force in the lives of the
three, sometimes desperate and as often lost, meandering people.
She was the invisible oil on the roiled sea of their emotions, the

source of common sense when those emotions were in danger of taking a high road. Some years ago, she was even a shoulder little Hey needed to cry on. (I had no one else.) For Mary, those last had been the toughest moments. To lull baby Hey to sleep, in her arms, yet not learn to love the girl beyond her station. She would never admit to herself that she loved me beyond her own life. I think I knew that, instinctively, though I didn't understand it at the time.

Over the years, Mary Bodkins became so very much more than an English Nanny.

To be precise, I didn't attend any school.

When I'd come of age to attend one, father had called on the Administration and asked if the Centre intended to open a High School for the growing number of teenagers within the complex. By the time I was ready for High School, the overall scientific staff of the Centre already counted in the hundreds. In addition, there was the support staff: the administrators, maintenance engineers, gardeners, cleaners, cooks, waitresses and people of less-defined responsibilities who seemed to live off the fat of Federal coffers. At father's instigation, it was decided that the children would be tutored at home by a select group of full time teachers. The expenses would be shared by the parents, and would be supplemented by a partial grant from Ottawa. To cut costs still further, as many children as possible would share in the same class, or classes, wherever possible. So, in a way, it was a school, only the schoolhouse was missing. So were the associated costs, and particularly the salaries of the school administrators, who, elsewhere, invariably exceeded those of the teaching staff. Father, as had his colleagues, always found this fact unnerving.

"Those who know nothing, get the fattest salaries. The world would be better off without them."

"Oy vey! But who vill tell us vat to do?" David asked father in his best Yiddish accent.

"Precisely! They do nothing but tell others what to do. Parasites!"

As it happened, Dr. Mendel's children were already attending the University in Calgary and Aunt Miriam had time on her hands. She offered to help. Under her smiling banner parents got together once a month, and Miriam passed on their decisions to the teaching staff. The parents were lucky. They also benefited from Miriam's practical wisdom. The method has worked smoothly ever since.

After the birthday party, at about ten, father, as so often happened, left for the Observatory. The Mendels and Dad's assistants left with him, while my school chums lingered on for a while, and then left also. After all, the party had started at four in the afternoon, and six hours of fun and games was plenty for one day. Mary conscripted JJ and me to help her clean up and then left us, the siblings, to our own devices.

During the last few years JJ had matured a great deal. He had always been tall; he'd inherited the posture of a professional athlete, and he'd made good use of the gifts nature bestowed on him. Unlike Dad, however, as I'd already mentioned, JJ loved sports. In fact, he loved all activities in which he excelled. Surely, that was natural enough. Only JJ actually enjoyed being better than others. He enjoyed his innate superiority. He liked being a leader and in most things he'd attempted, he had become one. No matter what the cost. If it lost him friends, so be it. There were always other friends. He'd discovered early on that the world was full of lonely people yearning for companionship. This knowledge he also put to good use. He bestowed his own friendship like a badge of honour on those in his wake. It amused him, since he was a very self-sufficient young man – once he was accorded due respect and admiration.

Only with me his mask of studied superiority invariably shattered. His outward self-assurance seemed to evaporate into thin air. I was always much too smart not to see through his calm, carefully contrived persona. I knew him through and through, and he knew that. At one time, JJ was close to hating me for feeling naked in my presence. But, even fleas have their fleas, and even emperors occasionally need a kind word. He knew that any praise from me was not the result of his machinations, but for some real trait of character that I truly admired. A trait he was hardly aware of. It was like receiving something for nothing. He liked that too.

Once we finished cleaning up, we relaxed out on the balcony. It was obviously outside our condo yet still within the three hundred-meter dome which housed the houses, so to speak. The advantage was that no weather conditions ever threatened the terrace furniture while the feeling of being outdoors was as close to the real thing as anyone could imagine. Even the sky looked natural through the continuous glass panes, which stretched as far as the eye could see. At night, the shimmering stars added glitter from above between the branches of full-grown trees.

"Tell me about our mother," I asked him without any preambles. We were used to speaking to each other directly, though on this occasion, JJ looked startled.

"I don't remember her," he blurted out. Then his contrary nature came forth, "you mean your mother or mine?"

I remained silent, allowing an amiable smile to play about my lips. I knew my brother well enough to know that I must ignore most of his first reactions. Slowly the protective sheaths JJ had erected around himself, which he'd maintained throughout the party, melted away.

"You mean, Heidi, don't you?" he said after a pause.

My smile got wider.

"Well, I don't remember her either!" he announced. And immediately he regretted his words. "I really don't, Sis, I really don't...." And in that singular instant he shed the remainder of his mask.

"I can help you remember, if you like?" I said.

I felt him watching me intensely. I knew that he saw my eyes dancing among the stars. I did that often. I let my eyes take me so far away as to lose contact with the immediate environs. Slowly I directed my gaze to his face, peeked into his eyes, daring him to agree.

"I bet you can't," he said. And then he looked at me keenly. "Can you really?"

"Lean back and take a deep breath," I commanded. "You are all tense – as if you expect me to attack you."

JJ opened his mouth to contradict me, thought better of it and shrugged. Then, he did actually take a deep breath. Then another. After three of four repetitions he felt a nice feeling of relaxation freeing the tension in his muscles. I know, I did it myself, often.

"I think you may have something there," he muttered. "Now what?"

"Nothing. When you feel really comfortable, look into my eyes," I said, my voice barely above a whisper. "Just look into my eyes..."

"You want to hypnotize me, Sis?"

"Just look into my eyes..."

I spoke so quietly that he had to shut up to hear me. My voice seemed to be coming from afar, yet, in a peculiar way, it simultaneously seemed to originate within himself. It was a nice feeling. Not at all like anything he'd ever experienced. There was just enough light for him to see a glint under my long eyelashes. But rather than continuing to gaze into my eyes, his own lids slowly shut out the stars shimmering through the panes in the geodesic structure above. And then, quite unwittingly, he began talking...

"She was about your height, just a little taller... Her hair was a deep, lustrous chestnut, like fresh chestnuts just freed from their green aril. Neither red nor brown, but the colour was deep... like a very warm fire... She wore it long, nearly down to her waist... only when Dad and mom went out, then she would pin it up...." Then his voice changed, his lips pouting, "...when they got back I was always already asleep.... always.... but she still kissed me.... Dad didn't but she did.... she always kissed me good night...."

A slight cough made JJ sit up.

"She was a lot like you, Hey. No wonder your name is Heidi too!"

"My name is not Heiditwo," I said firmly.

Only then did JJ realize that he'd just experienced a most wonderful sensation. It was a form of inner relaxation quite unknown to him. Like releasing flood waters which had been held at bay for a long, long time. He seemed quite unaware that he'd been talking.

"Can you teach me to do that? This method of relaxing, I mean?"

His tone was urgent. Only now did it begin to dawn on him how very tense an existence he'd been leading. His only release had been during sports and that called for a different type of stress altogether, hyped on adrenaline.

"You already know how to do it. You know all you need to know." My smile was not intended to tease my brother but I couldn't help myself. "If only you wouldn't try so hard to impress people. Under that mask you're wearing, you're quite a nice fellow, you know."

"I bet you say that to all the men!"

We both laughed.

I was amused. JJ had said men, not boys. He was growing up. I completely lost the connotation that the same applied to me.

That night JJ slept like a newborn baby. His dreams were filled with images of our mother. Of Heidi. Somehow his real, biological mother didn't appear in them even once. Just before he dozed off, I went over to his bed, and kissed him good night.

"Good night, mother," he whispered. And a moment later he was fast asleep.

I had dreams of my own.

I was hovering over a vast mirrored surface. It was very huge, its sweep stretching in all directions to the horizon. Like looking over a calm ocean from above. The surface was completely featureless. Smooth, with a deep shimmer. As I moved my attention, various stars reflected off the lustrous surface. For a brief instant I had to overcome a spasm of gripping fear. A sort of mental vertigo. Of abject agoraphobia. I heard a familiar voice saying that heaven is not for cowards....

I was all right after that.

I recognized various constellations. I could view them as though through a camera equipped with a telescopic zoom lens. The reflections moved closer or receded at my will. Lyra, with her enormous Vega, Cygnus with the brightness of Deneb, then Cassiopeia with the colourful trio of stars flirting with different hues. They were all beautiful. Then my attention floated towards the reflection of Perceus and Auriga suspended against the background of a vast ocean of other stars, other worlds, spanning the celestial horizons. All set against the vast background of our Milky Way.

The most fantastic thing was that the stars, a myriad of them, shone with a thousand different hues. They were not at all like the stars I remembered seeing on Earth. Red, orange, light and dark blue, silvery yellow, shimmering green like the sky reflecting in the Nile... Yet there was something very familiar about them. I looked at them as I would at long lost friends. Like a family that, through no fault of their own, got scattered across the vastness of the universe. I waved to them. I blew them a kiss.

I saw all these wonders with eyes that were capable of closing in or retreating from the objects I regarded with equal facility. At moments, I saw reflections of whole galaxies, of millions of stars pressed together into vast globular clusters. Others were like shimmering discs, with a dark stripe wedged in the middle, along their entire length. One moment I saw a mighty galaxy motionless, frozen in time. The next instant the huge monster shuddered, stirred, and began to rotate slowly, in a stately, majestic motion. Even as I stared, spellbound, the rotation increased till the spin rivalled the fury of a hurricane. I screamed in joy, bewitched by the wonder. I felt like a child who'd been given stars, my brothers and sisters, as playmates, in a cosmic game of.... life?

Gradually time, even as motion, had slowed down. I lingered, enchanted, lost in paradise. A thought crossed my mind that Alice had her Wonderland and I, Hey, had my universe.

My Universe?

The very thought of it was staggering.

And then, once again, I lowered my attention to the reflective surface of the globe beneath me. I stretched out with my arm and, to my surprise, the mirror gave way. My ethereal arm disappeared within the outer skin of the shining surface. For some reason, I felt inexorably drawn to follow my arm. My will moved me into a realm of absolute darkness. Such darkness as is not shielded from but devoid of all light. I found myself in a realm where light had not yet been born.... Suddenly I heard again that familiar voice. A voice I'd never heard before. It was like a caress....

It was then that I saw my mother's face. And there was darkness no more.

A single ray of the morning sun found its way through the double pane of a geodesic triangle, wavered between the overhanging fronds of the majestic Royal palm, and gently kissed my face still filled with enchantment. I blinked my eyes open, then tried hard to dismiss the daylight. Gradually, unwillingly, I gave up my struggle. My chest heaved in a protracted sigh. The sky was meant for the gods. Men, women, even girls, are bound to the Earth.

The dream was gone. But the stars were still there. Waiting. Waiting.

***

11

Gossamer Wings

The Moon was as bright as the globular lamp at the main entrance
to the Observatory. That huge lamp symbolized the planet Earth,
perhaps the universe, or just the perfection of a spherical form. The
globe I was looking at was almost as large. The full Moon was just
rising above the horizon. It symbolized the reflected light of the
sun. It wasn't the Moon I saw. It was the light I saw. Borrowed
light fed from another source. Like all the planets, even the two
giants dominating our system, the Moon, without the Sun, would
remain invisible. Without the Sun, no poet would ever sing the
moon's praises. No wolf would howl at its alabaster image. It
would not really exist for us – inhabitants of Earth. The globular
light at the entrance, the Moon itself, they were both shams. Artificial creations. Figments of our imagination. That which we perceived with our senses was a lie. A subterfuge. A machination of
our technology and our senses.

What is reality? Could we ever define it with our senses?
Ever?

It all seemed just a little sad.

The Moon truly emits no light of its own. It is dead. A spherical rock suspended some 386,000 kilometres above our heads,
whose sole *raison d'être* is to inspire lovers. It served no other
purpose – except to interfere, at times, with my father's observations of other celestial objects.

Enigma, my Enigma, also displayed but a mere reflection of reality. Of the vast, sham Universe. I called it the astral reality. Of the light, of countless photons, which weren't really there – they'd left their innumerable sources millions, perhaps billions of years ago. Many stars might not be there anymore. Many would already be dead. Extinct. Withered into little brown dwarfs, lifeless neutron stars, perhaps even black holes. And like those stars, the Enigma was invisible. Even I couldn't really see it. No one could. Perhaps it wasn't there at all? We all live surrounded by mirrors. We all see what we want to see. We fool ourselves that it's real. It is hard to tell what is real and what is an image concocted in our minds.

Minutes later, the luminous sphere at the main entrance to the science complex was dimmed, the top part shielded by an opaque umbrella. All the other earth-lights throughout the CSC had been automatically cut in a similar fashion to reduce interference with the workings of the Monster Eye. From above, the Science Centre was now nearly invisible. Like the City of London under the blackout, during the last World War. I'd heard about it from Dad, who'd heard it from his father. Perhaps, at times London just wasn't there. Who could tell in total darkness?

My father said that London would have been a good place, during that war, to observe the sky. No glare, no interference. Except for some bombs, here and there, filling the sky with momentary fireworks. And then the flashes would be gone. Only the craters remained. Father said the craters were very real. But for a while there were no reflections. Like the Science Centre on a clear night.

It's funny that. My father could only see in the dark.

While the CSC general lights were dimmed, the counterfeit Moon remained as bright as ever. We stayed on the terrace. I was sipping orange juice, my father took the other lounge chair, caressing a stein of Molson. The computers would conduct tonight's observations automatically. They had all been programmed for maximum effect. The data would be recorded for later analysis.

Father looked happy. He looked as though he was counting his lucky stars that he'd been appointed to his present job, here, in this private paradise, in the middle of nowhere. Up above, the stars began to emerge from the descending penumbra. Having crossed the endless, seemingly impenetrable darkness, the itinerant photons punctured the polished surface of the telescope and were trapped, immediately, on a film, never to fly again. To me this was sad. Even scary. Who gave us the right to trap what wasn't ours? Tonight they fought back. They seemed not as bright in the pale glow of the moonlight. My mind drifted outwards again. I must have looked worried. Dad put down his glass and looked at me with questioning eyes.

"Penny for your thoughts?" he murmured.

I was parsecs away. Much further than the Moon. My mind was drifting as far as the shadow of Pluto, a place I'd begun calling my own. A very private place.

"Tell me about the Moon, Dad?"

By now the Moon was looking at us through the third row of triangles at the base of our dome. A few minutes ago it had been cut into regular sections, rounded *Vache qui rie* triangles, ready to serve. Now it seemed to shrink to the size of a single hexagon.

"What would you like to know, Pet?"

Dad had been wondering about the Moon on his own, lately. Since the late President of the United States had announced, some twelve years ago, that NASA would build a Moon Base from which further planetary exploration would be launched, the days of the Monster Eye were numbered. The Moon Base would also serve as a Way Station for interplanetary exploration. Or so President Twigg's successors continued to dream. None of the future presidents had realized, or perhaps they had been badly advised, that even if we could reach Mars, our nearest neighbour, the planet's gravity was such that there would be insufficient fuel to ever return to Earth. It would be a suicide mission. Some had suggested that the president himself should lead the way. But whatever the planetary aspirations, the Moon base made sense for quite a different reason. It would be a vastly superior location for an optical observatory of the whole universe. There would be no interference from pollution, diffused lighting or gasses in the atmosphere. None at all. The Moon is much too small to sustain any atmosphere.

"I've seen it many times, through the Monster Eye... It seemed so close – I could touch it. But it also seemed cold and forbidding..." I prodded him gently. Dad seemed lost in thoughts of his own.

I didn't tell Dad that the Moon didn't seem real to me. Few things did, lately. Yet, for some reason, the Moon drew me towards its mournful, pale surface.

"It is certainly closer to Earth than any other celestial body. But it still takes quite a while to get there. Why do you ask?"

For Dad, the sudden interest in the Moon had sprung from his own report. Last week, the Loonies, as the Canadians affectionately referred to the astronauts who were busy constructing the first operational dome on the Moon, survived a severe meteor shower, which had raised dust on the Moon from Mare Imbrium all the way to Mare Fecunditalis: more than half of the Moon's visible surface.

"I want to go there," I said. I had no idea why I'd said that.

Father sighed. His daughter had had many such requests lately. He knew that I had been taking many a trip, in my dreams, to outer reaches of the Solar System. We talked about my inner realities. Sometimes. Lately more often. I'd told father about some of my nocturnal excursions in great detail. Not all. Some had been too private. Also too enigmatic. Like those in which I'd met my mother. It wasn't easy. To keep some of my experiences from Dad, I mean. Also, all my dreams seemed related to a realm of darkness from which light emerged at most unexpected moments. Spontaneously. They didn't make much sense to me. They wouldn't to Dad, either. It seemed that I'd uncovered some sort of wormhole, a mental aberration, worthy of the best science-fiction thrillers, through which I seemed able to reach many places. Or realities. Strangely, all those places were somehow connected with Pluto. Or thereabouts. With the shadow of Pluto. The Enigma?

"Can't you go to Moon on your own?" Dad asked, a tolerant smile playing about his lips.

"I am serious, Dad. And you know that in my... my, you know, my dreams I do not choose where I go. I am...." I wanted to say 'taken' but I pulled short. I hadn't been taken. Certainly not abducted. Nothing ever happened against my will. I also hated using the word 'dreams', when referring to my enigmatic travels. They were nothing like dreams, even if they occurred, for the most part, during my sleep. No. They weren't just dreams. I'd tried to explain all that to Dad many times already.

"I'm sorry, Pet. I didn't mean...."

"It's OK Dad. I know."

I could never hold a grudge against my father. Not even for a few seconds. I'd learned early in life that such an attitude did not benefit anyone. I had learned a great deal about life. I had Mary to thank for some of that. And Aunt Miriam.

"Well, perhaps not in mine, but certainly during your lifetime, travel to the Moon will be as common as flying across the Pacific, if a tad more expensive. Why do you want to go there?"

All of a sudden my lounge chair was no longer comfortable. I didn't want to tell Dad that I actually saw the meteor shower which struck the Moon last week. Dad had problems enough coping with my, what he called, 'unbridled imagination'. The peculiar thing was that I hadn't imagined anything. I just *saw* things. I was strictly an observer. What I saw had been as real as anything or everything I'd witnessed right here, on Earth. Only more so. Some of the things that happened on Earth I had already forgotten. My 'extraterrestrial' experiences remained etched in my memory.

"Just tell me about the Moon. Like a scientist, I mean. Not like a travel agent."

Dad took a deep breath. Since he'd reported on the meteor shower, his videophone had acquired a new dedicated line, funded by the people from NASA. They also insisted, politely but firmly, on more Monster Eye time. The telescope was under Canadian jurisdiction, but it had been founded by an international consortium. Our southern friends had paid a lions share. Since father wanted still more money to equip the new Department requested by the Ministry of Agriculture but hated sharing his pet telescope, he'd demanded what he'd thought was a ridiculous price for Eye-time. The NASA people agreed without batting an eye, so to speak.

Anyway, this was why Dad was at home tonight, with me, as the Eye was directed at the Moon, and would continue to be so for the next three days. Up to six hours per night.

But that was not what I wanted to know. Who knew what I really wanted? I was sixteen then. Soon I would be choosing my subject to study. Perhaps I was developing a more scientific interest in astronomy. Poor Dad. He was likely to be the last to know.

"Well, Pet, the Moon is not very large. It's only 3476 kilometres in diameter, about Montreal to Vancouver. And it only has a fraction of the Earth's mass...."

He continued for some time slowly, pensively, as though thinking aloud. I listened – spellbound. I didn't interrupt even once.

The latest incursions into outer space by the US of A, affected Dad in many ways. The Hubble II Telescope, being outside the Earth's atmosphere, was able to provide the most fantastic photographs man had ever seen of our galaxy, and a great many other galaxies which man had never seen before. The Moon Base, if completed and equipped, would not only equal but also excel in the field of optical astronomy. Father's Monster Eye would still have its uses, but the frontier of astronomy would move some 384,623 kilometres from Mount Ogilvy. Actually the scientists defined the Moon's apogee, in its elliptical orbit, as 406,686 kilometres and its perigee as 356,400 kilometres. None of this would matter if it weren't for the fact that our Moon is tiny, so small that the combined centre of gravity for Earth and Moon *together* lies over 1600 kilometres under the Earth's surface. He paused.

"There is nothing intrinsically wrong with the American proposal," he said sounding apologetic. "The Moon is certainly close enough."

Man had visited its inhospitable terrain a number of times, albeit with dubious success. Probably the most conspicuous event took place when Commander Armstrong swung his golf club some decades ago. Since then, the scientists had concentrated on unmanned probes, which had, over four decades, begun to bear fruit. Cold, indigestible, icy fruit. But it was the iciness that was to become the very essence of success. Iciness meant water. And water meant life. Not life indigenous to a planet, or in this case a moon, but life to whoever chose to venture where no man had been before.

In spite of literally dozens of American, European, Chinese and South-American probes, no water had been heretofore discovered; none of the digs, or drillings, had been deep enough. The last one was. Finally. They drilled one hundred-ninety meters into the Moon's surface and discovered ice.

"My Fellow Americans! Once we have water, we can drink. Once we have water we also have oxygen. Once we have oxygen we can breathe.... Once we can breathe...."

President Richard Gowan had gone on (and on, and on) for quite a time. His logic was impeccable. It might have been better to breathe before attempting to drink, but that was a minor detail.

He was very, very enthusiastic. He was also freshly baked, or elected, and still basked in his own glory. Nevertheless, he was the 3rd President since Pres. Twigg set the Moon Base program in motion. The only thing he'd failed to provide, so far, was food. But who needs food when you can breathe and drink water?

Never mind. One thing at a time.

But again, strange though it may seem, it had been the Canadian Science Centre that provided the answer to the culinary dilemma. Geodesic domes can be constructed from very light material. They can be assembled from small, repetitive components; they can be made airtight and offer, in time, a controlled environment in which food could be grown. Given water, of course. And water, according to the President, was there galore. His NASA advisers hadn't been so sure. But, within two years, the first plants started growing under the second geodesic dome. There was hope. Of course, by then Twigg had been long out of office. Any office. Perhaps he'd gone to Mars?

At the time father had told me that he was still waiting for the scientists to confirm the announcement. About the water. President Gowan had been known to make politically convenient declarations, but ones which had little grounding in reality. Our cousins to the South, had always been incurable optimists. Their glasses were never half-empty. And now the Moon, to hear the President, was half full of water.

Father had been asked, informally, if he would be interested in taking charge of the optical observatory on the Moon Base, if and when it became operational. The job would only become viable in five years. Maybe sooner. Maybe not. And it would mean rotation with other scientists. Etc., etc., etc..

"So you see, my Pet, I could make a condition that you come with me. Would you like that?"

I recall being speechless. There is a fundamental difference between dreams and physical reality. In the first, one remained in one's bed. In the other, one had to get up and up, and up....

"Isn't it awfully cold up there?" Suddenly my enthusiasm palled.

"Awfully cold but also awfully hot. Depending on where you are. At the Equator, at midday, the temperature is plus 104° Centigrade. At night it falls to minus 157°. You'd have to cuddle up..."

"Dad!"

"I'm sorry, Pet. I'm sure they would take care of the variations in temperature inside the domes, of course."

My eyes left my father's face and drifted to the white face of the Moon, now much higher along the dome's surface. It was wedged between two branches of a palm tree. Like on picture postcards we get from Florida.

"Will they have palm trees there?"

"Plenty. And a lot more greenery than we have here. We have to reconvert the carbon dioxide we exhale into oxygen. The best way is to let nature do it for us."

Father got up to get himself another beer. I jumped to my feet.

"I'll get it for your, Dad."

I recall that when I came back, I was humming an old tune. Something about the Moon and gossamer wings. Dad didn't know he still had that tape. It must have been out of print for ages. And then he sat up and joined me, in a passable baritone, with another old favourite:

Fly me to the moon, and let me play upon a star...

Together we raised quite a rocket. I mean racket.

Some of our nearer neighbours came out on their balconies to listen. Then, for some unknown reason, one or two, then most of them joined in, in an extemporaneous choir. It wasn't half-bad.

My dreams, at least those I could recall with uncanny precision, were becoming more frequent. They didn't always take me to some shiny globes or multifarious reflections of our Milky Way. Some were very much down to earth. Seemingly insignificant. Only when seen in hindsight, they grew in importance and made sense.

The dreams became more significant when they invaded my subconscious in a serial form. I would dream of an event, then, the next night, and the one after that, I would dream the continuation. It was like switching on the TV on successive evenings and enjoying the serial. Such a dream, in three parts, I'd experienced a few weeks after talking to Dad about the Moon. Only it had no connection with that conversation. Or with anything else, for that matter.

I dreamt I was a veterinary doctor, as well as a zoologist dedicated to the creation of havens for chimpanzees which had been used, often abused, in laboratory experiments, and then discarded by the medical research teams to fend for themselves. According to the knowledge I held in my dream, such a course of action was common practice.

The safe grounds, which I'd helped to create, also called sanctuaries, consisted of fifty to a hundred acres of land, surrounded by an electrified fence. This precaution was there not only to stop the chimpanzees from leaving the protected area, but, more importantly, to stop poachers from harming the chimpanzees in my charge.

I must admit, that some of this knowledge became mine only after I'd awakened. It must have lain deep in my subconscious, perhaps even the unconscious that we seldom tap for information. At the time though, it felt as if I'd been exploring some distant past, perhaps another existence, another lifetime altogether. Yet the events in those three dreams had been as real, as rich in detail, as anything I'd ever experienced in my waken state.

Some primates were beyond saving. They sat motionless, ostensibly in a stupor, reminiscent of elderly people I'd met, sometime and somewhere in that somnambular reality, who were suffering from Alzheimer's disease. Such chimps remained very still for lengthy periods, often developed total incontinence, and inevitably died. I felt they'd lost all interest in life, or rather that that which imbued them with life had left the 'vessel' in which it heretofore had flourished. Other poor dears, other chimpanzees in my care, seemed to have forgotten who or what they were. They couldn't even feed themselves. Others? It took years to repair others, not only their bodies but also their severely damaged egos. Or personalities. To repair that which made one chimpanzee different from any other chimpanzee. What made each one of them unique. And in my somnambular experience, the differences between the members of a chimpanzee family were as profound as among my own kind.

"For crying out loud," a biochemist yelled, "they're just apes. Apes!"

This well-known researcher with a string of letters after his name shouted as though to explain his indifference to the chimpanzees' fate. He was in line for the Nobel Prize. For legalized torture. For being inhumane, even if so very human.

My dreams were filled with separate, seemingly unconnected snippets of information, all the more surprising because I'd never so much as seen a live chimpanzee in real life. Yet I clearly recall my anger gradually dissolving into an ocean of soul wrenching sorrow. I woke up more than once with my eyes filled with tears.

What made these three dreams unique, absurdly so, was that my point of view alternated between that of the zoologist I was, and Zoey, a female chimpanzee. With a facility that bordered on the absurd, I would ask a question, then change and reply to my own query with the sign language the primate had been taught. There was an eerie ease with which these jumps of consciousness occurred. It felt a little like conducting conversations with myself. Only it wasn't.

There was more.

As the somnambular zoologist, I developed warm affection for Zoey. The female chimpanzee felt like a sister, a close relative, for whose sake I was prepared to make considerable sacrifices. In many ways, I had. I'd given up the comforts of city life, of the so-called cultural amenities, to live in primitive conditions with my new, primate family. For family we were. We shared our joys and sorrows, as a close family should. One moment I would regard Zoey with concern and affection, and the next instant I would see myself through Zoey's eyes, and, lo and behold, the same waves of tenderness and friendship emanated from me toward my alter ego.

In all ways that mattered, Zoey, the primate female who'd also suffered at the scientist's cruel hands, a mother of two wonderful offspring, felt and acted like my sister. A favourite sister. In spite of many agonizing moments, I enjoyed the dreams enormously. I recounted them to myself, in a way relived them, until I could re-call the smell of the jungle, the moisture suspended in the air, the feel of Zoey's fur under my stroking hand. I enjoyed the dreams even if, in the light of day, they made no sense at all. Even though they also made me cry.

I've often wondered, since, what any of this could possibly have to do with my other visions. With the polished globe hovering around the environs of Pluto, of my desire to fly to the Moon on gossamer wings. Not until I reached the age of the scientist whose body I'd occupied in my jungle dreams so many years earlier, did I learn of what it had all been about. Yet, even now as I am writing this, I'm hard put to understand fully the enormity of their implications.

Until much, much later. Until now.

You'll see...

***

12

More about fish

It wasn't just the fish in Dr. Mendel's tank; it was Dr. Mendel himself who was getting nervous. He no longer worried about earthquakes, certainly not of any globe-shuttering magnitude. He was worried about his inability to make head or tail of his golden pets, which were not behaving like well brought up fish should. He'd consulted two zoologists, one with a subspecialty in marine life, all to no avail.

"Something makes your fish nervous, doctor," said one of them.

"Why do you make your fish nervous?" asked another.

Dr. Mendel never invited either or them to his house again.

The neurotic behaviour of his pets of the Cyprinidaen persuasion would have been of little consequence, if it weren't for the equivalent and simultaneously mysterious behaviour of his seismographs. Together, they contributed to a double mystery. Not only did his seismometers hardly pause in registering a near continuous if gentle jitters, but they also displayed a complete absence of major earthquakes anywhere in the world. For a while Dr. Mendel thought that his instruments had gone on the blink. He called in the

engineers, had the electrical supply double-checked, he even questioned the humidity levels in his laboratory to assure that the odd
behaviour of his electronics was not caused by micro-climatic conditions.

Later, he made a nuisance of himself to all his colleagues. Not
just at the Centre, but the world over. They began calling him Dr.
Meddling. He hated that. But he hated even more his inability to
come to terms with his own ignorance.

"How can I run a department when I cannot solve the most
simple problems?" he asked my father during one of their Sunday
dinners. I say 'their' because I still didn't count.

The question was rhetorical. The problems were so 'simple'
as to be considered banal by most of his colleagues. The other scientists assured Uncle Dave that the barely perceptible vibrations
indicated on the graph of the new generation of seismographs were
due to their greater sensitivity. This would make sense, to a degree. But roughly half of the 'old' machines, those dating back
fifty years, also showed some movement. Even this could be explained by allowing some extra latitude for the quality of materials,
variable voltages, and variations in temperature and such like.
What no one could explain was the total absence of any major
earthquakes for close to past ten years.

"Ten years, John! This hasn't happened in my lifetime!"
David threw his hands in the air in an effusive gesture rivalling To-
scanini.

Dad mumbled, "You are still young", and used this opportunity to press another glass of Scotch into David's open palm.
Father was counting on David's love of good malt to placate his
reflexes. It worked. David's hand returned to his lap at a much
lower velocity.

"Cheers!" he raised his hand, again, now armed with the pla-
cating spirit.

"Here's to your fish," Dad offered. "May they swim in
peace!"

"More like in their piss," Uncle Dave muttered.

At least I think that was what he said. I just giggled. I was
watching the fish at the time. They seemed perfectly happy if in-

different – at least to my face peering at them. Or it could be that they just didn't fully appreciate the faces I'd been making at them. I guess I'll never know.

Father had problems of his own. His Monster Eye, as well as all four of his smaller telescopes, had been reporting data that was a little hard to stomach. Just as with Uncle David's fish, the figures were not earth-shattering. They consisted of minuscule deviations in the orbits of some of the planets. Only some, because Dad still hadn't had time to check all of them. Once again, the new results could have been due to new technology, to a number of variables, which would result in minor adjustments. After all, all astronomical facts evolved from a constant flux of new, often contradictory observations. Astronomy, like all others, was a growing science. Expanding. The astronomers were dealing with moving objects, each affecting others.

What led father to take his anomalous readings more seriously was the fact that each time one added even a minute fraction of a parsec to the distance between the sun and the orbit of a particular planet, one had to compensate with an increase in the velocity of that planet's orbital trajectory. In addition, the orbits were all elliptical. Father had to recalculate the apogee as well as the perigee of each celestial body, while it continued in constant motion. It all took time. He wondered how Hipparchus of Nicaea, could have done it, over two thousand years ago, without the aid of computers. The ancient Greeks had calculated that the Moon is about thirty Earth's diameters away from the surface of our planet. If we accept that his predecessor Eratosthenes, an equally great contributor to the Alexandrian School, figure for the Earth's diameter was about 12,874 kilometres, then the average distance of the Moon from the surface of the Earth would be 386,232 kilometres. The best that modern science can offer is 384,388.86 kilometres, a difference of a mere 1843.14 kilometres. Less than a round trip by car from Montreal to Detroit. The Greeks had been accurate to within 0.479%. And they had been capable of such precision during the 2nd century BC. If Dad were to ignore the minute differentials, then the science of astronomy would surely come to a complete halt.

By the time Uncle David had blown his top over his fish, father had begun receiving confirmations of various velocities. The figures confirmed, to eleven decimal places, his previous calculations. That was pretty exact. And equally as worrying.

"I still have to do my exercises with the outer planets," he told Uncle David. "Mercury, Venus, Earth and Mars are relatively easy. They are practically next door. Saturn and Jupiter will take longer. But if the variations affect the whole of the Solar System, then God only knows what will be the consequences."

"Is it really as bad as....?"

Uncle David was hardly ignorant in those matters, but he couldn't compete with father in Dad's area of expertise.

"It's like with the butterfly..." father interrupted.

"The butterfly's wings flapping over the Amazon jungle creating a hurricane over the Atlantic?" David quoted the now famous supposition based on fractal projections and chaos theory. It was all very theoretical but, well, one had to start somewhere. I had to laugh. The same thought about the butterflies had crossed my mind only a few weeks ago.

"Something like that. The real problem is that even if all our computers were lined up together they do not have the capacity to compute the possible consequences of such a planetary adjustment. After all, the orbital differentials, minute as they are, affect all the other orbiting bodies, which in turn affect all the others, which in turn... and so on, and so forth. Where do you stop?"

"I suppose our predecessors were better of. They remained in total ignorance of any such possibilities and died happy."

"Yes, only they weren't all that ignorant. But even so, are you sure they lived happily in abject ignorance?"

"I'm sure of it. The various religions enforced men's abject feeble-mindedness. Learning and, God forbid, thinking, were actively discouraged."

"You know, my friend," Dad raised an eyebrow, a whimsical smile widening his mouth at a cocky angle, "I never thought of it before. But our religious leaders may well have been right!"

"Very funny!" Uncle David's attitude to religion was a peculiar mixture of total disdain and deferential fear. It really was
funny unless one lived in Uncle David's skin.

"Look at it this way," father pressed his point. "No matter
what we find out today, we are completely and absolutely helpless
in trying to do anything whatsoever about it. And even if we could,
we would not have the slightest idea what to do..."

"There's always a way," Uncle David dismissed father's argument with another wave of his hand.

"Then tell your fish to behave themselves," Dad countered.

For the next few minutes the only sound in the room was that
of ice cubes striking the sides of two crystal glasses. Not an unpleasant sound. It seemed to calm their wrought nerves. All good
scientists love puzzles. They hate being stumped by them. For
now, neither of the two friends wanted to break the silence. They
didn't have to. The doorbell rang and Miriam walked in with a
rustle of silk and a big smile. She was the medicine both men
needed.

After father poured Aunt Miriam a gin-and-It, Mary announced that we had eleven minutes and thirty seconds to dinner.
Dad and Uncle Dave must have inspired her to venture into precise
measurements. While Mary always sat with us at the table, before
and after dinner she preferred to make herself scarce.

"I didn't get many degrees, before I joined you, Dr. Hydon. I
don't often follow your mumbo-jumbo. I'll do my bit and you look
after our guests."

After all these years, Mary still refused to address Dad by his
first name. It was meant to be, he must have thought. Not that he
hadn't asked her. "Familiarity breeds contempt," she quoted
someone the last time Dad had proposed a more informal form of
address. "Then how about Mr. John?" he'd offered as a compromise, hoping that, in time, the Mister part would go by the wayside.
"Now that's just plain silly," she'd replied with conviction. "I
don't mind running a house for Doctor Hydon Ph. D., Director of
the Canadian Astronomical Observatory and what-have-you. I
would never work for a John. Or even a Mr. John, if you don't
mind, Doctor Hydon."

"So what have you two boys been up to?" Aunt Miriam asked innocently.

This brought them down to earth. In as few words as possible, father gave Aunt Miriam a quick recap. She didn't seem to understand what made them so depressed.

"If I may ask, John, how old are you?"

Dad confessed to completing his sixty-third year, come next birthday.

"David is already sixty-six. Just how long a time will pass, do you think, before these planetary adjustments will begin to affect us? If ever?" she asked.

"I really couldn't say! What are you driving at?"

"Well, it seems to me that neither David's fish nor we, the three of us, will live long enough to worry about what might never happen!"

I was ready to put my hand up in protest but thought better of it. The planetary adjustments might prove very interesting.

Even before Aunt Miriam finished talking, Uncle David was snorting, and now his high pitched laughter was shaking his belly. Father couldn't help chuckling himself. Miriam had a long-standing habit of hitting the nail on the head.

"I, he, he, warned you, John, he, he... I warned you about her... he, he, he..."

When Uncle David laughed it was always much more he, he, than ha, ha.

Father looked as though he had half a mind to deliver a lecture on advancing longevity, but evidently he thought better of it. He must have remembered that the longer one lived the greater the chance of contracting a debilitating disease like Alzheimer, or any number of equally hapless disorders. He'd decided that, at least for now, laughter was a much preferred remedy for most of their problems.

Mary's "dinner is served" announcement gave them an opportunity to get at hold of themselves. Actually, just the two of them. Both ladies remained perfectly serious. No one looked at me. I was becoming fairly good at remaining invisible.

Laughter is good, but it doesn't last. It is like the *Intermezzo* in *Cavalleria Rusticana*. A beautiful interlude before one has to get down to serious singing. Father got serious about programming the telescopes to follow the major planets, Jupiter and Saturn. He set up the remaining two sixty-centimetre lenses to point at Uranus and Neptune. Pluto would have to wait. Strange, isn't it, since it had all really begun with Pluto, that now Pluto had to wait its turn? He was just finishing when he sensed me peeking over his shoulder.

"Hi, Dad!"

"Hi, Hey! What brings you here?"

He swung his chair around to face me. Several months passed before he told me about the thoughts that crossed his mind at that particular moment. *She is a picture to behold. Almost twenty, with her mother's fresh colouring, a mass of chestnut hair cascading over her shoulders. Heidi.... She's her mother all over again. Only more beautiful, if that were possible.*

"Do you have a minute?"

"I'm just finishing. Shall we take a walk in the gardens?"

Since I finished high school two years ago, we'd been spending more time together than ever before. Dad acted as though he loved having me close by, and I also refused to leave him alone. Whether I did so consciously or just inherited innate concern from my mother, we shall never know. JJ had long ago left Brompton, (without having been kicked out), and Calgary was much too far to visit him on a regular basis. Father and daughter had gravitated together, like two planets tied to the same sun. While I had not formally studied astronomy, my knowledge of planetary geology was vast. I did benefit, of course, from all the amenities the Centre had to offer. I had already published some papers. Dad helped, but I wrote them on my own. Dad worried that I worked too hard, that I didn't have sufficient company of boys and girls my own age. I wasn't really that worried about it.

"Dad... I've had three proposals of marriage, and I'm not even twenty yet!"

"You what???" His voice rose while his eyes were in great danger of popping out.

That exchange took place only the week before. Now Dad wasn't sure if he should worry about his daughter a little more, or a little less. Anyway, that was last week. Today, he told me that I looked as radiant as ever.

Five minutes after we left the Observatory we were strolling down the winding pathways, inhaling the richness of vegetation. It might not be so bad, on the Moon, Dad had said. But my thoughts lay elsewhere.

"I've been talking to Dr. Mendel," I said at last.

"Shouldn't you be running around with someone younger?"

I ignored that one. "He told me that chimpanzees are psychic. Did you know that?"

"You mean like fish and birds and cockroaches?"

"What?"

Father told me about the various fish, bugs and animals which supposedly had the ability to sense vibrations or magnetic emanations which people couldn't.

"Why can't we?"

"I never thought about it, Pet."

"Could it be that evolution destroyed our primitive abilities while developing others?"

"I suppose so. Why do you ask?"

"I've been reading about the age of Kali," I told him. My eyes wandered to the lotus flower floating serenely on the pond.

"Hindu philosophy?" Dad had read about it many years ago. Mother liked reading about such things. Ever since the Jesuits, religion had never been Dad's cup of tea.

"It's not really their philosophy that struck me. Not as such. What I found fascinating was their premise that we, the human race, are in a state of devolution. Not the other way round."

"Darwin had something to say about that," Dad put in, evidently still not sure what I was driving at.

"But Darwin was talking about physical evolution. I assume the Hindus are referring to a different sort."

"What other sort is there? Even the Old Testament did not seem to differentiate between different types of evolution. And my old masters, the Jesuits, never raised the subject at all..." Dad was groping.

I could see that father suddenly wished mother was still alive. He'd learned to live in solitude but being both father and mother to me was beyond his capability. My mother had known all there was to know about all sorts of religions. Perhaps that was why she'd practised none.

"Dad, I am not studying to be a Hindu. Or a mystic. Or a religious zealot. I merely think that we can learn a great deal from some ancient myths. There must be something in them if they've survived thousands of years, don't you think?"

"The idea that Earth was the centre of the world..."

"And you thought that I was a lonely old maid!"

"*Touché*. We are all allowed a mistake or two. But what is all this leading to?"

"I was wondering if there is anything in science, any kind of parallel to the Hindu mysticism as regarding evolution."

"Well, there is the Big Crunch. The opposite of the Big Bang. But we are a long way from the reversal of the theory of the expanding universe. Assuming it will ever stop expanding."

"That's it?"

"We don't know. An infinite Universe should also be an eternal Universe. An infinite supply of hydrogen would forever fuse to form helium, and so forth. But this is not what you are asking, is it?"

I remained silent. Without saying a word, we were both drawn to the bench nesting under an overhanging willow. As we sat down, its weeping embrace offered us protection from the enormity of the dome. Rather like our Solar System, or even our Galaxy, protects us from the enormity of the Universe.

"There are also the laws or thermodynamics," father seemed to be thinking aloud. "The second law tells us that the amount of energy available for conversion decreases constantly."

"And that's it?" I still wasn't satisfied.

"As far as our knowledge of entropy and the improbability of an eternal universe is concerned, yes."

"What about the Black Holes?"

"What about them?" This time Dad's voice wavered. He hated being pinned down into a field that was still virtually unknown.

"Couldn't the Black Holes act as recycling..."

"As converting matter back into hydrogen?"

"For instance."

Dad smiled. "Do you know, Pet, that I've been wondering about that sort of thing for years? I could never accept the concept of a finite universe. Not so much finite in space as finite in time. It just felt wrong to me."

"And to some four million Jains, the followers of Jainism – syncretistic religion combining elements of both, Hinduism and Buddhism. They gravitate towards the Oscillating Universe philosophy, rather than the bang-and-crunch or Fred Hoyle's Steady-State universe pithy alternatives."

"They do? Aren't they thinking of a sort of *perpetuum mobile?*"

"A universe of perpetual motion? It's an elegant idea, but no. Not in as many words, though the consequences are the same. But let's stick to the Black Holes," I insisted.

"We certainly would. Stick like crazy glue."

"Be serious Dad?"

Father nodded apologetically. He remembered racking his brains to make up some sort of law, any law, which would satisfy the conditions that might exist in the heart of a Black Hole. It wasn't easy. For matter to collapse into a Black Hole, the original star must have a mass greater than 3.2 that of our sun, which is the collapsed-neutron-star limit. Only then could a star enter the unknown state of ultimate stellar degeneration of a Black Hole, wherein gravity would take absolute dominance over matter, over all other laws known to man. Nothing could ever escape the event horizon of such a star. Neither radiation, nor matter. Nothing. Except, possibly, for the emission of gamma and x-rays, we still knew very little about them. All I knew was that the event horizon defined the proximity to such a collapsed star beyond which hid the unknown. Dad shared most of this with me in a quiet, dreamy voice.

"It has to do with gravity. But isn't there another state which matter abhors even more?"

Dad looked up from his reveries. "Such as what?"

"Doesn't nature abhor absolute vacuum?"

"There is no such thing in nature. Not absolute..."

"What if there were? We know that Black Holes do not compress matter into hydrogen atoms, or any other atoms or subatomic particles. Ergo vacuum. Absolute vacuum. What would nature endeavour to do about such a state?"

Father looked at me in grudging disbelief. I could see it in his eyes. His look said: I know all that only it doesn't make scientific sense. She couldn't possibly be thinking what I am thinking....

"Nature would do what is necessary to remove such a condition."

"To fill it with...."

"With wherever it took."

"Isn't this what we say a Black Hole is doing? At all costs? Without compromise?" I asked quietly.

Just then a large drop of condensation dropped from the glazed roof to the middle of the pond. Little concentric ringlets of water spread from the epicentre, expanded to the limits of the pond, and then tried to find a way to dissipate their energies on the way back. The funny thing was that by then the epicentre where the single droplet had touched the mirrored surface had become still. It was already perfectly calm. It had done its job. It had dissipated its energies throughout the tiny universe.

"What do you think, Dad?"

"I am thinking, Pet, that you are a very smart young lady." And then he asked out of the blue. "Who were those guys who asked you to marry them? Do I know them?"

My thoughts again drifted elsewhere. I'd entered the stage of trying to unravel my dreams. They had become so frequent, so regular, that I felt as if I'd been attending some sort of an educational course. Annoyingly, I had no idea how I'd been doing. Have I been learning or just observing events that in 'real' life had little or no meaning? I had a nagging feeling that soon, perhaps sooner than I might want, I would learn what my unconscious had been concocting. For some reason, seemingly unjustifiable, I was beginning to suspect that things as we know them, that the world as we know it, was about to undergo a drastic, dramatic change. What I didn't know was if the time modality was on an astronomical,

symbolic or down to earth, everyday time scale. Rather than knowing more, I really knew less.

When I'd talked to my father that day under the willow, I
really wanted to ask when and how we, the human species, had lost
our inner powers. Did such a loss alone define our devolution?
Was I, for reasons beyond my understanding, recovering some of
them? And if so, why? For what purpose?

My father had said that the Big Bang/Big Crunch theory was
still favoured by the scientific community. In a way, it seemed to
have some backing in both Hinduism and Jainism. I'd also found
some echoes of it in Esoteric Buddhism. Which came first, the
chicken or the egg? Did the ancient myths have basis in ancient
science? Or was the present day science influenced by the ancient
myths, which might have been intended merely as symbolic guide-
lines?

I found neither satisfying. Neither the ancient myths, if taken
literally, nor the present day science, which all too often pleaded
abject ignorance. As with the Black Holes.

I felt very alone. For some reason, my dreams filled me with
contradictory feelings. I experienced moments of euphoric, inexplicable pleasure, yet, at virtually the same time, I was filled with a
seemingly illogical sense of fear. Almost dread. I knew I had to
overcome the latter to continue deriving pleasure from the former.
At that stage, I had little control over my emotions.

Wherever my dreams led me, whatever I was to learn by
means that I couldn't really share with anyone, I was growing convinced of one thing. I felt that we, the people, or that which defined our humanity, did not originate on any time scale which
matched the astronomical calculations of our best scientists. And
what was more, I did not believe that we shall ever end. I was
growing in conviction that both time and space were just imaginary. Even as so many other aspects of our lives, of our everyday
assumptions, were imaginary. Like happiness, and love, and hate,
and the whole gamut of our emotions; even our unwitting thoughts,
ideas or reputedly dogmatic concepts.

I felt more and more like an observer.

I felt like a passer-by.

Father returned to his office to check on his programming, while I continued home. I needed time to think. My mind was not cooperating. Too many ideas kept fighting for attention.

Inside I became conscious of an eerie silence. No fans moving the air, no automatic sprinklers tending to the flowers. I left the lights off. With a shrug I clicked the remote control. The screen flickered and a tall man in a cassock down to his feet stared me in the eyes. On his head he wore a pointed hat resembling the Triple Crown, the sort the Popes used to wear before John XXIII had it sold and the proceeds distributed among the poor. Or so they said.

Then the man spoke.

"Behold, I give you a warning. The end is at hand. Beware...."

I flicked the off button. There were always more and more cranks able to buy TV time to flog their version of nonsense. I wondered what JJ was doing. At least my brother's doomsday scenarios were still all in good fun. Or were they ever? I hoped so. I was so mixed up lately.

And then the telephone rang.

"Hi Hey? I am flying over. Can you pick me up in Carmack? I'll be there at noon tomorrow. Thanks a million!" And he hung up. I had no time to ask him where or what was Carmack.

Carmack turned out to be a small town a good distance north of the nearest commercial airport. I wondered how JJ intended to get there. From Mount Ogilvy, it was less than an hour's drive, but still, JJ was taking too much for granted. I could have been busy. Or away – like he was going to be. But I couldn't deny, even to myself, that I was looking forward to seeing him. In the past JJ had been the epitome of level-headedness. He was cool to the point of stoic indifference. I needed his psychological analysis. Dad was knowledgeable, but he carried emotional baggage. He liked the results he'd already found. He was anchored in his own extensive knowledge.

I hoped JJ's education hadn't interfered with his ability to think creatively.

Just before going to sleep my mind returned to the discussion I had with my Dad under the weeping willow. Funny, I thought, in the universe, gravity is said to be the ultimate power. In all the myths I'd ever read, the greatest power was said to be love. Not gravity... Unless? Unless it was not gravity at all that pulled all things inexorably towards the overpowering heart of a Black Hole. Unless it was really just an Eye of the Storm. A galactic storm. An eye of infinite serenity.

Of inexplicable peace.

***

ZERO MINUS 10

13

Tit for Tat

At the University of Alberta, in Calgary, from the very first day,
JJ had adapted to his new environment. It was as though his home
was wherever he was at the time. He felt neither attachment nor
allegiance to any place, any person. In his own way he loved his
father and, I suspected, he felt a strange affinity towards me, although this affection, he was hard put to explain even to himself.
After a while, he stopped trying. To him I must have personified
his personal enigma.

"You seem to be the only person in my life who never expected anything from me," he'd once told me. "Even Dad expected
me to behave myself, as with the S.J.'s, for instance. As if it mattered." There was a suggestion of a sneer in the curve of his
mouth.

"Are you sure there is no one in your life, JJ?" I'd asked him.

Years later he confessed that he could seldom stop thinking
about my little questions. They came out of the blue, invariably at
a tangent to whatever mindset controlled him at the time. Or was it
he who controlled his mindset? He thought he did but sometimes
wasn't so sure.

JJ felt that the University Campus was a little like being at Brompton, but without the Jesuits looking over his shoulder. The other fundamental, basic, unsurpassed difference between the two institutions of learning was girls: their conspicuous absence followed by an equally conspicuous presence. Most men go through a stage in their life that can only be described as hormonal. JJ was no exception. For a while, he became colour-blind. It was of no consequence if the current love of his life was a blonde, a redhead, a brunette, or any of the fashionable mixtures of all three. *"Mada-mina, il catalogo el questo,"* he sang in his full bas-baritone, returning at early hours of the morning to his digs. During one such ad hoc performance, a policemen stopped him.

"Just what do you think you are doing, sir?" the officer asked, himself little older than JJ.

"I believe I've been confessing my guilt," JJ replied with a straight face.

"So you should. Mozart wrote *il* questo, not *el questo!*"

As it turned out, the young officer was of mixed parentage, German and Italian, and an opera buff to boot. For a while they became friends.

But this phase in JJ's young life went as quickly as it came. He got tired of being an animal. Of having no control over his own body. How he'd managed to avoid being infected must be assigned to a higher, inexplicable, kind and generous power to which he still refused to pledge any allegiance. He took precautions, of course. But even then, he was luckier than most.

In the meantime, the First World Electronic Church of the Adventist was growing in leaps and bounds. After five years in operation, JJ issued his first e-mail request for money. Frankly, he had no need for additional finances, but again, he was interested in the degree of human gullibility. He did not specify the amount. He merely informed his prospective or already hooked members that, should they feel the need to contribute to the gathering of information they had been receiving over the years, they could send a donation to an e-mail account. Contrary to the initial 'scare tactics' which had been as much a joke as anything else, the information the 'church' was now sending out actually took some effort to gather and disseminate. Just in case, JJ had already registered his church as a non-profit organization, and appointed a firm of accountants to keep his books. Even after the first million dollars had been deposited into his electronic coffers, he still considered that it was all a good joke. The three boys, now men, he'd conscripted to the 'church' at Brompton, still acted as the only officials running the organization.

Ah, for the wonder of electronics!

The three men had researched volumes of ancient as well as relatively new prophecies, assembled from around the world, mostly through the Internet, and extracted such information as suited their purposes. Each quotation they'd passed on to the Electronic Fraternity was carefully referenced to its original source. It was all perfectly above board and looked practically scientific. In a strange way it was honest, and, as JJ told me repeatedly, it was filling a niche in the ecclesiastic market. No hanky-panky, no embroidery, no additional revelations which Madame Zuzu had just pulled out of her nylon boa. The mailing list, originally a random spam, had grown to over a hundred thousand, not counting the numerous Internet chat-rooms which flourished the world over. Furthermore, the list had been growing daily, or in direct proportion to the established, orthodox churches generally getting cold feet about the state of the world.

"Not without reason," I told him once, and immediately regretted my words. Luckily, he ignored me.

People needed someone who was willing and able to do their thinking for them.

The funny thing was that the initial undercover organization JJ had started at Brompton was now recognized as a perfectly legal entity. The Jesuits still had no idea that the whole thing had grown out of JJ's desire to screw Father Martin. Or at least to get even with him. For his meddling. JJ'd finished his stint at the Jesuits with distinction, in the top five in his year, *Victor Ludorum* in sports, and as far as Fr. Martin was concerned, JJ had faded into the world outside without further incident. As it happened, Fr. Martin's compromised computer was replaced by a new piece of hardware, and the old model discarded without ever having its memory banks searched. *Sic transit gloria mundi.* All the trouble JJ had gone to turned out to be for nothing. He didn't even get the final satisfaction of a good laugh. Except for that single burst in the corridor when he'd initially bugged Fr. Martin's computer.

"Ah, well... Win some, lose some," he told me and dismissed the matter from his mind. But for a moment or two, he didn't look too happy about it.

For the last three years, JJ had been studying Political Science, Group Psychology and History of Philosophy. He'd managed to handle all three disciplines without undue hardship. To be honest, JJ loved work. He was only bored when he had nothing to do. When he worked, conducted research, delved into whatever unknown, particularly into any unknowns affecting human behaviour, he was happy. Happy and satisfied. Like after a good meal. Or like when scoring a winning home run for the U. of C..

I glanced at my watch trying to decide where JJ was most likely to be waiting for me. The next instant I heard the unmistakable roar of a single-propeller engine, buzzing overhead. "I don't believe it!" I whispered as I caught my breath. He wouldn't. He couldn't. He must have. I followed the plane towards the tiny landing strip just along the highway. By the time I got there, the little plane was taxiing towards the hangars. A moment later I saw JJ running towards me.

"Been waiting long?"

"Where did you come from?"

"Oh, just dropped out of the blue." His smile said the rest. "I had to show off, a little. You wouldn't have had a surprise if I'd told you before." Then he pointed to the red and white airplane parked at the corrugated metal shed. "How do you like her?"

This was too much. Even though I had witnessed many of JJ's pranks before.

"Turbo Skylane. The turbo-charger packs 235 horsepower right up to an operating altitude of 20,000 feet!" He let it all out in one breath.

"Did you steal it?" I asked in as serious a tone of voice as I could muster.

"I did. Got it for less than half price. The last owner got the jitters during a snowstorm."

I shook my head. "And you are going to leave it just like that?" I'd never flown a small plane, but the very idea of flying gave me goose bumps. It's the sort of thing I did only in my dreams.

"I called ahead. Radio, you know? They'll look after her well enough. People at small airstrips are much more efficient than at large commercial airports. Trust me." With that he climbed into my car.

JJ didn't own the Cessna. Well, he did and he didn't. It belonged to the... The First World Electronic Church of the Adventist.

"Really, JJ. You are not milking people out of their hard earned money, are you?" I knew the answer before I asked.

"Would you say that if I were offering an electronic advisory service on stocks and bonds? Believe me, they've milked a lot more people of their savings than I ever could. Or would. In fact, I told the boys to put a cap of a hundred dollars on donations. That should leave sufficient money for the old age of my goats."

"Goats?"

"I don't like sheep. Have you tried that cheese...?"

"I thought that you were telling them that they'll never reach their old age, weren't you?"

"Nothing of the sort. I'm not telling them anything new. I am passing on the result of our research, which they want to hear. As accurately as I know how."

I wanted to laugh. I didn't. Not because of what he'd said but at the superb pout he was trying on me now, as he had so many times before. I did my best to look grave and dignified.

"I'm not fooling you, am I?" he said after a pause.

I didn't answer. What my brother did was his business. I shook my head from left to right, as though studying the alternate directions at the crossroads. I took the left fork and some forty minutes later parked the car at the Centre's entry dome. It was the only dome open to the elements. From the sides. The cars still benefited from a curved roof overhead. In ten more minutes we were both fondling steins of golden liquid with a small head. We both thought Canadian beer was as good as it gets. As father was still taking his nap we remained on the terrace. He'd had a long night, last night.

"Staying long?" I asked examining my brother from head to toe.

JJ cut a handsome figure of a man. I wondered why he didn't prefer to spend his time off in the arms of some beautiful blond. Unless he preferred brunettes, of course. Chatting with a sister should hardly be a pastime of choice for an athletic man of twenty-three. Not that I wasn't flattered. Then I shook my head. For a brief moment, thinking about the lucky females who might have experienced the strength of my brother's embrace, filled me with jealousy. Just a pang but it was distinctly jealousy.

"You know, Sis, there is nowhere I'd rather be than chatting with you," he said eyeing me with equal interest. He must have read my mind. Luckily, not all of it.

"There goes my theory!" I said and told what I'd been thinking.

"There are dozens of blondes, brunettes and even redheads, some a little like you, but there is only one you."

"Thank you, Sir Galahad. And is that the only reason you came? To pay me a complement?"

"Where's Mary?" He glanced around.

"Shopping? I don't know."

I had a distinct impression that JJ wanted to make sure that we were alone. Assured, he leaned back in his chair and grew pensive. Some minutes passed before he spoke again.

"Do I look sane to you?" he asked finally.

"Neither more nor less than usual," I assured him. I wondered what was coming.

JJ turned his face away from me, as though to avoid my eyes. Then slowly, in an unfamiliar half-tone, he said something I would have never expected.

"I am getting hooked on my own spiel."

"Political Science, Mass Psychology, or History of Philosophy?"

"None of the above." JJ was definitely uncomfortable. He then took a deep breath. "I am beginning to think that there may be something in all that stuff I'm sending out to the Adventists."

I sat up, then lay down again. This was not my brother speaking. Not the cooler-than-ice JJ.

"You are getting hooked on the doomsday scenario?" I did my best not to colour my voice with judgment. Live and let live was my creed. Particularly towards my family.

"Did you even read any of my stuff?"

"About five years ago, when you were trying to stick it to Father Martin. By the way, what happened to him?"

JJ dismissed my question with a wave of his empty hand. With the other, he finished his beer in a single gulp and put his glass down.

"Have you been following the news on TV, the Internet, or even our glorious free press?"

"Not much," I admitted.

"Well, dear sister, the free press is not as free as you think. I developed access to info, never mind how, which makes mincemeat of our information society. They are keeping things from us that could make you scream. And by the way, when I referred to a doomsday scenario, I didn't mean the end of the world but, most emphatically, the end of the world as we know it."

So that was it. He must have gotten onto some of the stuff uncle David and Dad have been talking about. I wondered how much he knew.

"Tell me more," I said.

"You sure you want to hear it all?"

"Perhaps just some of it. Go on..."

JJ told me, in his usual well-organized way, what he'd gathered recently from his 'sources'. He admitted that he could tap into both the Canadian and the American governmental computer communication. Both political and military. Some of what he said I knew already from overhearing Father and Dave. But other elements were less pleasant, making the hair stand up on the back of my neck. Apparently the illustrious guardians of our Confederation and the Constitution down south, had been making contingency plans one of which was the sterilization of masses of people, mostly in the third world countries. From the air.

"If you tell anyone, they'll never let me out of jail," he finished.

"Why would they be contemplating such a horrible thing?" I asked once I got over shock, then disgust, then shock again.

"We have overpopulated our planet, and the food supply is under attack from sources they cannot control."

"You mean viruses and such like?"

"So you've heard about it?"

"Some."

I wondered if I should share my own knowledge with my brother. Before I could decide, father walked in to join us. The men hugged, patted each other on their backs, and JJ went to get three more pints. I used his brief absence to ask Dad if there was anything in anyway hush-hush about his or David's work.

"What ever do you mean, pet? Of course not. David and I have nothing to hide, you know that?"

"Of course, father," I was immeasurably pleased. "I'm sorry, Dad. It's just that JJ has been filling my head..." I stopped when JJ came back.

"....with doomsday scenarios? Really JJ, have you been scaring your sister with your nonsense? She looks worried."

As JJ looked at me, I shook my head. He relaxed. He guessed that I hadn't told Dad about his latest revelations. We raised our glasses to each other and JJ proceeded to tell Dad about his studies.

When father eventually left for his office, JJ and I went for a walk. I led him to what became my favourite bench, under the weeping willow, by the pond. We walked in silence, inhaling the multitude of scents as we passed the diverse flowering beds and bushes. There is no wind inside to disperse the aromas. There is always spring, under the domes. As some flowers rested in their cycle, others exuded an array of perfumes that saturated the air around us. Finally we sat down.

"I suppose it's my turn to tell you about some problems that humanity is facing."

I didn't like talking about negative things. For three years now I'd been invited to attend the Sunday dinners at the Mendels. I

mean at the dinner table, not just the fish tank. I found them en-
lightening. They hadn't always been filled with foreboding and
imminent danger. I'd learned a great deal about a broad range of
scientific research being conducted at the Centre. But only recently
was I discovering that everything I'd learned was beginning to fit
into a matrix of order and harmony. Even that, which we regarded
as negative or frightening, fitted into an overall plan, if one could
only see it. My eyes were being opened slowly, carefully, as
though not to scare me into retreat.

"There is a great deal going on that is not exactly advertised in
the popular press," I resumed, "although if you scan some of the
inside pages, most of the information is available."

I then told JJ the rest of the stuff I'd heard from Dad about the
viruses attacking most livestock on most mega-farms throughout
the world. At the moment Canada was reasonably immune to the
worst of it but, from what I'd heard, it wouldn't last. The exorbi-
tant increase in international travel, in relation to the past century,
assured that nobody, nor any country, would remain immune for
long.

Then I described some of the more interesting aspects of father's recent work. The flyby pyrotechnics, the meteoric showers
on the Moon, the increased activity of tectonic plates, and some
other factors that were still under investigation.

"Do you know that according to Dad, there is a good chance
that most planetary orbits in our Solar System are also undergoing
some sort of adjustment? I don't know the details but the very idea
is staggering. At least to me," I finished lamely.

"I think I should raise my maximum donation to one thousand
dollars..."

He was a really cool fish. Or a great actor. Perhaps both. "Be
careful, JJ, the future is not irrevocable," I felt compelled to change
my tack.

"What on earth do you mean, Sis?"

"You want to plan your future on the facts available today.
Indeed, we have little choice in the matter. But there is a great difference between projections and prognostications. The present is
our only term of reference," I tried to explain.

"And the past," he put in. "We can project the future on past performance. It is not a foolproof method but a lot better than nothing." As usual, JJ sounded very confident.

"That's not quite what I mean," I said in a quiet, relaxed, unemotional way.

JJ knew that tone of voice. When I'd used it before he knew that I demanded attention. He held his breath and waited.

"Be careful, JJ," I repeated. "The future is the projection of the present. However, only one actual present can be projected at a time. What I mean is that if you change the present, you also change the projection, that is to say, you change the future."

"And...?"

"Only the present is real. All else is supposition."

"And the past?"

"Interpretation. There are no two people who regard the past equally."

"If I understand your drift, you are telling me to stop planning, scheming, projecting and live more intensely in the present?" It was as much a question as a statement.

"If you want to survive," I added. I didn't mean to sound ominous.

"Survive!?" JJ laughed. "It may surprise you, Sis, but survival is not at the top of my list of priorities."

"I am not talking about..." and I stopped.

I didn't want to get into a philosophical discussion of non-physical or some sort of spiritual survival. He sensed that I wasn't ready to tackle this subject and let it alone. But I could see that JJ couldn't help wondering where the sentence I'd cut short would have taken me. He knew that, by the standard definition of the word, I was completely secular in my thinking. I'd studied some religions but they'd left no impression on me. He knew that too. At the same time, I was the antithesis of all things material. I wasn't so much spiritual as, to him, I seemed like the spirit itself. A presence that he felt even in Calgary, in moments of stress. A single thought, a fragmentary moment of redirecting his attention to me, had saved him from making some bad mistakes. He never told me about it till much later. But, if pressed, he would confess that, in a way he couldn't explain or even conceive of, I, his own sister, was his guardian angel.

I remember the time we'd touched on a similar subject. That time I'd asked if his stay with the Jesuits had given him any grounding in the Catholic faith. When I saw the expression on his face, I'd changed the train of my inquiry. I'd been reading some religious literature and wanted to compare my findings with JJ's expertise in prophecies.

"Did you find many prophecies which fulfilled themselves?" I didn't sound hopeful.

"All of them," he assured me confidently. "If not already then sooner or later they will *come to pass*."

"You mean, all things happen, sooner or later?"

"Precisely. Prophecies are like taxes. If you wait long enough, they will catch up with you."

I didn't say anything. It wasn't the answer I wanted to hear. In fact, it was precisely the time factor that interested me.

"So you see, Sis, I can never be wrong. I give the people the most likely scenarios as indicated by men or women who project their own vision of the future. I may offer some interpretation, but it is my gullible audience who interpret them still further and try to fit them into the time frame of today. I give them the fodder, they eat it."

"They sate their need...." I nodded. "I wonder what it is in the human psyche that calls for doomsday scenarios. Hollywood is full of them. The movie theatres can't get enough of them. They abound on the best seller lists. People make millions..."

"Just one million...." JJ corrected.

"....people make millions out of this inherent need. Is it some sort of death-wish planted in us by the gods of yesteryear?"

"It is the need to pay our dues. We all feel guilty for being imperfect," he said slowly. And after some moments he added, "that and the inherent transience of the present?"

I looked up at my brother with surprise. "Why, JJ, you sound like a Roman Catholic!" I was referring to the first part of his statement. The second part demanded more analysis.

"CC, not RC. Calgarian Catholic. We adapt the past to the present. There is more money in it that way."

"What do you mean?"

"Come on, Sis! You know as well as I do that for thousands of years churches have been making oodles of money out of their faithful. The Egyptians were no worse at it than the Vatican. It's just that modern technology has given us an edge. The churches are too conservative to take advantage of the cutting edge..."

"Surely JJ, you cannot relegate all religions to just money?"

"I don't. They do. And not all. There are saints in the cesspool of religions. There are giants. But they are few and far between."

I thought of Mother Theresa. And then I thought of hundreds of nameless doctors without borders, of the Coast Guard men and women who daily risked their lives to help others. Perhaps those were the saints of today?

"And the people?" I asked instead.

"The people take what they want. What they don't want, they don't take. It is a free market economy. The churches can no longer fleece their sheep by selling them plenary indulgences or absolutions. I would never sink that low. But I can give them what they want."

"It still sounds..." I didn't want to use the word dishonest. It wasn't really. JJ never demanded money, never threatened anyone with hell fire or some other mental perversion, to extract money from them. Admittedly some of the Churches had done so.

"And I promise you, Hey, I shall never burn anyone at the stake just because they don't like my little e-mails."

JJ lowered his eyes against the glare of the setting sun cutting its way through the prisms of the geodesic panels. Individual rays played and sparkled in the tiny ripples of the serene pond. A single duckling cruising effortlessly toward the other shore riled the water, but gently. Soon two more of her siblings appeared out of nowhere, and made haste to catch up with their leader. JJ never realized that life could be so peaceful. So relaxing. The world might come to an end, but here each moment counted as a lifetime, as a fragment so still as to embrace the eternity. He realized, for the first time in his life, that eternity is not an extremely long time, but a condition of timelessness. Of being outside time. And the second thing he realized was that it was precisely this truth that I'd been trying so hard to convey to him.

"You are a very strange little sister, Hey," he blurted out of the blue.

"And you are a very strange big brother, JJ," I countered.

A moment later we got up and slowly strolled back to the condo. Father was already back from the Observatory and supper was waiting for us all. JJ found the smell of home cooking intoxicating. Except for the three pints of Molson and some potato chips, he hadn't eaten since early morning. He took a deep breath and made for the kitchen. Without a word of warning he picked Mary up by her elbows, lifted her bodily to the level of his face, and planted two big kisses on each of her rosy cheeks.

"I love you nanny," he affirmed with great conviction, his nostrils filling with the culinary delights.

"You do nothing of the sort," Mary said irritably. "I am much too old for you."

But you could see that under her poorly disguise exasperation, the English Nanny was pleased as Punch.

***

14

The puzzle

The jungle drums beat everywhere. In shopping centres, in local malls, in the pretentious atria of office buildings, in the elevators, on busses, trains, airplanes, street corners and in-between corners, in parks, skating rinks, and yes, in a number of churches. Apparently all of God's children had gone deaf.

Radio and television interviews, discussions, sport reports, business data, even dramatic performances were aired against a background, often drowned by, illiterate morons smashing a metal pan against a kitchen wall. Films, comedies, tragedies, were set against overpowering sound-tracks which seemed bent on making any, if rare, intelligent dialogues between the actors all but impossible to follow. To the masses of teenagers, at whose lugubrious taste the market was principally directed, this was of no consequence. They didn't listen anyway – lest it accidentally force them to think. No. Explosions, the rattle of machine guns, wailing of police sirens with the accompanying screech of tires sufficed to sate their vitiated brains. Their proud possessors were busy chewing their gum, stomping their feet in stupefying rhythm, echoing the jungle strains.

"I am glad I'm not part of the world at large any more," JJ told us having just returned one final whirlwind tour of the 'outside' world. We were discussing what we were purportedly missing by remaining, for the most part, within the confines of the CSC. We were at the Mendels, with David presiding over our little gathering of scientists.

This was the first time that JJ had joined father and me on the first Sunday of the month. During his brief description of the various aspects of life 'outside', his listeners had remained speechless. Finally he sat down.

"Surely, you're joking. How on earth could people live in such conditions?" an elderly research chemist asked, disbelief in his eyes. He hadn't been outside the Centre for three years. Then, shaking his head he added, "How quickly we forget. Our mind has an amazing capacity to erase the unpleasant memories as soon as possible."

"That's what living in the present is all about," I whispered to my father. I wouldn't dream of taking part in the discussion. I was just glad I'd been invited. To listen.

"You all forget, I dare say, that for the first few months, after we'd moved here, we thought of ourselves as refugees from an ocean of madness," David nodded looking at his two sons. Both of them now held jobs at the Centre. Aaron the younger as teacher, his brother, Matt, as a gardener. Matthew had completed his studies of botany, but felt the need to savour the earth in his hands. There was no shame at the Centre in doing what one loved most. Providing one did it well. Both young men regarded themselves as refugees. Paradoxically, within less than two years of that supper, they'd both moved out. Their desire to dip their feet in the ocean was just too overwhelming. To each his own, I think. To each his own. But I missed them.

After a few more incredulous comments from the older members of tonight's guests, JJ resumed his narrative. He didn't paint a pleasant picture.

"The days when a beautiful melody was the prerequisite for success in the marketing of an LP, a tape, or now a CD, are long gone. All that belongs to the past. The only instruments revered nowadays by the senseless throngs are those of the percussion family. Drums – snare or bongo, tambours or timpani, a pair of metal plates or any other noise making device are greatly and grossly amplified by electronic paraphernalia, which aid their operators in multiplying the decibels to unprecedented levels. Parents give their three-year-olds drums for Christmas, and encourage them to raise din, so that their misbegotten litter might become inure to constant clamour and thus fit into the world to come." JJ paused for breath.

"But why?" someone put in.

"Well," Dave answered for JJ, misunderstanding the crux of the question, "the major advantage of such a course is that the little ones much prefer striking the drum with their sticks, than to derive innocent joy from their previous practice of striking everything with whatever was within reach of their tiny hands. Once committed to percussion, their parents, I'll have you know, smile in gratitude! There are savings in furniture. As for the noise, they've already achieved a condition of being half-deaf, of course, and their children are joyfully taking care of the other half."

"Thank you, Doctor Mendel. I couldn't have put it better myself," JJ said with a broad smile.

But Uncle David was just warming up. He raised his hands to his ears. "About sixty years ago," he continued, "there was a musical called 'Stop the world I wanna get off!' I thought it was a comedy. Now it seems that the disease was already spreading, even then. The mad carrousel had already begun its gyrations."

JJ didn't tell us everything. He was amazed how very shielded we'd all become within our crystal domes. Everything he told us taxed our credulity. Yet noise wasn't the only symptom of decadence. The rise in percentages of dropouts from schools was staggering. The rise in the ranks of the homeless as well as the mental condition of the impoverished was symptomatic of an uncaring society. And, ironically, against this background, there was an extraordinary rise in obesity. The fat and the starving. A strange balancing act. In the States, Canada, Western Europe and to only a slightly lesser degree in Asia, diseases directly related to obesity had quadrupled during the last twenty years. If we add to that eleven different strains of influenza, triple the number of people already infected with HIV, and double the varieties of venereal diseases, we have the reason why Ogilvy inhabitants did not thirst after the 'rich' life outside in the 'free' world. We wouldn't have even if we hadn't been aware of all that was going on outside.

"I strongly suspect that you people are in no way infected with the cancer eating at humanity's innards," JJ whispered to me. He made sure no one else could hear him. "You are like innocents who are protected even from the knowledge of evil." The next instant I detected a pang of guilt on JJ's face, for having told me the truth. He must have thought he'd tampered with my purity of heart. I kissed his cheek to reassure him. His smile lacked something of his usual boisterous joy.

As for the wide-open spaces, I must confess that, now and again, I cheated. Mostly at night. I would sneak out through the escape hatches and, with my eyes roam the sky from one horizon to the other. No matter what glorious detail the Monster Eye offered, I could only take in the magnificence, the utter grandeur of the universe with unaided eyes, with my heart and mind open yet silent. Just watching, and listening, and absorbing without thought or judgement. It was through these excursions that the universe and I became one. And we remained. Forever.

My eyes drifted to the serene garden just outside the Mendels' living room. The balmy air stood almost still. There was a barely perceptible zephyr moving the branches, created by a number of fans, which silently circulated the air. The warm air from above was directed downwards, only to rise again, naturally, and gather new warmth while basking under the solar panels. I loved my little world within a world. I found it difficult to accept that from his tiny sanctuary the Monster Eye looked further out into space than any optical devise in man's history. The tiny and the limitless met here in perfect harmony.

If there was such a thing as regression or devolution threatening the human race as foretold by the ancient Hindus, then surely, the devolution in music was at the forefront of the oncoming doom. Kali, the black goddess, was bent on destroying our eardrums. Not ours – theirs. Those outside. Shakespeare once wrote that if music be the food of love – we should play on. Well, according to JJ – no more. Play not, oh mighty bard, for the lovers have gone deaf. Deaf to harmony, blind to beauty, indifferent to order and the pursuit of happiness, deaf even to the summons of love itself. Rather, the present generation practised indifference, escape from responsibility, and disdain for any effort which might raise them above their level of a vegetative existence.

Devolution?

At the Centre, we seemed to have escaped the prophecies of the ancient Hindus. The prophecies of cyclic regression. But we had to hurry. Brahma was no longer sleepy. Soon he would awaken from his slumber and we would all disappear like the insignificant figments of his chimerical nightmare that we are.

For a long time we sat in uneasy silence.

John Hydon, a great deal on his shoulders, looked thoughtfully at his children. How close he'd grown to us these last few years. At long last I think he felt a deep sense of satisfaction. He knew that JJ and I had both escaped the worst. If discordant noise was the herald of decadence, then JJ had been spared the monstrosity of racial declivity under the vigilant eye, or really vigilant ear, of the Jesuits. At Brompton hard rock, steel bands, or any form of excessive and offensive discord was firmly discouraged. Even when walking up and down the many long corridors in the institution of learning, the boys kept the decibels down to a reasonable level. JJ had no idea how much he owed to the priests whom he'd long held in such low esteem. "Silence is golden," they affirmed sternly. *Silentium Altum.*

While Dad's eyes drifted to my face, my eyes, in turn, were fixed on my brother. I was absorbing his every word. I was fascinated though incredulous. JJ was my only contact with the world outside. It wasn't my world any more. Out there. It never had been, really. It must have been evident from my expression, that what JJ had described was foreign to me. Foreign and repulsive. Not the people. Only the manner in which they'd chosen to live. My father must have seen that. He exchanged glances with JJ. They smiled at each other as if to say, "Yes, she does look lovely."

I think I blushed.

"You look absolutely lovely, Pet," Dad whispered in my ear.

JJ nodded and turned his head away, as though embarrassed. I wondered why. One thing was certain. If I looked good, then he was, surely, the most handsome man I'd ever seen. My brother.

Father was right. Other than on my nocturnal trysts with the stars, I seldom left the confines of the Centre, the Sanctuary, which had been developing, more and more, into a haven for the remnants of beleaguered humanity. The remnants of people who still laid claim to sanity. Dad was very proud of his part in the development of the Centre. Admission was no longer limited just to the fields of sciences. Now we had the arts also. A repertory theatre alternated between the old classics and the best of the recent playwrights. Recent meant going back some fifty years. The same was true of music. Wolfgang Amadeus, Ludwig, Johann Sebastian, and their later colleagues, found a new lease on life here – long denied them on the outside. Painters were carefully screened to eliminate riff-raff and encouraged to exhibit at the Sanctuary, year round. The same was true of sculptors, of dancers, and even an occasional opera was presented in one of the major domes. On those nights the echoes of *Nessun Dorma* would wind their way from dome to dome, through the protected archways, then expanding again, from dome to dome, to dome... *Questa notte nessun dorma in Sanctuario....* The arias, melodies, travelled as though by magic, denying the passage of time, bringing Italian sunshine, or bewitching moonlight, into and through the crystal vaults, lingering, reverberating, dissipating slowly in the furthest parts of the Crystal City. Those were wonderful moments. People would flock out onto their balconies, hold their breath to partake in the feast.

Yes, I was very proud of my city. As was my father. He was its heart, its inspiration.

By now, there were many crystal domes straddling the long crest of Ogilvy Mountain. From the satellites orbiting our planet, the Mountain looked like a colony on the Moon, wedged between rolling hills and sharp crags, creeping around the inaccessible peeks and deep chasms, only to spread out again along a terrain that offered a broader foothold. It was the modern, the ultra modern Machu Picchu. Only the fog of the rain forest was missing. Here the air was as pure as the crystal that enclosed it. And the gods still lingered here.

The original Astronomical Observatory, the Monster Eye, had given birth to a community of thousands, a tightly knit society of scientists, artists and other intense seekers of knowledge. Of knowledge and beauty. JJ said the 'normal' men and women, the average Joe and Jane, had no desire to join the select few. Even those who knew something of Ogilvy Mountain, and they were relatively few, thought of us as pathetic eccentrics, eggheads, missing out on the latest in life.

"Poor saps," they would comment. "They're living in a prison."

But people at Ogilvy never closed their walls to those who wished to join them. In spite of the mild conditions of entry there were few candidates. You had to love your work. You had to be good at what you did. You had to be totally committed to whatever you were doing. You had to strive for your personal best, without appreciable financial rewards. No one was rich here. No one was poor. Yet all were so very different. You had to harbour a deep desire to join the inner society just for the privilege of being allowed to do what you really and truly wanted to do. Just for the joy of it. Work here was not an occupation. It was a condition of life. It was a reward for being true to your inner self. To your creative spirit. And whatever it was, whatever your passion, it could never flourish at the expense of another. That was all. These were all the conditions.

Quite easy, really.

To a considerable degree the Centre became self-sufficient. The controlled climate inside supplied most of the comestibles, grown the year round in seven domes dedicated to that purpose. People found here that eating less than half of what people were used to eating on the outside was more than satisfying. No one ate here out of boredom. No one stuffed their innards to compensate for neurotic hang-ups. Unbeknownst to outsiders, Ogilvians did, however, make their own wine, brewed their own beer, even distilled their own 'Scotch' from a recipe provided by my father's grand uncle; a recipe to be kept secret under the penalty of the Highlander's Venerable Curse.

The Scotch, with McTavish's proudly piratical features adorning each of the bottles brewed at the Sanctuary, was probably the only secret the Ogilvians ever kept from the outside world. The rest of the news they wanted to share with the 'others'; all too often falling on deaf ears. People at large didn't want to be bothered with scientific facts, which might upset their long cultivated ennui; not to mention the interference with their TV soap operas. "You do your bit, and we'll do ours," was their motto.

The night was drawing to a close. The moon continued to pierce the triangular crystals with filigree of sparkling light and shadows. Uncle David stifled a yawn.

"Only they don't do much of anything," JJ was nearing the end of another report. He was one of the few outsiders allowed unrestricted access to the Centre, without having to fill out entrance questionnaires. "I've noticed that people, out there, find work tiring. They question what is the purpose of civilization if unpleasant tasks could not be automated? Apparently they regard most tasks as unpleasant. Luckily for them, most chores are carried out by robots. The Trade Unions fought hard to achieve a universal three day week with a maximum of eighteen hours of what resembled work. Less bi-annual leave, illnesses, public holidays and lame excuses, of course. And none that I've met seemed aware that here, at the Centre, you're provided with much, if not most, of the means by which they stay alive, let alone healthy. It is your research that keeps their bodies and soul together. That's if they are still expressions of soul. That, ladies and gentlemen, is the world you have left behind, for this...." he made a broad gesture towards the gardens, the laboratories and the artists' studios. "Makes you wonder...."

But no one did.

It wasn't until JJ's next visit that father shared his latest concerns with his children. He'd been very busy lately. On average, Dad had flown to and from the Moon's Operational Base at John F. Kennedy's Space Centre at least once a month. And last month, he'd flown to NASA headquarters twice at their invitation. Since the first dome had been erected on the Moon over ten years ago, six more had been added, new water sources had been tapped, and the first four domes had been sealed with a rarefied but breathable atmosphere about the equivalent to that at say six thousand meters above the sea level on Earth. There are some, in Tibet or in the Andes, who find this sort of air quite acceptable. But it wasn't as bad as it sounds. People working on the Moon also benefit from only one-sixth of the Earth's gravity, and thus require much less energy to perform their tasks.

All facets of construction were on schedule and advancing smoothly.

Nevertheless, father's friends down South were worried about quite a different account. Although the economy was still humming, there was a growing concern over the welfare of citizens who had been losing their zest for work. The USA still dominated the world in the get-rich-quick department, but the politicians were finding it harder to usurp countless millions into their private coffers, at the expense of the common working man. The middle class had all but disappeared. At least in this field, China had already caught up with the Super-race. India was quite another story. Their development followed more on the American lines. They formed a fast-growing subcontinent of the have and the have-nots. But the States still led the world.

"Let them eat cake," a dictum which had worked for so many years in growing industrial societies, suddenly, or at least over the last twenty years, had lost some of its momentum. Industrial societies catered to the many who *wanted* to work. The Technological society did the very opposite. Particularly if cheaper labour could be commandeered under the World Trade Organization permits. Little work was actually performed in the USA. The proud members of the Super-race were too busy spending the money they'd made overseas.

The White House was desperately trying to awaken the old *esprit de corps*, the days of Glory, Glory, Alleluia. They found it hard, near impossible. The idea of space exploration had caught fire – for a while. For about ten years it stimulated young minds.

Now, the Moon Base was already well advanced and the initial excitement was replaced by the exigencies of hard work.

This was where father came in. So far, his consultation had centred on his knowledge of astronomy, planetary geology and, to a large extent, on his knowledge of the instrumentation required to equip the New World Observatory. Now, as of about three months, he'd been called in as the consultant planning the new settlement on the Moon. Father wasn't alone, of course, but he did have twenty years of experience of practically running the Ogilvy Mountain. To do justice to Uncle Sam, they did treat Dad with all due decorum. From the moment he'd set foot in NASA, he had been pampered like a national treasure, given all the privileges of a three-star General, and accorded diplomatic immunity to boot. Though why he might have needed the latter, only they knew.

"I'm telling you kids, I've never been so important in my life. Sometimes I wonder if I appreciate myself enough," he told us grinning from ear to ear.

Over the years, father hadn't changed physically. Not much. Except for a short trimmed beard and a slightly swashbuckling mustachio, which he allowed to grow a little too long, he looked like his old self. He maintained his moustache in memory of his grand uncle, the benefactor of the Scotch recipe.

"It is the least I can do, my friends," he'd announced at one of David's Sunday dinners twirling the ends of his handlebars. They'd all raised their glasses in solemn approval.

"Long live the Great Uncle!" they exclaimed in unison. May he live long and prosper, wherever he is.

But not all things were as cheerful as the golden liquid in their tumblers.

During dinner Dad told us about the problems the Americans were facing. For years the strength of their economy, of their tremendous success in practically all fields, had been due, at least in part, to their ability to centralize their production. Centralization had not been as advanced as in the old USSR, but the underlying causes which brought the Soviet Union to its knees, were now more than evident in the USA. In fact they were in evidence across the

Americas. In addition, all the other advantages of centralization, including those of mega-cities, international-organizations, mega-conglomerates, were now showing signs of dangerous structural weakness.

"They no longer have the money to redo the infrastructure which made their cities feasible. To rebuild the systems now, the very life of the megalopolises would have to come to a halt for extended periods of time. New York, Chicago, Detroit, San Francisco, Seattle, a dozen others, would all come to a stultifying standstill. Poor blighters...."

"Are we any better off?" JJ asked.

"Not to my knowledge," father shook his head. "And if you look further south, the eighteen million in Mexico City, the twenty-two in Sao Paulo, and many other once great cities are in their death-throes. Europe, China, India, Egypt, all face the same problems. Decentralize – or die a slow, painful death. The question is how. Nobody wants to move."

"And I presume, they can't be moved by force," JJ mused.

"Nor should they be. We all create our own heavens and hells. The point is, if they were to move where would they go? What would they do? There are no easy answers."

"Are there difficult answers?"

"Well, they have some horrid ideas which belong in Hollywood horror movies, but nothing a civilized man could stomach."

For a while there was silence. JJ's face, normally full of life, to whom nothing ever seemed impossible, looked frazzled. Adults usually develop the capacity to accept the inevitable. JJ was still too young for that. In his heart, though he would never admit it, he felt pity for those countless millions. On a global scale, more like billions.

"They must have some idea what to do about it," he searched Dad's face.

"Not really, JJ. The western civilization has worked for generations to reach this condition. We have all lived on credit. Enjoy now – pay later has been the overwhelming motto. Now we've got the account."

"We? Why must the new generation pay for the sins of their fathers?"

"You carry my genes, JJ. As does Hey. Neither of you has to pay. Unless you want to."

"I though you said we don't have a choice?"

"We all have choices. But there are always consequences. The forefathers of our friends, down South, could have stayed in Europe, or risk their lives crossing the Atlantic, or the vast continent to the Pacific. Many died trying. But their efforts and sacrifices assured many generations of a life of plenty. Even now not all has to be lost. If they take immediate action to decentralize, to free themselves from their ingrained urban mentality, to make do with less, to eat less, spend less, drink less, walk rather than drive, put on a sweater rather then raise the thermostat..."

"C'mon, Dad. Nobody in the US of A is going to do any such thing, you know that?"

Father didn't answer. There were some, not many, he'd met, who might. But it was contrary to the American mindset. They'd had too much gravy for too long. They'd never saved for the lean years. And they'd never really respected the environment.

"And us?" I looked up from staring at my lap. I hated bad news of any kind.

"I have some ideas," Dad said. "In a way, we've already done it. This is a Sanctuary for the sciences, the arts, for whatever we believe makes us human. Don't you agree, Hey?"

My face must have lit up and then, almost as quickly, I'm sure, lost its lustre.

"Didn't you tell us, Dad, that it's not just our Earth that is in the throes of a deep malady?"

"You are referring to our Solar System?"

I nodded.

"The diagnosis is still vague. Frankly, we still don't know what is going on. But let me tell you something. Since I left my old school, in the Old Country, I've never suffered from an effusion of religious convictions. But, when I analyze the stupidity of the human race, of the countless Empires, which have come and gone, of the plagues and calamities which we, as people, have survived, I cannot accept that there isn't some sort of inherent intelligence that occasionally manifests interest in our welfare. If you

wish to spell that inherent intelligence with capital 'I', feel free to
do so. But it's there."

We talked for a while longer.

Father reminisced about the old days when the free world
counted on the USA for their security. Not so long ago. Now,
there were no more Evil Empires, no Axes of Evil, no Devils Incarnate. The petty tyrants had grown old, tired, often sick, de-
jected. Most of them had died, as had their successors. Nobody
wanted to attack anyone anymore. It would take too much effort.
No one was stirred enough, or cared enough to fight, to invade
other people's land. The Giant had no one to bully into submission. There wasn't any point. For years the USA could not only
buy out any country with their spare change, but also beat them
into submission with one hand tied behind their back.

"The American Empire is like a Giant Ball. It obeys New-
ton's first Law of Motion. The Law of Inertia. The Giant Ball,
once set in motion, will continue to roll until a greater force stands
in its way. There is no such force. There are few influences diffus-
ing its momentum. The present motion will gradually dissipate and
die by attrition. A long, whimpering death. Short of a major miracle, it will die in the foreseeable future."

"That's a bad analogy," I put in. "Why, if there is no force to
stop the ball, would the ball ever stop? The idea you want is that of
a fire that has used up it's fuel or a bully who having no one left to
bully lies down to take a nap."

JJ nodded somewhat grudgingly. He refilled our tall glasses.
He cleared his throat repeatedly.

"But the remnants of the momentum are still there. This is
how the Moon concept, the Lunar Base, was born," Dad continued.
"They will continue building it. Perhaps also just from sheer momentum. But they already lack ideas. And most of all, they lack
men. Young men. Men of vision. Men who are not dedicated to
creature comforts. Men who carry the genes of the first settlers,
frontiersman, who once crossed the Atlantic and then the savage
continent to reach the Pacific Ocean. Such men and women, seem
all gone...."

JJ smiled sadly. "They've become a nation of quarterly results," he murmured.

After that we didn't feel like taking anymore. We sat in silence, lost in thought. It was not a happy evening. It was like attending a wake. The wake of a noble idea. Of something very beautiful. It was like holding a wake over a nation.

I dreamed that night that I was sitting on my balcony, on the Moon, looking up at Earth. She was just rising over the eastern horizon. She was beautiful.

***

15

Enigma

JJ was back in Calgary. Father was busy with the latest observations of what was now officially named The Enigma Effect. By recording the emissions of light in the sky close to Pluto and then photographing the apparent movement of stars immediately next to the planet, they had confirmed that there was an object, possibly a gaseous globe rather like Jupiter only with a diameter some twenty times smaller and infinitely more rarefied, following the orbit of Pluto. Or it might have been some sort of energy field, which not only reflected other celestial objects, but shielded whatever lay behind it. The strangest thing was that it neither emitted nor seemed to absorb any energy and thus did not register at all on the infrared spectrum. But it was very good at reflecting photons as well as shielding those that were behind it.

Frankly, to me it still didn't make too much sense.

When father and I were alone, he confessed to me that the best way to describe The Enigma Effect was to compare it to the Fata Morgana, which can best be seen in the Strait of Messina, between the coasts of Sicily and the Southwestern tip of Italy, near Reggio di Calabria. Fata Morgana is so called because it had once been thought to be the work of Morgan le Fay, the fairy of Arthurian legend. Originally, Morgan le Fay had been King Arthur's sister and an accomplished enchantress.

"It is a peculiar type of complex mirage," Dad said, his eyes drifting into the land of enchantment he was describing, "one that on occasion gives the impression of a castle suspended in the air or partially submerged in the sea. Morgan le Fay was known to live in a marvellous castle under the sea. The images she conjured to appear in the air, caused seamen to mistake them for safe harbour, and lured them to their deaths on the rocks."

Even as I too felt drawn into the magic, Dad's voice recovered a more scientific tone.

"The mirage is one that can occur only where there are alternating warm and cold layers of air near the ground or water surface. Actually it is a superposition of several images of one object. The images may undergo rapid changes as the air layers move slightly up and down relative to the observer. Just a complicated illusion, really. In case of the our Pluto, the question remains what image, and what layers...."

The Enigma Effect had all the hallmarks of a capricious fairy playing tricks on whoever was trying to see its machinations. The stars seemingly changed in shape, position and luminosity, suggesting the surface of a complex shape of unpredictable density, which may have accounted for the stars being there one moment, and the next disappearing into oblivion. They might have been just reflections.

I loved it when Dad told me stories like that. In fact, I loved all the fables.

"Few people know that the Arthurian legends date back to at least 600 AD., and that Arthur was not only a King of Britain but the head of a magnificent Court and Master of Europe. He reputedly dipped his fingers in the legends of the romances of Tristan and Isolde and that which later became the story of Parcifal, while his sister dipped hers in the Stretto di Messina."

It had been mother who'd enjoyed all that was fabulous, allegorical or romantic. I must have inherited a great many of my mother's tastes. And apparently many things that had to do with mother had remained indelibly imprinted in Father's memory.

"I thought that Fata Morgana was a bona fide mirage caused by the reflection of light through layers of air of different densities and temperatures. Are you suggesting that the effect is caused by the atmosphere of Pluto?"

"Even if Pluto did have one, an atmosphere I mean, we would hardly be able to see. At a mean distance of almost three billion kilometres, even the Monster Eye would be hard put to spot it, let alone analyze it."

"Then...?"

"Then it can't be that. What we are doing is rather like studying subatomic particles, such as quarks, in a cyclotron. We can't see them but we can record and study the trails they leave behind. What we see around Pluto are the consequences of a presence, without being able to see the presence itself."

Maybe Dad remembered me comparing 'my' Enigma to a mirror ball. This is exactly how the object of the reflective field was behaving. Yet he could hardly have taken my description of a three-dimensional Enigma on my say so. Although the reflections may have been those of a curved surface, there was no such phenomenon in nature that he knew of. Thus, as far as he was concerned, for now the Enigma remained an enigma.

That afternoon, after lunch, I returned with Dad to the Observatory. I was always there when one of the minor telescopes was free later on in the evening. Actually at night. I would set my own program on the computer, and then come back later to watch it unfold 'live'. It was the sort of thing that I found the greatest fun. Father would remain with me for a few hours. He would check the results from the previous night, reset the lenses and wait for me to finish my work.

On the way back we stopped at our favourite bench. For a while we sat, in silence, breathing in the serenity all around us. Father found it amazing that in a world torn by seemingly irreconcilable social and economical problems, we were spared all of its strife. It was almost like having died and now observing the physical world, without in fact participating in it. Like being in but not of the world. It really was like being in heaven.

And then, out of the blue, I felt inspired. to paraphrase Shakespeare.

"What's in a name?" I asked quietly. "Is rose not a rose that smells the same?

"That which we call a rose by any other name..."

Father began correcting me then stopped, evidently waiting to see what was coming next. I was in one of my philosophical moods.

"The name invariably symbolizes the nature of the object considered. You can find that throughout the Bible," I affirmed authoritatively. "Buddha, on the other hand, would question the wisdom of recognizing a rose simply by its smell. Or by its outward manifestation for that matter."

I looked at Dad's face. He nodded remaining noncommittal.

"Buddha, would say that a rose is not a rose. He would say that a rose is made up of non-rose elements. Of water and earth, of space and time, of chemicals and minerals. It is also made up of the effort of a gardener who tended to it with his love." I looked up at the crystal dome. "The rose that is not a rose contains the elements of the stars. It incorporates the Universe within itself. Remove one element, even our concept of a rose, and a rose is no more. Thus only when a rose is not a rose, it becomes a rose. By the same token my mother was not my mother. That is why I recognized her as my mother. Remember?

"You were nine then, Hey. You were nine... how on earth can you remember that?"

"You can," I replied simply.

More and more often I felt compelled to venture into a field that was quite strange to Dad. It seems that I reminded him so much of mother. He once told me that I was so very real, yet, simultaneously ethereal, delicate to the point of intense fragility. Dad had known that this sounded like an oxymoron yet this was exactly how he'd thought of me. Intense fragility. I knew that I was the very opposite of my brother. JJ was real almost to the denial of anything non-material. He was the personification of robust physical life. I, according to Dad, of what lay within.

Like my mother, I too had often been dreamy, wandering through the ethers on gossamer wings. Like that trip to the Moon. Father had often wondered where it had all come from. Neither of the two women in his life, neither of the two Heidis, had been or were in the least bit religious. Yet we were as much at home in the clouds, dissecting or imbibing the esoteric lives of great saints, great avatars, as he was among the stars. Was there a connection? Did gods really inhabit the stars of the Milky Way. Could so many myths be wrong? Created to tease the human mind? Imagination?

When I was little, Dad told me about Via Lactis. His own un-fulfilled passion. Was there heaven at its core? Could heaven be described not only as a state of consciousness, but also as a spatial entity? Perhaps heaven was a location where no other state of con-sciousness was possible.... I knew that Dad would have given half his life to do what I seemed capable of. Of meeting mother. His wife. Just once more. Only... only I had said that Heidi was noth-ing. Or no-thing. That she wasn't there. Like the rose that was only a rose because it was not a rose. Perhaps when I saw mother, I'd been recreating her in my mind from the trails she'd left behind. Like the quarks in an atom-smasher.

"Tell me about Pluto?" I asked playing with a twig overhang-ing our little pond. As I pulled on it, the starlight reflected in the mirror surface shimmered in response.

Father smiled to his distant memories. He'd learned of the basic characteristics of Solar System so very long ago. For the most part, his work of the last twenty years lay much further afield, reaching out to distant galaxies.

"Pluto has doubled the diameter of our Solar system. From the time of Giovani Domenico Cassini it was accepted that the So-lar System was defined by the orbit of Saturn. From one end of its orbit to the other, it measured nearly three billion kilometres. The Solar System doubled again with the discovery of Uranus. Then, only as recently as 1930, Clyde William Tombaugh discovered Pluto. This discovery doubled our home again. The Solar System grew from six to twelve billion kilometres overnight. A ray of light, a photon, which can circumnavigate the earth in one seventh of a second, would now take almost half-a-day to span the Solar

System. The god of the Underworld has doubled our Outerworld. He's doubled our myopic vision."

"Why myopic?"

"We, as a race, are still preoccupied with our belly buttons. We contemplate the tips of our racial noses. We lack greater vision. Even such as some people of the past had. The poets, composers, great sculptors, painters..." his voice trailed off.

"You're a bit of a poet yourself, Dad. Why do you hide it so much?"

Father looked embarrassed. He sat up, adjusted his jacket and shook his head. Then he relaxed again.

"It's all your fault, Pet," he affirmed with new confidence.

"Not Pluto's?"

"It is you, and only you, I might add, who invokes in me the stirring of my romantic past."

There was a moment's silence. Then I said very quietly, "It's mother, isn't it?"

This time I didn't have to wait for my answer.

"Every atom in my body is impregnated with the memory of your mother. From the moment I met her, and it will remain so till I die." He then looked at me with something more than love. It seemed closer to worship. "You seem to incorporate her soul within your own, Hey. How do you do it?" This time his voice sounded lonesome.

"She is within all of us. All you have to do is open your heart, father. She is everywhere..."

"...and nowhere. You've told me that before. Everywhere and no-where."

What could I do? I smiled a little sadly. There was so little time for talking as we did right then, under the weeping willow. Dad was growing older and busier at the same time. "I didn't mean nowhere in the colloquial sense, Dad. You know that? I meant that you couldn't limit her presence to a single place. A single location."

"Then how can I find her, Pet? How can I find her?"

I could have told him that his wife, my mother, was right here, right now, even as she was everywhere else. Wherever we invoked her presence. Why was it so difficult for people to understand this simple fact? I also could have told Dad that my mother was not my mother, and only then she was my mother. It sounded too much like the dialectics expounded by a Buddhist monk. Yet there was no other way to explain it.

Just like the rose, Mother was as much part of the universe now as she'd ever been. As much as she had been when she'd walked the Earth. Only we, then, had chosen to see the image of her which we had created with our senses. We diminished her by our conceptualization. She who walked the Earth was not my mother. That was a mere image of her. Like a mirage. Like Enigma suspended nowhere, yet perceived by us in the vicinity of Pluto.

I already knew all the things father had told me about Pluto. I'd asked him to tell me about it for two reasons. First, I saw Dad visibly relaxing when asked to just sit and talk astronomy. And secondly, I kept hoping against hope that one day his eyes might open to a greater reality in which he would find progressively more peace. The nature of this inner peace is difficult to share with someone. With anyone. And I so wanted to impart it to Dad by any means possible. He'd given me so much.

"Did you ever think that the Enigma might be a construct of our minds? A focal point, a term of reference we need to explain the changes which are occurring in the world? In our Solar system?"

"A chicken and the egg?" father smiled. "Frankly, it never crossed my mind."

I waited for more. It came in a way I hadn't expected.

"Enigma was more enigmatic, to me, before other astronomers confirmed my findings. The emission, or the reflection of photons in a spectral range, didn't make any sense. Yet that was all it was. Admittedly, the enormous activity in the behaviour of outer planetary giants didn't make sense either, even after I was ready to accept some inaccuracies in the calculations of the orbital data pertaining to the inner planets. At that time I was alone. I might have allowed my imagination to stray from the purely scientific route. My findings may have been taken as being subjective. They weren't, but they may have been taken as such. And now....?"

"Now your findings have become objective. Supported by other astronomers?"

"You see the difference?"

"Yes, Dad. I see the difference. But isn't there room for both? The subjective and the objective? For the inner and the outer? For the scientist and the poet? Do the two have to live in direct opposition?

"You would have loved talking to your mother. She always saw the hand of the divine in every star, every planet, every flower opening its bud to inhale the world. She would have told you that gods have brought the Enigma into our midst to bring us closer to them."

"Could there be any truth in her... in her...?"

"...in her vision? My dear Hey, your mother saw divinity in the frog at the bottom of the garden!"

"The Zen Buddhists still do," I said quietly.

"Your mother wasn't a Buddhist. She was..." father was going to say 'normal' and caught himself. He never meant to imply that the Buddhists were not normal. Perhaps very much so. But there was something very unnerving about living with someone who rubbed shoulders with the gods of ancient India, China, Egypt, Persia, Palestine... even ancient Greece. Heidi's gods had been everywhere. And then Dad finished his sentence aloud: "...everywhere and nowhere. Like the ancient gods who once trod this earth...."

I think he'd finally begun to understand.

The world continued to unfold itself.

Under father's guidance as the newly-appointed overseer, and inspired by an article that reported that forty to fifty people in the Third World countries could live comfortably from items discarded by a single man, woman or child in North America, the Sanctuary gained still greater independence from the world outside. There was a regular traffic of goods, in and out of the Sanctuary, to be sure. But this traffic was kept to an absolute minimum. The Ogil-vians, just didn't waste as much as they used to; reuse was their preferred mode of operation, reduction came second, recycling was next, and finally elimination of redundancy completed the cycle.

The planets continued their minute adjustments, those observable only to the Monster Eye. And the stream of asteroids continued to fly past and miss the Earth. I liked to think, they were clearing up the space around Mars. Even the sun seemed to be up to something, generating unusual sunspots causing outstanding Aurora Borealis as far south as Washington DC.

Summer followed spring, winter succeeded autumn in an orderly fashion. Days extended into weeks, months into years, as Dad and I met under the weeping willow, to sit, to feel, to share brief moments torn out of the fabric of time. We both reached, each in our own way, beyond the glittering stars, whirling galaxies, stormy primordial dust-clouds where suns still waited patiently for their turn to be born. Slowly, ever so slowly, carefully, step by step, I led my father into my private alluring universe. Beckoning gently, beguiling, with words laden with promise, I drew him into my strange, elusive, enchanting reality.

Dad, like a child in a mother's arms, grew to trust me completely. Perhaps because I'd done nothing to impose my ideas on him. On his mindset. I stated my truth, as I knew it, as my mother knew it before me. Father sensed that. He sensed that somehow, by some means beyond his understanding, the two Heidis, his wife and his daughter, were both present at our little sessions, participating in his laborious journey towards a reality which did not deny his own world, yet had its being beyond both time and space. More and more, this universe which was – though it wasn't, vibrant – yet more still than the eye of a storm, commanded his attention. It was beyond the reach of the Monster Eye, beyond human eyes, beyond any senses that were integral with human personality. To reach it, he had to shed not only his senses, his body, his emotions, but even to rid himself of his awareness of ego, of that which meant John Hydon, down here, on Earth, in the palpable universe he'd so loved since childhood. Then, equally as slowly, I led him to merge with that that was both him and not him, which felt like John, yet regarded him, or himself, from without – also from within, detached, non-judgmental, indifferent yet caring, within – yet without the universe he'd once known.

It was the same universe he'd known and loved, but he saw it now as it was, had been, before it succumbed to fractal fragmentation, differentiation, when it was still one, even as he was really one, as he and I were one....

And then, one day, after years of those elusive moments under always the very same weeping willow his heart wept no more. For the briefest of moments, a shred of eternity, he and Heidi, both mother and daughter merged into a unity, which no gods could ever tear asunder. He'd learned, there and then, wherever there was and whenever then was, that time is not time, even as space is not space, and only when he accepted these truths, each individually, both merged into one, a single truth, indivisible, substantial, real.

When this merging happened for the very first time, Dad thought that he'd died. His own image of himself, the concept of who he was, had been, all his life, became hazy, indistinct, and then erased itself as though it, or he, had never existed. He sat next to his daughter, stupefied, astounded, lost, not knowing what to do with his new knowledge, which even now began receding into the realm he'd already left behind. I kissed him on the cheek, put my head on his shoulder and waited. In time he came back, alive, for time existed once more, even as the bench we sat on existed within space, within the solid, yet so diluted reality. At the same time, he felt more vibrantly alive than ever before.

For a little while he held my head to his chest, stroked my hair, unknowingly, finding his feet again in the imitation world he still loved so much. He held me close, trying to hold on to that which he'd left an instant before. Then we both rose, without a word and walked hand in hand to our home. By the time we reached our condo, father had finally recovered the rest of his senses.

"What was that?" he asked, his voice hardly above a whisper.

"You met yourself, father. Isn't it wonderful?"

***

16

Orthodoxy

The dictionary states that the word orthodox is derived, like so many of our semi-comprehensible words, from ancient Greek. Our Hellenic patriarchs were great thinkers, held fascinating opinions and, after centuries tested by time, they have often been proven right. We might say, that the ancient Greeks were orthodox.

The word is made up of *orthos*, meaning correct and *doxa*, opinion, from *dokein* meaning to think. Thus if you hold the right opinions, if you think correctly, you are orthodox. Which is exactly the claim the countless churches throughout the world held regarding themselves, thus proving, irrevocably, that perhaps none of them were orthodox.

JJ found that that which he'd started as a joke, developed as a challenge, sustained out of fascination – was not orthodox. His First World Electronic Church of the Adventist never lied, never knowingly misled its followers, never skinned them alive, burnt them at the stake, sent them into bankruptcy nor grew disgustingly and filthily rich on its ill-gotten gains. Whatever money people parted with, and that was quite substantial, was recycled into the church's activities, or distributed directly by the accountants to worthy causes. JJ's opinion of what constituted worthiness may have differed from the 'orthodox' view of things. Nevertheless, he did not grow fat, did not install solid gold bathroom fittings, did not drive a Rolls Royce, even if the car which for at least a century had stood for the splendour of the British Empire was now manufactured by the lowly Volkswagen. Even the Cessna which he'd used for his own convenience for a year or two had now been sold, at a profit, and the money returned to the electronic account.

JJ may not have been orthodox, but he was scrupulously honest. He also held no aspirations of becoming bigger and better, or richer than other churches, although that last he might have found an easy, if vaguely amusing, challenge. To be honest, JJ was tiring of his teenage prank.

"Not so," affirmed his three assistants. They had been generously rewarded for their efforts. Perhaps, too generously.

In his lighter moments JJ called them his bishops. They, due to his effortless capacity to oversee each of their contributions, referred to JJ as the *Trimurti*, from Sanskrit *Tri* and *Mûrti*, the latter meaning body or shape. Thus the three bishops were JJ's body while he was the brain.

Under the auspices of the FWECA and with JJ's approval though without his active participation, his official Triumvirate had published a half-dozen books, all playing on the theme of an imminent doomsday as supported by ancient prophecies. JJ had read the manuscripts, made sure that his name didn't appear anywhere, that the substance was honest within its own context, and gave his electronic blessing. The first three books were still riding the crest of the New York bestseller lists when the sixth and last title went to print. Orthodox or not, people hungered for what the books had to offer.

"Why do you think this happens?" he'd asked me at one of his visits.

I was at as much of a loss as he was. "Frankly, I find people quite unbelievable," I admitted. I meant the masses outside.

JJ had finished his studies at Calgary and had soon become usefully engaged at the Centre as a liaison officer with the 'Outside'. He became the shield, the rampart 'outsiders' had to jump over to gain entry for themselves, or for whatever product they were selling. As his first contribution to the welfare of the Sanctu-

ary, JJ offered, for a substantial amount of money, selective
sponsorship to various manufacturers. The Sanctuary's official
name carried a lot of clout in North America, including the USA,
even if no one really knew why. Rather like the *By appointment to
His Majesty the King* in Britain, or the Papal Auspices in the rest of
Europe. These manufacturers were allowed to use the Centre's
official designation, on condition that they would never again try to
sell their product inside the Centre itself. Father thought the whole
deal was pushing the envelope of good taste, but at that particular
time, the lens of the Monster Eye needed to be re-polished, and
Ottawa had been dragging her centipede feet with the allocation of
funds. He agreed that JJ wasn't really doing anything against anybody's will. Dad insisted, however, that it be clear that the Sanctuary was not actually using the product. His only other condition
was that the word Centre continue to be spelled the Canadian way,
with RE, not ER on the end, even on the products directed at the
American market. JJ, as usual, came up with an answer. The logo
read:

NOT TO BE SOLD AT THE
CANADIAN SCIENCE CENTRE
WITHOUT PRIOR AUTHORIZATION

What the manufacturer wanted was the name, 'Canadian Science Centre' on his label. It was spelled out in large capitals. As
for the rest of the logo, "People never read the stuff," the CEO said,
handing over a check for two million dollars.

Perhaps people really did not read that stuff. They simply
wanted some sort of affirmation of importance. JJ remembered the
countless chemicals, which were still flooding the market, each
plastered with all sorts of warnings. No one appeared to read the
small type. You could write in very small letters:

NOT TO BE TAKEN INTERNALLY UNDER ANY CIRCUMSTANCES

or perhaps even a warning that the drug is:

DANGEROUS FOR PEOPLE WHO ARE STILL ALIVE

providing you added below, or above, or anywhere in large, bold
type:

USE AS RECOMMENDED BY YOUR DOCTOR

you were all right. For years, no one could get to within shouting
distance of 'their' doctor. Four-hour waits in the emergency and
three-minute consultations with GP's didn't really allow for reliable diagnoses. People would continue to pop pills at regular intervals, in case they survived. Perhaps their inherent death-wish was
responsible for the unmitigated success of JJ's First World Electronic Church of the Adventist.

At first, the other churches disapproved of JJ's ecclesiastic activities. Rather like the Jesuits, so many years ago. Then, they tried to
emulate JJ's methods. After all, they were mostly Orthodox. They
had to be right. Righteous. Infallible. Above all others. JJ wasn't
– nor was his Church. The only reason he didn't invite discussion
was that neither he, nor his full time lieutenants had the time nor
the inclination to enter into personal polemics. The official Internet
Page of the Church did, however, encourage active participation in
about three hundred chat-rooms, which had sprung up since JJ himself had initiated the original two.

So the Orthodoxy fought a loosing battle. And they'd so
wanted to join the bandwagon. The near calamitous economic state
of many countries, the pessimistic prognoses of oncoming famines,
plagues, earthquakes, extensive conflagrations of forests, inundations of tens of thousands of acres, made people immune to the vast
assortment of dreary consequences of "Not being members of this
or that particular Church". The tried and tested orthodox scare tactics no longer worked. People were not afraid to go to hell when
they were already in it. Or nearly so.

Also, there is an art to scaring people.

You must show them, whenever possible, that maybe, just
maybe there is a way out. An escape from the mess they got them-

selves into. That some of them will survive. Only JJ did not offer
salvation within his Church, but through knowledge he'd provided
over the years. After all, we still lived in the Information Society.
Knowledge was money and money was... Well, he'd never got to
explain what money really was. Money never interested JJ, except
as a game of outwitting the world. To other churches, doomsday
was no laughing matter. What threatened the survival of their particular sect was much more gloomy than whatever might happen to
the world.

And then, one day a group of very orthodox churches got together, pooled their resources, and began a campaign against any
form of exploration outside the panting, polluted, abused Mother
Earth. God created man to live and prosper on Earth, they said, to
take command of his environment and all that walks and runs and
creeps and flies and swims on within or above the earth. This was
their version of Genesis.

> *Be fruitful and multiply, said God, and replenish*
> *the earth, and subdue it, said God, and have dominion*
> *over the fish of the sea and over the fowl of the air and*
> *over every living thing that moveth upon the earth, said*
> *God. He said nothing about flying higher up, or to the*
> *Moon or anywhere higher than that. Nor did God say*
> *anything about peeking higher than the God-given eye*
> *could see.*

The 'higher up' had been defined as above the *fowl of the air*,
but lower than the upper atmosphere. They had to offer some latitude as they needed the communication satellites to promulgate
their orthodox message.

JJ saw red.

He took their ravings as a personal attack on the very nucleus
of the Sanctuary, which was still the Monster Eye. And the Eye
was his own father's right hand tool, his life, his pleasure and satisfaction. It also amused his sister, and there was little JJ wouldn't
have done for his sister.

JJ's reaction was swift and furious. With his expertise in Ancient Prophecies he extracted from his now extensive electronic library a number passages which prophesied that man was intended to venture to the stars, that all who were ignorant of this fact were in danger of Eternal Fire. That last threat he borrowed from his opposition. They loved threatening their faithful with Eternal Fire. It was like a popular sport with them. The Orthodoxy loved all things that couldn't be proven or disproved. It gave them all the latitude they needed to be eminently orthodox. JJ sent out his reply to his millions of readers and waited.

In contrast to JJ's own reaction, the counterattack was relatively slow coming. It took a year before people began to write threatening letters to the Orthodox Coalition. They objected to being scared by Hell or any other institution of posthumous correction. Twelve months to the day that the Orthodoxy had begun their propaganda, their righteousness, not to mention explicit opinions, had become more subdued. They went back to the angels in Heaven, and Heaven was once more way up there, and we should all try to rise up the best way we knew how.

"For those who are serious, of course, the best way is offered right here, on these pages, adorning your computer screen," said the Coalition.

Indeed the new, completely redesigned Internet Page of the Orthodox Coalition was awash with cute little pink cupids, baby angels, with tiny wings propelling their plump little bodies all over the computer screen. Heaven was back in style. The orthodox style. Way up there and even further.

According to JJ, orthodoxy wasn't limited to the established churches. There was also another orthodoxy determined to stop any branch of science from evolving. JJ thought that this trend might have originated in the days when the Church and the Protectors of knowledge had been one and the same. In ancient Egypt, the two were synonymous. Centuries later, Socrates was among the first lambs to be sacrificed on the altar of orthodoxy. The ancient priests of Rome guarded their knowledge from the eyes of the

masses lest they lose their ignorance and start thinking for themselves. As late as in the 16th century, Galileo paid with his freedom
for daring to publish *De Revolutionibus Orbium Coelestium,* without the churches approval. The scientific/religious establishment
afforded equal contempt to any and all supporters of 'wild raving'
that dared to oppose the Aristotelian geocentric view of the universe. Giordano Bruno's belief in the plurality of inhabited worlds
derived from Copernican theories cost him his life.

Orthodoxy . . . the scourge on human intellect.

In time, there was a gradual separation of Church and Knowledge but not without the two repeatedly crossing swords. The
stories of Galileo's reputed peccadilloes against the ruling sacerdotal Orthodoxy were well known. What was less known was the
ongoing battle that ensued soon after the various scientific orthodox factions lost their grip or control over peoples' minds. In early
Italian Renaissance of 15th and 16th centuries, Dante still steeped in
medieval thought, gave people the Divine Comedy which he wrote
in a vulgar tongue, not in Latin, that kept the common man in abject ignorance and reliance on the Church. Boccacio and Petrarch
followed, directing man's mind to secular ideas. This war led directly to The Reformation, Protestantism, mass emigrations to the
North American Continent and the liberation of the Northern States
of Europe from the Orthodoxy of the Church.

This wasn't an anti-religious movement, merely anti-
orthodoxy. People demanded freedom to pursue knowledge. On
their own.

The scientists, he'd told me, had not waited long to initiate
their own hierarchy based on exclusion. Each generation held on
tightly to the established norms, standing in direct opposition to
younger scientists who not only rejected the old, erroneous assumptions, but actually began publishing their own findings in the so-
called popular press. This time Secular Orthodoxy lost its claim to
exclusivity. JJ recalled reading about young Einstein who had
found himself the pariah of the scientific establishment. Apart
from the scientific disdain he'd been afforded for his unorthodox
theories, the German scientific community rejected him because he
was a Jew, the French, because he wasn't French and only the

USA, brand new on the horizon of orthodoxy, embraced him with relative warmth.

Finally, Quantum Mechanics all but destroyed the scientific orthodoxy with a single blow. After the orderly world in which "God did not play dice with the universe", to lean on Albert's sentiment, the Quantum Theory upset not only all previous scholarship, but reduced it to little more than intelligent speculation.

"Nothing is certain, they said, we can only approximate our knowledge of the universe. We can't be sure, we shall always have to live with the uncertainty principle." JJ's eyes shone with holy, or perhaps unholy, fervour.

There were just too many unknowns, too many factors to take into consideration. One thing affected another, the world was in a constant flux. What was right one minute, might be wrong the next. For a scientific classicist, an orthodox scholar, this was most upsetting. They needed to rely on things that were indisputable, reliable, solid and permanent. This fluid universe full of motion and change was all wrong. It was really upsetting. Reality was becoming hazy.

"Jung said that the individual is the only reality. There is none other," JJ muttered under his breath.

While at the University of Calgary, JJ had met some of the orthodox scientists. It wasn't that they'd openly denied the latest rungs on the scientific scale, it was that they did not really believe that those rungs led anywhere. Like some of their sacerdotal forefathers, they thought, or at least hoped, that the latest discoveries would turn out to be just a passing fad, like dozens of Protestant factions, each laying claim, at least for a while, to orthodoxy. To being right. To having the right opinion.

They weren't right. But they had the right to claim righteousness. Thanks to those they'd quietly despised, they now lived in a free world. Scientifically speaking, of course. He or she, the young and inexperienced scientists may be right, they conceded. But deep down they knew that it wouldn't be for long. That the old and the tried would prevail. Be vindicated. As if the truth was a liquid which one could pour from one laboratory test tube to another.

"**It all had its root** in the uncertainty. People, the so-called common man, man lacking higher education, had to learn to live in un-
certain times, and they found it difficult. They searched for sta-
bility. No longer just the priests or the scientists, but all people.
The masses. They all needed to be right. To find a rock to lean on.
The world had become too fluid. Like the inundations brought
about by the melting polar icecaps, which had swept thousands of
coastal acres under the advancing oceans, only to heave and push
up new lands, close by, as though to make up for previous loss," JJ
said at the end of his review of the Orthodoxy. He'd been asked to
do so by the CSC as a private commission.

"I think the Earth is cleansing herself," I said thinking of the
inundations. "She is doing her spring cleaning."

We had finished dinner and were enjoying a *digestif.*

David smiled but he did not have a scientific theory to offer.
Indeed. If the Earth wanted to cleanse her lands of human waste
there was hardly a better method. He'd racked his brains to find an
answer that would satisfy his intellect, not just his heart. I could
easily do the latter. But he was as helpless as Dad was with his
planetary adjustments.

The dinner had not been imbued with the same relaxed atmosphere that usually made our get-togethers such a delightful escape
from everyday problems. We all felt the weight of the uncon-
trolled, unexplainable changes, in which the human spirit could
perhaps thrive, but caused the mind and the body to rebel. Dad
also felt out of sorts. As long as he was left to his Monster Eye,
and had time to delve into the mysteries of the Central Halo, the
core, the heart, perhaps the Black Hole, he was happy. Lately the
exigencies of his office, let alone the constant trips to NASA, were
taking a heavy toll on his slowly but irrevocably advancing years.

"If they only got their hands dirty with some honest work,
they wouldn't have time to worry." Dad was referring to his last
trip south. "We have the trade unions to thank for that. They gave
the masses cake, but they forgot that by bread alone a man liveth
not. Not even by a chocolate cake with a double layer of sugar
candy."

This was the frustration talking. The kind he felt whenever he'd left the Sanctuary for any length of time.

"You know, they spend half the time telling me when they last ate a good steak? Or a chicken? Or any meat? Would you believe that? And they are scientists! They are engaged in the most fascinating project in man's history and they worry about their menu!" Father's voice rose uncharacteristically, "I'm telling you, they are mad. Plain stark MAD!"

The Americans, who had been used to affluence and abundance, could not be altogether blamed. Their herds of cows, extensive chicken farms, sheep, even millions of salmon raised in artificial pools, had all developed contagious diseases. Before their produce was eliminated from the market, people had died by the hundreds of thousands. It was even worse in Asia. There – millions died. All for the want of a chicken wing. But in the United States mass production was the byword of industry. They lived by it. They obeyed its laws. The National Banks, International Conglomerates had bought out the small farmers long before there was any danger of infection. Decentralization remained the only hope.

"Only, some said, it was already too late," father continued. "No farmer would go back to rising at dawn, working eighty-hour weeks, just to feed the obese masses. Yes, still obese. How do they do it? Let them eat cake, they said. Or junk food. We've done our bit. Talk to the banks. They've screwed me, was their answer. Can we blame them? Can anyone?"

It all came out of Dad's lips like venom. He needed to stay in the Sanctuary. He needed a rest.

No one made any comments.

There were a few small farmers left. They supplied the market at prices, which a decade ago would have boggled the mind. The few remaining peasants had become the new barons, lords of the manor, commanding their own price.

"And who can blame them?" Dad repeated his own question. "For years they've been squeezed to within an inch of their life by the rich and powerful, and now they want their share. Only.... it's all based on greed. Greed and indifference to other people's fate."

"Like in the good old days," JJ put in with a smirk. "Only now the shoe is on the other foot."

"Boys! Boys! I'll have none of that!"

This was Miriam. I'd remained silent throughout Dad's eulogy over the human race, but Miriam would not have it any more.
She felt responsible for the atmosphere in her house. "We mustn't
wallow in our own misery. Or anybody else's. Whatever happens,
happens for our good. It's an opportunity to learn."

I got up, walked around the table and planted a big kiss on
Aunt Miriam's cheek. "I should have said that, Miriam. Thank
you."

"I really mean it, my dear. There have been tough moments
in human history before. Look at the holocaust of my people.
Look at the Black Hole of Calcutta, the World Wars, even the cycles of Ice Ages. Imagine what they must have been like. They
survived. We survived. Not all, but enough of us to continue."

"Continue what?" JJ asked in half tone. "To keep making the
same mistakes?"

"No JJ. To keep making new ones. Mistakes are by far the
best way to learn. If we open our eyes and ears to the possibilities."

"I agree one hundred percent," Father joined in. "And there
are worse things that can happen to man than death. It is the death
of the spirit. And here, in the Sanctuary it will not happen." Father
got up and stretched his legs.

"One thing is certain," he said, "that the only poison which
threatens our survival is stasis, or remaining in the same mindset
for any length of time. Look where such attitude led in the past.
Nature demands mutation, progress, evolution. We've all grown
too comfortable. Too content with the life of Riley. It is time to
pull up our sleeves."

We all agreed. Only no one was sure where exactly we were
to channel our particular talents. We all had our assigned tasks,
and we all loved our work. Our efforts, for the most part, kept us
happy and satisfied. But none of us had any idea how to help the
rest of the world, so bent on self-annihilation. Was this how it was
meant to be? Will only those who refuse to follow the trend survive?

By the time we got home, we were considerably more relaxed. JJ had come in just to say goodnight. Dad clicked on the
TV News.

"The End is at Hand!" was splashed across the screen.

"My goodness," I couldn't help exclaiming. "JJ, is this
yours?"

It wasn't. With a feeling of disgust, Dad switched off the offensive title. The world was still beautiful, full of challenges. Full
of problems to solve. What more could one ask? JJ said he'd
wondered if he shouldn't scrap his Adventist Church and start an
Electronic Church of Immortality. To research the same prophecies and interpret them with a new twist. They say that the Bible
is a book of all things to all men. Perhaps the other Scriptures
would offer the same flexibility.

"It would be a new challenge for my spare time," he said.
"What there is of it. What if I could prove to people, millions of
them the world over, that they are inherently immortal? Like their
genes? Like their spirit?" There was a gleam in his eye.

I was flabbergasted. He was on a roll:

"Only – if I do venture into such a new unknown, I would assure my followers that my version of reality is not orthodox. That
it is as fluid, as free, as the uncertainty principle of the Quantum
Theory. Didn't Matthew write that according to your faith be it
unto you? Something like that. Even he agreed that reality is
whatever you believe in. Eh, Sis?"

Again I felt stunned. "Is there nothing you cannot prove by
using the scriptures?"

"I don't know," he answered shrugging. "I've never tried to
prove *nothing* yet. "

He had to dodge my slipper aimed at his head.

I strongly suspected that JJ didn't feel in the least bit guilty.
He had noted, over the years, that most people he'd met lived in a
constant struggle between the desire to remain firmly attached to
their traditions, and an equal and opposite urge to be, what they
referred to as being: born again. Not just the Christians, nor even
in terms of reincarnation so firmly imbedded in practically all
Asian philosophies. The Hindus overtly claimed to want to get off
the Wheel of Awagawan, the Cycle of Reincarnation, but they did

little to accomplish this end. JJ thought it had its base in the innate
longing for new ideas. For a new lease on life. A future. Right
down here. On Earth.

By the time he finished raving, I'd told him that it was much
easier to be born again than to grow up. I knew I was right. But
not everybody wanted to leave the racial kindergarten.

"But, it really does sound like an interesting idea," JJ's eyes
reached out to some distant star. "Not the 'nothing', but the 'immortality'. I can see it now, splashed across the computer screen in
large letters: THE FIRST ELECTRONIC CHURCH OF
IMMORTALITY!"

By then, I'd given up. There was no keeping up with my brother. But, grudgingly, I couldn't help admiring his inexhaustible
mental energy.

"Perhaps the word Immortality could be spelled out in large
capital letters. It has a nice ring to it. Immortality always fasci-
nates people. The masses have always refused to recognize death
as an integral part of life. I often wondered why?"

He could go on like this for hours....

I dreamt I was walking in the Garden of Eden. There were so
very few people around that I felt lonely. The next day JJ took me
for a drive to Whitehorse. He needed to pick up some computer
stuff. Waiting for him, I walked the shopping mall. I felt the same
way I'd felt in the Garden of Eden. Only the beauty was missing.

It was really strange. In spite of the mulling masses, I felt just
as lonely as I did in my dream.

***

17

NASA

Father's first impression of Florida was one of disappointment. He found it flat, dull and boring. He changed his opinion somewhat after he'd met the people at the Kennedy Space Centre. They were a race apart. They were much closer to his own way of thinking than virtually anyone else he'd met in the USA. One fundamental difference remained. Most Americans he'd met were result oriented. This was the American way, after all. Father had always regarded the trip more fascinating. The people down south, preferred the destination.

There is a bit of that desire in all of us. We all need an occasional pat on the back. We need to see the results of our labours. For Dad it was harder. After all, for many years he'd spent the majority of his time on, often futile, observations. He hadn't created the galaxies, the stars he'd been observing. It was more like writing a book, which could never be finished. Not for as long as the universe remained infinite.

But Dad still liked his southern counterparts.

Not that they were all astronomers, but like at home, at the Sanctuary, they were scientists striving for knowledge. In a way, by learning about the universe, he was learning about himself. Carl

Sagan once said that we are the Universe's way of knowing about itself.

Father shared this sentiment. The scientists he met at NASA were a divers group of people. Some were more open to knowledge, for its own sake, others were driven almost exclusively by the end result. "Never mind why or who, just tell me how," they would say. How to design, how to construct, how to make it safe, last, durable, airtight, thermally adequate, fire-resistant, and a great many other 'hows'. The 'hows' consumed ninety percent of their life. 'Why' was controlled by a different department. Probably in Washington.

"They are to us, what the Romans were to the Greeks," Dad told us after one of his first trips south.

Of course, their methods yielded results. It was just that NASA results were always very specific. There was nothing general about them. They dealt with a part, not with the whole. But, to repeat, their method yielded results. It had given them the Moon Base. Or at least a good beginning towards one.

With Dad's help.

Father thought this orientation towards tangible results had a detrimental effect on seeing the big picture. They, the scientists, chopped up projects into several departments, each working their fingers to the bone, while neglecting the over all coordination. They each epitomized the age of specialization, where every team knew almost everything about almost nothing. The administration, of which Washington remained the shining example, epitomized the very opposite. They knew next to nothing about almost everything. Regrettably, it had been the administrators who had assigned, or 'administered', vast sums of money exclusively at their own insidious discretion, with the understanding that they, for the most part, were bereft of any sense of discretion whatsoever.

Until some five years ago, the Americans had been obsessed with the idea of a manned landing on Mars. It has been known for generations that Mars's orbit is some 35 million miles from Earth. At 25,000 miles an hour, the escape velocity from Earth, it would take at least two months to get there. Yet in spite of all these well known facts, apparently no one thought of the volume of food needed to maintain the astronauts' bodies and soul together. A vastly preferred condition, even in space. They were busy preparing best possible menus, rather than calculating the staggering volume required. That, at NASA, would be a different department.

Dad thought it would be near impossible to feed the astronauts on the way to Mars, let alone to keep them there for, say, another two months, and then during another two months on the way back. That's six months of food for, say, six astronauts, or the equivalent of what one man or woman would eat and drink in three years on Earth.

"Did you look into your refrigerator lately?"

He smiled at his listeners. All the eyes were directed at him, hanging on his every word.

"Mary told me that food and drink in our fridge usually lasts for about three days, say a little under a week for one person. Now multiply that by thirty-six, arrange the freezers side by side and you have a fridge some ninety feet long. Don't forget to add breathable air and additional fuel required to reach an escape velocity from Mars of at least 5,600 meters/second, or 12,600 miles per hour." Dad's tone oscillated between incredulity and abject exasperation.

"Couldn't they find return fuel on Mars?" I tried to help.

"Perhaps. Given a few years to find it, adapt it and find a means of storing it, they might. But then multiply your fridges by a factor of six, as in six astronauts." Father shook his head. Of course, neither Dad nor myself knew anything much about astronauts. But there was such a thing as common sense. Or was that also a different department?

"It would seem," father just mused aloud, "that it would be a lot easier to move the Moon Base into Mars's orbit and go on from there. There would be no rush if the Base were self-sufficient. Of course some people might object to loosing their Blue Moon and all the resultant pregnancies, but, perhaps, in time, the Moon Base, together with the attendant and firmly attached Moon, would return to inspire forlorn lovers...."

I tried to imagine the Moon drifting leisurely towards Mars.... The logistics were verging on the absurd.

On the other hand.... I was hard put to silence the stirrings of unbridled imagination.

"As for the air required by the crew," Dad was still talking, "this is another very special problem. Our Sanctuary devotes over seventy percent of its surface area to the generation of oxygen, and the air is still being supplemented with exterior vents. There wouldn't be any on Mars, let alone in transit. All the oxygen and other gasses for breathable air would have to be carted to and fro." Again father's voice was approaching exasperation. He sounded defeated.

"Hibernation?" I put in hopefully.

"Perhaps," he nodded but wouldn't discuss the matter any further.

I only learned later why. Scientists found it much easier to put someone into deep hibernation than to bring them out of it. After seven years of experiments, and eleven untimely deaths, the research program had been scrapped. To give the Americans their due, all the human guinea pigs had been volunteers.

Yet, in spite of all of the challenges, there were still people at NASA obsessed with the idea of a manned landing. It was too late to send Twigg himself. He was long gone to the big spaceship in the sky. At least he couldn't do any more harm. While common people hated stupidity, this trait, under many different guises, had become synonymous with politics. They called them the Senate Appropriation Committees, Jurisdictional Committees, Budgetary Committees, Bi-partisan Committees, Get-me-out-of-this-mess Committees and such like, which corresponded in Canada to the single vast subject of innumerable Royal Commissions and Public Inquiries. In the meantime, Earth, as a whole, was falling on hard times. Since Twigg, four presidents had come and gone, but the Martian bug he'd planted still infected some of the best minds in NASA. They just wouldn't be denied. At least, quite recently, at some 400 feet below the surface, they'd found ice. It took seventeen unmanned missions, trillions of dollars, but they'd found it. By drilling. I remember Dad telling Dr. Mendel about it, back home. He'd put it in a peculiar way.

"You know Dave, divinity is like water, it always finds its lowest level," he'd said.

But again, I'm running ahead of myself.

Actually father may have been thinking of little *moi* lurking under the shining surface of Enigma. Can we really define divinity, I wondered? Perhaps gods do not reside among the stars but lurk below Earth's surface. Perhaps, like Orpheus, they've been lured into the underworld in search of Eurydice....

Scientists at NASA seemed detached from common sense, even as we were from the exigencies of the world outside the Sanctuary. They had splendid achievements, to be sure, but those achievements had always been in fields that were relatively narrow. When greater coordination was required, they seemed to loose the ground under their feet. Their loss was my father's gain. They needed his mind, his character, his vision to convert a dozen geodesic domes into a Moon Colony. And it took all of father's talents and experience to accomplish this noble aim.

The reason for this latest trip to NASA was as exciting for Dad as for everyone involved with the Moon Base. Last week, men working in the sixth dome – the largest so far and almost twice the diameter of the largest one at CSC – had discovered an underground lake and, by sonar, the engineers had already confirmed that the frozen lake would quintuple the assumed water availability on the Moon. The sixth dome just touched the very edge of the lake and the first drilling confirmed that the new source was potable. This in itself was a near miracle, as the previous tappings had required considerable purification.

NASA had many questions for father.

"What should we do with all this bounty?"

"Should we save it for later?"

"Extract it and hold it on the surface?"

"Increase the number of domes?"

"Apply it to the creation of a new biosphere?"

Save it for later? They suddenly became obsessed with savings. Most un-American.

The Americans still tended to regard the Moon Base only as a staging ground for further exploration of the Solar System. The engineers had done their job. Father had been presented with a neatly typed list of one hundred-eighty questions, which he had been expected to arrange in order of priority. They could have sent him the list by Internet, but they felt the need for personal consultation to set the general direction.

"Frankly, Johnny, we have no idea what to do with all that water. We don't really need a pool for the staff yet," one of the men quipped. This was the first time in fifty years that anyone had addressed Dr. John Hydon as Johnny. People down south liked to be informal. Sometimes.

No one laughed. It had cost them over seventy million dollars just to drill for that water. All energy had been imported. Father couldn't believe they still hadn't made effective use of solar power. With temperature on the Moon rising to over a 100° C and complete absence of any cloud cover, it must have been possible. As for the water, it might cost even more to bring it to the surface. The specialists needed someone to set them on the straight and narrow.

They were in dire need of a Big Picture.

Dad wouldn't put it plainly, not yet, but he would lead them towards building a Sanctuary. Yes, a Sanctuary on the Moon. Not just an astronomical observatory, or a Staging Station for further space exploration – as some of them still considered it – but a *bona fide* Sanctuary. With all it entailed. Why not? If he didn't, the Appropriation Committee would only disperse the funds to their favourite charities, which consisted mostly of their private interests, succeeding only in to making the rich richer.

Father had told me that he would have to play his cards close to his chest. To tell them immediately that he could see some fifty domes, of which half would be there for the sole purpose of generating breathable air and food, would be met with instant rejection. He would have to tread gently yet accelerate the construction program as much as possible. He'd decided to ask JJ to join him. Father knew well enough how to talk to his own people. JJ could also handle strangers, or relative strangers, with ease. A strange sort of talent.

By noon the next day, JJ knocked on father's door. By 1600 hours he had all the necessary security clearances and was now the official liaison officer, between NASA and John Hydon, the Head Honcho of the Canadian Science Centre. By 1900 hours, that same day, JJ and father were having dinner in father's NASA suite. When a very pretty corporal had finally cleared the plates, Dad leaned over the table and asked JJ a seemingly innocent question. His voice was conspiratorial, his eyes shining.

"How would you like to go to the Moon, son?"

"I would rather visit Andromeda, Dad. Could I finish this first?" JJ was still sipping his coffee.

A moment later JJ realized that his father wasn't joking. He opened his mouth to speak but Dad shook his head. "I still feel stiff from the flight," he said, "Let's go for a stroll."

Outside father told JJ that while he liked and admired his NASA friends, he suspected that since a certain date in September, some three decades ago, they'd suffered from a hefty dose of persecution mania. Although there had been no reported acts of terrorism for over seven years, at least not in the USA, they still liked to bug all rooms where any classified information might be disseminated. Anyway, father really wanted to take a walk.

It was strange strolling under an open sky, without the protective latticework of tubes overhead. He'd never realized he'd actually missed it till about five years ago on his first visit to Florida. His Ottawa trips consisted of a series of transfers from one vehicle to another, to a conference room and then back again. Other than a few times in Florida, he hadn't taken a stroll in Ottawa, or anywhere else outside the Sanctuary, in at least twenty years. And now, not only the deep blue of the sky but the endless horizon of the Atlantic brought back memories of his youth. It was hard to believe that he'd spent half of his adult life under a glass dome. When he'd arrived in Canada he'd just turned forty-three. Now, he was on the wrong side of sixty. Except that he felt just as young as thirty years ago. He truly did.

"So Dad," JJ asked once they'd cleared the buildings, "what bee is humming under your bonnet this time?"

Father told JJ about the underground lake. "We still can't be sure about the precise volume of water, but if contained and recycled fully..."

"...it would last forever?" JJ was already ahead of his boss. "So when are you planning to move us, Dad?"

Father laughed. He loved his son's enthusiasm. There was never any hesitation in JJ's voice. No 'are you sure, Dad?' 'Did you examine all the factors?' Just: 'let's go!' attitude. Contrary to the NASA people, JJ never asked how. He asked when.

"It's going to take some clever insider trading." Father used the stock market expression. "We must offer them what they haven't got, and want to trade for it at a profit. Also, we must make *them* make an offer to *us*. Otherwise, Washington will push their own people."

"We can offer our lives," JJ suggested.

Dad told me later that he'd looked at his son with renewed admiration. It had been this sort of spirit that had won the West. Now, it could win us the Moon.

"That's not a bad bargain. Judging by the problems they have with getting people to build the base, it could be a good trade."

Father hadn't told JJ, as yet, that fully one half of the cost of the Moon Base went to the salaries, insurance and bonuses for the crew. Americans still had it so good, that few of them wanted to sacrifice their relative wealth. The days of conscription were long gone. In this day and age, when a professional athlete could command an annual twenty million-dollar salary, getting people to risk their lives on the Moon did not come cheap. They had no more volunteers. They only had scalpers.

"It would save them a fortune..." JJ mused aloud.

Actually JJ had read the budget breakdowns a year ago. Since that time, the figures must have gone up. After all, Washington didn't make any secret of them. The allocation of funds was one of few budgetary appropriations the President and the Senate Committees had been proud of. JJ recalled the original announcement. He was a boy then. The President and the House Leader had been holding hands: "We do it for Mankind!" the House Leader announced proudly. "It is our gift to Humanity," added the President raising the House Leader's arm in a victorious greeting.

"Today the Moon, tomorrow the World!"

This announcement raised the roof. The chamber roared in unrestrained elation.

"I've been thinking along the same lines. Only.... are you sure our people would go for it?" Father didn't quite share JJ's youthful enthusiasm.

"Just how far do you think *they* would go?" JJ studied his father's face. He was referring to the Americans, not the Canadian volunteers.

"I don't know. But as far as water is concerned, my first calculations suggest a possibility of some forty domes, each up to a kilometre in diameter. Remember that the Moon has only one-sixth our gravity. It would be relatively easy to go up to two kilometres although I don't see the need..."

Father told me later that JJ's eyes were shining like never before. He must have felt like he was back in school planning subterfuge behind the Jesuits' back. Only this time it was Washington. And NASA. But the fun was the same.

"I think we must think this out at Dave's. With closed doors."

"Will you give them anything now?" JJ asked.

"The NASA people? I must. Any ideas?"

JJ was there because of his ideas. "Tell them that they should plan for doubling the appropriations. Maybe more. Say.... tripling them. Tell them that the President, the Senate, the House of Representatives and all the higher echelons of NASA will go down in history. For ever. Maybe longer."

Father remembered smiling. JJ had studied both psychology and history of philosophy. He knew more about human nature than most people at the Sanctuary.

"You think this will work?"

"Americans understand money. They're good at it. What they long for is immortality."

JJ grinned to himself. He never realized that his chat with me about immortality might take this little twist. "Perhaps I could... no, that would be pushing it..." He discarded the idea of stringing the Washington crowd onto the First World Electronic Church of Immortality. After all, you can't fool all the people all the time. And anyway, this was serious.

"It might work at that," Dad conceded. There was less and less one could be proud of in the field of politics. No new continents to conquer, no new wars to fight, no economical breakthroughs. Nothing much to excite anyone. There was the Moon. There and then, father decided to make the President of the United States immortal.

"Long live President Black!" JJ raised and imaginary glass.

"May he live long and prosper!" Father joined in the toast.

"If not longer..."

JJ had not been so excited for years. What a wonderful idea Dad had. To move the whole Sanctuary to the Moon. At least that was what he'd imagined. What else? Just wait 'til I tell Hey. Imagine jumping up in one-sixth Earth's gravity. Imagine flying with your own wings. Imagine being a bird. Imagine the view!

How do I know all this?

JJ did tell me all, in minute detail, the moment he'd returned. In fact he hadn't finished telling me till the early hours the next morning. And he came back the next day to tell me more. He was like a kid who had been just given his favourite toy. The best toy in the world.

So that's about the size of it," father concluded. "It wouldn't have to be a permanent arrangement for all of us, but the centre of operations, so to speak, would move higher up."

There was a momentary silence. Then, first David then the other three men around the table raised their hands and began a slow clap. Then they rose to their feet and each in turn walked to father and gave him a hug. They were the old brigade. The founding fathers of the Sanctuary.

"You're a genius, my friend!"

"There is nowhere I would rather die!"

"I can't wait!"

"Good luck! To all of us!"

Finally father raised his hand to sit them down. "Don't jump to any conclusion. We are on the right track. But we haven't crossed all the t's nor put dots over all the i's. My friend at NASA has submitted a report to Washington asking for the requisite appropriations. I told them that if approved, I can cut their maintenance costs by more than half."

"You mean we would get paid for working up there?"

This was Miriam. Even her eyes, not as young and sparkling as some years ago, seemed to have acquired a new gleam.

Dad nodded. "Not as much as the Americans. But... well, these are details."

He couldn't get over these people. Apart from JJ and myself, they were no longer young. Middle aged at best. Yet not a single question had been asked about any inherent dangers or about danger money. These people were of a very different breed.

I recall father looking around the table. What a difference he must have observed in the eyes of his friends and colleagues. Regardless of age, they all seemed to have asked 'when'. Never mind 'how'. There was always a way, within reason, of course. Not one of them would volunteer to go to Mars. They were not stupid. But the Moon? Why, the Moon was practically next door.

David Mendel stood up and raised his glass.

"Here's to John, our friend, our leader, our inspiration!"

"He keeps us young!" added Miriam.

They all raised their glasses. Yes, Dad must have thought, smiling in satisfaction. It was good to have friends. It was good to be young. Again.

JJ no longer lived with us. I had twice moved out to my own apartment, and twice I'd come back. I simply wasn't interested in proving my maturity to anyone. The other reason I'd decided to remain sharing a condo with Dad was Mary. For so many years she had looked after me, now she needed a little help herself. There was no question of letting her go because she no longer coped with some of her duties. Mary Bodkins was family. She was Grandma; a friend. And frankly, she was no hardship for me either. All she needed was a little help with shopping, particularly when Dr. Hydon had 'formal' guests. Other than that, she was pretty well self-sufficient.

I spent most of my time running various astronomical tasks for father. By then, I was a fully accredited astronomer, if not in letters, then in practice. In fact, when anyone had problems understanding some particularly difficult results, I often took over and usually managed to find answers. I seemed capable of sublimating myself completely and become, so to speak, one with the object of my study. Father told me that he'd never seen such powers of concentration. It was good to hear.

"You are the best acquisition the Observatory has ever made," he told me.

"Since they got you, Dad," I smiled back.

JJ, on the other hand, moved out the moment he'd been offered the position of the liaison. He was the roving ambassador, an ambassador at large, often roaming the world in the interests of the Sanctuary. Occasionally there was need of rare specialized electronic equipment, the latest medical diagnostic paraphernalia, or even the very latest in portable computers. Those monsters went out of date faster then he could buy them. JJ would disappear for a week at a time, and come back with a delivery date, often in half the time and for half the money. JJ was very good with people.

Sometimes, when Dad visited the Mendels, JJ dropped in on me. We would split a pizza on the terrace, with a good Sanctuary beer to wash it down. Asking me for confidence, he kept me up to date about the Moon Base possibilities. He was surprised at my apparent lack of enthusiasm. Of course, I'd already heard all about it from Dad.

"It would be fantastic," he assured me. "Can you just imagine?"

"Yes, JJ. I can. The universe is a magnificent place."

"But..."

"JJ, I've told you before. My personal happiness is not related to external conditions. I shall be as happy on the Moon as I am right here, right now."

He tried to infect me with his own enthusiasm. He failed. I was happy for him, for Dad. For the opportunities such a venture would offer. But those things were not really what made me tick. I knew that I could close my eyes and, in no time at all fly to the Moon. It was that easy. And it was getting easier every day. Only I still wasn't clear what was the purpose of my peculiar abilities. My body seemed necessary only for my activities down here, on

Earth. My mind, or soul, or whatever it was when I was not I, was quite another matter. Like Dad, I had already met myself. Many times. But I doubted there would be a time when I would get to know myself fully. But the search was what fascinated me most.

**

18

Enigma once more

This time I hadn't moved at all. At least, I hadn't experienced
any sensation of movement. The lustrous globe, previously giving
an impression of a medium sized planet, had now shrunk to a large
ball, no more than a few feet in diameter. There it hung, silently,
just a yard or two above my head.

It wasn't as though I could actually see it.

The only way I knew it was there at all was by observing the
reflections on its surface. The walls of my bedroom curved upwards on all sides away from me, upwards, extending from the
image of my body, reclining on the bed. This arched, distorted
spherical reflection of, unmistakably, my own body, was the only
awareness of my outer self that I recognized. Slim, ethereal, lying
prone, motionless, perfectly relaxed. It seemed to belong to someone else. The moment I saw the globe, or the reflections in it, I
knew it was the Enigma – the mysterious sphere heretofore at-

tached by invisible strings to the other side of Pluto. Only much, much smaller. It seemed tailor-made for my bedroom.

It was only at that moment, when the idea of its size crossed my disembodied mind that I became aware of its scale. Never before had I thought of the Enigma in terms of size. It was what it was. It reflected physical reality. The universe. Or my bedroom. It reflected reality yet remained apart from it. Time and space, and therefore size as such, seemed to have bypassed it, ignored it. And now, apparently, so did the movement and distance from its original source. Or position. It just was. Irrelevant to the normal, everyday, material actuality. Heretofore, the Enigma had been experienced as a physical object, albeit of unique properties, but a phenomenon observable by my five senses. This was an aspect of Enigma that so far had remained hidden. Or, as I learned later, it remained the same whereas I have changed. Evolved? My own senses have developed to a higher or at least different level of perception.

I kept very still waiting for what, if anything, would happen next.

For an indefinite period, though I had no awareness of the passage of time, nothing did. It was there, I was there, reflected, inanimate, in abeyance. It remained as motionless, as intangible as I felt at that moment. The only thing I recognized was the strange affinity I held for it. It was as though I was not really apart from the effulgent sphere. Not that there was light emanating from it. It was as black as blackness itself. The globe, a beautiful black mirror registered in my mind more like an absence than a presence. Whatever it reflected on its surface had light of its own. I felt more affinity with my reflection in the Enigma than with the body lying on my bed. I didn't touch the deep darkness above me yet, in a strange way, it, the absence, touched me. It drew me inexorably inside itself. Engulfed me.

The next moment it was gone. That, which wasn't completely there, wasn't there any more. Absurd?

Later, I tried to decide if the globe had been there for an hour or a dozen heartbeats. I had no term of reference. Only the darkness around me was no longer complete. It was the usual night we think of as dark, yet within its embrace we are always aware of some forgotten photons lingering from the previous day. Perhaps, lost, overlooked, trying to return to their realm of light, of sunshine. They might have been just my own reflections slowly dissolving into the night. Perhaps, I'd only imagined the sphere. But if so, why had it been so real?

I began to suspect that the Enigma was my link to that part of me which straddled the inner and the outer reality. Where I neither was nor wasn't. Where the reflections of reality were the reality. How real was my reflection in a mirror? Was I real, or was I a mere reflection of some reality to which I had, as yet, no access.

I asked myself again and again: isn't reality that which I perceive as such? Or does it have an independent existence. Isn't reality in constant flux? In a state of turmoil, continuously dying and being reborn? Like virtual universes? Like cells in my physical body?

"And why do I remember every detail now, in the light of day?" I asked myself a dozen times next morning. Could it be that my soul had been attempting to create an escape for my lonesome heart? Was I really that lonely?

I shook my head. I was happy, contented – or tried to be. What I longed for, sometimes, was the forbidden fruit. It was not to be. Ever.

I suppose, by any standard definition, I could be considered a lonely woman. Though in my late twenties, I continued to reject advances from a number of men, who had persistently sought my favours. Many of my overt admirers counted among truly eligible bachelors, endowed with the very best credentials. Many also displayed good looks, even charm, often good breeding – if one can use such a turn of phrase in the middle of the twenty-first century. They were truly nice men, fully qualified in every way imaginable to assure me of a loving, comfortable, secure future.

Unfortunately for them, the very concept of future lay completely outside my term of reference. My attachment to the Present, with a capital P, had, by all the usual standards, become nothing short of an obsession. I suppose being so intensely alive, so intensely involved in every second of every hour, every day, that the future was absolutely of no interest to me. Even JJ couldn't quite understand me. I seemed essentially indifferent to his and my father's intention of taking over the Moon Base. It was their dream and dreams are not always realized. Dreams, such as these, belonged in the future and I felt apart from anything that was not anchored firmly in the Now. I wished them all the luck in the world, of course. In the world and outside it. Or above it. I offered any help that might be mine to give. But no more. It was part of what could be. Not part of what is.

It did not stir fires in my heart.

Could this have been the real cause of my suppressed longing? My overwhelming detachment? All the young men I'd met could not match the elusive image embedded somewhere deep in my subconscious. Lately I was just beginning to open myself to the possibility that, to put it bluntly, none of the young men I'd met could match an amalgam of my father and JJ rolled into a single entity, a congruence that, by its very nature, could not exist. I would not allow this hunger to take over my conscious awareness. There had been moments when I had suspicions of my inordinate weakness, but I suppressed such thoughts quickly, decisively, as I tried to suppress all my other weaknesses. No one else seemed aware of my obvious flaws. I knew that what my father saw in me was perfection. But that was false. What Dad saw was a reflection of Heidi, my mother. Only the dead can remain perfect. As for my brother, well, I suspected I might have been the only person he secretly admired. By the majority of men and women at the Sanctuary, I was treated like a goddess: sublime, untouched by the foibles of human nature. Or could it be.... like the Director's daughter?

What foolishness!

I tried to be my own person, offering all that I had, myself if need be, but only now, today. I did not think of myself as someone who can age, grow wrinkled and unattractive. In fact, I didn't think of myself much at all. I was too busy. My own image of myself had undergone a number of diametric adjustments, of realignments, rather like the planets that continued to realign themselves in relation to one another.

For years I'd tried to match the reflection I'd seen in the Enigma. To blend into the inherent transiency of that reflection. To grasp the concept of non-being, or at least, non-becoming. The first, I know now, was absurd. Being, by definition, is paramount to immortality. Becoming? That was the question. To be, I must, but what of becoming?

Enigma aided me to recognize an image of myself when I was no longer limited by my own concept of who or what I was. It exposed my little self for what it really was. There were moments when I was imbued with such an awareness of life that my everyday existence palled into insignificance.

Then the irrevocable dawn came and I reverted to doing the very best I could. I no longer just was. I reverted to the condition of becoming.

Since my first excursion, if one could call it that, to the environs of Enigma, on the other side of Pluto, so many years ago, I'd felt unsatisfied. I felt a gnawing hunger. Even before I'd introduced Dad to the inner realm, that day, under the weeping willow, I'd grown in understanding of that very reality in which my father until and since that day showed little interest. He wasn't ready. Is anyone, I wondered? Is anyone ever really ready to meet themselves face to face? Really?

To each his own, I sighed, and continued to love my father with total commitment even as I loved the world, the stars, the universe itself. And as I loved JJ.

I did a lot more sighing then.

On the other hand, there were no means by which I could be, in the normal sense of the word, lonely. Lonely people are detached from reality. The true reality. Whatever that might be! People who feel apart, rejected, unwanted. I'd experienced none of these. In fact, unbeknownst to all, as there was no way I could explain this in words, I felt an uncompromising thread or connection linking me with all people, all animals, things, even stars and the black void in which we all have our being. There were moments, rare but recurrent, when I no longer felt that I was an observer. Not even when regarding myself in the mirror of the Enigma. During those timeless moments I'd experienced an even more powerful, almost overwhelming unity with all there was. Or is. Or could ever be. During those precious fragments of eternity I'd savoured the taste of being strangely alive, awakened to a reality greater than my mind could embrace. There were no words in my vocabulary to express such flashes of understanding, there were no people with whom they could be shared. It could be that in those instances I'd experienced Infinity.

There was, however, a price to pay. I suffered from a total inability to share them. If God there was, He must be a lonely God. Allah is One, proclaimed the prophet.

One and One only. I am that I am. And none other.

None other.

Alone.

Such pensive musings accounted for my moments of melancholy. Particularly when I was physically tired, usually after work, after all night observations. Later there were further payments extracted – awareness of separation, of incompleteness.... When my sense of individuality grew stronger than my perception of oneness, I would escape to my room, close the door and close my eyes to shut out the offensive actuality. I knew it to be false, transient, unreal, but even now, on occasion, I succumb to it. Regardless where gods take me, I remain very human.

There were other tests, usually at night, when I became acutely aware of my body – from the tiny bones at the tips of my toes, through my legs, my torso, down my arms and up my neck to the top of my head. I could trace my awareness as a tourist inspecting a new, if vaguely familiar city, full of winding streets, broad avenues, gardens overlooking large plazas, rolling pulsating fields, brooks, rills, and powerful rivers, and other domains dwarfed by densely packed structures.

At other times, I wouldn't identify with any particular part of my body, but as my thoughts lingered on any detail for any length of time, my attention seemed to zoom in on that part, that fragment of the whole, inspecting it with utter commitment. My mind would enter the cellular structure, zoom further into the molecular alliances, and finally descend to the most complex matrices of atomic order. Each particle confined itself to its assigned function, each in perfect discipline imposed by my unconscious will, each gyrating as a sign of life, for life in my inner world meant change and change implied continuous motion. What fascinated me most were the vast areas of space, of void as great, in scale, as the incredible distances between the stars and their planets. I, or my body, consisted mostly of void. Mimicking the Universe? The electrons obeying their nuclei remained at preordained distances, orbiting the source of their attraction even as Earth paid obeisance to the sun.

I saw, no, I heard my body as a celestial symphony. It was the soul of harmony. Even as notes follow each other to form a cogent accord, extend by playful arpeggios, cascading scales and enchanted unions, so did the individual atoms gravitate towards their molecular structures. There they developed new allegiances, complex harmonies, slowly as though even at that scale, time had no meaning, yet gradually becoming cellular structures, then organs, organized system, all enlivened by countless trillions of electrochemical reactions. Vibrant. A structure of order and harmony.

And this was just my body?

Yet the point of reference from which I regarded those complex relationships of my physical enclosure, my personal universe, remained very static. My mind, my awareness, in a state of awe, in surprise and wonder, remained still, perfectly still, and only my disembodied attention seemed to move from my head to my toes, and back, wandering and wondering, admiring as a god admires his or her own creation. Like a microscopic eye at the end of a surgeon's needle, I peeked at the expression of my being.

"Am I this I am?" I'd asked myself facing the mirror some time later. "Is this the I am that I truly am?"

There was another aspect I noticed during those nocturnal journeys – the complete absence of scale. Time, space or distance served only to illustrate what was already known to me. Those measurements had no meaning in their own right. This much became obvious, later, when I recounted my experiences in daylight. But at the time, particularly the first time or two, it was disturbing. Even unnerving. Yes. I still expected the laws of logic to apply to my inner realm. They didn't. They didn't apply at all. Depending on the interest expressed by my will at any particular moment, I would see myself as a tiny fragment of a greater reality. Or an in-

significant aspect of my own awareness. Or else witness my physical body expanding over many light-years, perhaps thousands, dis-
placing the whole universe, as I had heretofore known it. It was the
same universe, only this time it seemed contained within me. The
two became one. For now. The next instant the image of my body,
for it wasn't my real self, it was merely an image, would retreat
once again to my physical form, reclining on my bed, breathing
softly, effortlessly, accepting my present place in the matrix of time
and space.

There had been many such wonders.

None tangible, none I could discuss with anyone, not even
with my father, nor my brother, but absorb, store in my memory,
relish or despise. I was slowly learning to live with my loneliness.

How can God abide all alone, I wondered?

How lonely You must be?

Dad called Brad Morton at NASA within minutes of receiving
the latest data. Enigma had performed a dance on both sides of
Pluto. One moment the reflections had been on one side, the next
on the other. It made no astronomical sense. None at all. But
other astronomers confirmed the observations.

As for NASA, Dad had continued to play hard to get. He'd
agreed to give them the benefit of his unique expertise for the
Moon Base, in exchange for access to the successor of the younger
brother of Hubble. Father wanted to cast its eye, at regular intervals, toward Pluto. Of course it wasn't Pluto that father was after.
It was Enigma. It paid.

Just as Hubble III turned its unblinking eye at Pluto, the reflecting surface of the object behind it danced a short jig around it's
orbit.

"What the hell is going on?" Brad Morton, the man in charge
of the orbiting telescope asked him. "Are your people playing
hanky-panky with Pluto?"

In spite of Dr. Morton's jovial vocabulary, his tone sounded
dead serious.

"I've been telling your people about Pluto's, ah... hanky-panky, for several years," Dad said unabashedly. "You are not in the habit of taking your northern cousins very seriously."

"Your what?"

"Your northern cousins."

"Ah, yes, John. Ha, ha. Oh yes. Very droll." Dr. Morton cleared his throat. "I guess you're right at that. Ha, ha. Well, we shall put a stop to that. Right now. Is there anything else you would like me to peek at? Just say the word, John. Just say the word."

There was more, slightly embarrassed, throat clearing.

"Not at the moment, thank you. But I would appreciate your continued scrutiny of Pluto's environs."

"I hear you're giving our boys on the Moon a hard time, John." Morton had suddenly changed the subject. "Those little domes you're building there look real pretty through my Roving Eye. Just like those bubbles you have way up there in Yukon."

In spite of himself John blurted out in sheer disbelief.

"You're aiming the Roving Eye at us, here on Earth?"

The Americans had been wasting the most expensive and advanced piece of equipment ever put into orbit, to steal Canadian ideas. Wonders will never cease!

(The Roving Eye was Dr. Morton's pet name for Hubble III. All astronomers have pet names for their favourite toys). The doctor was alluding to father's successful insistence that the number of domes on the Moon should be doubled, then tripled, then extended still further as fresh water became available. Two years after they'd discovered the underground lake, the number of domes had grown to seventeen. They were being assembled at the rate of two a month – and counting.

Father quickly returned to the previous subject. To the expanding Moon Base.

"We need oxygen, Brad. Lots of green stuff to give us oxygen."

"I dare say that you do, John. I dare say that you do. You want to move all your people up there, John? Ha, ha..."

While Dr. Morton was laughing, father later admitted that the hair on his neck had assumed the stance of attention. It had been father's intention to introduce the possible participation of his staff in the Moon Colony only next year, when there would be at least a dozen more domes. Poor Dad caught his breath, then breathed deeply. Could it be that the American had guessed his surreptitious designs? His, as JJ would say, Machiavellian ruse? Had they been so much smarter, or suspicious, than he'd expected?

"Ha, ha... that's a good one, Brad," he said quickly to cover his unease. "Though, you know, Brad, it would save you guys an awful lot of money. Ha, ha..." His laughter still sounded a bit nervous. He hadn't yet bounced the idea off JJ. JJ was the whiz-kid in public relations. Or in Machiavellian stratagems for that matter.

"Will be talking to ya!" Brad said and his vi-phone went blank.

Father wiped his forehead. If he'd let the cat out of the bag too quickly it might have made things a lot more difficult. But the opportunity presented itself. He took it. If the idea of a Canadian contingent on the Moon originated with the Americans, he would hold all the aces. He could virtually name his price. Not in financial terms, but in equipment and staff.

"I must speak to JJ," he said out loud, and dialled JJ's extension.

It took minutes for Brad Morton to realize that his joke may have been quite a clever idea. Money was getting tight in Washington. Maybe I should talk to some people, he thought. Might score a point or two. Might even score a home run. It took Dr. Morton a lot longer to realize that father hadn't told him anything about the funny stuff going on around Pluto. He had been so preoccupied with scoring a home run that he'd forgotten all about it.

Dr. Morton hummed his favourite song all the way to the NASA cafeteria. He'd scheduled a lunch with General Hoffendorff. It could prove fruitful, he thought. I might just score an ace. Dr. Morton was very keen on all sorts of sports. On TV, that is. He'd had no time to participate in any since he was appointed to lead the Roving Eye team. But there was a chance, here, to rise up in the ranks.

"If I just load all the bases..." he mused.

I hadn't 'seen' my mother for three years. Frankly I'd had so
many new experiences with Enigma that I hadn't felt the need. I
had also been very busy at the Observatory. Dad had given me the
job of trying to assess the rate at which Enigma had been changing
locations by superimposing the infinitely small fluctuations in reflections in relation to one another. Though computers do most of
the work, there is an old adage about our electronic friends: garbage in – garbage out. It took a good amount of brainwork to get
the most out of the processing units. More so once they were
linked together into a single powerful brain. And particularly when
answers I sought often stretched to eleven decimal places. In astronomy exactitude was everything.

Of course, none of this had anything to do with my private
dealings with Enigma, let alone with my mother.

My mother appeared to me in a normal dream. We all dream
about out dear ones, from time to time. The only difference was
that I had never met my mother. I had been much too small to do
so. My consciousness was still in the process of installing itself
into my infant body. Of course, in a manner of speaking, we had
spent the previous nine months together, but genetic memory is not
really concerned with non-physiological traits, at least not at the
very beginning of entering a new body.

And thus my recollections of Heidi had little to do with Heidi,
or the role she had played in my life. Let alone with who or what I
really was. Or had been. Or am. What Heidi, the mother, really is
remains unchangeable, eternal, immortal. Over the years I had
learned that this was true of every one of us, from the moment we
become fully aware of who we really are. Until then, until the
moment of realization, practically all of our life's events will be re-
absorbed into the fabric of the universe, to be used for other purposes, by other people, if and when they find such traits useful for
their eventual advancement.

It all became fairly simple once I began looking at reality from
the right vantage point. I was amazed how few people did that.

Some had a vague idea that there was more to them than their body, their likes and dislikes. But few stopped to wonder if those predispositions were merely physiological reactions to some sort of inbred traits, or something they'd had the previous evening for supper, or if there was more to it than that.

By that time I knew, without a shadow of doubt, that the Heidi contained within my physical envelope was but a fragment of my true self, an insignificant shard of immortal crystal of my soul.

In that dream, I saw my mother quite differently. She appeared in her physical form. I didn't understand, at first, how I'd known it was my mother. But on reflection, the many photographs I'd seen over the years could easily dispel this mystery. Yet, at the same time, what I recognized as my mother was hardly her physical appearance. I'd known from my own past what made my mother, my mother. It went deep beyond any outer appearance.

In my dream, Heidi, my mother, sat at the edge of my bed, and told me stories. As though I was still a girl, bewitched by bedtime fables. In her first story she told me about Isis and Osiris, of their love for each other.

"And out of their union came Horus," she said. "They called him the sun-god. And he was. He brought light to his people." The words seemingly flowed from mother directly into my soul.

Then Heidi told little Hey all about Krishna frolicking in the fragrant groves of Vrindavan, and of his deeply erotic love for the beautiful Radha. Mother talked of other gods and goddesses who, through great commitment and love for each other, brought great blessings down to Earth, great bounty, which to this day enrich people of our planet.

"Had they remained celibate, none of this would have happened", she concluded.

And then she added one more thought that remains in my mind vivid to this day. "We all have our being, little one," she said, stroking my face. "We also have our becoming. In some ways, they are one and the same. Remember that."

When I woke up the next morning, I still felt the gentle touch of mother's hand on my cheek. I also understood something new.

At least one enigma in my life had been resolved. I'd learned that love flows onto this Earth through a variety of channels, and that, for some reason I couldn't quite explain, I had to get married. For love.

***

19

Signs

"There is a great deal more going on between heaven and earth than meets the eye," father told JJ when the three of us were alone. This portentous announcement was particularly significant coming from an astronomer. "I want you to put together some thoughts on the state of the world today. I think our friends down there need a little shaking up." Dad pointed south over his shoulder with his thumb.

"They won't like it very much," JJ smiled sadly.

Dad nodded.

The signs were everywhere. Either the human race would mend its ways, or the ways would mend the human race. It was looking more and more as if only radical surgery would cut out the cancer gnawing at our innards. For years we, as a species, had been far too decadent. Most ecclesiastic authorities had been warning of our problems: our indifference towards others, our lack of ethics, our moral decay, abuse of power, even pollution. And they might have sounded more convincing had they practised what they'd preached. Modern-day soothsayers talked about the Kingdom of Mu, about Lemuria and Atlantis. About past glory. They spoke of the inerrant cycles of great, ancient mystery religions, with their secret rites and doctrines known only to the initiated.

Others, those straddling science and religion, cited recurring ice ages, or great, biblical, cleansing floods mounting at our doorsteps. They all talked about disasters. Imminent disasters.

None came.

The world was, surely, slipping downhill, but not in a calamitous leap to end all leaps, not in a mad dash towards self-annihilation. It was much worse. The world was aging. Our global arteries had slowly been calcifying. For generations we had been growing decrepit. Loosing our vim, our *joie de vivre*. Or even our will to live. To advance. To reach beyond mediocrity.

We, the people, were growing old. Rapidly. With few exceptions, at an accelerated pace.

People died in the millions, tens of millions, but other millions were born to take their place. Out of habit. Like bacteria when placed on an agar culture in a Petri-dish. Instinctively. Without forethought. Many believed that eleven billion people was more than the Earth could support. Apparently, not so. No matter how many plagues swept through civilization, more innocent babies were born than Nature managed to get rid of. At long last, Mother Nature had called our bluff. She was doing her best to balance the odds, to restore some semblance of sanity to the once beauteous home of the impendingly-late Homo sapiens. We were no longer sapient, sage, sagacious, discerning. We had lost. There was a time when we were an integral part of her bounty. No more. Man had grown stronger, more resilient, more powerful than Nature herself. Plagues no longer sufficed. We had become the plague. The pollutant. We were the viral culture destroying the earth that fed us. The end must surely be near.

Would we get lucky?

Would Nature bide her time for a last ditch effort? To save us from ourselves?

Would we allow her to act in our stead?

After a break of two months during which father had built up a closer relationship with NASA to advance our interests in the development of the Moon Base, the Sunday dinners resumed. To make up for Dad's absence, we'd decided to meet more often. Until further notice, on a weekly basis. That was in addition to whatever Miriam and Mary put together just for the 'boys'. That is David and father and JJ and I if we were around. Just like in the old days. For some reason, in spite of my work at the observatory, at dinners I remained a little girl of nineteen. There are advantages to being the baby of the family. Of both families. I was pampered more than was probably good for me. But I knew that it wouldn't last. As for Dr. Mendel's sons, now adults, they'd both chosen to live in California – under the open skies. They visited every month. But it wasn't enough. Miriam missed them.

"Our people are always scattered all over the world," she repeated sadly each time Dad or I saw her. "JJ is too practical – he wouldn't understand," she confided to us when the three of us were alone.

"To each his own," father made an effort to defend his son's sensibility. "Live and let live." He would soon run out of things to say. I continued to nod in sympathy.

At the 'think-tank' dinners, there was always a great deal to discuss, mostly pertaining to the day-to-day operation of the Sanctuary. Father updated his inner circle on the latest developments and discussed matters of general interest. The others, heads of various departments, shared news connected with their own research. There was a great camaraderie, an *esprit de corps*. The principle of Complexity, once referred to as the Emerging Science at the Edge of Order and Chaos which had its birth in the Christo Rey Convent, in Santa Fe, found its fruition in the Crystal City. All members of the scientific community, regardless of their specialization, firmly believed in the interlocking nature of all disciplines. Father noted several times, with a degree of pride, that what had begun as a strictly *Canadian* Science Centre, was soon attracting the very best brains from around the world.

"There is only one Book of Science," father admonished repeatedly at annual meetings. "Your departments are just chapters of the same story."

We all believed him.

The day Dad appointed JJ, officially John Hydon Jr., Ph.D., to be the liaison officer for the Centre, the discussion took them along a pathway they hadn't discussed before. They had all been so intent on their work that the overall picture, the Big Picture, as JJ called it, had been left to unfold on its own. They kept in touch with each other, of course, but they'd long chosen to ignore the world outside. Their concept of Complexity was limited to the interdepartmental exchange of ideas. In a way, that was why they'd chosen to be here. At the Sanctuary. To be honest, the scientists took advantage of their seclusion to liberate themselves. To dismiss the influx of news pertaining to the world outside from their attention.

"Let the politicians take care of the world. I've got to take care of my bugs," announced the virologist who had just succeeded in designing a new vaccine for one of many strains of influenza circling the world.

"I don't think we can afford to dismiss eleven billion people from our minds," father suggested, looking to JJ for support. His colleagues seemed only partially aware of the dismal state into which the world was rapidly descending. They reminded me of a group of very smart ostriches with their heads firmly embedded in the sand. They'd all developed a false sense of security.

JJ gave them a brief update on reality outside the Sanctuary. They all listened attentively. But, other than David Mendel who'd always been willing and able to worry about most things, the scientists gave an impression of agreeing only for the sake of form. Perhaps, as people, they were all just too nice. They couldn't quite accept the depth of depravity to which our civilization had sunk over the last twenty or thirty years.

"As you all know, the rise and fall of empires has accelerated enormously. The USA rose to world prominence, not to say domination, around the middle nineteen-eighties. Less than seventy years later, there are unmistakable signs of decay. Decay or decadence. Compare this to the first colony, Newfoundland, which Cabot discovered in 1497 and which gave birth to the British Empire. That Empire lasted some three hundred and fifty years – till the Second World War. The Brits had only reached their zenith during the late 19th and early 20th century."

JJ looked around. The mood had changed. All eyes were on him. Finally he held their attention. JJ smiled. To date, the doctoral theses he'd written in Political Science and History of Philosophy, had been gathering dust on the shelves at the National Library. He cleared his throat and continued.

"I shall not bore you with ancient history, but let us note, in passing, that the Old Kingdom of Egypt spanned a whole millennium. Six dynasties lapsed while their people lived in perfect accord." There were a few aaahs.. and ooohs.. and 'reallys'. JJ was having fun. "Think of the scale, of the past and recent centuries. What we must consider now is the present. As I've mentioned, the USA appears to be on a downward spiral. China is an even more astounding example. There, the symptoms of decline are coming to the surface before they've even reached their full potential. A fall before the quintessential rise."

"And India?" Dave Mendel asked.

"India is a puzzle. Thirty-five percent of their population now enjoys the highest standard of living in the world. The remaining sixty-five percent are starving. Or live on the edge of starvation. Their caste system was abolished and then re-abolished by nine consecutive parliaments, but continues to thrive. It is almost as though their ancient beliefs are etched into their genes. India provides us with the supreme example of the haves and the have-nots."

"Do you think it will last? The haves and the have-nots, I mean," dad put in.

"No. It never has in the past – such disparity, I mean," JJ said. "The fact is that there are unmistakable signs, throughout the world, that things cannot and will not last, as they are."

There was a prolonged silence. Finally Frank Gray, a relative newcomer from England cleared his throat. All eyes turned to him as though in expectation of protracted salvation.

"And what of Europe?" he asked. "We, I mean to say, *they* match the USA in population, you know?"

JJ smiled. "A good point," he said. "There is, however, a problem. The Europeans, regardless of their partial, ever-changing, fermenting union, are still writing memoirs about Napoleonic Wars. You cannot erase the memories of a thousand years of wars with a few economically motivated political alliances. By the time they rise above their garrulous traditions, the world will be in its dying throes."

It pretty well is now, he'd almost added but bit his tongue. His job was to awaken them to outside reality, not depress them into inaction.

Nevertheless, the new silence extended even longer.

They ate without enthusiasm. The forks and knives scraped, quietly, the glasses still shone with that inimitable blood-red lustre of rich wine, especially when held up against the candlelight. It isn't pleasant to be awakened and see that the world is not at all as one imagined it. At least the guests' apparent loss of appetite would not be taken as an affront to Miriam. Since last year, she had been awarded a regular cook, a maid and a general factotum-butler who took care of serving, wine, laying the table, and all the attendant duties necessary to make the Sunday dinners a success. As for Miriam, she loved playing the hostess and now she did so even better than before.

When the last fork found its resting place, and the table was cleared, father decided that it was time for him to either make or brake the backbone of the little gathering.

So far Dad had discussed the possibility of the Moon Base as their new Sanctuary only with Dave, JJ, me, and three senior scientists, the founding fathers who had been sworn to secrecy. Father and JJ truly believed that the idea of moving as many of us as the Americans would allow to the Moon was an idea worthy of The Tales from the Arabian Nights. For JJ it was the jaunt of a lifetime, for Dad the very best conditions to continue his research. He still hadn't given up his idea that at the heart of each and every galaxy there beat a Black Hole. The idea had bugged him since childhood. And now, finally, the conditions on the Moon with complete absence of any refracted photon pollution, devoid of any semblance of Earth's atmosphere, stratosphere or even thermosphere, would be a dream come true. No water vapour. And finally there would be no sodium atoms which, at a hundred kilometres above the Earth produced sodium air glow, which interfered with the photography of faint stars.... well, this really was a dream in the making. From the moment the idea of a Moon Sanctuary crossed his mind, Dad's whole life became infected with a new, compulsive, nagging desire. He felt young again. Fresh blood stirred in his veins, his eyes took on the shine he'd had when first looking through the magic lens of the telescope at Cambridge. At least, so I imagined.

"I'll be closer to home..." I'd muttered at the time.

JJ had been flabbergasted. "What on earth do you mean, Hey?" he'd asked.

Some months ago he'd stopped calling me 'his Sis'. He told me I was just too beautiful, too unique, to be appropriated by the equivalent of a possessive pronoun. I'd never thought JJ could make me blush.

At the time I'd made my inane remark I'd also been embarrassed. "I am sorry.... I have no idea why I said that," I assured him. When I saw the expression in JJ's eyes, I sighed and added: "Really, JJ. Really."

I mention this exchange because for some reason I'd found it difficult to sustain my brother's gaze. There had been something in his eyes I didn't understand. It seemed more than just admiration. Or brotherly love. Whatever it was it made me lower my eyes. I'd first noticed something strange about the way JJ looked at me when he'd left Calgary, after his doctorates, and came back to live at the Centre. Within two days he'd moved out of the family condo.

"Need to spread out," he'd said at the time.

But his eyes said something quite different. I still didn't really understand what made my brother tick. But whatever it was I found him the most fascinating man I'd ever met. JJ was that elusive combination of the inner and the outer personas, which lived in separate clearly defined compartments, yet, seemingly, in perfect harmony. He was also very much his own man. No matter what trends, influences or fashions abounded in his vicinity, he remained an observer. When he acted, he was always decisive, relying on his own cognizance. I liked that.

"So there is no hope?" This was Frank once more. He'd only taken over the Department of Physics two years ago. The physicists had to be young, or they were apt to drown in their own knowledge. He was the youngest, the most resilient but by the same token he had the most to lose.

"There is always hope...." father said, slowly rising from his chair. JJ had given them the pitfalls, he would offer them a soft landing. Only Dave had an inkling of what was coming. The other three scientists who had advance notice, had previous commitments.

"The cultures on Earth will no doubt unfold themselves as they should." Dad now took a deep breath and hit the nail squarely on the head. "How would you chaps like to move our work to the Moon?"

There was a series of gasps, a few mouths opened wide, then closed only to open again. Father had expected no less. The scientists had led very sheltered lives.

"As I am sure you know," father continued vaguely amused by the whole gamut of facial expressions, "the Americans have been building a base on the Moon, what they call the Way Station, an intermediate staging ground for further exploration of our Solar System. I managed to persuade them, some years ago, that there might be advantages to conducting scientific research on the Moon. The research facilities will be quite unique." Father handed each one of them a brochure he and JJ had put together over the last few months. "Now don't be disappointed if it all fizzles out. But at the moment, I have been given a preliminary nod to start putting together a team of scientists willing to take the trip."

At first there was resounding silence. Then – they all spoke at once.

"Would this be a permanent move?"

"When?"

"For how long?"

"Are you serious?"

"Sounds fantastic!"

"What about our families?"

"It's a little hard to believe... really!?

"Yippee!" This last was our recent arrival from England.

There were dozens more questions. Father handled them one by one, with able assistance from JJ. There was no doubt that the offer had come as a shock. One is just not used to being asked to move to the Moon, particularly for an indefinite length of time. Perhaps for a lifetime. The strangest thing for JJ was that no one asked if it was safe. They wanted to know a great deal about the working conditions, but not from ease or comfort point of view, rather if they would retain independence in their individual fields.

Finally Miriam raised her hand.

"Shall I be able to continue with our Sunday get-togethers? They are very important to me...." her voice trailed off as though embarrassed.

"I would certainly refuse to go if I couldn't visit you on a regular basis," father assured her in a grave tone. "I am sure this goes for all of us!"

This was the sign for a new wave of veritable pandemonium.

The serious nature of the meeting was over. They all rose, drank to Miriam's health, raised their glasses to The Brain, which father was still being called behind his back. They loved Dad as children love their father. A good caring father – even though some of them were less than twenty years younger than Dad, and David a few years older. Dad was their patriarch. Their leader. There was never a question of not taking advantage of father's offer. Their sole concern was directed towards maintaining their work along the lines already developed. Or better. Much better. What new, incredible horizons this would open, they all raved. When the festivities came to an end, father asked them to keep the news under wraps until further say so.

"We mustn't scare the coop by trying to grab the bird," he told them.

It had all gone as well as he'd imagined. Frankly, he'd never doubted his staff. His friends. He'd chosen his colleagues well. They were the future of mankind. Wherever they went.

"So what do you think, JJ?"

JJ sighed deeply, glanced at me with vague disbelief, then looked away as though trying to avoid my eyes. This wasn't like JJ. He was never so quiet; not when someone offered a friendly ear. A moment later he inhaled deeply again, seemed about to say something, only to slowly empty his lungs without a single word. Moments later he cleared his throat, sat up, looked at dad, and again collapsed against the deckchair.

I had no idea what was wrong.

Father too was reclining on the terrace, a book in his hand. He opened it, turned some pages, then let it lie idle on his lap. As he leaned back, his eyes wandered along the crystal panes, shimmering in the dim moonlight. The new moon offered little light. Under normal circumstances, he would be in his observatory, directing the Monster Eye at distant secrets. Perhaps even at Pluto. At my Enigma?

Not today. Perhaps he felt as he must have felt when he was about to leave England to come to Canada. It seemed like centuries ago. Before I was even born. He was now almost seventy, jogs five a week, and looks and acts like a man half his age. Well . . . almost.

I knew all that, but his behaviour, his apparent detachment from the here and now seemed to have its origin somewhere much deeper. JJ echoed the same, inexplicable silence that seemed to pulsate with something portentous, yet something that no one seemed able, or willing to name. I recalled an ancient Hollywood classic, The Silence of the Lambs. In it, the woman, the female lead, lived in fear of silence. It, the silence itself, meant the end of something. Something dreadful. I began to fear the silence that seemed to emanate from the two men so close to me yet who, at this moment, seemed so very far away.

Somehow, even as they apparently rested on the laurels of their forthcoming achievement, I felt, as I am sure both father and JJ did, a strange stirring deep inside me. A dread of something inevitable, irrevocable, something which once set in motion could not be stopped nor avoided.

Time dragged on as we all sat in silence; father and JJ lost in their thoughts, I trying vainly to decipher their mood from their facial expressions. I suspected that whatever had set them so far apart, had nothing to do with our exciting, indeed exhilarating, future.

Slowly, as I also looked up at the glints of the aluminium tubes cutting the ceiling into a tapestry of light and shadow, their mood began to dawn on me.

If only we were Irish, I thought....

Had we been Irish, we would have celebrated the occasion not only with an all night vigil, but also with some ritual, perhaps very formal festivities, as they do on the eve of burial. The house would be full of guests; food and drink would abound. We would not be sad, not even introspective, but would rejoice in our lives, the lives that had ended, that were about to end, never to return.

Never to return....

Only there was no corpse. No one had laid it out, no one had washed it, no one covered it with a habit. No one had placed a crucifix on its breast, or rosary beads on its cold fingers. Not a single candle had been lit near its remains.

There was no sound of women weeping, no loud wailing, not even muffled sobs of sorrow. There was only silence. Deep, painful, resigned acceptance. The joy of a few moments ago was gone. The pain remained.

It dawned on me, that my father and my dear bother were holding a singular wake. They were holding a wake for their own lives, for their memories, their loves and hates alike. Over all that they drew out of what Mother Earth had to offer, all that made them whatever they were today. They were both, each in the deepest recesses of their heart, burying themselves.

It was at this moment that my own life flashed before my eyes, even as it is said to flash at the very moment of death.

A brush with bushes outside the bedroom window. The touch of my father's hands, loving, unknown, the pulse of the heart in his chest. Mary's reserved love, yet so welcome, so needed.... My Mother's face... The fish in Uncle David's tank. Enigma. The dinners every Sunday. Enigma....

Enimga....

I began to fit in. I examined my world. My Earth....

There had developed a strange disparity between the majority of people and the few dedicated to intensive work at the Crystal City – people who, to this day, populate my world. While the scientists, artists, writers, explorers, were blessed with relative longevity, upwards of a century, the vast masses lost their vitality in

their early fifties. They lingered on for a while in innumerable institutions created for that purpose, and died. Probably out of sheer
boredom. By contrast, only last week I'd attended a lecture given
by one of our resident centenarians.

Yet, protected as I have been, I am going to miss this Earth.
My home.

It will probably be easiest for Dad. He would take all that he
loved with him. He'd already said goodbye to mother. So long
ago. Thirty years? And not his whole world, his work, even the
future to him usually lay in the hoary past. Light-years away. Millions of years....

JJ and I would make sure he would miss nothing else.

Dear Dad. He still liked jogging better than any other exer-
cise. To keep fit. "It oxygenates my brain", he'd said many-a-
time. He could think while he ran, he'd told me. And he liked
thinking. He liked thinking a lot.

"It's up to them, Dad, the Yankees."

That it was. Father had made sure that the Sanctuary on the
Moon would be large enough to house at least a third of his staff, in
addition to the original plans set out by NASA. There were now a
total of twenty-three enormous domes, a full half-a-diameter larger
than the average dome on Mount Ogilvy. A third of his staff would
be holding a wake. Today. Or soon after....

Poor Earth.

We have been destroying our rain forests, our planet's lungs.
There – on the Moon, Nature was producing oxygen to save us
from ourselves. I wished we could take Mother Earth with us. To
drift slowly away, to leave our sins behind.

I glanced at JJ. His face gave nothing away. The exemplary
extrovert crawled into his skin and shut out the outside world completely. Even me, his sister.

I think I could guess his thoughts. At least, some of them.

For his part, JJ no longer enjoyed misleading the NASA people. The days when he gloried in his Machiavellian schemes were
long past. He was no longer a boy toying with other peoples' lives.
Perhaps, at this moment of soul searching, he'd even regretted

some of his youthful peccadilloes. He was sure that the sharper among the Americans had been fully aware, for some time, that father had officially proposed was a bit of thinly disguised subterfuge. They were intelligent, resourceful and still full of energy. If they did have a weakness, well, they were overly oriented towards making and accumulating money. Towards profits for the sake of profits. On the other hand, if it hadn't been for this very trait, the Moon Base would never have happened. Only a trillion-dollar budget could even attempt such a venture.

Year, after year, after year.

Poor JJ.

I'd known for some time that my brother admired the Americans for their capacity and ability to get things done. Admittedly, the *crème de la crème* of their scientific community has been dwindling for years, but so it has everywhere. Science required money. And for money they had to compete with countless armies of charitable organizations, who held that it was infinitely more important to save countless millions of sex-starved proliferators of venereal diseases from untimely self- imposed death, than to send a single man to the moon.

The Americans were so clever. Yet they couldn't save the Earth. Our Home. For a day or two....

JJ knew that the Earth was dying.

And in that moment a realization struck me with a force that made me wince. Father and JJ weren't holding a silent wake for Earth at all. They were indeed holding a wake. But the Earth would live on. They were holding a wake for humanity.

***

NOW

20

Reisefieber

There is a great problem with Now. It has neither past nor future. It all happens when it happens. To understand it we must see it in the context of other events, but only those which also belong, at least peripherally, in the present. To experience the context of Now we must look at a curved surface. Only that which is directly in front of us is perfect. That which is to the left or right, or up or down in relation to the head-on reflection is distorted. It may have been perfect an instant ago, or it will be perfect an instant from now, but only that which is directly in front of us is authentic.

If we are sitting at our breakfast table, we know what we are eating, right now, but unless we are creatures of habit, treading water, we have to make an effort to remember what we had for lunch three days ago. Yet, at the time, it was so real – so very 'now'. It is not a question of memory. It has to do with the reality of Now. Today is fact, all else is speculation. Like the uncertainty principle in quantum mechanics.

Now that I am thirty, my childhood memories are a series of events, seldom arranged in any chronological order. They seem to have happened at random, each fulfilling their preordained function to get me to wherever I am now. We don't seem to realize that everything always happens now. Nothing can happen in the past or the future. Now is where it's at. Now is the instant of constant becoming. Now is life itself.

The Germans call it the *Reisefieber*. It is the nervousness on the eve of travelling that stops us from getting a good night's sleep. It usually happens when we infringe on our biological clock, upsetting our rhythm, our routine. One of the many differences between people living in the Sanctuary and the average members of humanity living an average life outside is that on Mount Ogilvy few people follow any routine. Whatever work is called for takes priority. People, not just the scientists but gardeners, cleaners, cooks and waiters, all acquired the art of catching catnaps, whenever opportunity presented itself. Rather like old-time sailors, whose sleep periods had been chopped up into intervals of ten minutes at a time, or whatever the exigencies of the merciless seas had allowed. On the other hand, unlike those old time sailors, or any kind of seafarers or globetrotters, the members of the CSC seldom travel at all.

The first ability mentioned, that of thriving on catnaps, is true of JJ, the second is not. Neither father nor I slept well the night before JJ left for the moon. JJ slept like a baby. He's travelled more than most people and has absolutely no problem with getting up at two a.m., being whisked off by an army VTAL jet to Florida, and three hours later being strapped into his astronaut's seat, a mere half-hour before the final countdown. For the uninitiated, the VTAL jet is an acronym for Vertical Takeoff And Landing craft, which is used almost exclusively by the American army. The U.S. Airforce, on the other hand, sneers at anything slower than Mach 3, and which can generate a noise at the level of 'come-from-behind' win at the Super Bowl.

While JJ is taking all this in his stride, father and I, are getting more and more nervous as the time of JJ's first flight to the Moon approaches. Father's suddenly realized how much he's learned to rely on JJ for daily advice. He doesn't dare to even think about him in terms of paternal affection, as that would probably disable him for the duration of JJ's absence. Deep down Dad is a softy. We all seem to suffer from hang-ups when faced with the unknown. Not when we first think of challenges, nor even when we strive to fulfil them. The doubts come only when we actually stand face to face with the results of our labours. Then we get nervous.

It is called stage fright.

During his studies in Cambridge, Dad met an operatic basso who had studied singing for years. He had gone through countless hours of vocal exercises – scales, arpeggios and suchlike. He'd even attended classes in drama and opera production, then . . . countless rehearsals. He'd gone through the script a thousand times – both the lyrics and the music. He'd faced no fear during his studies, not even the possibility of failure. And then the time came. The now. The first operatic performance. Father was there. He saw his friend walk to the centre of the stage and stop dead. Frozen in time, in space. Frozen in the now. The basso told Dad later that he'd been aware of having stepped on stage but that he'd left his voice behind in the dressing room.

"It wasn't a question of courage," he'd assured Dad after what turned out to be a brilliant performance. "At the time, in that first instant of seeing the row upon row of faces staring at me, a vise griped my throat, my bronchial tube became devoid of any moisture, my legs had been reassembled from butter. I leaned on my sword for support. I wasn't really present. Not fully. The strange thing was that the moment the first note left my lips, all was fine. I was finally fully there."

Finally in the magic reality of Now.

Father's never had the inclination to go on stage. But on a number of occasions he's had to face an audience of his peers and total strangers. It had been the fear of failure that kept him going in moments immediately preceding the performance. Stage fright is even worse than *Reisefieber*. But right now, each time father thinks of JJ sitting in a shuttle with nothing but a thin sheet of metal and insulation between himself and the void, he feels as though he is about to face a large, unforgiving mass of staring faces. There are a thousand 'what ifs' crowding his mind, forcing their way to and from his aberrant imagination. But unlike stage fright, the feelings, pangs and constrictions don't pass. They linger. They return with each passing thought until finally father tires, losing himself in work. An hour later disturbing thoughts seem to return with renewed vigour. They are not really the old thoughts. New thoughts, fired by new imagination, force their way into Dad's emotions in the present.

"It's the unknown, damn it," he swears at himself. "But I like the unknown," he argues against his own logic. "I love it. I love it. JJ loves it too. We all love it...."

It doesn't help much. We are still creatures of habit. Of illusion. We don't know how to live in the present. In the eternal Now.

My own reaction to JJ's first extraterrestrial trip has been quite different.

I am blessed with a tremendous faith in the benevolence of fate. At least, that's how I think of it. I believe that the universe abounds with omnipresent intelligence that oversees its rational unfolding. Although I am conversant with the underlying principles of the Quantum Theory, emotionally I still side with the classicists, such as Albert Einstein, who held that God doesn't play dice with the universe. I do not necessarily recognize the Benevolent Intelligence as God, but.... what's in a name? My vision impregnates all space, all time, eternity beyond both space and time with this ubiquitous predisposition towards order and harmony. The fact that I am far from understanding my own tenets in no way diminishes, in my mind, their inherent efficacy.

"Whatever happens to him or to any one of us, is bound to be for the best," I tried to console Dad.

"What? When! What might happen? What?!" He was only half listening.

For now, I'll leave Dad to fend for himself. There are times when we must face our demons on our own. I have my own dilemmas to resolve, even if they are quite different from father's or JJ's for that matter. Assuming JJ has any demons to resolve. He seems much to busy, too much in the thick of all things (in the now), to have time for demons. Of any sort. If he does have any, he is the type who would walk up to one and face him there and then. Wherever there and then was at the time. JJ seems to live in the present, quite naturally.

I refuse to allow the thought of ever loosing JJ to enter my mind. I know that Dad's nervousness is tied up with carrying the whole of the Sanctuary on his shoulders. Both here, and possibly up there, way up there...

"Surely, space travel is no longer fraught with danger. Is it? Why hadn't I thought of it before? Why doesn't anyone raise the question of safety? Physical safety?"

The demons never sleep. The demons knock on the door of my mind, or is it my heart, even if I manage to dismiss them in seconds. I have to. I have my father to look after. Regardless of how healthy he is, he turned seventy-three earlier this year. He still looks and acts like a man in his early fifties, can run a mile in under nine minutes, and hold his own against any man 'on the outside' in practically any field. But, well, *tempus fugit*.

JJ has to go to the Moon, has to take a trip which has become, for some people, as regular as going to work. I know all that. But, universal benevolence notwithstanding, I'm still worried. A little. *Reisefieber*, I tell myself. Just *Reisefieber*. He's all right.

"He'll be all right," father echoes my thoughts seeing a frown on my usually smooth forehead. "Trust me," he adds unnecessarily.

Will be? He *is* all right, I have to repeat for my own sake.

This has nothing to do with trust. It has to do with *Reisefieber* – the inexplicable. It is supposed to affect only those who are actually taking a trip, and make *them* too nervous to sleep on the eve of their departure. I've taken the experience to a new level. I must be the first Sanctuarian who's managed to develop the symptoms vicariously, and endow them with a much richer set of syndromes. In my case, *Reisefieber* originates in my stomach, moves up and down my windpipe, constricts my forehead and finally settles somewhere behind my eyes, resulting in a slight headache. And I don't even have to travel. I just send JJ to the Moon.

In moments of such stress, I tend to escape.

I cast my mind back to my ephemeral Enigma, to my haven in the outer reaches of our Solar System. True, it all takes place in my imagination, or in some other somnambular reality, but... to me my trips are very real. More than real. They are as much part of my life, my psyche, my emotional make up as my relationship to my father or to JJ.

"What is my relationship to JJ?"

I'd never asked myself this question before. Surely, it is obvious. He is my brother. My relationship is defined by our consan-
guinity. What else?

Is there an else?

Why did he move out so quickly on coming back from Calgary? Why did I find it so hard to look him in the eyes? Is he
someone I don't really know? Someone I only think I know?
Whatever happened to JJ in Calgary remains an enigma. He is not
the same boy, man, he was before he left Brompton, and certainly
different from the brother I'd known in the past.

Why is it that when I think about him my pulse goes up? Am
I running a fever? *Reisefieber?*

The junk orbiting the Moon is, for the want of a better word, dis-
gusting. The three-dozen shuttles, which deliver construction materials from Earth on a continual basis, dump their loads into a pre-
determined orbit around the Moon. There they remain until needed
down below. Then, a sort of glorified taxi service ignites its engines on the Moon's surface. The robots rise up, load what is
needed, and deposit the junk safely on the surface below. It is not
junk, of course. It is building materials.

There is virtually no danger in these operations since human
intervention is required only occasionally. NASA has not lost a
single man, or woman, though there have been a number of broken
legs and arms from the construction crew attempting to fly inside
the pressurized domes on wing attachments.

Also orbiting the Moon is the Stage Station, where JJ's shuttle
has just docked, to transfer him, in due time, to the taxi which will
come up from the Moon to bring him down to the lunar surface. It
is all beautifully organized, running flawlessly, as only the Americans can organize. Whatever one has to say about NASA people,
they know and understand the 'how' of things.

While waiting to go down, JJ remains glued to the visor panels
which, unfortunately, are mostly facing down. Though the station
enjoys the condition of weightlessness, the 'floor' is oriented
'downwards' – towards the Moon. To look down one has to lean

over trapezoid structures equipped with magnifying lenses, which display the Moon's surface. The Stage Station is in an orbit at right angles to the orbit of the Moon itself, thus showing alternatively the dark and the light side of the Moon.

"Commander Hydon?"

JJ ignores the voice until a hand touches his shoulder.

"Sir? We are ready to go down, Sir."

Commander? Then he remembers. As the representative of NASA, in order to have freedom of movement on the Moon, he has to be of a certain rank. Otherwise all the higher ranks would have priority over his requests. He smiles at his thoughts. Since donning his uniform earth-side, he hasn't seen a mirror. He wonders what he looks like. Judging by the glint in the ensign's eyes, I must strike an impressive figure, he muses shamelessly.

Ten minutes later he is strapped into the much more confined seat of the shuttle taxi, and moment's later they silently cut the umbilical cord which tied them to the Station. The pilot actually asks him "Where to, Sir?" as if he was taking a real taxi down on Earth.

JJ gives the man the coordinates. For a while the taxi remains in orbit until they approach the most propitious position for descent. Once the engines are fired, they make it down in less than fifteen minutes. Again JJ is impressed with the American know-how.

"How often do you go up and down?" he asks the pilot.

"We are five hours on and five hours off, Sir. After six rotations we have six rotations off. And so on. In each rotation I might do as many as seven trips, Sir."

Just like a taxi. JJ already knew that the lowest salary up here is $500,000 US per three months period. A cool two million dollars a year. About a tenth of what a baseball player gets on Earth. Still, it isn't bad for a taxi driver. And it's a lot better than all the early astronauts. They were Airforce. These guys are union.

There are moments in most people's lives that seem to have their being in some sort of suspended animation. JJ had experienced such moments when listening to great music, once or twice when lost in the magic of an operatic performance. Such moments stretch out ignoring the criteria established by science. JJ is not a scientist. He is unaware that time is not supposed to stop, to hover in the present for an indefinite period. Yet his stay on the Moon fits just into such a category.

"You can take off your helmet now, Commander," the ensign tells him.

JJ does as told and looks around. He then shakes his head, blinks a few times and starts laughing.

"Is something wrong, Sir?" The ensign looks worried. People have different reactions when they first remove their helmets, but never quite like this.

"I'm sorry, Ensign. It's just that for a moment I thought that I'd forgotten to take the shuttle to the Moon." JJ is sill awed.

"You must have visited CSC, Sir?"

"Why, yes. How did you know?"

"I've also visited the Canadian Centre of Science, Sir. It is part of our basic training. I had the same impression when I first got here."

There were a number of visitors taking regular tours of the CSC, but JJ never thought of them as Americans undergoing space training. He said as much.

"We have been told to keep our mouths shut, Sir."

And they certainly had. "You are very smart people," JJ murmured in spite of himself.

"Thank you, Sir. Most of what we've learned has been from the Canadians. They are up in the Yukon...."

"Yes, I know."

JJ had to hold tight not to become exasperated. This was ridiculous. They had actually recreated an exact copy, to the details of landscaping, condo layouts, and the pools of the Sanctuary. And all this time we thought that we were pulling a fast one on the Americans!

"Well?" The unspoken question vibrates in the air.

The gathering of at least thirty people fills Dave's condo to the brim. The scientists and a number of their spouses spill onto the balcony, some sit on the floor, others crowd the kitchen. There is an air of buoyant expectancy. Almost nervousness. But mostly of undisguised curiosity.

"Well?" This time father speaks for all of us.

JJ hardly knows where or how to start. The single day's trip to the Moon and back has left him drained of energy, but mostly of emotions. He's still flabbergasted. The Americans have been planning all along to have us, their Canadian friends, take over the Moon Base. And what a reception they had in mind!

"You will never believe it," JJ starts tentatively, then immediately launches into a euphoric flood of praise for the Americans. The words "you wouldn't believe" recur a dozen times.

"And those are just some of the similarities. In fact, I challenge anyone of you to tell the difference between our Sanctuary and the Moon Base in the first three hours of arriving up there. Really. It's... it's... it's a miracle. It has been, it is, tailor made for us. In every detail."

JJ, usually displaying an extremely well organized mind, this time sounds like a schoolboy allowed to talk after a long, tedious lecture. Words seem to explode out of him, mixed metaphors abound, superlatives alternate with his arms waving as though searching for other, even bigger and better words.

"Believe me, you just wouldn't believe it!" he repeats yet another time.

"I think he likes it," Dad whispers in my ear, a mischievous grin on his face, "I strongly suspect that the lad likes it" he repeats giving me a puerile wink.

"I think I speak for all of us when I conclude that you like what you saw?" father says out loud just a little facetiously. But his eyes are filled with joy.

"Love it Dad! Just love it!" JJ still sounds like a schoolboy. He can hardly contain his enthusiasm. "And the view! Have I told you about the view?" He seems ready to plunge into another eulogy.

"I think we all know what Earth looks like from the Moon, son." This time father cannot contain his own broad grin.

The next day, JJ joins Dad and me for lunch. He has recovered fully from his trip and has reverted to his usual energetic but well organized self.

"You know, Hey, a strange thing happened on the way back from the Moon Base. I looked out the aft window and saw a dark cloud following us. Then it broke up and passed us on all sides. Later, it seemed like it burned-up on the re-entry. I wonder what it was."

I recall a dream I had some time ago.

"Discarded debris orbiting the moon?" I offer.

"Very likely. They must have dumped a load into the Moon orbit just a bit too far out. But how come it just broke up on either side of us?"

"That, JJ, will probably forever remain a mystery."

And for those of little faith it probably will.

**

21

The Last Prophet

We often think that our leaders are overpaid. We are often right. Yet there are cases on record which prove that after a particular CEO left a company, it quickly went bankrupt, although under the guidance of the lately departed CEO it thrived. The same appears to be true of churches. Even the kind that began and thrived on the ethereal wings of the Internet.

JJ resigned his leadership of the First World Electronic Church of the Adventist. What had once assured the unprecedented success of the 'church', had been JJ's scrupulous honesty, his overt disdain for money, and the meticulous research on which he'd insisted over the years. Hence the shock when the 'bishops' decided, unilaterally, to take over the initiative. Their first message consisted of just two words:

MEMENTO MORI

The Latin avocation to Remember Death, was splashed in thick, vibrating letters across my computer screen. Before I put the offensive spam in Trash, I couldn't help glancing at the lead article below the flashing sign. It started with an announcement that John Hydon Jr., the Renowned Philosopher and Sociologist had been unanimously elected the Elder of the FWECA. He was now the Last Prophet of the Last Days which, by the way the message and the warning sign of *Memento Mori* were presented together, seemed to imply that The Last Days are here and now. Threatening, looming and eminently imminent.

I have a powerful firewall, which stops 90% of the spam attempting to invade my electronic privacy. Somehow this stuff got through. I strongly suspect that JJ himself had taught his Triumvirate to punch holes through the electronic barriers. We always pay for everything. It is the immutable law of Karma. At first sight, I strongly suspect, JJ could well be in serious trouble. Our NASA friends might not look kindly on having our liaison officer elevated to the position of the Last Prophet of any church, let alone, what JJ referred to in his lighter moments as, the Church of Doomsday.

"This is not funny at all," he says even as he charges into my room unannounced. He's never done that before. He always calls or at least knocks on my door. "Did you see it?"

"Didn't everyone?"

"Yea, not funny." JJ's face is a mask of concentration and rage. He must be mulling over alternate strategies for a counter attack.

"I'll do it!" he says through his teeth not explaining what he is about to do. "After all I've done for them...."

"For the Triumvirate?"

He doesn't answer but rushes out of my room. Two hours later he calls me on my viphone.

"Did you see it?" His voice sounds excited. I tell him that I'd already seen it.

"No, no, not that. Switch on you Mac, your e-mail," he sounds breathless.

I do as he asks. There is another announcement filling the whole screen. It is of the usual spam category, though again it manages to get through my electronic defenses. My eyes grew wide when I saw and read the warning. Actually it could be read as a warning or a promise.

Rapture
MYSTERY UNVEILED

ALL MEMBERS OF THE FIRST
WORLD ELECTRONIC CHURCH OF THE ADVENTIST
WILL FULFILL THE ANCIENT MYSTERY
WITHIN SEVEN DAYS
By order of the Last Prophet

"I've sent it out as a virus. All you need to do is open your computer to send my message out to all your e-mail addresses. Firewalls notwithstanding. Well, most of them."

Only now do I have a chance to read the rest of the 'announcement'. Apparently there are people who interpret some biblical writings as the promise of the 'church' being whisked up, 'in the twinkling of an eye', bodily, to heaven and thus to immortality. JJ has quoted number and verse of Paul's letters to Corinthians and Thessalonians as evidence. What is missing in Paul's verses, as usual, is the date of the event. JJ has supplied one. A week from today.

"You're telling those poor saps that they will be 'caught up to meet the Lord in the air'? But that's silly," I tell him. "You know it will never happen!"

"Exactly!"

"What do you mean? Have you decided to feed people garbage?"

"I have to. But it's the last garbage they'll ever read." JJ looks smug. Actually he looks on my viphone like a boy who's just pulled a fast one.

"Because they will be whisked up into heaven?"

JJ continues grinning. And then it dawns on me. The moment people realize that nothing's happened, they will ignore all future announcements issued by the Triumvirate, and by any Last Prophet. JJ created a dragon, and now he's killed it. Or at least it will be dead in seven days, which is roughly the time a virus needs to circle the globe seven times. It should be enough to destroy the FWECA permanently.

"Will they believe you?"

"Up to the time I resigned as the invisible honcho of the church, there were forty-two million dollars that said they believe

anything I say. At least that's how much my accountants have distributed to charities over the years."

"Wow!"

"Yea. Not bad for a joke I started just to get even with Father
Martin." JJ grinned but there was no humour in his eyes. He was
still angry. "I don't think they'll ever use my name again," he adds
tightening his lips. "And NASA people will never suspect me of
being that stupid," he added murmuring under his breath.

I agree. Especially if they're all sitting up above on a heavenly cloud. I think I'll wave to them on the way to the Moon.

The ceremony will take place at Dome #7, at 0300 hours, reads
the official announcement. We all line up at the main dome. The
air is festive, though mixed with an undertone of sadness. Not all
of us can go. Not even remotely so. As the Good Book says, many
are called but few are chosen. In this case, few indeed.

There is room on the Moon Base for 2,600 permanent personnel. Our Sanctuary now houses over 14,000. It will be great but it
won't be the same.

Three weeks after JJ got back from the Moon, the cat was officially let out of the bag. General Kevin J. Hoffendorff had been
empowered by the President of the USA to officially appoint John
Hydon Ph.D., Director of the CSC as the new Director of the Lunar
Science Centre, the LSC, and to select his own staff to accompany
him on this mission.

"We both knew this was going to happen, John." I could tell
that the General had grown genuinely fond of my father. They are
about the same age and the General is quietly jealous of Dad's appointment. There is no way, however that the General can match
my father's physical fitness, dexterity, or just plain good health.
And, of course, the General is no scientist.

"I know, Kevin," Dad tells the General embracing him like a
long lost brother. "We can't all go..." Dad is well aware of the
General's hankering.

"Send me a postcard, will you?"

They both smile. The ceremony of the official announcement is arranged for the benefit of the International Press. Anybody who is anybody in the News Media is here.

"Tomorrow we are initiating the genetic analysis," father tells General Hoffendorff, but, in a way, the old soldier has lost interest. He has been working for thirty years to bring the Moon Base into reality. He's done his job. At seventy-three, he's ready to put his feet up.

"I don't suppose you guys would put me up here for a while? It would be like going with you, a bit. Wouldn't it?"

"Kevin. You are welcome to my condo. I would be proud to have you as my successor," Dad assures him. The General blinks his eyes to get rid of an influx of some annoying moisture seeping from under his lids. "Must be the air, here," he murmurs wiping his eyes with his thumbs. "I'm sure I'll get use to it," he hastens to assure my father.

Three thousand five hundred people have been selected for DNA testing. They stay close to their video-phones and try to keep busy. They are all a little nervous. Anyone of them, all volunteers for the greatest adventure of their lives, might be rejected. And even if they pass, there will be a final selection process. It isn't just a question of hereditary diseases, but also of any predisposition which might endanger a completely enclosed environment on the Moon. Whatever we put under the lunar domes – there it will remain. Before the first permanent inhabitant moves in, all the domes will be sterilized with the usual American efficiency. Then the ebullient flora will be allowed to rebuild the freshness of the air. The necessary bacterial cultures will be carefully screened and reintroduced into the enclosed environment.

"They think of everything," Dad says as I express my doubts about all the prophylactic steps the Americans have planned.

"Is it all really necessary? All this medical scrutiny?" I ask him later that evening.

"We must let them do their job," father affirms. His consolatory smile suggests that we are of one mind.

Finally father, JJ and I are alone. Mary is somewhere about, but lately she's been keeping her own counsel. I think she is reconciling herself to the inevitable. She simply cannot face leaving Mother Earth. She's too set in her ways. I spoke to Aunt Miriam. They are staying too. After initial enthusiasm, they thought better of it. With the boys in California and David pushing eighty, this was just not a good idea. Not any more. Ten years earlier they would have come running. Miriam had guessed my concern.

"She'll come to live with us," she said. "After all, she's family. Like you are."

For the next few minutes I was holding Miriam's head to my chest endeavouring to quiet her sobs. We'd all grown very close. I'd known Miriam since I was born.

"It's all right, Miriam, dear auntie. We shall only be a fraction of a parsec away."

At this she finally smiled. "It doesn't sound so bad that way," she admitted.

By astronomical standards, the Moon really is an arm's length away. Literally next door. Our sun is only 0.000005 of a parsec away from us. Alpha Centauri, 1.32 parsecs. At any rate, my attempt at humour had worked. Aunt Miriam wouldn't miss us as much any more. Not as much.

"We must do all that's possible," Dad says. He's been looking tired lately. They are discussing the latest medical reports from around the world.

"And there really are all those viruses about," JJ adds pensively. He'll be joining us for dinner.

"More so than usual?"

"More so than in recent history." If I didn't know better I would think that JJ looked worried. The second time this month.

He takes a deep breath. "In 1918 an influenza pandemic killed, worldwide, between forty and fifty million people. People died of a virus that managed to circle the world twice before fizzling out. This took place without the benefit of our modern-day air travel. The population of the world, then, was about one billion. Over the last few years the population has been stable at around at eleven billion, so we can expect eleven times as many deaths, or, in round figures, about half a billion people. If we add to this the frequency of air travel we enjoy today, the vastly depleted immune system due to the sedentary lifestyle, we are talking in billions. Add to this the ensuing bacteria running rampant on the countless decomposing corpses and we can at least double or triple this number," JJ sounds deadly serious.

"Just from one virus...?" I purposefully omit the adjective 'lethal'.

"As best we can assess, the flu-bug in 1918 evolved from a virus in birds, which had found its way through mutation into pigs, which, as you know, have an immune system extremely similar to the human. You will note that the flu virus which has destroyed millions of birds and pigs already, is expanding at an alarming rate in East Asia."

"We're next?" I interrupt again, impressed with his knowledge. Apparently I didn't sound like posing a question. It was an answer begging to be contradicted.

"The sooner we move out of here the better," JJ says with a wry smile.

Lately, it wasn't often that JJ smiled. And when he did, it seemed at inappropriate moments. I had a strange feeling that JJ would be one of the few people who wouldn't miss Earth. In spite of his mobility in the course of his duties, his frequent trips outside the Sanctuary, he was becoming more withdrawn, more content just to remain within the Crystal Walls. As I covertly study his face, I think that perhaps he knows something we don't. But I can't read it. Simultaneously to growing withdrawn, JJ is becoming more inaccessible. We don't talk anymore, like we used to. Occasionally I even have the feeling that he is avoiding me.

"JJ?" I try again to break through his armour. For a moment I manage to get him alone on the balcony. "Is something wrong?"

He takes one quick look at me, smiles, shakes his head and goes inside. He's been like that, on and off, lately.

The first time it was fun. Now, it's a little unnerving. Eden is just as splendid as before. I am hovering above it, seemingly unaided, rather as I'd hovered before over the Enigma. Or was it in the future? There is no term of reference. I could have been anywhere – at any time. As for my hovering above the Enigma, well, in fact, it feels exactly the same. Since I know, I assume it must have already happened. At least to me.

As my mind is attracted by a specific object, a mountain or a river, or anything at all, I zoom in on it. Exactly as I did once, so many years ago, when I was zooming over the black mirror to see the various constellations up above Pluto. Yes, it must have been in the past. Is there a past? Or is it just a question of an orderly arrangement of events? I had a similar experience when I was studying my own body. Only in reverse. I would zoom into the sub-cellular structure, even into the subatomic matrix of life just to study the...

To study what? I wonder.

[Sometimes I think the whole universe exists only in my head. I could blink my eyes and it would dissolve into an impenetrable void. I gather my courage and I blink. It is still there. Fancy that!]

To study the Truth – the answer comes out of nowhere.

The truth seems to have no monopoly on space/time scale. One minute it can span the vastness of outer space only to delve into the sublime vision of an electron microscope the next.

I wonder what I am doing here.

Eden, the Garden of Eden, seems to enclose the whole globe. The whole Earth. I see no cities, no signs of a highly developed civilization. The Earth is as pristine as it must have been before it all started. Before what started?

Before the first coming, I hear my own thoughts.

Before the First Coming. This time, in my mind, I capitalize the letters. Before God created Adam. And Eve. The two of them had the run of Paradise. Was that the purpose? To run around naked and do nothing much? Like a couple of pets? Or to grow and evolve till finally we could pollute the planet into a state of decadent depravity.

In the past I'd always reached forward, to new horizons, new ideas. To Enigma. Why am I going back in time?

There is no time – it's that insistent part of me which seems to know all the answers again. There is no time.

And what about seeing my mother?

There is no time, the thought insists.

I refuse to argue with myself.

At this I feel something equivalent to an electric jolt. Surely, this is the same Earth. My Earth. The Earth of my father. Yet... why so many eons ago? Is this really what it was, before man took over? What if man didn't choose to build civilizations based on material needs. There might have been fewer of us. What if we'd developed a civilization, even a culture, like the dolphins? Just swimming in the vast ocean, in harmony with nature, with our environment. What if we could do this sort of thing on Earth? As land-dwellers. Is technological development inevitable?

Only to save us from the industrial revolution.

Who said that?

There is no one around. My mind is playing tricks on me. I look down to see if there is any life, down there, below me. I take a spin around the globe, then two or three more. I see nothing. Once or twice I think I saw some animal scurrying to hide behind some bushes. Can they see me? Surely... I can't even see myself.

I feel my invisible lips parting in a wide grin. I have to get used to this. It's eerie. If I had any hair, it would stand up on my neck. Only I don't have a neck.

Help!

I can see, but I don't have any eyes.

"It's our turn," the voice is right next to me. But it's not my own.

Dad is standing over me, smiling, doing his best to look carefree. "The DNA," he adds seeing I'm miles away. Miles? Eons? I refuse to think about it.

"I'll be up in a jiffy, Dad," I say. "I must have dozed off."

We go out together to the bio lab. As usual we walk. It's hard to believe that soon all this will be a quarter of a million miles away. We pass by our bench. The weeping willow is still weeping. She must be as old as I am. At least thirty. The ducklings are large now. I wonder how many generations of ducklings have graced this little pond. Soon they will be taken out and placed in a different environment. Like ourselves. If we're lucky. If we pass all the tests. There is no hiding it. I shall miss it. I shall miss every palm tree, every flowering bush, every shrub, every ripple on the small pond. Our pond. Dad's and mine. And JJ's. I'll even miss the birds frolicking up above, amid the latticework of aluminium tubes. I'll miss it all.

For an instant I remember the wake Dad and JJ held on the terrace that night. I sigh and shake my head. I am not alone, I realize.

I wonder if I really want to go. I guess I wouldn't, if it weren't for Dad and JJ. We are family. For thirty years. That's a long time to be together. Poor Mary. Thank goodness for Miriam. *Que sera sera*, I start humming. I haven't heard this song since I was a little girl. Mary sang it for me. Now Mary will sing it for someone else.

A nurse takes my temperature, blood pressure, then blood itself, then swabs inside my mouth, and lets me go. Someone else examines my teeth. Then they take X-rays – some other scanners glide over my body. I hate being naked, even in a hospital. Finally I'm done. I feel abused. Violated. One should only be poked when one is sick. Not when perfectly healthy. Next time I'll poke them right back. I would do it now if it weren't for Dad. I can't let him go up there alone. Dad is seventy-three now. Didn't I already say that? God knows he's healthy, but he is seventy-three. With luck, he might be active for another twenty, thirty years. God, how time flies! On the other hand, so many things feel as though they happened only yesterday. Like when we sat for the first time under the weeping willow. I suppose I'll miss her most. When I sit under her drooping branches, I feel as though I am back in a womb. I feel embraced, protected. Alone yet never lonely. I am with the green twigs, and the pond, and the ducklings. You just can't be lonely on that bench.

They're finished with Dad. He took longer. Must have checked on more things. They probably couldn't believe he's in such a good shape. As we walk back, Dad pulls me towards our bench. I smile. I knew he would.

"I saw her on my own," he says once we sit down. "It was different, but it was, well, she was even more real."

"It's often up to you how real you make her," I say. I know we are talking about mother. About Dad's wife.

"I make her?" he asks.

"We have the whole universe within us, Dad. We only experience what we want to experience. It's just that few of us realize that it is the other 'I' that does the choosing."

We sit watching the ducks. We are not allowed to feed them. I miss that.

"I am that I am," Dad says slowly. "So that's what it means."

This is a wonderful moment. Dad understands. At last.

"I love you Daddy," I say.

Little more is necessary. Just love. Lots of love.

***

22

Another Enigma?

The first contingent is scheduled to leave for the Moon early in
June. JJ, or Commander John Hydon Jr., as he is now referred to
by the Lunies, will be leading the support staff, engineers, maintenance workers, gardeners, dieticians and such like, who are to pave
the way. The front assault group. The Marines or Green Berets.
Only the Marines never had it so good. With the exception of a
few, this team have all signed contracts for six months. JJ's and his
immediate staff of six have open-ended contracts. No restrictions
on either side. It was JJ's idea. He argued that this arrangement
would foster the very best in his people. In people that count.

"No one is indispensable," JJ told Kevin Hoffendorff in a rare
tête-à-tête they had in Florida. "But some are more indispensable
than others."

It was a very non army-like idea.

The General had never married, but he'd told Dad that had he
ever tied the knot, he would have liked to have had a son like JJ.
"Splendid young man," he'd said pulling in his stomach in a vein
attempt to emulate JJ's contour. "He would go far in the army,"
he'd added as though bestowing a medal on JJ's chest. Dad had no
heart to tell him that JJ wouldn't be caught dead in the army. "Too
many orders, not enough initiative," JJ had said, "and when you

can finally act on your own, you have neither the energy nor the heart to enjoy it."

"I don't really find myself too old to enjoy anything, son," father looked a tad offended.

"Precisely my point," JJ concurred. "That's because you're not in the army, Dad."

JJ is leaving today. Dad and I are saying our so-longs right here, at home. I cannot bear to see him to the VTAL pad. His team has already left. JJ is the last. In Florida the order will be reversed. JJ will take the first shuttle. The twenty-seven others will follow. They will be on the Moon Base the same day, sipping drinks in their new homes. I suppose there will be drinks on the Moon? Perhaps, like down here – our own. Our own wine and beer. It's hard to tell. Will we need beer? Is there a summer on the Moon? I mean with the Moon always facing the same way, do they have seasons? I know the temperature differentials are staggering. At noon, on the Equator, the temperature rises to 104^0C, but at night it plummets to minus 157^0C.

"That's enough to freeze off your *cojones*," Dad had once said to JJ. "Remember your thermal underwear!" They'd both laughed. They didn't know I was listening.

Funny how we say up there or down here. The Moon is just as often down or at the side as is it up. Only, when it's down, we can't see it. Unless we take a quick trip to Rio. We don't take many trips any more. Frankly, we never did. How come I know so much about our Solar System, about distant galaxies and so little about the Moon? Or about Earth, for that matter? I feel like a person living in a city which boasts a magnificent museum, but who never visits its treasures because they are so close. So easily accessible. "We can always go tomorrow, or the day after." Or next week, or month. It's the same with the Moon. It's so close to us that I feel I can learn about it any time. Tomorrow, or the day after.

I've seen the pictures, of course. Craters dominate lunar topography. Their floors are usually lower than the surrounding terrain and I've often seen mounds rising at their centres. On the outside of the impact craters there are frequently lines radiating in all directions. They run for hundreds of kilometres, across mountains and valleys and other craters. Another common feature are the rilles. They are long and narrow depressions, also extending from tens to hundreds of kilometres. They also cut across other features. Then there is the Straight Wall. A cliff that looks like an artefact, like a manmade construction. Other 'walls', not quite as straight, can rise from a few to a few thousand feet. My colleagues refer to them as scraps.

And then there are the ridges. They form a network of low relief over the *maria*, the flat surfaces of the lunar seas. They often form crisscross patterns adding variety to the otherwise bleak landscape.

The rarest are the domes. Until the pictures Dad took with the Monster Eye, few had been seen from Earth. The circular domes are not high, and thus they cast little shadow. They range in diameter from 5 to 20 kilometres. Those that are irregular in shape, more elliptical, extend to some 50 kilometres.

And finally, at the brink between eternal light and eternal darkness there are some crystal jewels scattered in a seemingly random pattern. The Moon always offers the same face to the sun. To study both sides, it has been deemed propitious to place construction where access to the exploration of both sides of the Moon would be easiest. It had been a wise decision. The face of the Moon exposed to the sun seems to have lost its water. It must have evaporated through deep cervices caused by extreme variations in temperature.

And there it lay.

The Lunar Science Centre. LSC. Sill with Canadian spelling. Close to the water found on the side of perpetual darkness, yet open to the sunlight for the plants, heat and light. And perfectly positioned to explore both sides. It looks like a series of jewels because, at night, the domes catch sunlight. They sparkle with reflected light. The sandwich consisting of four layers of transparent plastic keeps the heat from escaping the colossal geodesic domes. But at noon – the Moon's noon – silver-coated mirrors slide over the most exposed areas to protect the inhabitants from the scorching sun. From Earth, those silvery panels combine to look like diamond dust scattered on the Moon's surface. They give people on Earth a focus, a connection to those already up there.

Moon's Noon... I am sure there is a song there somewhere.

The DNA tests of the first group revealed no surprises. The first contingent was judged healthy, with no negative traits that could be passed on. At least, what negative traits there were seemed non-contagious. Even the psychiatric evaluation produced no pronounced deviations from the accepted norm. JJ took that as a personal affront.

"How dare they call me normal! Never in my life have I done anything that was normal," he insisted.

Dad went to see JJ off and then continued to his office. "He'll be busy for some time," he said. I wish I were busy. During the last month, my duties at the Observatory have been phased out. A young man will be doing my work.

I am looking forward to receiving my own genome analysis and comparing it to Dad's and JJ's. It could be interesting to see how we differ. When I get the phone call, I drop my work and run to the lab. Something is pushing me there, something undefined yet urgent, like an itch in the middle of my back that I cannot quite reach. Dr. Brown is expecting me.

"You've passed Miss Heidi. So has your father," he announces the moment I cross the door of his office.

I want to ask him something but I don't know how to formulate my question.

"Was there anything unusual about my father's or my genome? Something that we should know?" I don't know why I'm asking.

Dr. Brown looks distinctly uncomfortable.

"Well, not exactly," he avoids meeting my eyes. He glances towards the geodesic structure spanning over the suspended ceiling, as though looking for inspiration. He appears to share in my own unease. "There is one thing that we find hard to account for..." he starts but his voice trails off into silence.

"Well? Am I dying? Mad?" I prod. I am not really serious, but I feel that itch again.

"Oh, no, Miss Heidi. It's nothing like that." Now he looks embarrassed.

I get to my feet. "Out with it, doctor! I really do not have all day."

He also gets up still looking as though he would like to avoid answering my question.

"Well?"

"Oh, ah, yes. Well, Miss Heidi, perhaps I should talk to your father first," he's still hedging.

"I am perfectly capable of conveying whatever you have to say to my father myself, doctor." It's been years since I've raised my voice to anyone.

"John Hydon is not JJ's father," he blurts out turning his back on me.

I stand still, then try to sit down on the chair I think is still behind me. I must have pushed it back getting up in a huff. I miss it by two inches. I slide to the floor and remain there trying to collect my thoughts.

The next thing I am aware of is Dr. Brown doing his best to lift me to my feet.

"I am sorry, Miss Heidi. Really, I am sorry. I didn't want to tell you. It's all my fault..."

He goes on like this till I find myself safely in the chair, not under it. As I look up, the doctor is trying hard not to look disconcerted.

"If you don't mind, doctor, I'll go and see my father now."

But father is busy elsewhere.

I walk to my bench. I sit down and try hard to reduce the pounding of my heart. Neither the willow, nor the serene pond offer any solace. JJ is not my brother. But how? Margaret must have played around. Would father be hurt? Offended? It was so long ago. And JJ? How would he take it? My heart is refusing to tone down its mad tattoo. I do some deep breathing. It helps. My mind is a mad whirl of bits and pieces of memories. Disjointed fragments torn out of my recent past. JJ's avoidance of my eyes. His moving out after finishing Calgary. His strange aloofness on

occasions when in the past he was just a boisterous brother. Brother? JJ is not my brother.

JJ is not my brother.

He is not my father's son. Who is he? Of course I know that.
I already thought of it. Margaret's. And some playboy's with a
good posture and high forehead. I can see the lines splashed across
the front page of British rags. The Daily Mirror, the News of the
World, would have a field day.

MARGARET'S HEIR SCOOTS TO THE MOON, a sort of
play on words of 'heir' and 'hare', or A TALE OF MARGARET'S
TAIL, even worse.

They can be cruel. The paparazzi. Margaret had been cruel.
Or perhaps... or perhaps she'd done Dad a great favour. Let's face
it. After the initial problems of the first three years, JJ had given
Dad a great deal of joy. And now, a great deal to be proud of.

He'd avoided my eyes.

And if it hadn't been for Margaret then, in a way, I would
never have been born. Dad wouldn't have tried to escape from her
to the Lake District. He wouldn't have met my mother... Life can
be so complicated. It must be true that time doesn't really exist and
all things, all events, even ideas and emotions already exist in the
matrix beyond space and time. In the heart of a black hole. Or in
Enigma. It is our job to arrange those events, those ideas and emotions into a comprehensive, sensible order. We must restore or
even create order within chaos. The primordial chaos in which all
that ever has or is or could be is rolled into one.

He avoided my eyes....

Does JJ have feelings for me? Non-brotherly feelings?

There is that stupid heart of mine going nineteen to a dozen. I
take a few more deep breaths. I don't even notice when Dad sits
down next to me on our bench.

"You all right, Pet?" he asks gently.

I open my mouth to tell him. He holds up his hand. "Dr.
Brown called me. He was worried about you."

We sit for a while in silence. I begin to notice, again, the willow, the tremulous ripple on the pond, the yellowish-white lilies

amid the flat green pads. It's all coming back. The world will continue to unfold itself.

"How do you think he'll take it?" Dad asks.

Good old Dad. Maybe he's figured as much already. They
don't call him The Brain for nothing. He must have. And he's
kept it all to himself. "No one need know," he adds and then turns
to face me. "Unless..." he stops there.

"You've noticed?"

"It wasn't that hard to see. But I've never been sure. Had I
been, I would have had the DNA checked long ago. So that you
two could be together."

"So it wasn't that obvious after all," I murmur not quite knowing what to say.

"Only since JJ returned from Calgary. Did something happen
between you two?"

"No, Dad. Nothing happened between us. Nor would it ever.
Somehow, it would be wrong."

He nods. We seem to think alike. No one could be sure. Not
just of the DNA, nor of Margaret's peccadilloes, nor even of JJ's or
my own feelings. It has all been unspoken, hypothetical, not allowed to enter our full awareness.

"We shall have to tell him?" I form the sentence in a question.

"It's only fair. After all, he's old enough to take care of himself. I hardly think he'll run to Suffolk to claim his dubious title."

That was it. For some reason we are both laughing. We sit on
'our' bench, rolling with laughter. Most of it is the release of pent
up nerves. But trying to imagine JJ running after a British title is
more than we can take seriously. Now or ever.

Finally. Finally at least one enigma has been resolved.

"It's time to go back, Pet," Dad gets up wearily. We are now
relaxed but also drained of energy. "I'm sure Mary is ready with
our supper."

I rise, unwillingly, then sit down again. I hate to leave our
spot. Who knows how many more times we shall sit here?

"I don't suppose, Dad, they would take our bench up to the
Moon, do you?"

Suddenly I feel very tired. I pull Dad down again, next to me
and lean my head on his shoulder. I close my eyes.

The view of the Earth is fantastic. I say this knowing that we use this adjective too freely. Fantastic means beyond reality. Existing only in imagination. It also means fanciful, whimsical, capricious, and seemingly impossible. The Earth is all of these. Only it's real.

We sit on our balcony, JJ's arm rests possessively over my shoulder. The view changes, from hour to hour, showing us the green and brown of the continents as they interrupt the blue of the oceans. A kaleidoscope of colours. Here and there, over the night side, the eruptions of light mark our cities. Their cities. We don't belong there any more. The sunrays glance off the Arctic with blinding intensity only to reappear, a minute later, on the other side of the globe with a gentler, more satin caress. And all this is held in a veil of divergent shapes, of a gossamer tulle of clouds, drifting along at their own easy pace from the far west to the far east, never stopping, just metamorphosing themselves into different configurations, different adornments. Our Earth. Our long-suffering, abused, exhausted Earth.

How do I love thee....

Thou hast given us so much. Thou hast brought us sons so talented, so marvellous that they've been compared to gods. They all walked in Thy precious paradise. What once had been paradise. Now needing cleansing. Restoring to Thine illustrious glory. To start again. To begin a cycle of rebirth.

We are saying good-bye.

On each successive orbit the globe below us grows smaller. It remains as beautiful, as precious, only further away. And then, before our very eyes the wondrous Earth shrinks and retreats into the velvety darkness. It is no more a multihued sphere, nor even a celestial lantern, sharing it's reflected glory. It is little more than a moon, a round luminous disk, we had seen, so recently, from its surface. And then, just moments later, the Earth joins the other planets, then the other twinkling points of light on the dark garment of the universe.

Father had said it would happen. I didn't believe him. I don't really believe him even now. I'm sure that the next time I blink my eyes, the Earth will be there again. It must be. It is my Earth. My home. It will be as verdant, as blue, as fragile in its veil of clouds as it has been for billions of years.

What is time anyway? The Earth is not just a planet. The Earth is an Enigma. An idea. An inexhaustible compendium of ideas. Of problems to be resolved. There was a time when gods descended to her womb and seeded a desire for knowledge. The desire to evolve, to rise above what was. They breathed real life into our mouths.

I don't have to be there any more. But I must see it. Caress it with my eyes. So many memories. I close my eyes.

I run to the balcony. The Moon is still there. Thank God! Dad must have carried me home.

Another dream, another vision.

Will they ever stop? Why me? Why have I been chosen to witness the past or the future, or both all mixed up in a cauldron of events untouched by reality? Are such things still to happen?

JJ would know. He's studied all the prophecies. I should have listened, read his Internet messages. It's too late now. He's destroyed the church of his own creation. The Lord giveth, the Lord taketh away. He had a right to destroy it, I suppose. But what am I to do? Seeing myself on the Moon was one thing, but to tear the Moon from its orbit was quite another.

Why did I have to witness myself bidding farewell to my Earth? I suppose it must have been precipitated by our imminent departure to the Moon.

(I hate saying good-byes).

Perhaps the dreams get mixed up sometimes. Or jumbled up in time. I'd like to forget them all. Well, almost all. I always want to remember my mother. And the Enigma. What it sands for. It's beauty. I also want to remember JJ's arm draped over my shoulder.

***

23

Zero Minus Ten Days

Before leaving, JJ had asked me to take care of his email in his absence. He'd expected that within a month or two, his inbox would dry up by its own momentum. Or lack of it. He hardly cared who would look after the electronic mail once we all moved to our celestial abode. He had no more secrets. Anyway, I'm told that there is some way of redirecting email through radio waves.

We'll see.

JJ's inbox is much fuller than mine ever was. I relegate some forty spam items, which have managed to get through his elaborate firewalls, to the trash bin. They are mostly adverts of ways guaranteed to lose all excessive kilos with the aid of popping pills just before eating. Apparently you can still enjoy your food, only you don't absorb any. A sort of gastric masturbation. You make love to yourself and you don't even get pregnant.

It's time to move out and up. Way up.

To the Moon.

Talking of masturbation. Checking JJ's email over the last few days I've discovered, quite unwittingly, that there are now over fifty products competing with the original Viagra, all designed to heighten man's libidinous prowess. They sound more like lecherous prowess – assuming there is a difference. Apparently the products enable men to perform adequately even with the ugliest of women. It's guaranteed or money back.

Even as I sit in front of JJ's computer screen, a funny sound, a bit like a lost duckling, announces the arrival of more email. I click them open. The first letter makes me laugh. JJ will love this one. I reach for the radiophone. We have been told to use it only in an emergency, but I haven't spoken to JJ in a week. I tell myself that I deserve to hear his voice.

Then I change my mind.

I simply couldn't speak to him and not let the DNA stuff out of the bag. It will have to wait; though I'm sure JJ would be delighted at the news. The email, in a nutshell, advises JJ that he's been excommunicated from the First World Electronic Church of the Adventist. The reason quoted is "insufficiently religious". I dare say the accusation is not without substance. JJ is probably the most irreligious person I know. He's been an avowed atheist for as long as I can remember.

"Yes, Hey," he'd said in a noncommittal tone of voice. "I believe in the Absolute, but only as an aim, a purpose or an unattainable destination. Unattainable because this destination lies in infinity, and thus it remains forever only a direction, never a point of arrival. The seed of that Absolute or the Ultimate, which you can spell with a capital A or U if you wish, is anchored in every one of us. Or, at least, it has the potential to flourish in everyone of us."

"Do you imagine that people are aware of this, ah.... this potential?" I recall asking.

"I can't speak for others. But I believe that if you discover this seed, it will grow in you, expand, and virtually take over your will. A religionist would say that it would save us, but I reject this metaphor, because most adherents of religions consider saving as a means of going to heaven and remaining there, bored stiff, for ever-after."

"So you don't believe in heaven either?" I asked.

"I don't believe in getting to heaven. I equate being in heaven with being consciously aware of taking an active part in the journey. It is the process of becoming that fills me with bliss. Not having become and going to nowhere."

"So the process for you is eternal?"

"As I understand it now, yes. If we consciously embark on a journey without placing on it any limitations, then this seed I referred to before will assure us of the continuity of travel. Remember that the aim, the goal, lies in infinity, which, by definition is unattainable. Rather like a black hole that attracts matter to itself, regardless of how it metamorphoses itself over eons of time. You can orbit a black hole for eternity, but should you fall into one, you're dead. Your journey, your becoming, is over. You've reached stagnation. A stasis. Maybe I'm not expressing myself clearly. Anyway, we must discover this potential within ourselves or remain, well, sort of half-dead...."

I'd never realized that JJ had such 'deep' thoughts. Usually he sounded more like an entrenched cynic than a free thinker. But then, I guess studying History of Philosophy in Calgary had left its mark.

But I tend to agree with him. Once you stop becoming – you're dead. Also by definition. Which, as such, is no problem; only in a state of being, as against becoming, you shed your personality. Probably also your individuality. You become a nonentity. One with all. Make that All with a capital A. That which identifies you as you is a function of becoming. So you as you is no more. Ever.

"But, you know," he'd added after a pause, "if we fail to discover it, this seed, this potential within our consciousness, then its very absence will cause our consciousness to atrophy. What little there is of it will disseminate itself into the fabric of the universe without leaving any discernible trace."

"The eternal death?" I murmured. I was going to say damnation but that's not what he meant. He meant an absence, not any form of suffering.

"Only of that particular segment of the journey. After all, the travel takes place at a conscious level. If you stand still, then you don't get anywhere. There is nothing to record, to keep. Or to save."

It sounded as if JJ had it all worked out. Whatever his personal philosophy, or set of beliefs, it made him a very effective co-traveller. Wherever the journey took him. Also, I may be wrong, but it seems to me that the only god, or God, JJ believes in is, and must be, anchored deep in his heart. It, or He, can never be relegated to some exterior Entity judging us or patting us on the back.

In this sense JJ was, and remains, an exemplary atheist. I am sure that he'll be delighted at having been excommunicated by the Triumvirate. After all, there was at least a peripheral purpose behind his Internet doomsday announcement. They wanted him out. They got him out. Hopefully, everyone is happy.

Sometime after JJ and I discussed the subject of being and becoming, I was drawn into the Enigma. It might be wiser to say: into my enigmatic state of consciousness. This time I seemed to be in a non-participatory condition. I just looked and listened.

The thought, which must have precipitated my vision, was my inability to fully integrate into my consciousness the concept of being with the process of becoming. Specifically, I'd been wondering, not for the first time, how my mother could be visible to me and yet not be in a state of becoming.

The next instant I saw myself changing shapes, rather as colours change in a kaleidoscope. They rotated at a frantic rate, sliding or metamorphosing from one to another. It seems that my enigmatic state enabled me to witness the hundreds of thousands of incarnations I'd experienced since my consciousness had become individualized.

As I watched in my disembodied state, the process accelerated still more, finally becoming a vibrating source of light. I had my being within this light. It represented the process of evolutions, the countless incarnations, all rolled into one. I began to realize that I am this light. That the light is me. It is the sum total of all that I have ever been.

And then, with a shock that brought me out of my vision, I had an instant of realization, that, in the condition I'd just experienced, I was also all that I ever shall be. I was the process of becoming. I was life itself.

I am the Process, I whispered as my eyes searched for a witness to my vision. All that I have ever been, or shall be, I am. So is my mother. So is every individualized consciousness.

I am the Process.

I am life Itself.

Dad says that there's been a great increase in chunks of matter, some as large as football fields, slamming into Mars. He says they must originate in the Asteroid belt. There is no other possibility. I'm a bit nervous about the Moon. Earth has an atmosphere that can burn up all but the largest meteors, or globs of whatever might be falling down on our heads, but the Moon has no such protection. That, surely, must be why the whole of the Moon's surface is peppered with craters of every size and description. I tell Dad as much.

"We have nothing to worry about," father puts his hand on my shoulder reassuringly. He is assuming that JJ is at the root of my anxiety. "Apparently Mars has been singled out for the avalanche of space debris. As I mentioned before, Mars is by far the most exposed planet to asteroid bombardment. Considering the composition of a lot of that stuff, Mars' surface will be replete with heavy metals, chunks of ice and all sorts of interesting minerals."

Father is trying to reassure all of us, particularly those scheduled to leave for the Moon within days. No one comments. They all look to him for leadership.

"And don't forget that on the Moon, each dome can be cut off from every other at a moment's notice. The meteor would have to strike you practically on your head to do you any harm." And so on, and so forth. Dad really does care about every one of us. So much so, that he carefully omitted to tell us about the impact craters. Why worry about the inevitable? *Que sera, sera*, he murmured.

We are at the Mendels' condo, trying hard to enjoy what is probably the last regular Sunday dinner. Not surprisingly, the atmosphere is a little down. Everyone is trying hard to say something funny, something light and carefree. Not for the sake of those going, but for those who are to be left behind.

"If Twigg were still alive he would raise this as an additional argument for putting a man on Mars," David offers, inconsequentially I think, until I understand that he is referring to Dad's previous comment about the interesting minerals on Mars. Not only is Twigg long dead, but so is the Mars program. For now. Finally they've redirected all their efforts towards the construction of the

Moon Base. Only the name, Way Station, remains, but even that is
confined to just four of the domes.

"How true," someone agrees.

No one seems to care very much, one way or another. Even as
light conversation fills the frequent silences, an absurd thought
comes to my mind. I ask myself how does one make love in one-
sixth of the earth's gravity? I feel my cheeks turning red. I have
no idea why such lewd thoughts entered my mind. But my imagination takes off on its own tangent. I visualize all sorts of contortions quite impossible to realize on Earth. I see myself flying,
bouncing, turning somersaults, all in a passionate clinch with...

"What about the pandemic reported in China?" someone
wants to know.

"I haven't heard much more, but as of next week I am shutting
down unrestricted access to the Sanctuary. It seems necessary to
take some steps. I've got Ottawa's OK," David says. He looks a
little embarrassed. His sons are both on the outside. "As of next
week, everyone will have to go through a decontamination proced-
ure to get into the Crystal City. It won't be foolproof but at least it
will provide a line of defence."

Dr. Mendel is taking over from Dad. Not the day to day operation of the whole Sanctuary but he will be the Godfather, the
Spiritual Leader, so to speak. He will decide on the direction the
Sanctuary will take, while the Administration will decide how to
get there. That was more or less how father had been running
things. He and Dave have been very close. For many years. In a
way they are like brothers. David refers to their relationship as
partners in crime.

"We get away with murder, here, my friend," he'd said many
a time.

"Quite true," my father'd agreed. "Only we don't do it for our
own sake."

That was also true. Neither father nor Dave had accumulated
any money, any jewels, or gold over the thirty years they'd been
working together.

"My diamonds are infinite in number," Dad would say pointing up with his thumb.

"And I could never dig out all the gold from under my feet," David would add.

They understood each other. "And what of the rainy day?" I'd asked once half-seriously. "It doesn't rain here, darling," Dad replied. "Least, not very often."

It did, however, rain regularly; from four a.m. to four-thirty a.m., watering the lush gardens. Only the astronomers really knew about it. The others slept through it.

I see Dave pulling Dad towards the balcony. I edge towards them. Dave tells Dad, quietly, about his latest readings. By the time I get to them, I can only hear his conclusions.

"At this rate, in roughly eighty to ninety years, the climate will change diametrically. We shall be as the moon. Our North Pole will permanently face away from the sun."

"No more four seasons?" Dad asks.

"Not as we know them today. On the other hand, the continents will have drifted closer together. All northward."

"Any loss of life?"

"Not if they stock up on heating oil," Dave smiles but there's no mirth in his eyes.

"You're sure about all this?" Dad asks, shaking his head from side to side.

"97.03% probability."

I guess the rest. For years now, Dr. Mendel's department has been studying minute deviations in Earth's axis angle of rotation. Lately the rate of change had increased substantially. Not anything people at large would notice with the naked eye, so to speak, but the trend was, apparently, quite substantial. If Dr. Mendel's people were right, then the Sanctuary would need a lot more heating during the near-permanent winter. The solar energy would offer little heat. The one consolation is that, by the time the change was felt physically, Uncle Dave and Aunt Miriam would be long dead.

I pretend I haven't overheard anything and go to mix with the crowd.

Today, we all drink just a little too much. No one gets drunk, of course, but the extra glass of wine helps to alleviate some sorrows. Shakespeare said that parting is such sweet sorrow. That's

not true. There is nothing sweet about parting. It's just sorrow.
Plain and simple, sad, gut wrenching sorrow.

On the way back, Dad drops by his office. I go with him. He
looks at some printouts and says he'll have to hang around for a
little while. I decide to wait for him in JJ's office. It seems so very
empty with JJ not there. I check and clear his email. There's nothing worth keeping. Reports, bills, and more reports. They'll all be
taken over by JJ's successor. A nice girl. A woman about my age.
There are more women staying behind than man. I wonder why
that is?

I am about to leave JJ's old office when the radiophone makes
an unholy racket, like a wailing siren. I dare not touch it. It is the
one assigned for emergencies to and from the Moon. Only two
such radiophones have been installed, one in Dad's office, one here
in JJ's. I look around but there is no one. A little tentatively I
press the receiving button. There is some interference and then I
hear JJ's voice.

"Hey?"

"Yes, JJ! How are you? Is everything OK? Why...."

"Hey?"

"Yes, it's me," I've never had an extra-planetary conversation.

"Hey, will you marry me?"

I must have been silent for longer than I realize; on the other
end his voice sounds worried. Very worried. It's strange. I've
known JJ for my thirty years and I've never seen him worried. Annoyed, but not worried. Not once.

"Hey? Hey! Are you there?"

"Yes, JJ."

"Yes you will, or yes you are there?" I never thought I would
hear JJ exasperated on my account.

"Yes to both, JJ." And the moment I say it the r'phone goes
dead. Which is about the way I feel at this moment. Dead. Or at
least half-dead. My head feels woozy. I try to get up but my legs
are weak. I don't know what is going on. JJ asked me to marry
him. He is not my brother. He can ask me anything he wants.
Oh... my God. I... I said yes....

He must have heard about the DNA. Absurdly, I wonder when. I wonder how long he'd waited before calling me. JJ's a fast thinker. His mind is superbly organized. I bet the report is still lying in front of him. He must have taken it with him but had no time to look at it. Poor JJ. He's got so much on his shoulders. I'll have to take good care of him. I'll make him slow down, take things easy.

And then he's bound to learn to hate me in no time at all, I tell myself. A strange sound escapes my throat. I think others would call it hysterical laughter. It stops the moment I realize that I am going just a little mad. It could be that I am happier than I've ever been. More than I thought it possible to be. It is...

I have no idea what it is like. I've never been engaged before. I've never been proposed to from the moon, by phone!

It's new to me.

The telephone rings again. This time it's the real phone. I pick it up like grabbing a lifeline. It's my father. He tells me that when the radiophone went dead, it was because the Moon had just cleared the horizon. We were blocked by the curve of the Earth. We're also blocked by an abyss of space. Some 364,000 kilometres of it. At least I'll end up in the Guinness Book of Records. I've heard of long engagements but this beats them all. At the time, it didn't cross my mind that Dad must have been listening in on our conversation. I am a bit absent-minded. OK. Very absent-minded.

I'm engaged.

"Dad?"

"Yes?" Dad is holding something back.

"Guess who called?" I can't help being coy. I feel like a little girl. I feel like singing. Or dancing. Gosh, I'll have to learn to dance. How come I never did?

"I told him you were in his office," Dad says in a peculiar voice. At least to me it sounds peculiar. Then he poses a very noncommittal question. He just says "Well?" with a definite question mark.

"I'm engaged, Dad," I say it outright.

"To your brother?" This time he sounds incredulous. He's lying. Or acting. I know Dad. He never sounds incredulous. When you spend your lifetime studying light, from stars and whole galaxies, that originated millions of years ago, nothing can surprise you. You've seen it all, so to speak.

"Yes, Dad. Do you approve?"

"I love you, Pet. I also love JJ. How could I possibly not approve?"

I take that in. I still feel tipsy. Drunk on.... I don't know what I'm drunk on.

"I love you too, Dad. We both love you."

I suddenly realize what an incredible relief it is to be able to admit to myself that I love JJ. For years I have had to suppress my feelings even before they reached my frontal lobe. Love should be open. Visible. Not squeezed into a dark nook of one's soul. Well, no more.

"We both love you very, very much, Dad," I repeat.

Three minutes later father joins me in JJ's old office. I'm still too weak to walk. And the next moment for some reason I seek the comfort of Dad's arms and start crying. My tears flow unabated. Dad says nothing. Just stands there, his arms around me, trying his best to protect me from whatever brought on the deluge. He need not have worried. The floods had been held at bay for a long, long time. Now, finally, it's out. What a relief. I'll be all right for the next ten years. For a lifetime.

"Love you, Pet," he whispers.

"Me, too," I manage as my heaving chest calms down. "We too," I correct myself again. I must always say that to Dad for the both of us. Men are no good at this sort of thing.

We really do love Dad. I suspect that wherever our journey will take us, we always shall. We walk home in silence. Dad, if he'd thought far enough ahead, must be happy. What was happening to JJ and me should assure him that he'll never lose us. We would be under the same roof. Or, at the very least, under the same geodesic dome.

"Dad?" I ask as we enter our condo, practically for the last time. Only days are left to our departure.

"Yes, Pet?"

"Do you think there will be a padre on the Moon?"

Father grins. It is his first broad smile this evening. "We'll just have to get you one, Pet," he says. "Even if I have to don a dog collar myself."

It all happened too smoothly. It was just too easy. Something had to happen to balance the scales of duality. It did.

Radiophones are not like ordinary telephones. They do not assure the parties of any reasonable privacy. The radio wave impulses travel the open ethers. Anyone with the right equipment can tune in and listen to our conversation. They had.

The day after JJ asked me to marry him, I am awakened at five a.m. by the insistent ringing of my telephone. An hour later I learn that I am not the only one to be torn out of blissful sleep. All the telephones, all the email receivers, all the radiophones are jammed. I'm told that three million people had listened in to JJ's proposal. And now, more than double that number are rushing in to congratulate us. It seems that the decadent world, which we are so ready to leave behind, still feels the need to partake in my joy. They have been decent enough to wait until five a.m. They just couldn't wait any longer, many had said. They had been afraid that later . . . the lines might be jammed!

Lack of sleep notwithstanding, it was the most wonderful present I'd ever received. It also played havoc with communications. It was utter hell for the Administration. From Mount Ogilvy all the way to Florida. And back.

Somehow, no one seems to have minded.

Not too much.

***

24

Enigma Unveiled

It is a good feeling, even if a trifle selfish, when you observe people other than yourself who seem a little strange. Over the years,
I've had my share of visions. Over twenty just of the Enigma itself. Large and small. On occasion, I've had the impression that
the lights, which formed in a circle around the central darkness
within the mysterious globe, radiated auras of some past avatars,
philosophers, or perhaps very wise men. But apart from these
vague impressions, I've never experienced any actual apparitions
or spectres of those or any other ancients.

Today, reading the news on the Internet, I found that people,
ordinary people from across different continents, reported having
seen Moses or the Christ, or even Buddha, and get this, also Isis
and Osiris. They'd spotted them in different circumstances, not
limited to dreams. Someone claimed that he'd seen Jalaluddin
Rumi strolling, arm in arm, with Shams of Tabriz through the vine-
yards of Meram. A young girl in the North of Italy swore she'd
seen Francis of Assisi in deep discussion with Meister Eckhart, although she gave no explanation as to how she'd recognized them
for who they were. As for Isis and Osiris, that story sounded even
more bizarre. They, the two deities, had been seen floating down
the Nile, not on a Royal Barge or some Egyptian skiff, but just an

inch or two above the water, reclining on thin air, apparently deep in conversation with each other.

Now that, even by my standards, is pushing it.

I know that our minds are well capable of conjuring images of men or women we hold dear, even as I had done of my own mother. But Isis and Osiris? Weren't they just legends? Or is it that people are starving for something other than catering to their ailing bodies, falling, year after year, into a state of hopeless disrepair.

Give me a break!

By those standards my own visions, dreams if you prefer, were and are extraordinarily ordinary. Had I laid any claims to being a visionary – not that I'd ever told anyone outside my family about my own dreams – I would have been locked up long ago, and the key to my padded cell would have been thrown away. Nevertheless, I must admit that I derive a degree of perverse pleasure from the knowledge that I am not the only one suffering from an overactive imagination. Either that, or there is some sort of malady sweeping the world which is affecting our minds. And I am not talking about any avian, swine, bovine or any other pestilent influenza. The flu virus might well kill our bodies, but these visions seem to be eating at the human soul. Theirs – not mine. Or perhaps, just perhaps, they are feeding our soul. Who can tell, these days?

But I ask you, Isis? Wasn't she symbolized by a cow? Perhaps the seers saw a cow floating down the Nile and mistook her for the Egyptian goddess? No disrespect to Isis, but, really!

As for the rampant swine flu pandemic, it really is sweeping the world. Many of the principal cities are semi-deserted. Looting is widespread, as is murder and general mayhem. It seems that, in time, all civilizations are destined to fall. But this? This is not a question of an empire outliving its time. This is a global collapse of civilized behaviour. No wonder people's minds are escaping to reassuring visions. Perhaps it is only natural.

Anyway, what father had suggested a good twenty years ago is finally taking place. People are escaping from cities like rats from a sinking ship. Decentralization is catching on as the only answer to the spread of diseases. The governments, both the politicians and the bureaucrats, have been doing their utmost to contain the widespread panic. They can't follow the mass exodus of their citizens with their tax forms. They may be forced to cut down on their own plush pensions. Tough.

I am sorry for all of them. I mean for all who have become refugees within their own countries. Really sorry. The bureaucrats can stew in their own fat. God knows they have enough of it. I only hope that the Sanctuary will be spared this breakdown of civilization. We are virtually self contained. We grow our own food, we have air and water. The essentials. A true Sanctuary. We, or those who will remain behind, will need each other. No matter how bad things become, there is always room for sanity. And Mount Ogilvy shows no signs of weakening. Some departments have been reduced to essential personnel, or even eliminated, but the principle of Complexity lives on. Anyway, we shall keep in touch from the Moon. As for the visions of those outside? Well, finally, I am not alone. For better of for worse, they've made me feel better.

Though, not for long.

Some time ago I dreamed about Eden. The first time I just walked around and, I clearly recall, there were very few people around. I felt lonely. The next time, I dreamed of the Earth being completely deserted, except for some animals scurrying under abundant bushes. And then, there was that other daydream. I am referring to my dream years ago, where I was a zoologist, somewhere in Africa, and I was looking after abused chimpanzees. I remember little Zoey. If I close my eyes, I can still feel her soft fur against my chest. I feel her warmth as I stroke her head, I feel her heartbeat as her arms cling around my neck. She seemed so frightened, then. Together, all three of these visions, these dreams, prepared me for the dream I had last night. At least that's my impression.

And what a strange dream it was!

I feel it even now.... As real, as though happening all over again. The same sights.... the same thoughts, ideas, questions, emotions... I am weightless, unreal.... It is as if time has preserved this moment for posterity.

I'm floating in the air....
As is usual in my chimerical experiences, I have no body to call my own. I am pure consciousness, motionless, yet finding myself wherever my attention takes me. The vegetation is abundant, luxuriant, absurdly verdant, as befits the Garden of Eden. There are no signs of any cities, any advanced civilization. I see a village or two, nestling over crystal-clear waters of gracefully bubbling brooks. There are a few people around. They look relaxed, going about their business. Mostly tending their garden.

It all looks very idyllic. But the people are not my purpose here.

I float effortlessly over the rolling ground until I spot a group of chimpanzees clearly taking their afternoon siesta. Calm and serenity abound. They are all visibly relaxed, some striking most grotesque poses. No matter.

I hover over their heads, making sure they are all asleep. Then, very gently so as not to disturb them, I insinuate myself into their thought patterns. Don't ask me how. In dreams, things don't have to make perfect sense. On the other hand, I recall an instant when I'd wondered if this was what had been happening to me over the years. That someone has been invading *my* subconscious.

Anyway, I seem capable of touching the seat of their intelligence. Collectively. These are already sentient creatures quite unaware of my presence. I touch them with my thoughts, my consciousness. What cannot be accepted by an awakened mind is often quite easily metabolized by one that is dormant. There is no opposition, no defence mechanism to confront new ideas. I open their inner vision to the world outside their self-centered reality. Beyond their egos. And, believe me, they have powerful egos. I recall from my previous dreams how hard they'd worked to establish their pecking order. Alpha male and Alpha female are absolute leaders in their community. Then come the Betas and so on down the line. Ego, at this stage in their development, is both the greatest gift and an arresting scourge. It is that which will one day help them to discover the potential within, yet it is also that which will set and keep them apart. Apart from the truth and from each other.

It will be a long journey.

I know that I am not here to strengthen nor to destroy their egos. I have come to raise the stakes.

I'm here to awaken their awareness to the potential that heretofore had lain dormant within them. To broaden their horizons. To initiate the toughest, most demanding period in their development. It will lead them, step by step, to the formulation of concepts of universal unity. It will enable them to reach beyond themselves, beyond the limitations of their egos.

Even as I fulfil my function, I wonder how I know these things... It is I yet not I that fills their minds with new light... who am I?

Your conceptual duality will remain, I say to them. For now. It accelerates your learning process.

I'm worried that their concept of ego sets them against each other. That it will challenge the seeds of their subliminal knowledge. My doubts seem to permeate their dormant minds. I must be more careful.

A trait necessary for your physical survival... you will go through the painful process of setting up groups, one against the other, hordes against hordes, masses against masses... For those that survive, religion, or the process of re-linking to your original source, will become the next necessary step and your greatest challenge. I am your source...

I try to saturate their adolescent minds. Evolution is such a strange journey. And then there is that doubt again.

Who am I to teach them anything?

I tell them about the pitfalls. I tell them that losses make us richer, that they release us from fetters. I tell them, silently, that they should strive for a state of balance. I offer them a way of life, a path towards freedom, towards the awareness of their individuality. Never as a means of subjecting others to one's will. I try to tell them that freedom and responsibility are two sides of the same coin. It isn't easy. They have no coins. No, it isn't easy.

I know so little myself, but I must try...

Most importantly, I came to plant the seed of awareness in you... awareness of your true nature. Of your potential. Of an affinity for life itself. I came to implant in your mind the concept of the incontrovertible union with the world you live in.

I try hard. It isn't easy.... *Who am I?* They are like babes in the woods....

I was in a semi-waken state when I withdrew from their paradise. I knew that only time would show if I'd succeeded. I hope that from this moment on the wonderful chimpanzees would possess a greater awareness of their potential. They would also be aware of a far greater choice in all their endeavours. But more than that, they would become much more aware of the dictates of free will.

I wipe a tear forming on my cheek in slow motion.

As I withdrew from their minds I felt a pang of sorrow. I had compromised their inherent simplicity. They would no longer abide as Innocents in Paradise. I'd given them food from the tree of knowledge. In time, over many eons, they will learn to reach for knowledge within their own selves. For the knowledge I'd planted there, in their deepest unconscious. When they do, they will sense my presence. Even as I sense, now, the presence of those who have come before me.

This is my greatest mystery. My personal enigma. Throughout the dream, I felt that I was no more than a messenger delivering a preordained message. I didn't know of its source, though I have my suspicions. At the periphery of my emotive vision I was conscious of a reflective, elusive, presence hovering within me and without me. Like a sphere of invisible light. I could never quite see it. My attention was elsewhere. But I knew it was there. Within me and outside of me. How strange. How beautiful.

I was never alone.

What is Enigma? I wonder for the thousandth time, even as I come fully awake.

Who am I, for that matter?

I am a channel. A means. A messenger. I am a mode through which the ocean of infinite possibilities manifests in the objective reality. Am I indispensable? Is anyone?

I am still searching.

After we scan the heavens, experiment with great religions, offer our lives for the sake of gods we created in our own image and likeness, we discover infinity within our own hearts. So will my children, my chimpanzees. In time they will develop empires, pay homage to idols and icons, and then one day, seemingly out of nowhere, they will come face to face with their own wondrous Selves. They will discover their own Enigma. They will look long and hard, and they will say, I am that I am. And even that will be just the beginning. It is an endless journey.

Now, in the light of day, I know that on Earth, evolution has run its course. That it is time for another experiment. I hope it will be more successful.

JJ's first report from the Moon Base left little to be desired. As before, on a personal level, he is full of praise for the Americans. I wonder if the fact that a radiophone, not being a protected means of communication, has anything to do with it. In spite of JJ's inherent openness, he can be a good politician when he feels it's necessary.

This time his report is much more technical than that of his first impressions some weeks ago. While his first trip left an indelible mark on his, and our, emotions, this time the lists of facts and figures is evidently meant principally for the Americans.

He enumerates requisitions in order of priority, mostly concerning the equipment for the laboratories, which, he says, are beautifully equipped but do not, in his opinion, take sufficient note of experiments which might be possible to carry out exclusively under the Moon's conditions.

"The abundant vacuum, the minimal gravity, the extremes of temperature should offer very specific advantages for the scientists," he suggests.

Next he speaks of the Big Picture. Of the uniqueness which could benefit the USA. Which could benefit mankind. This includes some suggestions regarding the exploitation of probable Moon ores, with particular regard to supplementing the solar energy with other, chemically based means of propulsion.

"If you guys ever want to touch down on Mars, you'd better ship this stuff to me pronto," he says in his usual direct way.

"That's not exactly the way I would have put it myself," Dad comments under his breath, but he cannot help grinning. "He sure knows their language," he adds, nodding south.

We are all, about twenty of us, jammed into Dad's office, all anxious to hear JJ's voice. Two recording devices make simultaneous transcripts for distribution to others.

"There is one other thing," says my brother who is not my brother. (I must stop thinking in those terms). I detect a change in his tone. "Dad, this is for you. Please convey my best sentiments to General Kevin and ask him about shipping up here grand uncle's equipment. It can get quite nippy up here at night and grand uncle would be nice to have around."

This raises a minor storm of applause from all the 'in' people. Grand Uncle McTavish's Scotch. Evidently JJ thought it wise to leave the precise meaning of his request in Dad's hands. Dad and Kevin had become really close friends, and an extra half-million dollars for such a noble cause would better be done on a *tête-à-tête* basis.

At this Dad thinks it appropriate to give the moustache he'd grown in honour of the very same Grand Uncle McTavish an extra twirl. "Only hurry, Dad," JJ hastens to add. "We're expecting you up here any minute now."

At that, JJ cuts the transmission.

This brings us all down to Earth. The clock is ticking. The rest of us are on standing orders. Every day some fifty people leave for the Moon. Dad is supposed to go last. Back home, though we're alone, he whispers in my ear.

"Like a rat from a sinking ship...."

"No, Dad, like a captain who always leaves the sinking ship last," I reply as quietly. We both feel very uneasy about the great spaceship Earth. More so about so many friends we are about to leave behind.

Neither of us would share our thoughts outside our little balcony, and even then only after a good bottle or wine. Will there be wine up there? And then I can't help laughing at my qualms. With two thousand of the world's best brains and six hundred support staff, everything will be up there. They will make wine out of

Moon-dust, if need be. They will squeeze it out of a rock. Like
Moses.

Or was that water?

"Did you ever stop to wonder, Dad," I muse aloud, "how
come we are leaving Earth when at the same time our Ancient
Home seems to be falling apart? Are there powers at play we still
know nothing about?"

"Easy, girl," Dad smiles but avoids my eyes. "Things are not
as bad as they seem..."

I take a nap after lunch. The dream last night drained me of energy.

A thought crosses my mind that one day the chimpanzees will
write their first scripture. They will refer to this day, to last night,
as the mysterious Second Coming. No one would have seen me.
No one would have seen my face. I would be a member of the
mysterious Elohim, a member of the gods, perhaps a new dynasty,
who descended upon the Earth, the New Earth, from a new and
different heaven above them, to help their people. My people. The
Chimpanzees. Perhaps little Zoey will be their Eve. She would
consciously choose her first lover, her Adam, not by the exigencies
of instinct but as an act of her free will. I hope they'll prosper better then we did. I hope they will live in accord with Nature. With
the beautiful Earth which for millions of years took our, took
man's, abuse.

When I woke up this morning, I was covered in sweat. Funny
that, I thought. I may have been in Africa, to visit Zoey, but surely,
my body remained in my bed. And the temperature here is quite
normal. Furthermore, if Uncle David were right, Africa would end
up much closer to the North Pole.

And then I realized that I hadn't seen Zoey. Zoey couldn't
possibly be still alive. Perhaps her spirit lives. For ever? We can
prophesy events, but we cannot prophesy when they will come to
fruition. Perhaps, some of them had already occurred. Perhaps I
have been given to see a distant past. There are so many possibilities.

Infinite numbers.

I am beginning to understand the concept of Enigma. It is not really a thing. It is a state of mind. It is anything we make it. And when a number of minds put their heads together, even their ethereal heads, then the Enigma swells to a planetary size. It is not really there, but it reflects the whole universe. The whole objective reality. Perhaps at the heart of our galaxy there are many gods, their hoary, ageless heads close together, inspiring the worlds, orbiting billions upon billions of stars, to higher aims, greater aspirations. In a million years or so, I might find out.

Perhaps this is what attracts my father to the central halo, to the heart of our own and every other galaxy. The irrepressible draw of the Enigma. Of the unknown.

There is one other thing I've learned about this Riddle. It is a condition outside both, time and space. It is a state of mind without any limitations – wherein nothing is impossible. It is a condition wherein you are as powerful as the spirit within you. Yet, simultaneously, it is a state of consummate balance. Though there is nothing to stop you, you can never abuse your power. Perhaps one could as easily call this condition heaven. Only religions have destroyed this concept. Enigma is accessible to all. Not only the goody-goodies, nor those who live in constant fear of a divine super-being. Nor even those who maltreat their own bodies, live in a state of penance, or self-immolation. It is for people who reject limitations and thus free themselves of them. Where people are not saved by what is above them, but what is within their own being.

This is the effulgent fascination of Enigma.

David and Miriam drop by at suppertime. For the first time in thirty years, they come unannounced. They come in early. They want us all to be together. To talk.

"We brought the gefilte fish," Miriam says proffering a platter wrapped in transparent plastic.

"*Gefüllter fisch*," David corrects stressing the German pronunciation. I wonder if he can still speak any German, after all these years.

We saw them both yesterday. Yet the men embrace like long lost brothers. I hold Miriam close. As I mentioned before, there is no sweetness in parting. We all live on borrowed time.

"Just couldn't do any work," David says in a way of an excuse.

"The usual?"

Dad doesn't wait for an answer and pours two Scotches and a Gin-and-It for Miriam. I shake my head when he asks me with his eyes for my choice. I want to stay wide-awake. A drink or two would slow me down. And I shall serve Chablis to go with the fish.

Mary walks in with a tray of *canapés*. How did she know the Mendels would drop in?

"I know you like these," Mary says placing the colourful plate in front of Miriam.

Miriam stands up and kisses Mary on the cheek. The women are developing a certain rapport. They will probably spend days, months maybe, talking about us. About Dad and me. And JJ, of course. Mary will be the link. She's been with us the longest. Since I was born. Dear Mary.

"Here's to those who will hold the fort," Dad raises his tumbler. "Don't forget we may be back in a few weeks, if not sooner," he adds.

Nobody believes him. No one would give up his or her dream that easily. Both the Mendels know it. So does Mary. They smile vague, polite, crooked smiles.

"Here's to all of us, wherever we are," Miriam says. She looks a lot more relaxed than David. I suspect she has Mary to prop her up.

For a while we sit and chat and then Dad and David go out on the terrace. They get engrossed in something. When Miriam goes to the kitchen to help Mary finish the gefilte fish, I join the men.

"....up by 2.07°C and climbing. The icebergs are melting faster than ice-cream cones. There is no telling what the consequences will be," David scratches his head but does not seem unduly worried.

"It's not too late, Dave," Dad says, "I could pull a few strings, you know."

"Miriam would never leave the boys. She's a real Yiddisha mama.... She doesn't say so often enough, but she would rather die a thousand miles than two hundred-fifty thousand miles from the lads. And they are good boys, you know.... A pity you didn't have much of a chance to get to know them better," Dave says between sips of Scotch.

"I'm really very grateful to you both for taking care of Mary. She's been very good for us." There is a frog wedged somewhere in Dad's throat.

It all sounds rather kind and depressing. I go back in and put on a lively CD. I decide to open the wine now and give myself a glass. I have to do something to keep up with the others. I realize that I am the only one to whom the impending trip is a source of constant joy. JJ is there. There and waiting. God, how I miss him. I'd missed him before, in the past, but never like this. I don't care what else happens up there, or down here for that matter, I just want to be in his arms. Officially. Not brotherly arms. In my man's arms. I've waited long enough. I take my glass and return to the balcony.

"....ozone layer is breaking up and oxygen deficiency has been reported in Northern Hemisphere. I can but wonder where it will all end," David sounds positively cheerful. "A good thing we have the domes overhead," he adds smiling. For him, the whole mess we've made of the world is just a case study. He would probably enjoy a really good earthquake, to shake things up.

"Have I told you about the sun spots activity?" Dad asks with equal innocence.

Men! I can't stand their stoic detachment. I go to the kitchen to see how the ladies are doing. I find them lost in conversation. Mary is telling Miriam about her village, in England.

"The door lintels were so low my father had to duck each time he crossed the threshold," Mary illuminates Miriam. "And you should see the size of the rooms...."

"I know," Miriam interrupts, "We had the same problem in Russia. We couldn't get past the bed to reach the window," she says proudly.

I want to get lost. To fly to the Moon. Right know. I am too young to die. To talk about the past. On an ancient CD, Sinatra is

singing "Fly me to the moon...." Yes please, I murmur to myself.
Right now. Yes please.

I sit down in the living room, alone. My mind drifts back to Enigma. I wonder how the process actually works. Somehow consciousness transforms itself into thoughts, perhaps also emotions,
and then somehow they affect matter. Or maybe they just affect
what we recognize as matter. Aren't all solids not solid at all?
Doesn't all matter consist of atoms, and atoms consist, mostly, of
empty space?

The physicists have known this for more than a hundred years.
Somehow we never seem to think of matter in those terms. Yet
since my body, my physical body, is mostly empty space, I'm not
even limited by the velocity of light! No wonder I can travel to
Enigma, to Paradise, to the Moon – on gossamer wings...

At some level there must be some sort of transmutation, or
transubstantiation of the energy. At that level, time and space have
no meaning. Not in the accepted sense. Or perhaps we can only
experience this sort of thing, but not really understand it. This reality might be beyond thought and we associate thought with
understanding. Don't we? I wonder if anyone knows. Really
knows. Some avatars of the past appear to have known.

I close my eyes.

JJ is sitting at his desk, lost in thought. His computer is on,
and there is a small stack of papers to his left. I move towards him
and plant a kiss on his cheek. He doesn't move. Then, slowly he
raises his hand to his face, touches his cheek, and looks at my
photo in a silver frame standing next to the computer. I wonder if
he felt anything.

Well, I tell myself, I guess I'll never know.

"Dinner is served!" I hear from 380,000 kilometres away. It
is amazing how Mary's voice carries.

There is more, but it is not for public consumption. Please, keep this to yourself. After thirty years of living with Enigma, I've reached my own conclusions, which I cannot really share with anyone. Not if I want to stay out of a psychiatric ward for the criminally insane. But now, I feel safe. There is no such ward where I am going. So I'll tell you.

Enigma is a state of consciousness in which all things, all events, all ideas, emotions, concepts, even vibrations already exist. They are all there, suspended in a state of being, waiting to be resurrected and allowed to partake in a condition of becoming. In a way, they are all jumbled up. They all co-exist without differentiation. Little Hey used to call them no-things, existing no-where, yet everywhere. She had no way to explain the condition of being as against becoming. For becoming you need time. And there, in the state of Enigma, there is no time.

I am beginning to think that our lives are merely states of consciousness designed to arrange some of those conditions, suspended in the state of Enigma, into a higher state of heightened order. Into an orderly sequence. Like notes and chords in a beautiful melody. Surely, that is what life must be about. Order and harmony. An interrelation of things, events, feelings, vibrations to enhance the nature of those things, events, feeling and vibrations in such a way, that the sum of them becomes greater than their individual nature.

This is where we come in.

Sometimes we don't quite make it. We allow discord to find its way into our condition of becoming. Or even miss the harmony altogether. But surely, we must try. Try hard. Or should. The possibilities are truly infinite.

***

25

Zero hour

The vibration is a lot less than I expected. The next moment we
strap down, hardly more than when driving a car. The seats recline
backwards, the countdown ticks away, and I feel my back pressed
into the back of the chair. It is not an unpleasant feeling. A little
like taking off in an airplane only more so. Soon there is silence.
Complete silence.

I'm in space.

Dad reaches over and touches my hand. I see him looking
through the minute porthole and smiling. This is his dream also.
Not just to gain access to the universe without any atmospheric
interference, but to experience space itself. That's where his beloved stars are. That's where they are born – that is where they die.
But mostly that is where they live. Dad told me once that he thinks
of stars as being alive.

"Like we are, Hey. Just like we are. They have their planets
to look after, their visitors – their comets, their emotions, when the
dark spots rile with anger on their faces, their..."

Dad can go on like this for quite a while. When we are alone,
of course. The rest of the time he is the scientist. A damn good
one, everyone always said. Still is. Dad had turned seventy-three
four months ago. The youngest seventy-three I've ever seen. Still,
we have to overcome the gravity pulling us in the opposite direction at an acceleration of 32 feet per second and reach an escape

velocity of just over 40,500 kilometres per hour, or as the Americans call it, seven miles per second. Dad's aging heart must be working hard at five g's.

Exactly as described by JJ some weeks ago, we are transferred to the Orbital Station, and promptly whisked down to the surface. Four domes have airlock facilities to take in new arrivals. Good old Americans. As usual they've got the whole operation down pat. There is neither a hitch nor a glitch. The next thing I know I'm in JJ's arms. My helmet is still on. He is kissing the visor.

There are too many emotions. Too much is happening all at once.

As my helmet is removed, JJ lowers himself to one knee. In his hand he holds a ring. It is an uncut diamond in a white gold band.

"I picked it up on the Moon. Must be a meteorite." He puts it on my finger. And then, right there in front of all those people he....

Never mind. Use your imagination. This is not a Harlequin romance. But when I come up for air, over two hundred people are applauding. They are all our friends who had arrived before us. This crazy atmosphere continues. We are led through four domes, each filled to the brim with all sorts of vegetation, to a dome with buildings in it. Here we break up. Each group is taken by their guide to their particular quarters. Ours, Dad's and mine, are exact copies of our condo on Earth. Correction. Dad's has larger rooms but is smaller, just one bedroom. It's for Dad only. JJ picks me up in his arms and carries me up another flight of stairs, two or three at a time. We have two rooms, and a terrace above. It is a sort of penthouse. Like the domes we'd passed through, abundant vegetation is overflowing everywhere. It's like living in a jungle. The trees are only about ten years old but they've been planted at three levels, so they look much taller than they actually are. They will grow. I am sure of it. In Paradise everything grows. That's what makes it Paradise.

We are alone.

It is none of anybody's business what we did for the next hour. Enough said that I'd waited thirty years, and JJ, well, JJ for about ten. Maybe less. But I don't care. He will never have to wait again.

I hear an idyllic bell. I think I'm in love. Think? I've never been more sure of anything in my life. The ringing sounds like a cross between a chime and a distant village church. It must me in my head.

"Do you hear bells?" I ask.

"Yes, darling. It's time for supper."

"Already?" I'm a little disappointed. Not about the supper. About the bell.

"We shall be back in no time at all."

But we weren't. On the way down we went to pick up Dad but he was already gone. We walk another two kilometres to the canteen. That's the official name but it looks more like She-herazade's idea of eating at the Hanging Gardens of Babylon.

"Not one inch of space is wasted," JJ assures me. "We need every plant to produce enough oxygen for two thousand-six hundred people. Plus the Americans. They are still building more domes."

I spend half my time looking around, the other half stealing glances through the transparent roof panels at the enormity of the Universe. Its blackness is infinite. It is also intensely three-dimensional. It draws me in, cuts me off from my own self. It makes me insignificant. Suspended in this vastness are tiny points of light of different hues and intensity. They appear at variable distances from me. They really are suspended in space. Not painted on the firmament, as when seen from Earth. These beacons of light are a thousand times brighter than those I'm used to seeing. Even through the Monster Eye. Through the telescope they were detached from each other. Here, space is contiguous. Unfolding forever. This clarity is not resultant from the purity of air. A little under five hundred meters over my head, there is no air. No air at all. I reach for JJ's arm. In spite of my knowledge, of years of ex-perience in astronomy, I need reassurance. He takes this as an invi-tation for another kiss.

"Come now, young man," Dad says, his eyes as bright as I'm sure mine must be, "this is no way to treat your sister." How long has he been watching us?

We all laugh. We do a lot of laughing. It's our nerves, I suppose. It's not everyday that one is transported to Paradise in the middle of nowhere.

After supper we are given our first official tour of the four adjacent domes. They look identical to those we left behind on Earth, only larger, and there is more protection inherent in the structure. The elements of the geodesic structure seem stronger. Actually, they are manufactured from a lighter alloy. Each dome can be cut off from every other at a moment's notice. The airlocks shut automatically should there be any differential in air pressure. There are airtight compartments at each cardinal point, or 'corner', not that there are corners in the diameter at the base, and two dozen spacesuits in each compartment. Just in case. Also, I see stacks of compressed air in long tubes. They are portable life-savers. They unfold to offer up to ten mouth-pieces at each end, capable of providing air to twenty people for up to two hours.

We are also told not to look directly into the sun. In spite of Polaroid panels, the light is too blinding. It could burn out our retinas. A dangerous Paradise after all. But we can look everywhere else. I look at JJ. I like looking at JJ.

"Did you like it, Dad?" JJ asks.

While we were, ah.... upstairs, father had visited his new Observatory. Now his eyes take on a dreamy, far away look. He gives an impression of a boy who just got the keys to his first car. A sports car. Vroom, vroom is written all over his face.

"You wouldn't believe it. I only had an hour, but you wouldn't believe it...." that's all he said at the time. He'll have a great deal more to say tomorrow, I'm sure.

I don't know why, but I feel completely drained. Probably too much happening, all at once. We walk back – there is no moving sidewalk as we had earth-side – but the walk is an experience in itself. When you hop up, you rise about six feet in the air. Then you float down. Not fall, only float. I feel like a prima donna on the stage of the Bolshoy theatre. If this isn't Paradise, I wonder what is.

I am ready to collapse into bed.

It seems strange. So soon after our arrival.

As we stand together, I in-between Dad and JJ, we watch the Moon accelerate in its orbit. What we actually see is the Earth below us moving faster. First slowly, then with increasing velocity. Within an hour, Moon-time, a day below passes in just a few hours. The Moon changes its trajectory. The Earth is shrinking below us. Soon it is little more than a large Moon, as the Moon looked from Earth only yesterday. There must be something wrong.

Dad glances at the instrumentation in front of us.

"The velocity is now 35,000 kilometres per hour. We'll be there sooner than we thought," he says.

I seem to know what he is talking about. I nod and feel quite relaxed. I must be regressing. So far I've been discombobulated only in my dreams. Now I'm also lost when I'm wide-awake.

"Look, there!" JJ points to a large dot of light. "Isn't it beautiful?"

"Even now the light has a reddish tint. Of course. Now I remember. We are on our way to Mars.

I am covered in sweat. Again.

Instinctively I reach out for JJ. He's gone. Have I dreamt about coming to the Moon? Did we really make love? Have I gone mad? For a second I think that I am in a sanatorium for the mentally unhinged. Then I look around me. It is similar to my room at the Sanctuary, but.... perhaps in the sanatorium the rooms are also similar....

I jump out of bed and almost hit my head on the ceiling. I tick off one item. Different gravity. I still could be imagining it. I look out through the blinds. The sun is still there only much brighter. As it looks after a night of heavy drinking. Only I've never done a night of heavy drinking. Well, that once when.... Never mind. We live together now. Only he isn't here. I go to the other window. The Earth is here also. I mean there. So it was another vision. Another dream. Prophetic?

But why? And why so soon?

My first night on the Moon was an experience beyond words. We made love till the early hours. The gravity here gives a new meaning to the word light-headed. It also provides amazing uses for walls, and, although a little risky, the ceiling. With the aid of a chandelier. You don't tire so easily, either. Anyway, we gave up just before dawn. Only on the Moon, there is no dawn. There are no early hours. The Moon always offers the same face to the sun. There are those few days, in each lunar month, when the Earth casts a shadow on the Moon's surface. I suppose you could call it a night. I'm told it gets really cold then. Hence the McTavish. By the way, Dad says that it's coming.

Finally we both fell asleep. Exhausted. And then, there was that dream. Only something was missing.

I should be used to dreams by now. I've had them since I was a little girl. They never get any easier to ignore. Always as real, as engrossing, as demanding on my attention. I think I've learned a lot through them. But I cannot stop thinking that there must be another reason for them. A reason which, though it seems as distant as the Earth right now, scares me. I feel that some force that I cannot as yet control is invading me. I am either seeing the future, or the past, or I am worried about something. That last I doubt. Although some dreams are scary – like moving the Moon out of orbit – they still have an engrossing beauty about them. The same was true of the chimpanzees. Not to mention the reflections in the Enigma. And then it strikes me. All my dreams have always been imbued with beauty. Unparalleled, unearthly beauty.

Is Enigma responsible for all this? Shall I ever learn the truth?

The next moment a bizarre thought catches up with me. This was the first time ever that both Dad and JJ figured in my dream. Mother had, of course, but she's dead. And she is everywhere, and all that. JJ and Dad are eminently alive.

There is still something nagging at me.

I take a pressurized mist shower and get dressed. There is no one downstairs either. Dad is obviously in his Observatory. His telescope faces the other side, away from the sun. He won't be getting much sleep. I look down at the Base Layout posted on the door. I memorize the way to JJ's office and Dad's Observatory.

Then I realize that I'm hungry. In fact, I am ravishing. That's
what's been nagging at me. Food. Food! I feel like screaming. I
find my way to the canteen and gorge myself on fresh fruit. I wash
it down with some sort of drink I've never had before. I don't care.
It tastes good.

I am almost finished when JJ walks in.

I get a peck on the cheek, like an old married woman. "Slept
well?" he asks innocently. I feel like saying "you should know"
but that would be a cheap shot.

He looks very full of himself; like that time when he told me
about planting those bugs in Father Martin's computer. I don't answer but give him my best vamp look. I practiced it the last few
days earth-side. Just in case I would need it. It works. He looks a
little flustered.

A moment later Dad walks in. He looks and sounds gruff.

"You are both living in sin!" he starts without any preambles.
"The wedding will take place at 1800 hours Moontime, in dome
seven."

With that he turns on his heel and walks out. We wait till he
leaves the terrace before laughing out loud. I've never seen Dad so
pompous. Could it have been echoes of his Catholic upbringing?
Of course, his daughter has never lived in sin before either. Not for
a whole night.

"We'd better not be late," JJ warns and excuses himself. Apparently there are five more contingents scheduled for arrival today. He has to make sure all's ready for them. JJ takes his work
very seriously. I feel a little jealous.

I spend the morning walking around the Base. New arrivals are
all given three days off before reporting for duty. I need some rest
after the last few weeks on Earth. Not that I worked so much, but
they were emotionally wrenching. Draining. Around 1200 hours,
what would pass for noon on Earth, I bump into JJ. He stops in his
tracks, glances at his watch and grabs my elbow.

"Let's have lunch together..." He catches himself. "If you're
free, that is." He remembers I don't like being taken for granted.

"I shall be delighted, kind Sir," I acquiesce gracefully with a small curtsey.

"I must give you an officer's uniform," he says. "You will be able to give orders."

"To you?" I ask innocently.

JJ grins but doesn't answer. This is all so new to both of us. It is not at all like brother and sister. God, is it ever different!

After lunch he takes me for a stroll. In dome #7 there is a little bench half-hidden under a small weeping willow. In front of it, there is a tiny pond. No ducklings, but the rest is identical. My eyes fill with tears.

"They only finished it hours before your arrival, he says kissing my tears away.

It is not at all like brother and sister. It takes me a minute or two to get a hold of myself. "It's the most wonderful present I've ever had in my life, JJ," I whisper. I want to say more but can't. My lips are sealed. With his.

I decide that I don't want to look like a wet rag at my own wedding. I go back home to take the usual afternoon nap. I find a lieutenant commander's uniform laid out on the bed. It is sparkling white, like in the US Navy. I've never had a uniform before. I've never been a lieutenant before either. I try it on, approve it, take it off and lie down. I didn't even pull the blinds. I must have fallen asleep immediately.

The globe below looks enormous. Like Earth, only it seems bigger because it is more uniform. At least in colour. Or it could be that our orbit is lower down. As I keep studying the surface, I know I am right. We are moving much faster than we did around the Earth. We have to, that close.

The next instant the uniform surface explodes with a spectacular mountain. Everest, I exclaim! And then I feel silly. Everest rises less than nine kilometres above sea level. This is a very different kind of mountain. Olympus Mons seems to jump up at me. It is the largest mountain in the Solar System. Its base covers some

500 kilometres in diameter and it towers twenty-four kilometres above the surrounding plane. I am spell bound, holding my breath.
How do I know all this?
In a blink of my invisible eye the view changes again.

I'm still looking at the soaring giant but now I seem to see it through magic time-lapse lenses. The bottom of the mountain is hidden in a thick forbidding forest. The trees rise a few thousand meters, then are cut off as though by a magic wand. Some hardy bushes and grassy shrubbery make a feeble attempt to rise higher but soon they give up also. There is nothing to feed them. Not even water. For a while the rock rises unadorned until it too disappears in a thick, impenetrable fog. Impenetrable to human eyes. My eyes pierce through it effortlessly.

Two kilometres higher up, the shear ramparts of this colossus reappear and continue on and on, unchallenged. No wonder they call it Olympus Mons. The Olympian Mountain. Only gods would dare to scale such forbidding crags. Only angels would rise to such an impressive aerie. Angels, and men. Striving for supremacy?
Have I just witnessed a distant future?
Time has no meaning in Enigma.
For an instant I hover nowhere. I am no-thing, no-where. I am.... Who am I?
As quickly as doubts leave me, I recognize the next mountain: the soaring Tharsis. Ten kilometres towards the sky, four across its base. In seconds we're past it. My Lunar spaceship now soars over a land that drops, suddenly, by two, three, then seven kilometres. The bed of the forbidding chasm is hidden in ominous shadows. The canyon extends in brooding darkness, like the pit of hell.
"Four thousand kilometres..." I hear myself recording my observations.
These are the Valles Marineris. What mysteries lay buried in their inhospitable deeps? I concentrate on the surface so as not to slip into another fragment of past or future history. I have no desire to awaken old ghosts, to witness past deeds, valiant or malignant or deadly, still extant, suspended, in Enigma's infinite matrix.

"Let the dead bury their dead," I whisper. To us belongs the future. To be conquered with courage. Are we not to reawaken this arid, forlorn planet?

The Red Planet has born countless scars throughout its bellicose history. Just one impact crater, Hellas Planitia, could bury two of our Moons.

Are we really here?

I wondered when we arrived. When did we reach our present orbit? My sense of time has deserted me completely. I seem equally aware of the reddish surface below, of my office in dome #8, next to Dad's, and of my duties as assistant astronomer. Right now, an observer. I am to catalogue all surface features, from one kilometre in diameter upwards.

Where am I really? Am I still dreaming....

I glance at the data sheets. Mars is little more than half the Earth's diameter but its surface area is about the same. I look over my shoulder. I can see Earth in the screen of the telescope behind me. She looks forlorn without a moon. I feel guilty.

I reach out to the Asteroid belt and direct Ceres to the Earth orbit.

It moves obediently and in seconds stabilizes itself in the Earth's proximity. It is only some eight-hundred kilometres in diameter.

I drop its perigee lower, adjust the apogee to an elliptical orbit and double its orbital velocity.

The new moon will not be as large, but it will appear almost equal in diameter. And lovers will have the benefit of its allure at least twice during the night. I smile at all the Earth's lovers....

I wonder how I did it? How did I do it?

Ceres looks happy in its new location.

My mind drifts back to my present location. I have a job to do. No matter. Time is waiting for me.

So we are going to terra-form Mars. It must have been quite some time since we arrived here. I vaguely remember JJ saying that the taxis we'd brought with us should be ready in a few weeks.

Mars's gravity is greater than the Moon's. Escape velocity must be adjusted. About half of what we needed on Earth. Every three taxis will combine to make one. They are clever, those engineers.

I set my other telescope to follow the orbital path. I watch as the surface rushes past below me. Well, not exactly rushes, but I am well aware of its movement. The next moment I duck my head. I thought we were on a collision course with Phobos. I remind myself to keep a look out for the other Mars moon, Deimos. It's about half of Phobos's size, it will be harder to spot. And it is much further away from Mars' surface. I seem to have all the facts in my head. Deimos is at 23,000 and Phobos 9,000 kilometres. Compared to what the Moon had been from the Earth, they are both within arm's reach.

My mind wonders...

I think of the future. If we terra-form Mars, if we live long enough to terra-form Mars, we shall have a planet only slightly smaller than Earth, for less than three thousand people to live on. Assuming we shall all want to leave the Moon Base, which right now seems extremely unlikely. For some reason, the Americans, with Dad's participation, had selected an equal number of men and women to staff the Moon Base.

Are we the future Martians?

I try to imagine a planet without any animals, other than human. There will be plenty to eat, providing you're vegetarian. It just so happens, we all are. Not necessarily by choice but the Moon offers no other option. Will Mars breed the killer instinct out of us? Shall we pursue non-pugilistic aims? It would take thousands of years before anyone would want to play at empire building. After all there is more than enough room for everybody and this time we are not starting out in caves.

I try to imagine a world where man has no one to kill. No one to rob. To exploit. Back on Earth, most of us lived like rats. Not in the Sanctuary, but outside. It was paradoxical. We were enclosed, yet it was the outside that was overpopulated. We didn't close ourselves in. We closed them out. *Them.* The rest of the world. Was it fair? They had been caged in their own mire. When you cage rats, restrict their freedom, they fight each other. No matter what size the cage. The zoo? They become territorial. It's probably the prerogative for survival.

There is no question of this here. There is ample water some 100 to 400 meters below the surface. The present atmosphere, just seven millibars, less than 1% of Earth's. It already has traces of oxygen and water, as well as nitrogen and argon. Ninety-three percent consists of carbon dioxide, the most useful gas for growing plants.

Will this become the New Eden?

Will this become a New World of people living in peace? For the first time in human history?

Even as I sense that the alternate reality is releasing its hold on me, I feel a deep pain. It is like a great longing gnawing at me from within. My father has inspired us all. Still does. He's lead us all here, the Promised Land. Yet he will never taste of its bounty. Like Moses, he'll stay behind. In the deserts of space. Perhaps, when the time comes, we shall spread his ashes on Olympus Mons.

Perhaps, this is all but a dream....

"Darling!"

I thought my eyes were wide open all along. How do you open eyes that are already open? I did, just now. I saw JJ's face gazing down at me. I love his eyes. They really do change colour. They move from brown to hazel to almost green at times. Now they are dark brown. Like those of a Latin lover. Funny that. I've never had a Latin lover. I pull JJ towards me. He stops me. I pout.

"You must get dressed. It's 1700 hours already. We're getting ma...."

I jump out of bed pushing him aside. 1700 hours? My God! I only have an hour. I'll never make it. Help me!

"Help me!"

I must have screamed because JJ moves back, his hands extended before him for protection.

"Darling," his voice is as calm as the pond under the weeping willow, "all you need do is put on your uniform and walk less than fifteen minutes to dome number seven. We have plenty of time."

"Don't patronize me!" I say. Actually I screamed again. "You know very well that I'll never make it!"

And then I sit down on the bed and take a deep breath. I'm all right now. Reasonably all right. I got the jitters out of me. Ten minutes later I am ready. I had even put on some makeup, which I don't do as a rule. I'd bought the compact down below just for this occasion. For the wedding.

There is a knock on the door. JJ opens it and I see Dad framed in the doorway. He seems stuck between the aluminium jambs. His mouth is agape, his eyes even wider. He leans on the frame for support. He told me later that he thought he'd seen Heidi. My mother. Apparently he's carried her picture, dressed in white, all these years. Of course mother wore a dress to her wedding, but Dad, well, Dad was overpowered.

"You look very beautiful," he says finally. His voice is calm.

We all leave together.

As we are nearing dome #7, I can hear the Mendelssohn wedding march. Beyond, someone is chiming some bells. There must be over a five hundred people crammed into the dome. Many stand on one leg in order to avoid stomping on the plants. Others are propped up on the shoulders of those beneath them. It looks like a circus.

"Do you take this woman...." Dad starts, then clears his throat. JJ continues on his own. I follow. "By the power vested in me..." Dad again has problems with the frog. "You may now k-kiss the b-bride," he finally stammers.

It's too late. To the applause of five hundred people I'm already nestled in JJ's arms, carrying out the Admiral's orders. Didn't I tell you? Dad is an Admiral now. I am Lieutenant Commander, Admiral's daughter and the Commander's wife. Tomorrow Dad said he'll promote JJ to Captain. But only tomorrow. We've had quite enough for one day.

Even so, I like it here. A lot.

The reception is held at the Hanging Gardens. Actually most of the domes look like hanging gardens. There is one enormous wedding cake and everyone can have a slice while it lasts. On the way back, to my chagrin, JJ excuses himself. Just for a minute he says. I must get used to being a Captain's wife. I'd never imagined JJ could be so disciplined. I keep learning about JJ. He seems to have grown a great deal since he stopped being my brother.

"I'll see you at home," he says and storms off. He mutters something about a radiophone from Earth.

On the way back, Dad and I sit on our bench, under the weeping willow. Just to reminisce. About the old times. And then Dad goes back to his Observatory and I return to our place. To JJ. My JJ. My husband. I only learned later that JJ had insisted that Dad be selected to go the Moon. The NASA people thought he was much too old. The normal limit for both sexes was forty-five. Perhaps they were right. But Dad had seen the sky and the world with his own eyes and through the magic eye of the liquid telescope at the Moon Base. He told me that he could die happy now.

"Why not, Pet. I'm already in heaven."

But he didn't. None of us did. We just lived on and on and on....

Yes. Happily. I don't know about the ever after part, but for a very, very long time.

But that's another story.

JJ is back promptly as promised. I ask him about the radiophone.

"It was nothing, darling" he says. "George, at the Sanctuary, said something about the Moon accelerating in its orbit. Some nonsense about it increasing its perigee and apogee at the same time. I told him I was busy today. He'll check and call me back tomorrow."

***

EPILOGUE

Second Coming

My fingers are still poised lightly over the keys of my computer. My eyes, perhaps a little bleary from constant staring, are still mesmerized by the extraterrestrial sunset. I am still sitting breathless, enchanted by the beauty which I am privileged to behold. Surely, it must be real. Isn't all beauty real?

Surely I am gazing at my home, my late home, drifting away from me, even though I have absolutely no sensation of movement. It must be real. Surely, reality is what we perceive as genuine. The wondrous globe suspended in the endless depth of black velvet is the Earth, my Earth, my home. Or at least, now, home to my children. The second try. The Second Coming....

Even if I am drifting away, on my own journey, leaving them stranded. Poor orphans. But they will grow rich. They shall inherit the Earth.

"I think it all went rather well, don't you?"
I've been watching them for an hour now. Or it could have been a million years. Actually I am mostly listening rather than

watching. What I see must be a construct of my own mind. It can't be otherwise. Not here. It's just that events can be arranged almost at will. Sequentially or at random. It's up to you. I have a reasonably organized mind. I need a semblance of order. There is no time here. No space either. That is why they need someone like me to foster their will, to have their ideas translated into physical reality. They are almost pure Beings. Without a mode of Becoming they can do little. Perhaps nothing. I don't know. But every one of them said, at least I heard it as words in my head, that they had to take on a body through which to implement their plan. The body was of little consequence. It was the message that mattered.

Still is.

They had time enough. *Just like in my time.* *I wonder why they always pick the hard way.*

These may be words, or just wisps of the mind, like echoes of some forgotten tune, lingering behind in the mental reality to which I seem to have gained access. I am, of course, inside the Enigma. We've met before. You know me as Heidi. As Lieutenant Commander Heidi Hydon. Lately of the Earth, presently of the Moon, and who knows to what time and space she'll pay allegiance in times to come. Whatever the present decides, that future will be.

To get inside the Enigma I had to stop being what I am. I had to become nothing. Or almost nothing. Only then did I become the real me. Everywhere and nowhere. I remember trying to explain it to Dad. To my father on the Moon. Also on Earth.

"I neither see nor hear anything until I enter total darkness and absolute silence. Only then do I let go. I stop resisting. Only then can I leave the dark realm and see the light," I'd told him.

I had to smile when I heard his answer.

"How much it sounds like astronomy," he'd said. "I look into the darkness in order to see the light. The universe is darkness, yet light is born of this abyss of seeming nothingness."

My father is a very wise man.

Over the years I had learned to recognize various emanations of light inside the Enigma. In my mind they develop faces, sometimes even bodies, but mostly just emotions. My mind absorbs them, metabolizes their presence without converting their emanations into words. Those come later. Much later. After I'd regained my senses, I returned to my body. Here I am limited only by my own shortcomings. By my inability to sense that which is beyond senses.

But I'm learning. Always learning.

Sometimes I sense the long-bearded Moses, still concerned about people dispersing their energies over idols, still blind to the ineffable Truth. He imbues me with strength when overwhelming odds are against me.

I am that I am, he says. I believe him.

Another pulsation belongs to Krishna whose vibrations course through my veins, ever expanding, helping me to see divinity in a single blade of grass, in the roar of a mountain lion, or in the lightness a hovering swallow. He also taught me never to waver in the course of my duty.

I also perceive the presence of Jesus, whose love shimmers the brightest. His aura is synonymous with peoples' compassion for each other. He is still busy bringing to life those who are not yet awakened. He shows me how to regard my father, my husband, my neighbour. He rises daily above all illusion.

Beyond, there is Mohammed who sees, in this magnificent circle of light, his beloved *ummah*, where every Muslim is a Muslim's brother. His aura speaks of fellowship rising above all other; of wealth that has value only in the act of sharing.

And then there is Rumi.

From his unwavering light I sense an oscillation like breathing in and breathing out, simultaneously, like being absorbed by Infinity in his euphoric *fana*, only to return, triumphant, in *baqa*, to embrace the particular expression of the divine. He teaches me how to absorb beauty and then to reflect it back to its ineffable source.

Like my first contact with Enigma.

Next to him hovers the dispassionate effulgence of Buddha. Steadfast, like the flame of a candle on a windless night, immutable, balanced, asking naught while giving off his own inexhaustible light to whoever draws on it. He is my master of equanimity.

And then there is the Old Master.

Seemingly like an Old Fellow, Lao Tsu remains the most enigmatic. What his light conveys to me is an eternal smile, hovering impartially, caressing – never imposing, over all that is. And isn't. It had been he, the Old Master, who first taught me that I am that that I am not. That I am everywhere and nowhere. That anything that is, really isn't.

He helped me see my mother.

There are others, less distinct to my incipient vision. At the very least I can detect some two dozens. Many emanations are quite strange to me. They seem far beyond my powers of recognition. Perhaps with time...

Do you think they'll do better on Mars?

You want me to look again? Last time I did I saw over a million different futures. Frankly it makes my head spin!

(I sense their auras touching in strange conversation.)

They all laugh.

(Did you ever see a light laughing?)

Lao Tsu, for it must have been the Old Master who'd posed the question, hasn't had a head for at least two-and-a-half millennia. Still.... old habits die hard. When they do die, completely, we become re-absorbed. It is the last willful act. Like those who came and went before us. We shall join the Stream of Life from which all becoming draws its incessant vitality.

Once more I'm amongst them. Silent.

Only an observer.

I try, once again, to recognize their thought patterns. Over the years, particularly in my discussions with JJ, I found that we all educe different lessons from each of the past sages. I try to limit mine to those that repeatedly strike the most familiar echoes in my subconscious.

"They are not 'past' in Enigma," I tell JJ. "They have their becoming like us – in the present."

Around the central void I find familiar oscillating lights, advancing and ebbing like luminous waves of an infinite ocean. This is the way they communicate. I continue to recognize new patterns. At least I think I do. There is Osiris and Isis, next to them, I think, Hermes.

Hermes Tresmagistus?

Further down I sense the more familiar emanations. The ephemeral auras of Buddha, Jesus, Moses and Krishna seem to complement each other, as though bound by some resonant harmony. Still further I detect Mohammed and Rumi, and more to my right I recognize the unmistakable radiance of Lao Tsu's Tao. There are others I cannot recognize, but all are discussing what to do to save us. To save the human race. The Homo sapiens.

From our machinations. From ourselves.

They have such glorious potential...
I loved walking the earth...
Some are capable of such love...
It would be such a loss...
Aren't we responsible in some measure?

I hear many such comments. There is no joy in Enigma today.

The sages dwell, dim echoes of past becoming, in delicate vibrations approaching the most ephemeral of thought waves. Like photons at both outer extremes of the invisible spectrum. I don't know how else to describe the uniqueness of their auras.

This energy in which they have their being affects time, extending their individualized perceptions to millions of years. At least I believe so. At one time Lao Tsu intimated that there are still higher vibrations that can extend self-awareness to tens and even thousands of millions of years. To billions, I think he'd said. Such resonance would make them immortal. At least in my mind. But none of this matters. By human standards, there is no time here. Even now. None that a human mind could ever detect. Not for as long as the mind remains human. And, after all, they all abide in the Present.

We shall learn so much more in the infinity of time....

A thought touches me in direct contradiction to my speculations. What am I to think? Is time also infinite? Is this what the Present is all about?

I sense another thought. It is a smile. A smile of understanding. *There is so much to learn...*

The masters convey to me that every few thousand earth-years, the Enigma enters the physical plane to make certain adjustments. This probably accounts for the behaviour of some asteroids, or the sudden, by Earth's standards, relief of pressure in the tectonic matrix. I now strongly suspect that left to itself, Earth would soon look like the surface of the moon. Or Mars, for that matter. It did, before the ancients offered protection and guidance. Once the Earth had been as pockmarked as the Moon is today; only a million times more so. The atmosphere alone does not account for the difference. Those we know as Elohim were responsible for separating the single landmass into distinct continents, to minimize the lethal impact of the extraterrestrial bombardment. Then they moved the continents apart. Minutely, they are still drifting. Should a catastrophe occur, at least some life would be spared.

They'd made mistakes – hence the dinosaurs. Nobody's perfect. *We all live and learn...* I hear them echoing each other.

Since, some of the Ancients had moved on. Those arcane predecessors are now active at the galactic level, although 'now' is such a relative term. Like the past and the future. They all have their reality in the Infinite Present. Perhaps their home, their Enigma, is in the heart of the Galactic Halo. The blackest Black Hole from which all light emanates. As my Dad always wondered.

Our time will come... again I sense a vibration. *I wonder what it is like to ride herd to millions of star systems. I had problems enough with just twelve tribes and a bunch of Romans.*

I can guess who that is. He has such a sense of humour.

We've problems enough in the Present, a playful emanation nudges the two auras pulsating at its either side, as though lost in a private conversation. I now this is in jest. The obvious always is in Enigma.

Those two always wonder....

He left the sentence unfinished.

But all the auras lose some of the solemnity. Krishna and Jesus, and possibly Osiris are head and shoulders more punctilious than most others. Buddha is everybody's cerebral equal, but he disperses himself over myriad life-forms. He is a magnificent

Internist but a fastidious Surgeon. He literally cannot hurt a fly. Mohammed had done his job better than most others, but his message is gauged in time. Rumi lavishes in comparative knowledge, but he still didn't work out how to apply it on a larger scale.

And Lao Tsu?

The Old Master is in a world of his own. It is to him that most of these Titans reach out when they need mediation. He would remain silent for so long that they might assume that he'd forgotten the question. And then he offers an answer that staggers imagination. At least, my imagination. Lao Tsu always reaches out for the first principles. He is by far the most timeless in this timeless realm. It had been he who'd worked out the method of conscious manipulation of vibrations between their own and the mundane physical consciousness.

They too have no concept of time, he once said of our human foibles. The adverb *too* speaks volumes of his humility. *Just look how they help each other during the first twenty minutes after a calamity strikes them.*

His aura assumed a glow of pleasure.

Why, they act like human beings!

And for the next ten years they'll revert to their backward, egotistical ways... Jesus put in sadly. He backed up Mohammed more often then did other sages but he also appreciated the folly of stopgap solutions.

We must find a way... he would add soon after, but he still didn't find an answer to the human equation. He, like most of them here, had experience of handling only small groups of people. A few thousand at most. He knew how to inspire some, but not many. Only those who were ready for his particular message.

...we all live and learn....

This last must have been Hermes. His aura is not quite as brilliant. Could he be sad today? What is today in terms of eternity? I think they all care too much.

We all live and learn. Life is a learning process. Eternal life. Eternal learning.

I was there, in Enigma, when they made their decision about the Chimpanzees. It was long after I'd already done my job. As I mentioned, there is no time there. You can drop in and find yourself in the middle of a discussion of events spanning a thousand years either way. This time, as usual, it was Lao Tsu who found the most humane method.

I'd been selected to descend to Earth and plant advanced knowledge into the Chimpanzee mind. Not just self-awareness. They've had that for countless generations. I had been chosen to plant an awareness of oneness. Of being an inseparable part of the greater whole. To give them a sense of belonging. Not just on Earth, but in the Universe. I was to bring about, to fulfill the long awaited, as Lao Tsu called it, Second Coming. The first had almost failed.

Six million years ago, the Ancients had gathered a group of Chimps and breathed spirit into their nostrils. At least, that's how Rumi described it.

That was the First Coming.

The chosen few had quickly branched out into Australopithecus, then Homo habilis, erectus, and finally Homo sapiens. We, humans, are the end product of this portentous experiment although we still carry the DNA of the original Chimps. Over ninety-six percent of our bodies are of the original stock. Like the chimpanzees, the gorillas and the orang-utans. We are the same family.

We are all Hominidae.

"This spirit is static, yet it moves fast. The body moves fast, yet it remains almost static," Dr. Brown, the molecular biologist at Ogilvy, had told us.

Another mystery?

For six million years the Masters strove to direct us towards the Enigma. We had a thousand names for It. A thousand symbols. We had invented countless gods and immediately placed them in their inaccessible heavenly environs. We seldom looked for them within our own nature enhanced by the Ancients' vision. Throughout evolution, many sages had descended to Earth to inspire our ancestors to walk the straight and narrow. We didn't. Still don't.

And so the First Coming had failed. It hadn't taken hold. At least, not for most of us. Another mistake? Could I have done any better?

The elements had all been there, the message had been as great, but it didn't take hold. Perhaps the message is only as good as the messenger. Or the Word did not find amenable and fertile ground. I hope my message will take the Chimpanzees further. If not, they, the Saviours, will try again. And again. As I keep reminding myself, there is no time in Enigma. Not by physical standards. There is no passage of time in the heart of a galaxy, in a polished sphere outside the orbit of Pluto, or in the depth of a human heart. Nor in the heart of a Chimpanzee. It does not matter. By our reckoning, they are all outside the confines of space and time.

The sages are all lovers of Life. Lovers of the Process. Of Becoming.

The edge of Being is for everyone, but thy must make the effort, I felt one of them musing. Apparently Life, as we know it, is on the very edge of Being. It is in a constant process of mutation, fomenting on the boundary of stasis.

Everyone who dares to cross the unknown....

The thought hovers on the edge of my perception. Buddha's ideas are as light as his light itself.

On Earth, nothing had worked.

Decisions had to be made. The tidal waves generated by the sun were becoming so immense as to rise beyond the power of the ancients to protect us. Lao Tsu said those solar surges are only temporary. That they would last no more than two or three hundred years. Then, things would get back to normal. After a mini Ice Age and some tectonic adjustments things would get back to normal.

Normal? And what of humanity?

To be or not to be, to continue or to start from scratch, that is the question. The vast majority of the human race is nowhere near

ready to move into higher vibrations. The overwhelming majority
would be torn apart by their mental opposition to the unknown.
People still are like that. The unknown is still a threat to their mind
set. Had the ancients attempted to help them, they would be regarded as devils incarnate, destroying their customs, traditions, almost everything that people hold holy.

Thank goodness for the Chimes, Lao Tsu's aura assumed
prominence. *At least they withstood the test of time. In spite of our
children trying so hard to abuse them...*

So we have been their children.

Still are, I suppose.

And what of Mars?

For now Mars is a mystery. On Earth, the long journey had
begun with an amoeba and, over millions of years and countless
thousands of divergent mutations stumbled into a pattern that evolved into a human species. It could have been so wonderful. Already in the distant past our forefathers had aspired to the stars.
There had been Lemuria, Atlantis....

But Mars...?

Mars could be a different cauldron of the witch's brew. On
Mars man could grasp at the chance to develop still further, to
reach out beyond any dreams to which he'd aspired on the old
planet.

Or?

Or instead of rising from the amorphous pool of mono-cellular
amoebae to our present stature, we might choose to take a reverse
direction. We might turn a full circle. We might start at the top of
the ladder, bask for a while in our own glory, and then descent
slowly, over millions of years, to a primordial level of primitive life
forms.

It's been known to happen....

It could be worse. We might manipulate our genes to create
subservient animals. To serve us, their human masters. We might
choose to exploit them as we had, once, with so many on Earth.
Throughout the ages.

I wonder what Lao Tsu would have to say on the subject. He can perceive patterns in the matrix of Enigma of which I can but wonder.

The Old Master reminds me of my father.

Dad spends most of his time gazing at his beloved Universe. He likes to encode his own meaning onto what he observes. He can detect colour where others can see only brightness. His eyes detect subtle nuances of intensity recorded by the instruments, and then his mind seems to recreate images based as much on his knowledge as on the data emanating from the screens.

Now and again, my father comes with me to see mother. It makes him happy. I wonder if JJ will ever try to see me. Not as I am only as I am not. Everywhere and nowhere.

Is any of this real? Do all the ancient sages I perceive have their being merely in my mind? Am I, perhaps, no more than a figment of their imagination? If life is the recognition of sequential experiences, than I've already lived more or longer than any one I've ever met. More than I would ever dare imagine. I've visited the Moon, almost landed on Mars. I've examined the Universe, close by, in the curved surface of the mysterious Enigma. In a way, I've created a new race, a new Adam and a new Eve. Indeed, new worlds are coming into being before my eyes. Are they real? They are to me. And don't forget, I also married a man I love more than life itself.

Ah yes.

The last time I gazed into the ponderous mists of Enigma, I also saw that I am, or in terms of physical time I will be, a mother of three children. Beautiful children. As beautiful as JJ and my mother. Mother is everywhere and nowhere. She'll know.

And by the way. Thanks to the reality I claim as my own, my father did find the truth about the Black Hole at the centre of the Milky Way. He did so without the use of the most powerful telescope in human history. The Lunar Eye. As I expected, he doesn't talk about it. I think you can guess why. The Admiral has an image to uphold.

Before going back to wherever my physical body is in time and space, I decide to take a peek at my Chimpanzees. The problem with peeking while still in Enigma is that I have no idea at what chronological period I am looking at. I am well aware that I've been no more than an instrument the sages have used to help our cousins. I am curious, though. It may be presumptuous of me, but, in a way, I think of them as my children.

I find them in a village.

There they all are. Sitting on their haunches, by a bubbling brook, teaching people how to use medicinal plants. The humans look a little lost. They seem to have regressed somewhat. Lost some of their self-esteem. Perhaps they gained something it its stead? I am glad they have the Chimpanzees to help them. I am sure my children will be kind to my kind. They will not bear them grudges.

The Chimps are still using sign language, but only when communicating with men and women. I guess that verbal communication will come later. Or it might not. I am glad to see, or hear, or perceive, that between themselves the Chimpanzees communicate telepathically. Rather as we do, up here. On the Enigma. Or within the Enigma.

Within the enigmatic state of consciousness.

I hope that they will sense, intuitively, that the Second Coming does not refer to who is coming, only to whom the message is given. This is their second chance. I wish them well.

I have great hope for my children.

Earth too is given a second chance. She reminds me of Eden. I hope she will thrive and support the new recipients of Logos. I hope the Second Coming will bear abundant fruit. When it does, my children will inherit Enigma to continue in their becoming. After all, it is an endless journey. For all of us.

Are we not all one?

*****

Acknowledgment

I would be remiss were I not to thank Bryn Symonds and Madeleine Witthoeft for their diligent editing, each in his and her inimitable way. To my many friends my thanks for their meticulous proofreading. As always my gratitude to my wife, Bozena Happach, who put up with being a grass widow for weeks on end, for her insights,

Sincerely,

Stan I.S. Law

INHOUSEPRESS, CANADA
http://www.inhousepress.ca
107,244